THE GHOST AND SEBASTIAN

For your entertainment

THE GHOST AND SEBASTIAN

An Unsolved Murder Mystery And A Romantic Ghost

Original Novel By:

BERNICE CARSTENS

authorHOUSE®

AuthorHouse™
1663 Liberty Drive
Bloomington, IN 47403
www.authorhouse.com
Phone: 1-800-839-8640

© 2014 Bernice Carstens. All rights reserved.

No part of this book may be reproduced, stored in a retrieval system, or transmitted by any means without the written permission of the author.

Cover design by Jose Hontiveros

THE GHOST AND SEBASTIAN: An unsolved murder mystery and a romantic ghost original novel. Acknowledgments and Author's Biography Of Accomplishments. See Contents page.

This novel is totally fiction except for the brief mention of cities, states and airports.

All characters, names, actions and places are fiction created by the author. Anything similar is a coincidence.

Published by AuthorHouse 10/24/2014

ISBN: 978-1-4969-3437-6 (sc)
ISBN: 978-1-4969-3438-3 (hc)
ISBN: 978-1-4969-3436-9 (e)

Any people depicted in stock imagery provided by Thinkstock are models, and such images are being used for illustrative purposes only. Certain stock imagery © Thinkstock.

This book is printed on acid-free paper.

Because of the dynamic nature of the Internet, any web addresses or links contained in this book may have changed since publication and may no longer be valid. The views expressed in this work are solely those of the author and do not necessarily reflect the views of the publisher, and the publisher hereby disclaims any responsibility for them.

THE GHOST AND SEBASTIAN

This is a powerful story about a renowned mystery writer, Sebastian, an unsolved triple homicide, and, a romantic ghost Jenny. She, her boyfriend and her mother were murdered in a mansion in Marblehead Neck, MA in the year of 2006.

In January of 2010, the unsolved triple homicide peaks the interest of the renowned hotshot non-fiction mystery writer, Sebastian, from New York. His goal is to help find the murderer of Jenny, her boyfriend and her mother and write a book about it. He's also a criminal psychologist with a master's degree, a psychic medium and clairvoyant.

In the early spring of 2010, Sebastian temporarily moves to Marblehead and finds a place to stay at the Ultimate Inn. He hears about a VIP pitch party in Marblehead at his friend Alan's mansion who also has a mansion in Hollywood, CA and is a movie producer. After Sebastian arrives at the party, he mingles and meets, Samantha, a romance novelist that has magnetic blue eyes, dark hair and an uncontrollable temper.

Not long after the pitch party, Sebastian meets a beautiful real estate agent, Katherine, who rents him a spooky Victorian mansion which sits on a cliff overlooking the Atlantic Ocean.

While Sebastian lives in the spooky Victorian mansion, he encounters Jenny's pale lifelike ghostly apparitions that are stunning and unpredictable. His life becomes entwined with Jenny's ghost as she begs him to find her murderer, and, her spiritual power gives him strange love pleasure that shocks him. Katherine and Samantha seek psychotherapy and other powerful ghost sightings follow.

As the story nears its end, Sebastian plans to move out of the mansion and gets an overwhelming surprise that puzzles him. A different surprise follows!

Sebastian's persistence to reach his goal is inspirational and it often leads to success! This is a very captivating story and good entertainment.

A FASCINATING ROMANTIC GHOST STORY AND A MURDER MYSTERY THAT IS SPELLBINDING!

CAST OF CHARACTERS

STARRING
SEBASTIAN AND JENNY'S GHOST

Jenny's mother	SHANNON
Jenny's boyfriend before her death	PIERCE
Pierce's mother	MRS. MARLOW
Jenny's aunt/mother Shannon's sister	IRENE
Jenny's neighbor	MRS. NORTH
The gardener	CHARLIE
Previous tenants in Jenny's mansion	JOSH & CLAUDE
First tenant in Jenny's mansion	OSCAR
Real Estate Agent	KATHERINE
Sebastian's father	OLIVER
Oliver's girlfriend	ELAINA
Movie Producer	ALAN
Movie Producer	BRAD
Movie Director	MAX
Movie Director	JONATHAN
New female writer	SAMANTHA
Pierce's ex-girlfriend	VICKI
Old female writer	NINA
Tea Leaf Reader	ANNABEL
Producer Alan's Butler	WINSTON
Producer Alan's waiter	WESLEY
Producer Alan's waiter	BIGGS
Sebastian's nemesis	SAM
Restaurant waiter	JACQUE
Chief of Police	CHIEF BROOKS
Homicide Detective	LT. DARWIN

Police Officer .... OFFICER MARTIN
Ultimate Inn's Manager .... GERARD
Ultimate Inn's Security .... INSPECTOR BRADFORD
Ultimate Inn's Chef .... ANDRÉ
Ultimate Inn's dining room waiter .... BRUCE
Ultimate Inn's lounge bartender .... SAUL
Ultimate Inn's coffee shop/lounge waitress .... VERONICA
Ultimate Inn's lounge pianist .... DANNY
Ultimate Inn's lounge customer .... PHOEBE
Ultimate Inn's lounge/bar customer .... ALFRED
Ultimate Inn's lounge/bar customer .... DEX
Yacht Captain .... CARLOS
Yacht Captain's Companion .... HARVEY
Psychiatrist .... DR. LOUIS

CONTENTS

Page

INTRODUCTION: Put Mystery in Your Life xi
1. THE PITCH PARTY 1
2. SEBASTIAN'S NEW HOME 19
3. MRS. NORTH AND MRS. MARLOW 37
4. THE UNEXPECTED VISITOR 53
5. CHARLIE THE GARDENER 73
6. LOUIS THE PSYCHIATRIST 91
7. EAVESDROPPING - ULTIMATE INN 104
8. THE ATTIC AND THE CELLAR 118
9. BOMBSHELL IN PARADISE 138
10. PLEASURE 156
11. VALENTINE'S DAY 170
12. SHOCKING POLICE NEWS 184
13. COMPANY IS COMING 198
14. A SURPRISE ARREST 212
15. EARTHQUAKE 226
16. SOMETHING IS BREWING 240
17. CALLING DR. LOUIS! 254
18. EMOTIONS RUN WILD 268
19. BREAKING POLICE NEWS! 282
20. SEBASTIAN'S FATE 296
ACKNOWLEDGEMENTS 311
ABOUT THE AUTHOR 313

INTRODUCTION

Put Mystery in Your Life

Marblehead, Massachusetts was founded in 1629 and is perched on a dramatic finger of land on the Atlantic Ocean just 30 minutes north of Boston. It's a coastal community of over 19,000 residents and it has many ghost stories.

Marblehead is the birth place of the U. S. Navy and it also remains one of the east coast's premier yachting centers. It is an upscale place with lots of millionaire residents and it retains many historic homes, cemeteries and churches. Some Victorian mansions are perched along the east coast of Marblehead Neck near Castle Rock Park which can be reached by a path from Ocean Avenue.

Sebastian, who was born in New York and still resides there, is a renowned hot-shot non-fiction mystery writer. He's a charismatic single man in his 30s, tall, brown eyes, brown wavy hair and is now in his home office on his computer researching unsolved murder mysteries. He saw a particular one in Marblehead Neck of a triple homicide that occurred in 2006. After reading it, he became quite interested and wants to temporarily move there to try and help solve it and write a book about it. He therefore will lease out his home in New York because this is his new goal. He's also a criminal psychologist with a master's degree, a psychic medium and clairvoyant.

Sebastian first contacted his father Oliver who lives near him in New York to discuss his temporary departure to Marblehead.

Oliver is a widower and a wealthy jeweler who lives alone but has female companions.

It's now early spring in 2010. Sebastian has prepared himself to move to Marblehead for perhaps a year to see if he can help solve the triple homicide. After flying out to Logan Airport in Boston, MA, he rented a car and drove out to Marblehead which was 18 miles north of Boston. When he arrived there, he thought it looked like a fabulous place to live and it didn't take him long to check into the Ultimate Inn.

In a couple of days, Sebastian was in the Ultimate Inn's lounge and at the bar introducing himself to the bartender Saul who recognized him from his books. After Sebastian ordered a soft drink and it was served to him, he told Saul that he has temporarily moved to Marblehead to write about the unsolved triple homicide that took place in Marblehead Neck in 2006. Saul told him of a police officer who stops in the Ultimate Inn to see if there's any trouble and maybe he'd like to talk to him. Sebastian thanked him and then told him he is planning to hire some outsource police service.

Saul was quite happy to meet Sebastian and told him he was a fan of his murder mystery books. He also told Sebastian of a VIP pitch party that will be taking place very soon at a mansion in Marblehead. The mansion is a second home to a Hollywood Movie Producer named Alan who occasionally stops in the bar. Sebastian thanked him and told him he knows the producer and will give him a call.

Sebastian went back to his room in the Ultimate Inn where he's staying and called his friend Alan. Alan was thrilled to hear from him and invited him to his VIP pitch party and took his telephone number. It was a short call because Alan was on his way out. Sebastian thought about the lavish cocktail party and thinks it will be a great night!

1

THE PITCH PARTY

On this chilly spring evening in the year of 2010, Sebastian, the renowned mystery writer from New York, now staying at the Ultimate Inn in Marblehead, MA, has arrived at the writers' "VIP Pitch Party" being held at the Marblehead mansion of his friend and renowned movie producer, Alan. Sebastian is a dashingly handsome single man in his 30s, tall, with piercing brown eyes and wavy brown hair. He has come to the party stylishly dressed. As he entered the foyer of the mansion, Butler Winston greeted him, "Good evening, sir. May I have your invitation?" Sebastian gave it to him. After confirming it, Butler Winston said, "Follow me, sir." He then escorted him to the grand room and left.

Sebastian stood still for a moment to look at the décor, which was elegant, and the room was sparkling from the glow of beautiful crystal chandeliers. He looked at the guests and saw them stylishly dressed, and many authors, for sure, were engaged in conversations pitching their screenplays and books to some movie producers and directors seated at tables.

Sebastian suddenly spotted his friend Alan standing while conversing with guests. He is a famous Hollywood, California movie producer who also owns a mansion there. He's pleasant, single and in his 40s. Sebastian approached him and said, "Alan!" Alan looked at him with wide eyes and responded, "Sebastian! It's so good to see you!" They then hugged. Sebastian said, "It's good to see you too, Alan. Now that I'm in Marblehead to work on my book, we'll be able to visit. How have you been?" Just then, the young waiter, Wesley, came over and asked, "What can I get you gentlemen to drink?" Sebastian ordered a glass of champagne and Alan ordered scotch on the rocks. The waiter left. Alan answered Sebastian's question regarding how he has been and he told him he's been fine and then asked about his health. Sebastian went on to say that his health is good and he keeps writing which makes him happy. He also told Alan his mansion is beautiful. Wesley, the waiter, soon returned and approached Alan and Sebastian and served them their cocktails and beluga caviar with crackers on a silver tray.

A little later, after Alan and Sebastian enjoyed their caviar, Alan held his drink in one hand and put his other hand on Sebastian's shoulder and said, "Sebastian, now that I know you're in Marblehead to write a new book, tell me more about it." He then removed his hand and Sebastian told him his new goal is to try to help the police solve the triple homicide that took place in Marblehead Neck in 2006 and to gather more information so he can write a book which he hopes will end up a blockbuster movie. Alan looked happy to hear that. Sebastian suddenly had a clairvoyant moment of a dark haired intoxicated woman having a tantrum and he needs to beware! When it ended, he was silent. Alan noticed he was meditating and asked him if he was okay and Sebastian told him he was.

The waiter, Biggs, soon brought Alan and Sebastian more drinks and caviar. After they ate a little and sipped their drinks, they and other guests were suddenly startled by an argument coming from nearby. Alan and Sebastian looked and noticed it was their friend Brad and a woman arguing. Brad is a well known Hollywood producer, tall, handsome, in his 30's and stylishly dressed. Sebastian asked Alan who the good looking dark haired woman was who was arguing with Brad. Alan told him it was Samantha, a new romance writer he met at a pitch session in Los Angeles when she had an apartment there. She lived there a couple of years trying to make it as a novelist but found the competition too stiff for her plus she feared earthquakes. She's from the east coast and has since come back and bought a condo in Marblehead because they're friends. She's obsessed with him and wants him to make a movie of her novel. Alan told him he'll introduce him to her. Samantha is age 28, gorgeous looking, about 5 feet 5 inches tall, has beautiful magnetic blue eyes that draw you in, shoulder length dark brown hair and she's wearing a beautiful blue cocktail dress with silver 3 inch high-heeled shoes. Sebastian then started thinking about his clairvoyant moment he just had of an intoxicated out-of-control woman and knows it's this woman it was referring to.

Brad and Samantha are not completely visible to everyone as they argue but quite audible to some guests. Sebastian asked Alan, "Aside from Samantha's bad temper and what I can see of her from here, she's beautiful but I don't think it's a good time to be introduced to her." Alan told him she is feisty and quite argumentative but will calm down, and because of her explosive temper, he thinks she needs anger management classes.

Alan and Sebastian continued to focus on Samantha and Brad with some visibility as they looked between people. Alan suddenly said to Sebastian, "Oh, I'll tell you something else about Samantha. I've noticed a dark side to that woman."

Brad is now raising his voice in anger while swaying a cocktail in one hand, then taking gulps of it, then talking and swinging the other hand in mid-air. You could hear him tell Samantha that she's showing a bad temper because he told her that her manuscript was not well written. He also told her it was not ready to be published as a novel and it was not ready to adapt to a screenplay. Brad paused and then told her he wouldn't produce a movie from it if she paid him to do it.

Alan and Sebastian continued to listen and look at Samantha who looked very angry. She was swaying her cocktail in one hand and then taking a gulp of it, and then with her wild looking eyes, she looked at Brad and said, "Listen, Brad, you're nothing but a nasty arrogant egomaniac. And when I get a romance novel published and submit a screenplay, I won't ever let you produce a movie from it. I'd like to throw this drink at you right now but I won't."

Just then, Alan and Sebastian moved a little closer to Brad and Samantha while Alan looked furious. Sebastian said, "Wow! What a temper Samantha has, Alan. Are you sure you want me to meet her now and spend time talking? She'll probably throw her drink in my face." Alan again explained that she's safe once she calms down, but right now he needs to listen to them so he'll know more of what they're yelling about and then he can shut them both up. He's also very surprised that Brad is carrying on like he is in public and thinks that Samantha must have pushed his wrong buttons while they were intoxicated and that fueled the argument.

While Brad and Samantha continued to argue, they didn't notice that Alan and Sebastian were nearby watching them argue and sometimes stopping for a second to throw down swigs of hard alcohol. Alan suddenly decided to go over to Brad and get in his face and give him hell. As he did so, Samantha watched him while she looked so surprised yet she knew she was next. In anger, Alan said, "Brad, the both of you need to learn not to argue in public. What the hell's the matter with the two of you? Is it the alcohol?"

Brad looked relieved that he was interrupted. He told Alan he was sure the alcohol played a part in the argument and it was good that someone interrupted them because it made Samantha shut up. He then apologized for his arguing. After Alan accepted his apology, he said, "Brad, in the future, be the professional that you are." Alan then became silent, stepped back and they stared at each other a few moments and you could tell Alan was angry which was uncommon for him.

Sebastian quickly spoke up as he reached out to shake hands with Brad because they know each other. He told him how good it is to see him, other than witnessing the argument, and then asked him how he has been. Brad expressed things were going well for him and asked Sebastian about his writing. After they talked briefly about Sebastian's book, Brad told him he's looking forward to reading it. He then looked very irritated and said goodbye to him and not to anyone else as he quickly walked away.

Sebastian then watched Alan who began talking to Samantha as she stared at him with wild eyes and was definitely intoxicated. Alan kept on pointing his finger in her face as he said, "Samantha, you listen to me. If you ever do want to get anywhere in this business or another kind of business, you need to control your mouth. I will not stand for your anger in my presence here or anywhere. Do you understand me, Samantha?

Try to be more professional." She apologized to Alan and told him she wouldn't let it happen again and he accepted her apology, then, she became silent while staring at him for a few moments. As Sebastian watched them, his eyes were fixed on her unusual beauty which was very pleasing.

Now that Samantha is calm, Alan told her he'd like to introduce her to someone very special who unfortunately had to see her at her worst. And he's one of the finest non-fiction mystery writers there is and his name is Sebastian and he's from New York. Alan then stepped back.

Sebastian thanked Alan for his kind introduction and then put his hand out to Samantha and said, "I'm pleased to meet you, Samantha, and she said, "I'm happy to meet you, Sebastian." While shaking hands, their eyes met and the sexual chemistry was strong. After their hand-shaking, they stood there and just stared at each other while she was silent but physically flirting with him as he and Alan watched her and looked shocked. When she stopped flirting, she was swaying her cocktail a little with one hand and gently stroking her hair with the other hand due to her intoxication. Somehow, she still looked beautiful as she suddenly said, "Sebastian, I've heard a lot about you. What are you working on?" Sebastian was momentarily speechless because he was attracted to her magnetic blue eyes which put him in a trance.

Alan has been watching Sebastian and Samantha looking at each other like they want to get in bed, so he said, "I'll leave you two highly sexed creatures alone for awhile. I need to get myself a strong drink after this damn ridiculous and unprofessional behavior going on! It's unacceptable!" He then left.

Now that Alan has left Samantha and Sebastian to carry on, Sebastian soon landed back on earth after the intense sexual eye contact he and Samantha were locked into. He was now ready to answer her question.

Sebastian first said, "Samantha, I'm very pleased to meet you because I love meeting writers. To answer your question about what I'm working on, it's an unsolved triple homicide that happened in the year 2006 in Marblehead Neck of the young lady Jenny, her boyfriend and her mother." Samantha slightly perked up and said, "Oh, the mystery murder at the mansion on the cliff. I remember it well." Sebastian told her that he'll be doing a lot of research on it. He then asked her to tell him all she knows about it and she told him she is familiar with it because she read the whole story about it in the newspaper and magazines and watched it on television. She also added that it will never be solved. Sebastian is fascinated with information from Samantha and wants to know why she thinks it will never be solved. She told him it's because the murderer must have been very clever. Three people were shot in the same mansion, the same day, hours apart and no one knows who did it.

Sebastian then continued talking with Samantha about the unsolved triple homicide of four years ago and hopes she has more to say. He told her that he's determined to see if he can help solve it and went on and told her the mansion where the murders took place may be for sale or rent now with option to buy and that interests him. She asked, "Why does it? It will feel awfully spooky, Sebastian." He responded, "Well, it would be pretty neat writing about the murders if I'm living in the place where they happened. I'm a psychic medium and clairvoyant so I may sense and see something. It probably would scare some people." Samantha stared at him.

Sebastian shifted to a different conversation and told Samantha that he heard she was a new writer and the genre was romance. She answered, "Yes, romance. I'm presently writing a steamy novel." Sebastian's reaction was, "I always say, write from the heart." Sebastian suddenly started looking around the room. While he wasn't looking at Samantha, she deliberately spilled her drink on his suit. He was startled and speechless looking at her as she stared deep into his eyes for a second. She then said, "Oh, Sebastian, I'm very sorry and I don't know how that happened!" She quickly took his arm and said, "Come with me into the library so I can dry your suit off and it's also quiet in there where we can talk."

Sebastian and Samantha strolled over to the library without saying a word. Once in it, she took his hand and lead him over to a corner that was cozy. She took some napkins off of a nearby table and started tapping wet spots on his suit ever so gently as Sebastian watched. He soon asked her, "Are you sure you didn't deliberately spill that drink on me?" She got angry and threw the napkins down and started storming out of the library. Sebastian stopped her by grabbing her arm. He then held both her arms and they faced each other looking deep into each other's eyes. Sebastian said, "Don't be so sensitive, Samantha! I didn't mean that. By the way, I want you to know that those blue eyes of yours are gorgeous. They're like a magnet. They draw me in." With her piercing and angry stare into his eyes, she said, "That's why they're called magnetic blue. Listen, Sebastian, I'm not easy." He let go of her and started walking back and forth as she watched.

While Sebastian and Samantha are still in the library, he suddenly stopped walking back and forth and went over to her. He gave her a hug and then looked into her eyes and asked, "How would you like to go to dinner some night? Can I have your phone number?" Samantha answered, "It's yes to both questions. You've got yourself a date, Sebastian." She wrote her number down on a piece of paper that was on the table and handed it to him as they smiled. He told her he now wants to mingle a little more before he leaves so he kissed her cheek and they exited the library as he told her he'd call her.

While Sebastian is walking around through the crowd of people, he spotted two directors he knows who are talking to each other so he approached them. One is Max, a Hollywood director in his 30's and the other one is Jonathan, a Hollywood director in his 40s. Sebastian went to both of them and said, "Max and Jonathan! It's good to see both of you again! Are you guys keeping busy?" Max told him he most definitely is and has had some recent good movies that he enjoyed directing and they're getting good reviews. He asked Sebastian if he just came to Marblehead for the pitch party. Just then, Biggs, the young waiter, suddenly came over and asked them if they would like a cocktail. Sebastian ordered a soft drink and then Max and Jonathan ordered martinis. Sebastian then answered Max's question and told him he's in Marblehead to research and write about an unsolved triple homicide and he just found out about this pitch party. He added that it was perfect timing to pitch his future book and that he likes people to know that he's working on something special.

Jonathan told Sebastian that his new book idea sounds good and maybe it will make a good movie. He wants to know when he completes it so he can take a look at it. Sebastian told him he'll definitely let them know when it's all finished. He then mentioned how they have each other's cell phone number. He also told them he is temporarily staying at the Ultimate Inn until he finds a place to rent out for about a year in Marblehead because of all the information he needs.

After awhile, Biggs was back with the drinks and some appetizers for the men. They all took some and soon Sebastian wanted to leave. He said, "Max and Jonathan, I want to mingle around to see some other people I haven't seen for awhile. It was real nice seeing both of you." Sebastian, Max and Jonathan shook hands and said goodbye.

Later on, when Sebastian was on his way to see producer Alan before leaving the pitch party, he spotted a writer he wanted to stop to say hello to. Her name is Nina, she's 62 years old and is a famous Hollywood biography writer. She is petite, has gray hair, she's wearing diamond earrings and a classy suit. As he got near her, he approached her and said, "Nina! It's wonderful to see you again! Do you remember me?" She quickly answered, "Of course I do, Sebastian. How are you?" He told her he's just fine and asked her how she is and if she's still writing a lot? She told him she's quite healthy for a 62 year old and she keeps on writing about Hollywood. She then told him that it is great seeing him again and asked what he's working on. He told her how he's working on a new unsolved murder mystery and plans to stay in Marblehead for awhile. He then told her he was on his way out when he spotted her and wanted to say hello and he's sorry he has to cut their conversation short now but he'll see her another time. Sebastian started to leave and she called out, "Bye, Sebastian! Hope to see you again!"

Sebastian is making his last stop and it's over to Alan. He found him sitting alone looking around at the guests. He approached him and said, "Alan, I had a great time but it's time for me to leave. Call me when you would like us to visit again while I'm in Marblehead." Alan responded, "Sebastian, please don't hesitate to call me anytime. I'm interested in your new book and I want to read it!" Sebastian and Alan hugged goodbye and then Sebastian headed out the door of the awesome mansion filled with creative people he loves to be around.

Sebastian was in high spirits when he left the mansion and headed to his car. Once inside of it, and before he started his car up, he smiled and then said to himself, "What a wonderful night."

The next morning, Sebastian was in his room and had already showered and shaved and was dressed in casual clothes.

He was sitting on a Victorian armchair while he was talking on his cell phone with a real estate agent who introduced herself as Katherine. Sebastian introduced himself to her and asked about the Victorian mansion in Marblehead Neck where the 2006 triple homicide took place. They talked about it and it is available for rent or rent with option to buy. He was quite happy to hear that and asked when he could see it. Katherine looked at her calendar for a second and then told him he could see it this afternoon. He agreed to and told her he'd call her back shortly to confirm the time and address. He also gave her his phone number at the Ultimate Inn and his cell phone number in case she wanted to call him and then they hung up. He stayed sitting a few moments with a smile.

Sebastian then went to the Ultimate Inn's coffee shop which has customers and he's sitting in a booth alone. While waiting for the waitress, he looks content thinking about the appointment he has in the afternoon to look at the Victorian mansion where Jenny and her mother lived. The waitress, Veronica, who has her name pinned on her dress, came over to Sebastian. She's young, pretty, has long red hair, a bubbly personality and chews gum. While holding her pad and pen, she looked at Sebastian and said, "Good morning. Can I take your order, sir?" She then chewed her gum while waiting for his answer. He answered, "Yes. I'll have two eggs that are sunny side up, home-fries and whole wheat toast. Oh, and coffee with cream." She finished writing and left. Sebastian then took out a small book and started reading it about the different places in Marblehead and Marblehead Neck he wants to visit. After he eats, he wants to see Fort Sewall which was an armed fort used to defend against the British invaders in the war of 1812. After that, he wants to go to Crocker Park to watch the harbor boats, although he knows there are good views of the harbor from Fort Sewall.

Veronica, the waitress, soon arrived with Sebastian's breakfast. She smiled and then chewed her gum as she put his dishes down. She then stopped chewing gum and said, "Enjoy your breakfast, sir." He thanked her and she left.

After Sebastian relaxed and enjoyed his breakfast, Veronica was back with the bill. He signed for it, and after reading her name on her dress, he handed her a generous tip while saying, "Thank you, Veronica." After she smiled, she thanked him and chewed her gum as she walked away with her bubbly personality.

Sebastian then went to his rented car and headed out to Fort Sewall. When he arrived there, he spent a little time looking at a canon and the scenery but he soon went on to Crocker Park to sit and watch boats go by which he loves to do. He plans on having his father Oliver come down from New York and go boating with him as soon as he gets settled in a place to live. It's now early afternoon and Sebastian is still at Crocker Park. There are many boats in the water and he is watching them with pleasure while he's eating a hot dog.

After a good amount of time spent here, he wanted to go back to the Ultimate Inn where he's staying temporarily so he can freshen up for his appointment with the real estate agent, Katherine, whom he has never seen, so he left Crocker Park.

After Sebastian arrived back in his room, he took a shower and then put on some good looking casual clothes and some wonderful smelling cologne for his appointment. He said out loud to himself, "First impressions are important." He then gave Katherine a call and asked for the address and time to meet. She gave him the location of the Victorian mansion where Jenny and her mother lived when they were murdered and said she'd meet him in front of it in two hours.

It's late afternoon and almost time for Sebastian's real estate appointment with Katherine. He is well on his way to look for the Victorian mansion and can hardly wait to see it because this could be his home for a year. After awhile, he spotted it and parked nearby and just stared at it for a few moments. He was awe-struck! It is a three story mansion that's pale green with white trim and coral colored areas. It's a cornucopia of styles starting with the Victorian era and ending with wraparound porches, indicative of Queen Anne style. The porches are on the first and second floor on one side of the mansion. The late Jenny's Victorian mansion, with neighboring mansions, is perched along the east coast of Marblehead Neck near Castle Rock Park which is reached by a path from Ocean Avenue. It stands out among the others. It has two tall Victorian front doors and many tall windows along with a few stained glass ones. Sebastian got out of his car and stepped in front of the mansion and started pacing back and forth while waiting for Katherine to arrive.

A white real estate car suddenly pulled up to where Sebastian was standing. It was Katherine. He waited for her to get out of her car and then they looked at each other and smiled. She is wearing a pretty pale pink suit and he's surprised how beautiful she is. She's tall, shapely, in her 30s with shoulder length blonde hair and has green eyes. She walked up to Sebastian and they shook hands and you could tell they were attracted to each other.

Katherine spoke first and said, "Sebastian, I want you to know that this house hasn't been dusted for awhile so you'll have to use your imagination." He told her he would. She asked, "What do you think of the exterior?" He answered, "It looks mysterious and makes me curious to see the inside." She told him the Victorian era started in 1837 and that this mansion was built in 1850. In the 1900s, Jenny's mother Shannon became owner of the mansion. She also had a will stating, in case of her and her daughter's death, the mansion and her furnishings were to be donated to a specific town. Therefore, this mansion is all furnished and can be rented with option to buy. He said, "Okay." She then said, "Let's go inside." As they headed up towards the door, you could tell the lawn was well cared for. She told Sebastian that Charlie, the gardener, has been taking care of the mansion's landscape for 40 years. When they got to the front entrance and Katherine was about to open the door, she said, "I just love Victorian mansions." He said, "I do too."

As Katherine and Sebastian enter the mansion's foyer, they immediately see the large mahogany staircase that commands their attention. There's a Victorian style table in the center of the foyer and rose covered velvet chairs against the wall and dust and cobwebs everywhere. He said, "This place already feels spooky." Katherine and Sebastian then admired the beautiful mahogany wood, rose colored décor, wallpaper, and a wall full of oil paintings. Before they looked any further, she told him that all the rooms are large and there are ten. The first floor has one bedroom, large full-bath, half-bath, dining room, kitchen with a swinging door, and butler's living quarters. There's a huge room with pocket doors and it can be used as a living room and a library. The second floor has a sewing room, four bedrooms and three full-baths.

Katherine and Sebastian entered the huge burgundy themed living room. There's a fireplace, mantle, piano, desk, sculptures, huge bookcases but everything is dusty. There are brocaded satin drapes, lace curtains, oriental carpeting, two burgundy velvet sofas and two mahogany wing armchairs. The oil paintings are not of great value. The valuable ones were donated to a museum. Katherine said, "This was Shannon's authentic antique furniture which comes with the purchase of the mansion." He said, "This place is eerie."

The dining room is in rose. Katherine and Sebastian are looking at the mahogany table with ten chairs, a china cabinet with a mirror in it and full of china, a buffet and chandelier with cobwebs. As they entered the kitchen, he told her he read about Jenny's mother being murdered there but didn't know the spot. He walked around and suddenly sensed negative energy in a spot and said, "Katherine, this is where she was murdered." Katherine was silent. They continued to look in the kitchen which is white and blue with a butler swinging door. The appliances are updated and the cabinets have French doors and there's a white table with four chairs. They looked at the blue butler's quarters and laundry area.

Katherine and Sebastian moved on to the back of the mansion to the bedroom where Jenny slept. It's in raspberry with cream colored trim just as it was when she was alive. It has Victorian pillows on her bed which has a huge mahogany headboard. There's a dresser, a dressing table with a mirror, two large Victorian lamps, a stuffed chair with a coffee table

Sebastian told Katherine that he read about Jenny and Pierce being murdered in her bedroom and that he can now feel their presence at the time of their death. She just stared at him knowing he's psychic and clairvoyant.

Sebastian and Katherine moved on to the full-bath which is in berry and gold and has some updated things but still has the Victorian style. There's a huge marble shower in one area, in another area there's a claw foot tub to keep the Victorian theme going, there's a Victorian style sink and faucets, and a dressing table with a mirror and a vanity bench that you can imagine seeing Jenny sitting on. They also looked at the half-bath located off of a hallway done in peach and gold Victorian décor. That hallway has secret passages.

Katherine and Sebastian continued on to a long semi-dark hallway which lead to the staircase. They started up the beautiful mahogany staircase but the dark wood, cobwebs and dust made the mansion feel haunted. Katherine apologized to Sebastian about the dust as they went on to see the bedrooms. One was Shannon's, one was the housekeeper's quarters and two were guests bedrooms. They were all in pastel colors and furnished and had good size closets. The cobwebs didn't go un-noticed. Katherine and Sebastian saw the three full-baths, one in green, one in lilac, one in peach. All three had claw foot tubs and large separate shower areas. They also saw the sewing room. They then went to the attic. Sebastian said, "This feels spooky." It was full of cobwebs, boxes and a life-size naked female mannequin, the kind a tailor uses, with moveable torso parts for sizing. It also has arms and a head on it wearing a black bushy wig, red lipstick and had haunting large pale blue eyes. He said, "Let's get out of here."

The tour was almost over. The back yard and cellar still needed to be seen. Katherine and Sebastian have entered the cellar and that's pretty eerie too. It's dark and dusty with cobwebs and lots of antique frames and old furniture that have been left there. Sebastian said, "Let's get out of here too and check out the back yard."

Katherine and Sebastian are in the back yard and he's quite impressed. There's a place to sit with a table and chairs and gardens everywhere and a driveway and privacy. He then said to Katherine, "I want to live here." She said, "Let's go to my office and do the paper work." They smiled at each other and then Sebastian asked, "If you don't mind my asking, are you married?" She answered, "No and I have never been married. How about you?" He told her he's never been married either. He never found the right one. They soon left the mansion with Katherine locking the door. Once outside, she looked at Sebastian and said, "Follow me to my office." "Okay, Katherine. Maybe after the paper work you'd like to go to dinner." "Oh no, I can't. I have too much to do today. Maybe another time but thank you anyway, Sebastian." He smiled at her and went to his car and followed her.

After a lot of paper work in Katherine's real estate office, she told Sebastian that she needs to check a few things out and she'll get back to him either this evening or tomorrow morning with an answer as to whether or not he can rent the mansion for a year. They parted with a handshake. He went on to dinner at his Ultimate Inn's coffee shop. After dinner, he had a soft drink in the lounge at the bar and talked with Saul, the bartender, for awhile, then he went up to his room.

The next morning, after Sebastian woke up in bed, the first thing he thought about was that he never got a call from Katherine about the mansion rental and hopes she calls him this morning. He then got right out of bed, showered, shaved and dressed in his casual clothes and went to breakfast.

While Sebastian is in the coffee shop having breakfast, his cell phone is ringing. He answered it and Katherine said, "Good morning, Sebastian. I have an answer for you about the mansion rental." He responded, "I can hardly wait to hear it." She happily said, "You're the new mansion tenant!" Sebastian was elated and thanked her. She asked him if he could come to her office and he told her he'd be there shortly.

Sebastian was soon in Katherine's office and they're sitting across the table from each other smiling. She told him his rental stay will apply towards the "rent with option to buy" clause which includes an inspection before the purchase. He told her it will most likely be a one year rental because he has a home in New York. He also added that he wants to keep Charlie, the gardener. After the paper work, he paid the rental fee. She then said, "Well, here are your keys!" She dangled them in his face as they both smiled. He then said, "Thank you so much for your help, Katherine. When I settle in and get the mansion cleaned up, I'll have you over. Would you like that?" She certainly did like it and mentioned that he could hire housekeepers to clean the mansion up and he liked that idea. They stood up as he was ready to leave and he couldn't resist giving Katherine a hug goodbye. She looked surprised and smiled as she watched him leave her office.

After Sebastian got back to his Ultimate Inn room, he called his dad, Oliver, in New York and they were so happy to hear each other's voice. Sebastian told him about the wonderful pitch party, and, how he just got the keys to the murder mystery mansion on a rental basis with option to buy. His dad was delighted to hear this news. Sebastian said, "Dad, I want you to come down this summer and we'll rent a yacht! How's that sound?" "Sebastian, I would love that. Let me know when." After they hung up, Sebastian smiled and thought about what's to come when he moves in the mansion.

2

SEBASTIAN'S NEW HOME

Sebastian hired three housekeepers to get the Victorian mansion cleaned up which took a few days and it's now sparkling clean. He's gradually settling in where Jenny and her mother Shannon lived when they were alive. He also has introduced himself to Charlie, the 62 year old gardener.

Sebastian has been entering each room, the attic and the cellar in hopes of finding clues but more often goes in Jenny's bedroom where she and her boyfriend Pierce were shot. He's also sensing Jenny's bedroom is where he should sleep for the duration of his stay in hopes of finding clues to the murders. He admits that his first night sleeping in her king-size bed felt strange but he wants to feel a closeness to her. He also admires the lavish Victorian décor of her room.

This morning, Sebastian made himself a cup of tea and some toast in the cozy white and blue kitchen. Then, as he walked through the dining room, he looked in the china cabinet mirror for a few seconds, and in back of his reflection, he saw something pale and shadowy. He looked surprised and then quickly turned around to see if there was a ghost in the dining room and saw no one. He said to himself, "Maybe it was a cloudy spot on the mirror." He opened the china cabinet door and wiped the mirror and then looked in it and there was nothing in back of his reflection. He then left the mansion and went to Jenny's grave site to see if he could feel the presence of her spirit there.

Sebastian was soon at the cemetery where Jenny, her boyfriend Pierce and her mother Shannon were buried. He stood and looked at their headstones and sensed their energy, and then kneeled in front of Jenny's where he was hoping for some extra sensory perception but he didn't feel any. After leaving the cemetery, he drove off and found a spot where he could look out at the ocean and meditate, as he often does, to free his senses and open his mind up to deeper thoughts.

In late afternoon, at the mansion, Sebastian thought he'd get his manuscript started by writing notes in his red book and then entering them into the computer. He sat in the living room at his mahogany desk with the large bookcase in back of him and one on the side wall and then turned on the lights so he could start writing. For now, he named his story, "The Puzzling Murder of Jenny, Pierce and Shannon."

As Sebastian was writing, he suddenly sensed a light breeze in the room. He stopped writing and looked around and there were no windows open and the breeze continued. He said out loud, "There's paranormal activity in this room." Just then, the breeze stopped. He couldn't continue writing.

The next day, Sebastian called his friend Samantha, the writer, and asked her if she'd like to go to dinner and then visit his mansion. She quickly answered, "Yes! I'd love to!"

A few days later, on a warm June evening, Sebastian and Samantha were at a restaurant in Marblehead enjoying dinner near a window with an ocean view. He was dressed casually and she looked romantic in a short red dress with her dark brown hair pulled to one side. She stopped eating for a moment as she looked out the window and said, "Sebastian, the view is beautiful." He agreed and told her he's happy they got together for dinner and then asked her where on the east coast was she originally from and what got her into writing. She answered, "Because I moved so much on the east coast, I tell people I lived in several places, then in Los Angeles and I'm now living here in Marblehead and have a condo. And I've always wanted to write novels for therapeutic reasons and my choice was romance." Sebastian asked her if the writing helped her. She suddenly got angry and slammed her fork down and told him she didn't want to discuss it. He said, "Oh, I'm sorry! I didn't know you were so sensitive." She looked angry as her magnetic blue eyes made eye-contact with him while he wondered what was wrong with her mind.

Samantha started eating again but stopped to ask Sebastian if he was raised in New York. He answered, "Yes, in the Big Apple and I still live there." She told him she had never been to New York and has no desire to go there.

Samantha was then in deep thought while looking into Sebastian's eyes telling him she thinks he's wasting his time with an old murder case. He told her that he's not and he's happy he's renting the mansion where they took place because it will give him a sense of what led to them. She changed the subject and asked him if he was ever married. He told her no but now that he's in his 30s he'd like to be. He then asked her if she was ever married and she told him she never has been either but would like to be.

The young waiter, Jacque, walked by Sebastian and Samantha's table and accidently spilled his tray on it. She got alarmed and yelled, "What is wrong with you?" Jacque said, "I'm sorry, madam." He quickly cleaned up the table as they watched. Samantha was ready to leave in anger while Jacque told Sebastian to wait a minute while he talked to his manager. Jacque left and quickly returned and told Sebastian there would be no charge for their dinner because of the accident. Sebastian handed him a tip and Jacque thanked him and then Samantha and Sebastian left the restaurant rather quickly without having dessert.

Samantha and Sebastian soon arrived at his Victorian mansion and have just entered the foyer and she is impressed. After he gave her a tour of the ten rooms which she loved, he went to his bar area and poured them a night cap of an after dinner drink. They sat in the living room next to each other on one of the burgundy velvet sofas with their drinks and are now relaxed and have forgotten about their dinner they just had with the accident-prone waiter. While Samantha looked romantic in her short red silk dress with her legs crossed showing off her red high-heeled shoes, they suddenly looked at each other and locked eyes with a fire in their heart.

After rolling around on the sofa for awhile, Sebastian wanted to end the evening because of how much work he has to do on his book tomorrow. He kissed Samantha on the lips and she responded very passionately. He then said, "Let's call it a night." She said, "Let's. We have plenty of time to enjoy each other." He walked her to the door and they had another kiss with body contact and then they said goodnight.

It's early summer and Sebastian loves living in the three story Victorian mansion with five bedrooms. He is still sleeping on the first floor in Jenny's bedroom and it doesn't feel strange anymore and he loves her king-size bed and sheets. He soon got to love all the Victorian era and Queen Anne era style furnishings that were left there from Jenny and her mother.

One late afternoon, in the living room, there was soft lighting coming from the Victorian lamps making the room look warm and inviting. Sebastian was sitting on one of the large mahogany wing armchairs in burgundy velvet with his red hardcover book and meditating. Through tall Victorian windows, sunlight spilled onto the wall showing shadows of wind-blown tree branches with leaves that were moving across the wall. Sebastian noticed it and stopped to look but then continued meditating on what was the motive for the murders. He knows he needs the library, the police, and he needs to talk with neighbors and any living relatives that Jenny, her mother Shannon and her boyfriend Pierce left. He senses, by sleeping in Jenny's bedroom, he'll gain a closeness to her and it will give him information sooner or later.

While Sebastian was still sitting on his wing armchair and writing, his cell phone rang. He answered it and it was Samantha sounding angry as she yelled, "I need to see you, Sebastian! Something awful happened!" He asked, "What happened?" She told him she'd be right over and hung up.

Shortly after, Samantha stormed into Sebastian's living room and threw her purse on the sofa and started pacing the floor yelling out, "Sebastian, I found out someone stole my manuscript of one of my romance stories!" While he's still sitting on the wing armchair, he's watching her and trying to figure out why she is so high-strung. He told her to sit down while he gets her something to drink to calm her down so she can explain more about it. He then went to his bar. Samantha claimed that she couldn't sit down because she was too angry. She suddenly shouted, "Play with me and you play with fire!" Sebastian asked, "Hell, am I safe dating you, Samantha?"

    Sebastian is at his bar area pouring two glasses of wine so that he and Samantha can relax while she explains what happened to her manuscript. He brought the wine to the coffee table and said, "Sit down, Samantha, and tell me what happened." She finally sat down and explained that several months ago she took a manuscript to the copy center and made two copies. While there, she stopped to say hello to a person she didn't know well and then left. She got home and noticed she only had one copy so she returned to the copy center but the other one couldn't be found. She later mailed a copy to the registry for safety purposes until it gets published. She now just received a notice, several months later, that the title of her manuscript has already been registered by someone else. Sebastian said, "It's possible that someone else had that same title for a different story. If that's the case, you'll need to change the title. If someone tries to steal your story, then that becomes a lawsuit." She got up and paced the floor and couldn't stop.

    Sebastian stood up and grabbed Samantha by her two arms and stopped her from pacing. He looked into her eyes and she looked very evil at that moment while staying silent. He told her, if she finds the person who has the same title, she needs to stay calm while discussing it. He suggested they go to dinner tomorrow after she calms down. After pausing a moment, he said, "After the last scene you caused in the restaurant, let's not go to dinner for awhile. Let's just take a walk in a park and sit in a gazebo." She broke away from his hold on her arms, then went to the sofa and grabbed her purse and then stormed out the door while yelling out, "This is not a joke, Sebastian! A gazebo is not the answer!" She left while he was standing and watching her. He then sat back down and said out loud, "What a hell of a temper she has! I don't know if I should be dating her. And she does have a dark side like Alan said."

The next morning, Sebastian planned on going to the library but first wants to call Katherine, the real estate woman who rented him the mansion. While he's sitting in his kitchen with a coffee, he's on his cell phone talking with her. He told her how he took her advice and had the cleaning service clean the mansion and now it looks great. She said, "Oh good!" He went on and asked her if she'd like to see it and then they could go to a nice dining room for dinner later. He knows the chef at the Ultimate Inn who cooks very well. She said, "Thank you for the invitation and I can visit your new home today and have dinner with you later." Sebastian was thrilled and asked her what time would be convenient for her to come over. She told him in late afternoon she'll call him before coming over. They hung up and he left for the library.

While at the library, Sebastian is looking at microfilm of the 2006 murders. He came across a photo of Jenny, her boyfriend Pierce and her mother Shannon. It was blurred but good enough to tell what they looked like. The article read that all three victims were murdered on July 27, 2006. Pierce leaves behind his mother and father, Mr. and Mrs. Marlow, of Melrose, MA and Jenny's mother leaves behind a sister Irene of Rhode Island. The wake for the three victims was at the same funeral home on the same day in Melrose, MA. Sebastian was happy to find this article and photo but knows he has to visit the outsource police service he has already hired to get details of how the bodies were found. He printed everything and then left the library and went to his mansion.

While Sebastian was at his desk, he thought of calling the outsource police service he hired. He wants to talk with Chief Brooks who knows him as a renowned mystery writer, criminal psychologist with a master's degree who sometimes works with police, and a psychic medium and clairvoyant. Sebastian then made the call to the chief and asked him if he could visit him or another officer regarding the 2006 unsolved triple homicide. Chief Brooks scheduled him with Lt. Darwin for the following week and Sebastian thanked him and they hung up. The chief knows his mother was a psychic medium who worked for the police and solved a murder for them. She was able to tell them who the murderer was and he was later arrested, tried and found guilty and given a life sentence. While serving his time, he sought revenge and had someone outside the prison kill Sebastian's mother by shooting her.

Later on, Sebastian was waiting for Katherine to come over to see his mansion and then go home and change to have dinner with him later. He soon heard someone at the door and answered it and it was Katherine in a pretty white cotton dress. Her shoulder length blonde hair looked so nice with her beautiful green eyes as she stood there smiling. He also noticed she came in her white real estate car straight from her office. Sebastian said, "Come in, Katherine." She entered and said, "I can already tell the mansion has been cleaned."

Sebastian immediately started showing Katherine all of the ten rooms and she loved how sparkling clean they all looked. They then went into the rose dining room and sat down and had a cup of tea with fresh baked cookies from the bakery. He told her how he went to the library this morning and started to gather information on the murders he's writing about. After they finished their tea and then migrated into the living room and sat for awhile, he asked her what time she wanted to go to dinner and she answered, "Well, I'm going to need a couple of hours to get ready so I better go home, shower and get dressed." She also told him, that because she lives far from him, she's coming over to his mansion in her car and they can switch to his car to go to dinner. He was okay with that. She told Sebastian that she'd call him when she is ready. After he walked her to the door, they smiled and then said goodbye.

Later on, Sebastian and Katherine were in the Ultimate Inn's dining room and she was wearing yellow and looked beautiful. He looked handsome in a summer cream colored sport jacket with a matching colored shirt and tan pants. While they were complimenting each other on their perfume and cologne, Bruce, the waiter, came over and asked, "Would you both like to have a drink?" Sebastian asked Katherine what she would like and she answered, "I'll have a glass of Chablis." He said he wanted the same. Sebastian then told Katherine he's soon going to rent a luxurious motor yacht and this will be his first time renting one. And he found out that the yacht can drop anchor nearby the harbor to pick up people and drop them off. There are only boats in Marblehead Harbor although transient vessels can drop anchor on the Marblehead side of the inner harbor. Sebastian also told her his father would be joining him. He then asked her if she would like to go on the yachting cruise with them and she said, "Oh I would love to! I've always loved boating."

Bruce, the waiter, is back with their drinks and serving them. He asked, "Would you like to order your dinners now?" Sebastian answered, "We need a few more minutes." The waiter left. Katherine asked, "Sebastian, I want to know about your book." He told her it will take him some time to finish it and he'll tell her some things as he goes along writing it but some will remain private until the book is published. He needs to get a lot of information from different people. As they kept chatting, Bruce, the waiter was soon back and ready to take their orders. Sebastian and Katherine both ordered roast duck with orange sauce, baked potatoes with sour cream, asparagus and salads. Sebastian also asked the waiter to bring them some water.

In the kitchen, Chef André was standing over the stove cooking. He has an accent and is obese and all in white with his tall chef's hat on. Bruce, the waiter, went over to him and told him that Sebastian, the famous writer from New York, was in their dining room with a beautiful woman and they just ordered roast duck. He also gave the chef the rest of their order. Chef André quickly responded and said, "Make sure everything is perfect when you serve him." Bruce said, "Oh I will, Chef André. Don't worry about that. Maybe I can get his autograph." The chef looked at him and said, "I already have mine." Bruce energetically went and brought water to Sebastian's table and then waited on other people.

Sebastian and Katherine were talking and sharing their stories about school. She disliked it but hung in there to get a job she would like doing which was real estate work. She's now able to live alone and support herself. Sebastian told her school was easy for him because his father encouraged him to continue. Kathryn told him that she had a happy childhood and was an only child but was sad when her parents died in their 60s. He said, "I was an only child too. We all have to deal with the hand we're dealt." Kathryn said, "That's true."

After Bruce, the waiter, arrived with the roast duck dinners, he asked if Sebastian and Katherine would like more drinks and they didn't. He then left. Sebastian took a bite of duck and loved it, and when Katherine did, she thought it was perfectly cooked and so tasty. As they enjoyed their dinner and each other's company, it was soon time for dessert. They ordered chocolate ice cream and coffee. When they finished, Sebastian paid the bill and gave Bruce, the waiter, a well deserved tip. Bruce thanked him and then asked, "Can I have your autograph? I know you're a famous mystery writer from New York." Sebastian gladly gave him his autograph on a piece of paper the waiter provided. The waiter thanked him and Sebastian just smiled. He and Katherine got up from their table and left for the mansion to have a night cap.

At the mansion, Sebastian and Katherine strolled into the living room, and while she's now on the sofa and he's on an armchair, they're each holding a glass of Chablis. She thanked him for a wonderful dinner and he told her he hopes they have more together. She soon said, "I really need to go home now. I don't like staying out late because I like getting up early in the morning, therefore, I need to go to bed early." Sebastian agreed. He then told her he has to get busy with his book but he's waiting to meet with a police officer to get more information that will help him write his book. He hopes he can help solve the murder mystery. He got up and said, "Let's walk around before you leave and look at the oil paintings." She responded by telling him she loves art. They walked in the foyer and looked at the paintings and discussed them and then looked at the ones in the living room. Katherine told Sebastian, "These paintings are good, but like I told you, they replaced very valuable original masters that were here. The masters are now in a museum for safe keeping."

While standing in the living room, Katherine decided to leave but Sebastian stopped that from happening. He got close to her while staring into her eyes and soon embraced her. He kissed her lips and she let him but then stopped him. She said, "Let's wait awhile before we take this further, Sebastian." He said, "There will be another time, Katherine." They slowly walked to the door and then said goodnight. He also waited until she got into her car before he shut his door. He then went to the living room and sat on one of his plush armchairs and thought about Katherine. When he got sleepy, he took a shower and then went to bed in Jenny's room.

The next morning, after Sebastian had breakfast in his kitchen, he thought of things to document in his red book and he also wants to go to the library. He was later outside his door leaving and spotted Charlie so he called out to him and they waived to each other.

Sebastian soon entered the library and saw his rival, the flamboyant Sam, who is a wannabe writer in his 40s. Sam found out Sebastian was in town trying to solve the 2006 triple homicide so he's trying to solve it before he does so he can be the hero. Sam got thrown out of the Ultimate Inn coffee shop by the manager Gerard one morning because he was insulting Sebastian who was trying to eat breakfast.

As Sebastian walked by Sam to get to a computer, he quietly asked him, "How are you, Sam?" Sam was surprised to see Sebastian. He answered, "I'm fine. I'm doing research on the same murder mystery you're working on and I'll find the murderer before you do!" Sebastian just ignored his unprofessional nasty manner and went to another computer in the library. As he did, Sam blurted out, "Take a long hike off of a short pier, Sebastian." Sebastian found his ignorance quite laughable and then sat at a computer where he pulled up records of people in 2006 who were arrested for crimes in Marblehead Neck. He got some insight into what kind of people were living in Jenny's neighborhood. After a couple of hours, as he was leaving the library, he noticed his rival Sam still sitting in front of the computer. Sebastian has been aware for some time that Sam is a wannabe hero and trying to be the hero of the 2006 unsolved murder mystery.

A few days later, on a sunny day, Sebastian thought he'd surprise Samantha and show up at her condo in Marblehead that he has never been to. He is wearing shorts and a sport shirt as he entered her back yard. He saw her wearing shorts and a tank top sitting at a table with a cold drink writing her book. He called out, "Hi, Samantha!" She turned and looked at him and said, "Oh what a surprise, Sebastian!" He sat with her at the table.

Sebastian said, "I thought you'd like company today, Samantha." She told him he's always welcomed and then asked him if he wanted a beverage but he didn't. He asked her about the stolen copy of an older manuscript she left at the copy center and she told him she put it aside and will look into it later. She's still working on her new novel.

Sebastian said, "I know you're from the east coast, you lived in L.A. for two years and you've had your condo here in Marblehead for two years. How do you support yourself since you haven't published any novels?" She told him she saved her money when she worked in an office and lived rent-free with her parents. They later died in a car crash and left her their fortune. He said, "I'm sorry to hear how they died."

While Samantha is sitting down and has her hand on the table, Sebastian reached out and put his hand on hers and they both made passionate eye contact while remaining silent. He then leaned over and lifted her chin with his hand and kissed her lips. She made it a very long kiss.

A short while later, Sebastian and Samantha were in her king-size bed in her condo and were partially covered with a sheet. They were making passionate love like it was their last day on earth as she kept sighing. Samantha slowly said, "I knew you'd be this sexy from the moment I met you, Sebastian." He said, "You fascinate me with your romantic look, dark hair and magnetic blue eyes, Samantha, and there's a mystery about you that baffles me." They continued to slowly move around kissing and caressing each other and still sweating even though the air conditioner was set on cold. She softly told him that their love better not be a one-night-stand. While still making love to her, he said, "We're just attracted to each other and I don't know when it will end." Samantha was outraged at his response, and before he had a chance to go into ecstasy, she quickly sat up and yelled at him, "I'm not a piece of meat! I thought you had feelings for me! Get out! Get out now, Sebastian!" He grabbed his clothes on a chair and started putting them on fast. She quickly got out of bed and put her clothes on and then threw her hair brush at him as he was leaving and she kept yelling.

The next day, in late afternoon, Samantha was sitting in Sebastian's living room on the sofa slightly intoxicated while holding a glass of red wine. He was standing while looking out the window with no beverage.

Sebastian suddenly went over and stood in front of Samantha while she was still sitting on the sofa. He said, "Samantha, about last night, our first sexual encounter, I want you to keep this in perspective. I like you as a friend. Do you understand?" She answered, "You mean I'm your play toy?" She put her drink down on the coffee table and threw her head in her hands and then threw her head back which made her hair look wild. While she was in a fury and just staring at him, she suddenly jumped up off the sofa and stood in front of him and yelled out, "I never want to see you again, Sebastian! You're like all the rest! Bye, Sebastian! You're a creep!" She started to leave and he stopped her and put his hands on her arms and told her if she continues to show a temper like she's doing, he won't want to spend any time with her. He went on and told her he's a busy writer and he can't tolerate hot tempered people around him. They stared into each other's eyes while Sebastian was still holding her arms. She had a weird mysterious look in her eyes and he sensed there was something seriously wrong with her. He let go of her arms and said, "You really need anger management help, Samantha." She stormed out of the room and slammed the door quite hard.

Now that Samantha has just left, Sebastian went and sat on an armchair and thought about her temper and feels bad for her. He also believes there's a mystery about her.

Sebastian has decided to stay away from Samantha for awhile and then maybe try to help her get some professional help and medication to control her temper. He feels it's so uncomfortable for anyone to be around someone with an uncontrollable temper like hers yet he does feel bad about it. He soon got sleepy, so he went to take a shower and then wants to go right to bed and hopes he can sleep after the evening he just spent with Samantha.

A few days later, Sebastian was at the outsource police station that he hired and now has a license to work with them. He's sitting with Lt. Darwin who has just given him papers with information that he wanted on the unsolved triple homicide of 2006 so he can try and help solve it. He allowed him to do this because he knows all about Sebastian and he knew his mother and remembers how she worked for the police and helped solve a murder which later resulted in her being murdered. Sebastian mentioned to Lt. Darwin that he knows he and Officer Martin were on the 2006 triple homicide case. The lieutenant told him he was and it was a tough case. Sebastian went on and told him that he plans to write a book about it and hopes he can help solve it. He also asked him if he remembered the name of the woman Pierce was engaged to before he met Jenny. The lieutenant told him her name was Vicki, a redheaded masseuse, and it's in the papers he just gave him. Sebastian thanked him and stood up to leave and noticed Chief Brooks and Officer Martin nearby so he waived to them and then left the police station.

The next day, Sebastian was at this desk in the living room with papers sprawled out that he has been reading from the police. He had his red hardcover book ready. Sebastian's first thought was that Jenny and Pierce must have been shot in the bedroom because their blood stains were nowhere else. The same goes for Jenny's mother, her blood stains were only in the kitchen so she most likely was murdered there. He wonders what the motive was for these murders although he has some feelings of what could have happened. He needs to know for sure if Pierce was engaged to Vicki before going with Jenny, and if so, he wants to know more about her.

Sebastian referred to his papers he got from the police that quoted, "Pierce was 27 and from Melrose, MA and left his parents Mr. and Mrs. Marlow who were both interviewed and cleared. Pierce was previously engaged to 24 year old Vicki from Revere, MA and in 2006 was interviewed and cleared." Sebastian now knows that's true. The papers also quoted, "Jenny was 23, her mother Shannon was 50 and they were both from Marblehead, Neck. The only living relative was Shannon's sister Irene of Rhode Island who was cleared. Sebastian yelled, "Then who the hell killed them?"

Sebastian read more of his papers from the police and thinks there were possibly two murderers even though Jenny's mother Shannon's body showed she was dead not long before the other two bodies. Sebastian now wants to start from the beginning of when and how the police were notified.

The outsource police were called by Mrs. North, the neighbor, who heard the gunshots in the early afternoon on July 27, 2006. Two police officers, Lieutenant Darwin and Officer Martin, responded immediately to Mrs. North's call and went to Jenny's mansion and knocked on the door and no one answered so they kicked the door in. Lieutenant Darwin found Jenny's mother Shannon on the kitchen floor who was shot in the heart twice. He found Jenny in her bed on her back with two gunshot wounds to her heart and one to her chest. Pierce, her boyfriend, was found dead on the floor near the bedroom door. He perhaps went to the door to confront the intruder and was shot. He had one gunshot to his head and one to his heart. All three people were shot with the same type of gun, and bullet casings were found in the bedroom and kitchen from a 22 caliber. Officer Martin searched all ten rooms, attic and cellar. Lieutenant Darwin then called the police department and a coroner soon arrived and an ambulance and the bodies were moved to the morgue.

Sebastian doesn't believe Jenny, her mother and Pierce were murdered over a robbery because only the first floor was robbed. There has to be another reason for these murders.

After getting up from his desk, Sebastian paced the floor for awhile as he was in deep thought. He then walked over to an armchair and flopped onto it for several moments to think. He soon said, "Hell! That's damn interesting!" He stayed there a bit longer and thought to himself trying to make sense of all this.

In a few days, Sebastian was walking around Castle Rock Park with Katherine. They then went and sat on chairs not far from the edge of the cliff and looked out at the ocean. He said, "Katherine, I'm so happy we're still seeing each other." She responded, "I feel the same, Sebastian. I've been thinking about you." He then asked her if her real estate office had any photographs of Jenny, her mother Shannon or Pierce that he could look at. She told him Jenny's Aunt Irene in Rhode Island took them. Her aunt was not in the will to receive anything else. Jenny's mother's will stated, in case she and Jenny died, she wanted all her valuable paintings donated to a museum, and, her Victorian mansion and its furnishings to be donated to a specific town for historical preservation or sale. Sebastian was in deep thought.

In an hour or so, Katherine and Sebastian went back to the mansion to make salads. She helped him make them and they were quite comfortable doing that together. They took them to the rose dining room and started eating. Sebastian told Katherine that he wants to keep seeing her because she feels like his soul mate. She first looked surprised that he said that but then laughed a little and then said, "Wow! This sounds like the beginning of a romance, Sebastian. As I told you, I've only had one serious affair in my life and it was when I was 21." She stopped talking and he said, "You don't have to tell me everything if you don't want to. What I do want is to be closer to you." They were silent while they continued eating their salad and having coffee at the table. She soon said, "I have to get back to work, Sebastian." He told her to call him anytime and she told him to call her when he wants to. They finished their coffee and stood up and he gave her a hug and then walked her to the door where they kissed for a long time. He then watched her go to her white real estate car and drive off and head back to her office.

    Sebastian went and sat on one of his wing armchairs in his huge living room immediately after Katherine left. He looked quite relaxed and definitely happy as he smiled while thinking about her and already knows she's someone he seriously wants in his life.

3

MRS. NORTH AND MRS. MARLOW

On a spring morning, Sebastian thought it would be a good idea to introduce himself to Mrs. North, an elderly woman, who lives in the Victorian house next door. He went and knocked on her door and when she opened it, she asked, "Can I help you?" Sebastian identified himself and showed her his ID card. After she read it, she invited him in. She and Sebastian sat at her dining room table while she offered him muffins with jelly and tea which he accepted. He thanked her for sitting with him to discuss the murders. She suddenly said, "Jenny's boyfriend Pierce broke off his engagement with another woman when he met Jenny. Jenny was such a sweet lady." Sebastian asked, "Did you know, Vicki, the woman Pierce was engaged to?" After telling him no, she paused and then blurted out, "I miss not having tea with Jenny."

As Sebastian and Mrs. North were discussing the murders, she suddenly told him that after the murders, there was gossip that maybe Pierce's ex-girlfriend, Vicki, had something to do with them. Sebastian told her Vicki was cleared. He went on and asked her about the gunshots she heard in the afternoon that she reported to the police. She told him she heard them in the afternoon and the news said there were also gunshots in the morning, but she didn't hear them because she wasn't home. Sebastian asked Mrs. North if she ever saw Pierce get violent with Jenny. She said, "No, but Jenny told me he had a temper. I use to see him come and go into Jenny's mansion because I look out my window a lot." She then offered Sebastian more muffins and tea and he told her he had enough. After conversing about the case awhile longer, he thanked her for her help and the tea. He stood up and wished her a nice day and she, being elderly, slowly walked with him to the door and said, "Goodbye, Sebastian."

As Sebastian was leaving Mrs. North's house, he decided to drive to the police station and ask for a physical description of Vicki who was engaged to Pierce before he met Jenny. After receiving it from Lt. Darwin, he thanked him and left. Lt. Darwin has already allowed Sebastian to take notes from Mrs. North and Mrs. Marlow when he visits them.

Sebastian got back to the mansion and wrote in his red book the description of Vicki at the time of the murders. The files read: She was age 24, 5 feet 5 inches tall, overweight, short red hair, wore glasses, had a large nose and needed dental work. She was cooperative at times but had a bad temper and had a police record for physical violence. Sebastian looked into her record and didn't find anything alarming although she was in court a couple of times. As he looked up from his desk for a few moments, he admired the sunlight coming through the windows casting shadows on the wall of maple tree leaves swaying in the wind. He then thought for a moment of what a hell of a case this is. It happened four years ago and still no one knows who the murderer or murderers were.

Sebastian's first scenario was that a robber, in late morning, thinking no one was home, gained entry through the back door by swiping a card through the door lock. He started to rob valuables but Shannon, who was in the kitchen, heard him and came near the kitchen entrance and was startled by this scary robber. When he saw her, he quickly shot her twice. The robber knew the neighbor Mrs. North wasn't home in the morning to hear the gunshots because he saw her leave. The robber continued to rob the place of antiques and stash them in a hallway closet until he left. He soon heard Jenny and Pierce come in through the front door and go into her bedroom. She never knew her mother was dead in the kitchen. The robber hid in the house for awhile hoping they'd leave but they didn't. It could have been early afternoon by now and Mrs. North was home and was about to hear the gunshots. Jenny was in bed on her back dozing off, Pierce was in the bedroom and heard noise and walked to the bedroom door and opened it. He was shocked when he saw a robber at the door. The robber shot him. Then Jenny heard the noise, sat up and looked at the robber who then shot her so they couldn't identify him. He then left with antiques. Mrs. North heard gunshots and called the police.

After Sebastian thought for a moment, he said, "Maybe there were two separate robberies, even though the coroner said Shannon was dead awhile before Jenny and Pierce. One could have been late morning and the other could have been early afternoon when Mrs. North heard the gunshots.

Sebastian's second scenario was that the robber, in late morning, thinking no one was home, gained entry through the back door swiping a card. Shannon spotted him from the kitchen where she was standing, and he knew it so he shot her twice and then continued to rob the place. He knew the neighbor

Mrs. North wasn't home in the morning to hear the gunshots. He made several trips to his car with antiques and then left the mansion and got in his car and drove away.

Shortly after the above morning robbery, it was then early afternoon. Maybe a different robber gained entry through the back door swiping a card through the door lock. Maybe he thought the neighbor wasn't home in the afternoon. He first went into the living room, not knowing the mother was dead on the kitchen floor, and started to rob but suddenly heard someone come in the mansion. It was Jenny and Pierce who came in and went into her bedroom. She got on her bed, closed her eyes and was about to doze off while relaxing on her back and he stayed with her. Pierce suddenly heard noise and went to the bedroom door and opened it and was startled as he saw a robber at the door. The robber quickly shot him twice. Jenny heard the shots and sat up and saw the robber, so he shot her too so they couldn't identify him. He then maybe had second thoughts about the neighbor who might be home and heard the gunshots, so he robbed a few valuables and got out of the mansion fast, got in his car and drove away.

Sebastian was through with his scenarios. He went to his kitchen and poured himself a soft drink and then paced the floor with it. He soon went and sat on a chair to think.

The next day, Sebastian went to the cemetery to visit the graves of Jenny, her mother Shannon and her boyfriend Pierce. He spent more time sitting by Jenny's grave. He soon got a sense that someone was right in back of him. He quickly turned around but there was no one there. He then left.

A few days later, Sebastian's friend Alan, the movie producer from Hollywood, was visiting him. Sebastian just finished giving him a tour of the ten rooms and then they went and stood in the living room. Alan said, "Sebastian, I love the place. Let's have a drink to our friendship." Sebastian went to the bar area and asked, "What will it be, Alan?" "Oh, I'll have a glass red wine if you have it." Sebastian then poured them each one. They kept standing and talking about the very successful pitch party Alan just had. Sebastian soon said, "I've been with Samantha a few times since the pitch party and wow! You were so right about a dark side to her. Anyway, I'll probably stay friends with her. That's all I'm going to say right now, Alan." After Alan smiled, he asked, "Did you romance her?" Sebastian told him, "I have and that's as far as I want to go talking about it." Alan went on and asked him how his book was coming along and Sebastian told him he has a lot of information. After their drinks, they went to the harbor and walked around awhile to enjoy the scenery before going to dinner.

Later, Alan and Sebastian were at a restaurant near the harbor which had a beautiful view of all the boating activity. While enjoying oysters on the half shell and pasta with red clam sauce, they sipped wine and talked about old times and laughed a lot until late evening. They sure do like each other's company and are true friends.

The next morning, Sebastian made eggs with turkey sausage, raisin cinnamon toast, juice and coffee. When it was ready, he had it in his white and blue cozy kitchen that has a swinging door which he loves that only has access to the dining room. After breakfast, Sebastian planned to work on his manuscript and can hardly wait to put more ideas in it. He also wonders why many people have told him the mansion is haunted. He's not totally convinced, even though, at times, he has felt a strange breeze in the mansion. Then there was a time he looked in the china cabinet mirror and saw his reflection and something pale and shadowy in back of it. When he quickly turned around to see if someone was there, there was no one. He thought maybe the mirror needed cleaning so he wiped it and looked in it again and there was nothing in back of his reflection. However, he won't dismiss that from his thoughts.

Sebastian went to his desk and had his red hardcover book open and ready to continue writing his manuscript about the unsolved triple homicide that occurred in 2006. But his mind first drifted to the attic to the life-size naked female mannequin that has large haunting pale blue eyes, has a black bushy wig on and red lipstick. He's been to the attic several times since he has moved in the mansion and thinks it's quite mysterious, especially the mannequin which is fascinating and almost hypnotic. Sebastian wants to look in more boxes that are there to see if there are any clues to the murders, or, maybe he'll run across something strange that led to a private life Jenny had and no one knew about. And maybe he'll find something about Jenny's mother Shannon.

Now that Sebastian's mind has shifted back to his red hardcover book, he wants to get started writing at his desk, but as he did, his cell phone rang which was on a table next to a wing armchair. He went and answered it and it was Saul, the bartender, from the Ultimate Inn lounge and bar. He invited him to a special party that the lounge and bar will be having to celebrate the Ultimate Inn's 20 year anniversary. There will be food and entertainment and it's in two weeks on a Saturday night. He thought Sebastian might like to take a break from his writing to relax a little. Sebastian thanked him and told him he'd try to go but he may not be able to because he's very busy with his book. They soon hung up and he shut his cell phone off and returned to his desk and started writing. As he wrote the name Jenny, he suddenly got a premonition that something paranormal was about to happen. Then chills ran through his body.

When Sebastian started writing the name Jenny again, there was a breeze and scent of gardenias that filled the air. He immediately sensed there was a spirit in the room with him. Feeling that the mansion is haunted, he is anxiously waiting to see what will happen next. A moment later, he felt the presence of a spirit close by. He quickly turned around on his chair and experienced a ghostly encounter standing near the middle of the living room about eight feet from him. Even though he's a powerful psychic medium and clairvoyant which makes him able to communicate with the dead, and has the ability to perceive things that are not in sight, he's shocked because he has never seen a ghost. The disembodied spirit of this dead person was a pale lifelike ghostly apparition of a stunning female wearing a sheer pink nightgown which was long and loose-fitting. She was young, slender, pretty with dark eyes, long light brown hair and was staring at Sebastian.

While Sebastian stared at the ghost, he wasn't sure it was Jenny because the picture he saw of her in the newspaper wasn't clear. With his unusual power, he asked, "Are you Jenny?" She answered in a soft and gentle voice, "I'm Jenny. I know you've come to help me." She paused and then cried out to him, "Help me! Help me!" Jenny's ghost suddenly disappeared and so did the gardenia scent.

Sebastian was shocked. He got up from his chair and paced the floor while he said out loud, "I just saw Jenny's ghost and heard her talk to me, and, I saw her lips move! She almost looked alive. This is the first ghost I've ever seen. This is not a dream! I am really in a haunted mansion!"

As the day went on, Sebastian couldn't get it out of his mind that he saw Jenny's ghost and how stunning her apparition was. He documented his latest information in his red book and into the computer. By late afternoon, he made himself a cup of tea. He later drank a glass of wine and fell asleep on one of the beautiful mahogany wing armchairs.

The very next morning, Sebastian thought of Jenny's boyfriend Pierce, who was murdered with her, and decided to visit his mother who lives in Melrose, MA. He showered, shaved, had breakfast, got dressed and headed out to Melrose.

In Melrose, MA, not far from Marblehead, Sebastian arrived at Pierce's mother's house, Mrs. Marlow, and he's about to introduce himself to her. She is an elderly woman. After he knocked on her door, she answered it and just stared at him. Sebastian introduced himself and showed her his ID card, and after she read it, she then invited him into her colonial style living room. While she's sitting on a chair, Sebastian is sitting across from her on a sofa as she asked, "Sebastian, would you like some coffee or tea?" "Coffee would be nice, Mrs. Marlow." She left the room to make it and he got up and looked at the framed pictures that were displayed on a table. He spotted a picture of Pierce and Jenny. He now sees the resemblance of Jenny's ghost that he saw yesterday in his living room and this picture.

Mrs. Marlow returned with a tray of coffee, cream and sugar and some hermit cookies. Sebastian went back and sat on the sofa and said, "I was looking at your nice picture of Jenny and Pierce." She said, "Yes, I often look at it and cry."

While Mrs. Marlow and Sebastian are having coffee and cookies, she said, "I'm sorry my husband is not available right now but I hope I can be helpful." He said, "I'm sure you will. I want you to know the police have allowed me to take notes from our meeting, so please tell me about Vicki."

Mrs. Marlow went on and told Sebastian that it all started when her son Pierce was 26 years old and the manager of the Ultimate Inn in Marblehead and Vicki was 24, a redhead from Revere that worked as a masseuse in Boston. She use to stop in the Ultimate Inn lounge and got to know Pierce so she invited him for a free massage. He went and then soon started dating Vicki. After one year, they got engaged. Mrs. Marlow then told him that Pierce said Vicki had a terrible temper and she occasionally got physically violent with him but he continued to go with her. Then, one day Pierce went to a bookstore where Jenny worked and they right away were attracted to each other. He kept visiting her at the local bookstore and they wanted to date so Pierce broke off his engagement to Vicki and she didn't take it well.

Sebastian asked, "What do you mean? Vicki didn't take it well." Mrs. Marlow told him she kept calling Pierce and arguing with him, and maybe her temper came from something in her past. She then got up and took a picture out of a draw and showed him Vicki's picture. Sebastian looked at it and then asked, "Mrs. Marlow, what's the name of the place in Boston she worked at?" She couldn't remember. Sebastian told her he wants to contact Vicki but Mrs. Marlow said, "Oh you can't! Before the murders, her mother and father's house was up for sale because they were planning to sell it and retire in Los Angeles. Awhile after the murders, the house sold and Vicki moved with her parents so she could maybe become a cosmetologist to movie stars." Sebastian said, "Well, I don't want to take up all your time, Mrs. Marlow." She suddenly blurted out, "One more thing! Something strange happened at the wake!" Sebastian said, "Please go on and tell me." He is now very curious.

Mrs. Marlow began to tell Sebastian what happened at the wake which was held for Pierce, Jenny and Shannon. She told him that all three of them were at the same funeral home at the same time. Shannon's casket was on the left, Jenny's was placed in the middle and her son Pierce's was on the right. There were lots of people who came to mourn.

Sebastian kept listening to Mrs. Marlow go on. She suddenly looked a little spaced-out as she had a flashback of the wake.

She told Sebastian that Shannon's sister Irene from Rhode Island was there and was quite old. She was dressed in purple and had white hair and that they had a conversation about the deaths. Irene told her that she was devastated over the loss of her sister Shannon and her niece Jenny. Irene then went over and kneeled at her sister Shannon's casket and another mourner kneeled at Jenny's. She and her husband kneeled at their son Pierce's casket. All of a sudden, Mrs. Marlow's eyes got very large while staring into space as she told Sebastian that while they were all kneeling at the caskets, Jenny's body suddenly sprung up! She sat straight up and then moved one arm! All of the mourners got shocked and ran out of the funeral home while screaming and so did she and her husband. Sebastian kept listening to Mrs. Marlow and was fascinated by what she just told him. Mrs. Marlow suddenly came back to earth and stared right at Sebastian and said, "Some people say Jenny's spirit couldn't rest because she wanted the murderer found and have justice served." Mrs. Marlow then became silent as she stared at Sebastian and waited for his response.

Sebastian told Mrs. Marlow that Jenny's body maybe sprung up from a reflex or the way she was placed in the casket. He then told her that she was very helpful and thanked her for the coffee and hermit cookies but now he has to leave. She said, "They were homemade hermit cookies!"

He smiled and then she said, "It was such a pleasure to spend time with you, Sebastian, and maybe it was just a reflex that made Jenny spring up but I'm still scared." He told her not to worry about it. She slowly walked him to the door and they both said goodbye. Sebastian went back to his mansion and documented all his information he got from Mrs. Marlow and it certainly was a lot and he was quite happy with it.

A next day, Sebastian was at the library again but he didn't see his rival, the flamboyant wannabe writer, Sam. He went on and looked up robberies that took place in Marblehead and in Jenny's neighborhood in 2006 at the time of the mansion murders. He singled out a few and thought to himself that he has to get the police reports on some of these robbers and especially one in particular and that is Alfred. Sebastian is back at his mansion and sitting at his desk writing in his red hardcover book and also putting some information in his computer about the robbery reports.

For the next two days, Sebastian wants to step back from this murder case and take a break and then come back with a fresh new look at it. Today, he had the urge to go up in the attic to look around and take another look at the spooky mannequin that's up there. While he was on his way up there, he checked the four bedrooms, three baths and the sewing room on the second floor. Everything looked the same as the first time he saw it so he continued on up to the attic.

When Sebastian got to the attic, he just stood at the entrance and then scanned it looking for the naked female mannequin. He suddenly spotted it in the same place where he last saw it so now he knows that no ghost has moved it. He went over to it and stared at its head with its black bushy hair, red lipstick and large haunting pale blue eyes. Even though the mannequin is scary, Sebastian still thinks it should be in the sewing room because seamstresses use mannequins. He then went on and looked in a trunk and there were some blankets, doilies and an old dress in it which looked like it was from the 1800s. He thought it belonged to someone who lived in the mansion before Jenny and her mother. While looking at an antique frame, he suddenly heard a snap and then felt a chill so he quickly turned around and scanned the attic. He noticed the mannequin's head was now turned and staring at him! It wasn't that way when he looked at it a few minutes ago. He became curious. He then went over to it and looked at it up close, and, when he did, it snapped its head back to the original position it had always been in. He left the attic and went to his living room to sit and think about it.

The next day, Sebastian decided to give Samantha a call, and soon after that, they were sitting in a booth in a pizza house. While they were eating pizza and having red wine, he stopped and said, "I'm sorry I haven't called you for awhile but I've been so busy with this murder case and I don't like arguing with you. You need medication." Samantha said, "I'll try to control my temper and maybe see a doctor." He told her he'd take her to dinner some night which caused her to give him a passionate look and then wink at him.

Sebastian started telling Samantha what has been happening with his murder case. He told her that the mansion is an eerie place at times and that he gets chills and breezes and knows they're coming from a spirit. He didn't tell her that he saw Jenny's ghost because he wants to tell the police first. He also told her that one day while he was in the attic, the mannequin turned its head. Samantha's magnetic blue eyes popped while she held her pizza and stared at Sebastian. She said, "I wonder if anyone will believe that story about the mannequin, Sebastian. But I believe in ghosts." He knows some people won't believe him about the chills, breezes or the mannequin's head turning but he does and that's what matters to him. He knows the mansion is spooked.

After Sebastian and Samantha finished their pizza and salad, he told her he's glad they're still talking to each other. She told him she is too and that he can tell her anything he wants about the murders or the breezes and chills coming from spirits because it fascinates her. But the mannequin's head turning, she's not sure it's what he thinks. She thinks something broke in the neck area. He's skeptical about that and plans to look at the mannequin another day, however, he believes there'll be more strange breezes and chills.

Samantha went on and told Sebastian that the breezes and chills he got could have been from a very old spirit of someone who lived there fifty years ago. Sebastian said "Oh, no! I believe it was Jenny's spirit." While Samantha's holding her glass with a little wine in it, she suddenly dropped her glass and spilled wine on a small area on the table. They both took napkins and wiped it up. She and Sebastian then stared at each other for a moment while remaining silent because they both thought a spirit may have caused her to drop her glass. He and Samantha ordered another wine and lingered on it before leaving the pizza house. After they left, they walked to his car and before they got in it they hugged and kissed. They soon arrived at Samantha's condo and said goodnight in the car and he told her he'd call her. Sebastian then headed back to his mansion and called it a night.

The next day, late afternoon, Sebastian looked out his back window and saw Charlie moving shrubs to a strange dark area in the backyard that looked unusual so he wants to keep an eye on him. He then called Katherine and asked her if she would like to go with him to the Ultimate Inn's 20th anniversary party which is Saturday night. She declined but thanked him. He then told her he's happy she's going on the yachting cruise with him and his dad Oliver when he comes to visit him soon. She said, "It really sounds good to me and I'm looking forward to it. It would be wonderful to spend the day out on the ocean." Sebastian told her he'd let her know when and then she can tell him if it's convenient for her. He also needs to talk with his dad to see what is convenient for him, but meanwhile, he wants to get together with her. She told him she wants to, but right now, she's busy with paper work and they can talk later. After they said goodbye, Sebastian looked like he was going to jump for joy. He's sure that she's the kind of woman he wants to keep in his life. She's beautiful, classy, gentle and kind.

Saturday evening has arrived and Sebastian is dressing up for the Ultimate Inn's 20th anniversary party. He looks very handsome in a pink shirt, and his brown wavy hair and cologne smells wonderful. He is anxious just to get away from his writing and enjoy a party. He's also looking forward to seeing Saul, the bartender, who is in his 30s and who invited him to the party and who he sees once in awhile when he stops in the lounge. Sebastian is about ready to leave the mansion and this party is just what he needs to relax and have a little fun for a change.

When Sebastian arrived at the Ultimate Inn's lounge and sat at the bar, he couldn't help but notice the place was packed with people, balloons, and free food was placed all over the bar and tables. The young pianist, Danny, who always wears a hat while tickling the ivories, was playing a tune while Phoebe stood next to him and belted out a song as she faced the customers. She's a pretty girl in her 30s with dark brown hair, about 5 feet tall and slightly overweight. Saul came over to Sebastian and was happy to see him. He took his order for a soft drink and brought it to him, then left.

Sebastian kept watching Phoebe sing and loved it and he also liked Danny at the piano who suddenly yelled out to customers, "Give Phoebe a hand!" The customers applauded her. Saul was back and asking Sebastian how his book was coming along and he told him it's looking good because he has a lot of information. Just then, Gerard, the Ultimate Inn's manager came over. He is in his late 20s, stocky and pleasant and Saul introduced him to Sebastian. After they shook hands, Gerard told him he knows who he is and he's a fan of his non-fiction murder mysteries. Sebastian said, "Thank you. I remember you, Gerard. One morning, not long ago, I was trying to have breakfast while a customer named Sam kept harassing me and you threw him out." Gerard did remember and smiled. After they talked a little, Gerard left.

Sebastian noticed all the bar stools were occupied. He looked around at the crowd of people and saw Veronica, the young redheaded waitress with the bubbly personality, who was working and enjoying her gum. He gets a kick out of her. She spotted Sebastian at the bar and went over to him. She stopped chewing her gum and said, "It's so nice to see you again, Sebastian." He said, "Oh, I'm happy to see you too, Veronica. Nice party!" She agreed and told him she had to get back to work and so she left.

Saul came back over to Sebastian and asked him if he would like another soft drink but he didn't. Saul then said, "By the way, I'd like you to meet the Ultimate Inn's Security Inspector Bradford who just came in. I'll bring him over to meet you as soon as he finishes talking with some people he's with now." Sebastian told him he'd like that. Saul suddenly noticed the inspector wasn't talking with anyone so he called him over to the bar. He then introduced Sebastian to him and they shook hands and were pleased to meet each other. Inspector Bradford then said, "I can't talk now because I'm on security watch." Sebastian told him he understood so in a few minutes the inspector left. Sebastian then ate chicken wings that were placed in front of him.

There was soon loud noise coming from customers at the bar. They were Alfred, who's thin, wore glasses and had dark clothes on, his friend Dex who's obese and frumpy, and Sebastian's rival, Sam, wearing a red shirt and yellow pants.

While Sebastian was still at the bar, his rival Sam, the wannabe writer, was drunk and suddenly came over to him and yelled, "I'll solve the murders before you, Sebastian!" He then threw a punch in his face. Sebastian swiftly reacted by punching Sam in the jaw and knocking him onto the floor. The piano player, Danny, stopped playing and there was no laughter as people watched Sebastian hold Sam down on the floor. Officer Martin just came in and caught the whole incident and sees

Sebastian on top of Sam. He quickly took over and cuffed Sam and took him to the police station.

The Ultimate Inn's lounge and bar was now quiet while customers asked each other what happened. The Security Inspector Bradford and Gerard the manager were in another part of the Inn when they got a call about this and rushed right over to the lounge. Sebastian was back sitting at the bar and Saul asked, "Is your face in pain?" Sebastian answered, "I'm okay." Saul asked him if her wanted a beverage but he didn't want anything. Inspector Bradford and Gerard, the manager, are now talking with Sebastian and asking if he's alright and Sebastian told them he'll be okay. Saul told Gerard and Inspector Bradford that Sam threw the first punch. Sebastian soon wanted to leave so he said goodbye to Saul, Inspector Bradford and Gerard as they all shook hands. Gerard said, "You'll never see Sam here again." Sebastian gave him two thumbs up and left while many customers left with him.

4

THE UNEXPECTED VISITOR

    While Sebastian was driving home from the Ultimate Inn party, he was thinking of the violence that just happened there which was fueled by Sam's alcohol consumption.

    After Sebastian arrived at his mansion, he got out of his car and saw his living room lamp was still lit like he left it which was to let thieves think he was home. He entered the beautiful rose foyer and went into his living room and suddenly looked twice at one of the wing armchairs. To his amazement, a ghost was sitting on it. It was a pale lifelike ghostly apparition of a woman who looked to be around fifty years old who was sobbing. He sensed it was Jenny's mother Shannon's ghost which makes this the second ghost he has seen and leads him to wonder if there are more to come.

Sebastian quickly sat on the sofa and continued to stare at the ghost who had some gray hair and was wearing a house dress. He asked, "Are you Shannon, Jenny's mother?" As the ghost stared at Sebastian, she cried out to him as her face expressed tremendous fear, "Help! Help me! I'm Shannon! Help!" Sebastian's unusual power enabled them to hear each other. He then asked, "What happened to you, Shannon?" She was silent. Sebastian suddenly heard two loud gunshots and then Shannon's ghost slightly bent over and mumbled, "Ahhhhh. Help me. I've been shot." As blood was coming from her gunshot wounds that were to her heart, her ghost suddenly disappeared from the wing armchair. He yelled, "Wait! Don't go!" He was stunned over this apparition. Seeing ghosts is new to him, and since he has seen two so far and hears them talk, he believes it's because he's an unusual psychic medium and he's living where they were murdered.

The next morning, as Sebastian awakened in Jenny's bed and his face was sore from Sam's punch, he thought of Shannon's ghostly apparition and the blood he saw on her caused from the gunshots which saddened him. He went into the shower and continued to think about Shannon being shot and how senseless the murder was. After getting dressed, he headed out to the police station.

Sebastian is at the police station this morning and talking with Officer Martin and thanking him for taking care of Sam. He told him how his face is sore from Sam's punch. Officer Martin noticed his face was swollen and told him he was sorry he had to experience that incident. He went on and told him that Sam was held overnight and released early this morning, and if Sebastian decides to press charges for assault and battery, he needs to file a complaint and the court will give him a date to appear. Sebastian then said, "I most likely won't file a complaint. I have other things to think about are more important.

Meanwhile, I have more news for you." He handed the officer a report of the information.

Sebastian then told Officer Martin how he recently experienced ghostly encounters in the mansion The officer asked, "What?" Sebastian told him he saw Jenny's ghost and her mother Shannon's. They talked to him and he heard them because of his unusual psychic power. The officer looked shocked as he stared at him. Then Sebastian used Jenny as an example. He told him that Jenny's messages could lead him to the murderer, then he'll deliver her messages to the police. The officer just stared at him.

Sebastian went on and told Officer Martin that he now believes in ghosts because he just saw two. The officer then said, "Tell more about it." Sebastian told him how he saw the ghosts on separate days, a couple of weeks apart, and they were lifelike ghostly apparitions. He told him they were easy to communicate with. Officer Martin is fascinated at what he's telling him. Sebastian told him that when he arrived home from the Ultimate Inn party, he walked into his living room and saw Shannon's ghost which was a pale lifelike ghost sitting on a wing armchair. He asked her if she was Shannon and she told him she was. He heard her cries for help, two gunshots and then saw the blood, then she disappeared. The officer said, "Sebastian, maybe the eerie mansion is causing illusions." He said, "Not at all. I'm a psychic medium with unusual power and that's why I'm able to communicate with spirits, and, see and hear ghosts speak. I'm also clairvoyant." The officer said, "You have the ability to perceive things that are not in sight! That's a special gift."

After the long and lengthy ghost talk, Officer Martin thanked Sebastian for the update on Mrs. North and Mrs. Marlow's interviews he had with them.

Sebastian then asked Officer Martin if he could have a copy of the police reports on robberies that happened in Jenny's neighborhood at the time of the murders. He told him he read up on some on his computer and didn't like what he read about a particular guy named Alfred. Officer Martin said, "Oh yes, he's trouble but we couldn't link him to the triple homicide murders in 2006." He then gave Sebastian a printout and said, "I hope you find out something." Sebastian went on and told him he's renting the mansion for at least a year and maybe more, since he has had ghosts sightings. He then told him that he sleeps in Jenny's bed and thinks he'll sense something from sleeping there. The officer thanked him for his help and then they stood up and shook hands and Sebastian left the outsource police station.

It's late afternoon and Sebastian has just entered his mansion foyer with the police report on Alfred in his hand and went into the living room and put it down on his desk. At that moment, he noticed the scent of gardenias in the air and so he inhaled. While looking around the living room, he called out, "Jenny!" He inhaled again and then asked, "Is that you, Jenny?" No message was sent and there was no sign of Jenny's ghost and the gardenia scent faded. He dismissed that and headed to the full-bath in Jenny's bathroom.

After Sebastian got in the bathroom, he turned the shower on, and in seconds, he was in it while it was steamy and hot and it felt wonderful as he suds up all over. He soon got out of the shower and stood on the plush rug drying himself off and then tying a towel around his waist. Just then, he noticed the scent of gardenias. He quickly called out, "Jenny!" Shockingly, there she was, one foot in front of him. It was Jenny's pale lifelike ghostly apparition wearing a sheer pale green nightgown looking beautiful and mesmerizing. He thought for a moment, "This is her second apparition."

With his towel around him, Sebastian and Jenny's pale lifelike ghost are standing in the bathroom just staring at each other because her sheer pale green nightgown, long light brown hair, brown eyes and pretty face has made him immobile. She put her arms around him and this is when he was shocked that a ghost was embracing him. Without speaking, she seduced him by slowly and gently moving her body against his. While he could feel her doing this to him, he was suddenly propelled into ecstasy and was able to put his arms around her and feel her, even though she was a ghost! They kissed and slowly went down onto the plush rug and soon made passionate love. Her spiritual power gave him strange love pleasure like he never felt before and made him lose touch with the living world. He was now in the world of ghosts. While continuing their passion, he said, "Oh Jenny!" He was soon on his back looking fatigued as Jenny's ghost suddenly disappeared with the gardenia scent.

The next morning, Sebastian was sitting on the sofa in the living room holding a cup of coffee and he couldn't get his mind off of what happened with Jenny's ghost last night. He said, "I actually made love with a ghost! Who would ever believe this? I never felt anything like it in my life! She took me to her world. I also know the scent of gardenias in the air precedes her apparitions."

Later on, Sebastian got back to his work but found it hard to concentrate. He worked on his story documenting his new information about Jenny and her mother Shannon.

Now that Sebastian has the police report on Alfred, the alleged thief/murderer, he has decided to call him. In the afternoon, Sebastian was sitting on a wing armchair and using his cell phone while calling Alfred who now lives in Swampscott, MA. The phone rang but there was no answer.

Sebastian called Alfred again and there was no answer so he decided to go to his home in Swampscott and maybe he'll answer his door. Alfred is in his early 50s, small, thin, dark hair, wears glasses and looks suspicious. Sebastian arrived at his home and knocked on his door several times and then a man answered it fitting Alfred's description. He was wearing dark clothes and asked, "What do you want?" Sebastian asked, "Are you Alfred?" He said, "Yes, why? Who are you and what do you want?" Sebastian introduced himself and showed him his ID card. After Alfred read it, Sebastian told him he's a renowned mystery writer and he's writing a new book on the triple homicide which happened in the Marblehead Neck mansion in 2006. Alfred said, "Oh no. Not again! I've been out of trouble for years!" Sebastian told him that his new book will give him a chance to clear himself again and say something maybe he forgot to say. Sebastian then sensed that Alfred has been in the mansion.

While Alfred is still at the door with Sebastian, Alfred thought for a moment that maybe he can clear his name again so he invited Sebastian into his home for only a few minutes.

Sebastian is sitting on a chair holding a pad and pen and Alfred's smoking a cigarette while sitting on another chair across from him. Sebastian first said, "I appreciate your time, Alfred." He didn't respond. Sebastian then asked him if he minded if he taped their conversation and Alfred said, "Go ahead. I've done this before." Sebastian went on and asked him if he was presently married and Alfred answered, "No, why?" Sebastian told him it was just a question. He then asked him if his real name was Alfred and he told him it was. He asked him if he was ever in the Marblehead Neck mansion where Jenny lived and where the three murders took place in 2006. He answered, "Why should I tell you that? You're not a cop!" Sebastian explained that he's not a police officer but here's a chance to clear himself in his new book, many people read them. Alfred said, "Some questions, I won't answer."

While Sebastian was still interviewing Alfred, he just stopped for a second and got up and looked around the room they were sitting in and noticed valuable antiques. Sebastian suddenly had a clairvoyant moment of Alfred in his living room mansion. He then said, "Those are beautiful antiques you have!" Alfred told him he had them for years and wanted to know what else Sebastian wanted to ask him. Sebastian went back and sat down and asked him what he would like to say to anyone who reads his new book. Alfred answered, "I had nothing to do with those murders! It would be hard enough doing one!" Sebastian then asked, "Were you ever involved in 'one' murder?" Alfred got very angry with that question and quickly stood up. He threw his arm out and pointed his finger in Sebastian's face while yelling, "Okay, you're out of here, pal!" Sebastian got up and grabbed his recorder, pad and pen and walked to the door while Alfred was right behind him. Sebastian said, "I'm very sorry, Alfred. I didn't mean to upset you. One of your answers just led me to that last question." Alfred yelled at him again to get out and don't ever come back. He then slammed the door and you could hear him yelling from the street.

Sebastian left Alfred's home quite happy with all the information he got from him. He went back to his mansion and documented it in his red hardcover book. He also prepared a report to bring to Officer Martin or Lt. Darwin. The next morning, Sebastian was sitting with Officer Martin and has just handed him his new report on Alfred and a tape recording. He then told him he had a clairvoyant moment of Alfred in the mansion. Officer Martin thanked him and said, "Good job." They talked a little about the interview and then Sebastian stood up as they shook hands goodbye.

A few days later, in the early evening, Sebastian was out and forgot to take his cell phone with him, therefore, he didn't stay out long just in case someone was trying to reach him with important news.

When Sebastian got back to his mansion and looked at his phone messages, he saw that his dad Oliver left a message so he called him immediately and said, "Hi, dad! I got your message. How are you?" "I'm fine, Sebastian. I just called you to see how things were going with you" Sebastian told him everything was okay and he has lots of news to tell him when he visits. He asked his dad if he could come and see him and stay for a few weeks at his mansion. He wants to rent a yacht and bring Katherine, the woman who rented him the mansion. He told his dad that she's beautiful, in her 30s and he wishes he could have an affair with her but they're just friends now. Oliver told him he knows exactly what he means. He also told him that it's August now and a perfect time for boating or yachting and he can get away when he wants. That's the jewelry business he's in. Sebastian told him he'll get back to him with a date because he has to check with Katherine first to see what date in August is convenient for her. Oliver said, "No problem, Sebastian. Call me a week before we go so I can plan it. I'm anxious to see your mansion and to think I'll be sleeping in it." Sebastian said, "I'll get back to you, dad!" They then hung up.

It was soon after Sebastian's call to his dad that he was on the phone with Katherine. She was looking at her calendar for a vacation date. She suddenly said, "In two weeks it would be a good time to go yachting and I'm anxious to meet your father." He said, "I'm so happy that you're going on a yacht with us. We'll have a great day." They talked a bit and he told her he has news on the murders that he'll fill her in with when he sees her. They said goodbye and hung up.

The Ghost And Sebastian

Sebastian worked on his book for several days and stopped. He started thinking about the day he, Katherine and his dad will be going on a yacht cruise for a day. After looking at his calendar, he called Marblehead Harbormaster and was able to obtain a temporary permit for a motor yacht to drop anchor near the harbor to pick up guests. He rented a luxurious motor yacht that's 78 feet by 9 inches long that accommodates eight guests. It will have a captain who will be in complete control at the ergonomic and well appointed helm with seating for one companion. The date has been set.

Two weeks later, on a beautiful morning which was the day before the yachting day, Oliver was about to arrive at his son Sebastian's mansion but will only stay three days. While Sebastian was having coffee and toast in his white and blue kitchen, he thought about his dad who will be arriving this morning. Someone suddenly kept knocking on the door.

Sebastian quickly answered the door and it was his dad and he was not alone! He was standing there dressed in white and smiling with two small suitcases on the doorstep, and on his arm was a beautiful woman who was smiling. Sebastian immediately told them to come in and he and his dad hugged. Oliver is tall with brown wavy hair like his son Sebastian and a fun guy to be with. He's also a widower in his 60s and a wealthy jeweler in New York who has a few beautiful female companions. The woman Oliver is with now is a woman about 35 years old. She has very long blonde hair, very shapely and wearing daringly short and tight white shorts, pink tight tank top, pink lipstick and eye-makeup. She looks like a glamour girl. As they stood in the beautiful rose foyer, Oliver introduced Sebastian to his female companion whose name is Elaina and they shook hands and smiled. Sebastian put the suitcases aside and then led his father and Elaina into the huge Victorian burgundy living room.

Oliver's first reaction was, "Sebastian, this place is really gorgeous!" Elaina said, "Oh, it's beautiful." Sebastian told them he'll give them a tour of the mansion after they settle down. He then asked them if they wanted anything to eat or drink and they wanted something cold to drink but not alcohol at that hour. Sebastian left to get them all a tall glass of lemonade filled with ice. When he returned, they sat for awhile talking about Oliver and Elaina's flight from New York and how they're looking forward to their yachting day tomorrow. Sebastian said, "I am so looking forward to it and I have a date too. She is the real estate agent who rented me this mansion. Her name is Katherine and she's a beautiful blonde in her 30s. I'm quite attracted to her and hoping that something good will come of it." Oliver wished him the very best and expressed how he is anxious to meet her tomorrow.

Later, Sebastian was giving Oliver and Elaina a tour of the mansion. When he showed them the four bedrooms on the second floor, he told them they can share one or have separate rooms. Elaina said, "I'd rather snuggle with Oliver."

Oliver, Elaina and Sebastian were then on their way up to the attic. When they got there, Oliver spotted the naked female mannequin and went over to it and said, "I don't know if I like this mannequin. Her large haunting pale blue eyes look strange and so does her black bushy hair!" Sebastian told him he feels the same about it, and then told him, the mannequin turned its head by itself, two days ago. Oliver and Elaina looked stunned. Sebastian then said, "Maybe the neck is broken." He started feeling the neck all over and said, "I don't think it's broken. That means, I'll keep wondering if something weird's going on with this mannequin." All three of them became silent and left the attic.

In the kitchen, Sebastian is showing Oliver and Elaina the swinging door to the dining room. After that, they went into

Jenny's bedroom and Sebastian said to his dad Oliver, "I sleep here in Jenny's bed. I believe this is where I'm going to sense how the murders happened and it's a matter of time. I've already seen Jenny's ghost twice, dad! After that, I saw her mother Shannon's ghost. They were pale lifelike ghostly apparitions and we heard each other speak because of my power." Oliver was speechless for a moment but then told Sebastian that maybe he's drinking too much. Sebastian told him he's not, he's a powerful psychic medium and clairvoyant and that's why he can communicate with spirits, see and hear ghosts speak, and perceive things that are not in sight.

When the tour was over, Oliver told Sebastian that he thinks the mansion is amazing and wouldn't mind if he owned it. He went on and asked Sebastian if he would like to own it. Sebastian snapped and answered, "Of course not, dad! It's spooked with ghosts who come out! I don't want to be around them that much. And I don't know what the mannequin in the attic is going to do next!" While Oliver and Elaina were silent, Sebastian told them to change the subject because he has everything under control.

The evening arrived and Sebastian, his dad Oliver and Elaina are all having a wonderful dinner in the beautiful rose dining room by candlelight and a dimmed chandelier. The table was beautifully set with fine bone china, lead crystal goblets filled with red wine, sterling silver flatware and the pattern was Burgundy. Sebastian prepared a mushroom gravy with steaks, scalloped potatoes, asparagus, salads and warm rolls and butter. It was a wonderful dinner while they talked about tomorrow. When it was time for dessert, Sebastian said, "I hope everyone likes key lime pie, if not, I have coffee ice cream and strawberry. I also have fresh perked delicious vanilla flavored coffee." Oliver and Elaina want key lime pie and so does Sebastian. When they finished with dessert, Elaina got up and said, "I'll clear the table, Sebastian. Show me where the dishwasher is."

He showed her and he helped her clear the table as Oliver looked on and sipped his wine.

Later on, in the living room, Oliver and Elaina were sitting on a velvet sofa and Sebastian was sitting on a wing armchair and they were having red wine. Elaina couldn't resist telling Sebastian how beautiful the chair is he is sitting on. He told her he loves it too. Sebastian decided to call Katherine to see if she's ready to go yachting tomorrow. He got on the phone and talked with her and she is ready. She also asked about his father. He told her his father is looking forward to meeting her and he brought a girlfriend with him. Katherine said, "Oh, great! We'll be a foursome. That'll be more fun." He told her he can't wait until she sees the yacht he rented. She then said, "I have things to do now, Sebastian, so I'll see you tomorrow morning at 9:00 a.m. near the harbor where we decided to meet." They said goodnight and then hung up. Sebastian looked at Oliver and Elaina and said, "I'm anxious for the both of you to meet Katherine and I hope you both like her as much as I do." Oliver said, "Oh I'm sure we will." Elaina said, "I'm looking forward to meeting her."

Sebastian, Oliver and Elaina don't want to stay up late tonight because they have to get up early tomorrow. They need to meet Katherine at 9:00 a.m. near Marblehead Harbor and go to their yacht that's leaving at 10:00 a.m. and returning at 8:00 p.m. Therefore, they're leaving the mansion at 8:30 a.m. tomorrow. While they are having red wine before bed, Sebastian is telling them about the yacht he rented and said, "I saw pictures of it and it's beautiful. It's a luxurious motor yacht and is 78 feet by 9 inches long and has a stereo sound system, air-conditioning and it accommodates eight people." Oliver said, "It sounds like we're going to have a great day!"

It wasn't long before Oliver and Elaina went to their bedroom, took a shower, then got in bed and cuddled while enjoying their new mattress. Sebastian went to Jenny's bedroom, set the alarm for 6:30 a.m., got in Jenny's bed and fell asleep.

The morning arrived, and after Sebastian took his shower, he was in the kitchen making fresh perked coffee and the aroma was heavenly. Oliver and Elaina soon came into the kitchen dressed in casual clothes, and after they all said good morning, Oliver said, "That coffee smells so good." Sebastian asked them if they slept well in their new bedroom. Oliver answered, "We slept like babies." They laughed and then Sebastian gave them the choices of breakfast they could have. All of them wanted fresh perked coffee, juice, eggs over light, home-fried potatoes, sausages and wheat toast. In awhile, they were all sitting at the dining room table and were quiet because it was early in the morning. They had second cups of coffee and then went to their rooms to get ready. Sebastian had a big picnic basket packed and was waiting until they were ready to leave to put the refrigerator food in it. He had soft drinks, wine, champagne and after dinner drinks.

It was soon time to leave the mansion as Oliver was wearing a colorful shirt with white shorts, Elaina was wearing skin-tight red shorts with a bright yellow tight tank top and Sebastian was wearing a white shirt with blue shorts. He will carry the two tote bags with things they may need for the day, Elaina will carry the picnic basket and Oliver will carry the wine. After Sebastian called Katherine and told her they were on their way, they headed out to Sebastian's rented car.

It didn't take long to arrive near Marblehead Harbor where their luxury yacht will be waiting for them to board. Sebastian lead the way to where they were supposed to meet Katherine. He soon spotted the very pretty Katherine and she saw him and smiled as she quickly walked towards him. She was wearing red lipstick, a light blue tank top with white shorts and her beautiful green eyes were sparkling as her shoulder length blonde hair was slightly blowing in the wind. She was carrying a picnic basket in one hand and a tote bag in the other. After she and Sebastian met and looked into each other's eyes and smiled, they hugged and then he introduced her to his father Oliver and Elaina. They shook hands and were happy to meet each other and then went to the yacht. There it was. It was white with a blue stripe and it sure was a beauty. They went aboard and met Captain Carlos and his companion Harvey and they all shook hands. The captain will be in complete control at the ergonomic and well appointed helm. His companion Harvey will sit next to him.

After Katherine and Elaina went and put the food in the refrigerator, Captain Carlos gave them all a tour of the yacht and it was quite exciting to them. It's a luxurious motor yacht that's 78 feet by 9 inches, all air-conditioned, it has a stereo sound system and accommodates eight guest and will cruise at 28 of one nautical mile an hour. Sebastian rented this size so they'd have ample room to walk around.

In this yacht, there are four cabins plus a cabin for the two-man crew. Starting from the top of the yacht, there's a small sunning area, under that is the helm where the captain sits with his companion, and that leads to another level where there's a deck for walking, a sun lounge, a salon with two sofas and a separate dining area with a large table. On the same level is the galley with a refrigerator, freezer, icemaker, dishwasher and microwave/convection oven. Under that level is a master cabin in the center of the yacht which is elegant and has a large bath and shower. Sebastian and Katherine took that one. In the bow of the yacht is a VIP cabin with a double berth, bath and shower. Oliver and Elaina took that one. On the same level, there are two twin cabins with baths that will not be used. There is also the two-man crew cabin with two berths, a bath and shower, which Captain Carlos and Harvey will use. And last of all, there is a swim platform that has access to water or swimming which they are all happy about.

After that tour, Sebastian, Katherine, Oliver and Elaina are in heaven and can't stop smiling and don't know what to do first because it's only 9:45 in the morning now. Oliver said, "Let's have coffee with some muffins we brought and I'll warm them up. How about it?" Sebastian and the ladies were all for it. Oliver wanted to prepare it so the others went and sat on a sofa nearby. When everything was ready, they all sat at the dining table and talked a little until they finished their coffee and muffins which were delicious. Some were banana nut and some were blueberry.

The captain's companion, Harvey, soon came down to the galley to tell the guests that they'll be leaving shortly and cruising out into the Atlantic Ocean. He also told them they'll stop every now and then in case someone wants to go to the swim platform where there is access to the water. They might want to dive into the ocean. He explained to them that the entire day will be like that. Last of all, they'll return to Marblehead around 8:00 p.m. Sebastian told Harvey that he and Carlos can eat with them anytime or by themselves because there's plenty of food. Harvey thanked him and told him he'd tell Carlos, and before he left, he said, "I hope you all enjoy the day." They all thanked Harvey and told him to enjoy his day too. They were soon cruising.

Katherine suddenly said, "I feel like going to the sun lounge." Elaina commented, "Let's. And don't forget to use sunscreen, Katherine. I have plenty if you need some." They both changed into their bathing suits and went to the sun lounge and each had a chaise lounge. Katherine had a two-piece swimsuit that was white with gold trim and it looked beautiful on her with her shoulder length blonde hair. Elaina was wearing a purple bikini that looked good on her with all her curves and her very long blonde hair.

Sebastian and Oliver put their sunglasses on and just left their shorts on and joined the ladies in the sun lounge while having coffee. They were all talking and laughing and soon Sebastian was staring at Katherine and said, "Katherine, you look gorgeous in that white and gold swimsuit." "Thanks, Sebastian. I bought it for this ocean cruise." Oliver didn't forget to compliment Elaina on her purple bikini. He said, "Elaina, you're a knockout in that purple swimsuit." "Thanks Oliver. Are you going to put yours on?" He told her he will if he decides to go to the swim platform and dive in the ocean. She said, "Oh, I can't wait to see that because I'm afraid to dive in deep water." Katherine said she feels the same. Sebastian said that he'll probably go to the swim platform and dive in the ocean. Katherine and Elaina are anxious to see their men do that. Sebastian suddenly left the lounge to turn the stereo on and soon there was music. He returned to the lounge and had another coffee.

Sebastian, Oliver, Katherine and Elaina looked out at the ocean and thought it was so relaxing. It was a beautiful sunny day with a temperature of about 80. After a couple of hours, they all wanted a change of scenery. They went down to look at the swim platform in the rear of the yacht. There was an upper level to it with a small sunning area which had stairs to go up and down to the swim platform below it. While Katherine and Elaina sat down on seats on the swim platform, Oliver and Sebastian looked at it and they liked it and are planning to dive into the ocean later.

Katherine, Elaina, Sebastian and Oliver decided to take a good look at their cabins now and try out their berths and heads. They bounced on their beds and laughed and then flushed the toilets and said they were satisfied. After that, Katherine and Elaina put shorts and tank tops on over their swimsuits and then went to the dining area and galley to think about what they want to have for lunch. Katherine made fresh perked coffee as they all sat at the table and it was soon decided that they'll have cheeseburgers with pickles, chips and potato salad with a cold beverage about noontime. Katherine said, "Oh, and we need to give Captain Carlos and his companion Harvey some lunch. They can decide when they want to eat and they'll only have to microwave the cheeseburgers." Sebastian said, "I think that's nice of you to make that for them, Katherine." Elaina offered to make their next meal. She then stood up and said, "Let's all walk around the deck." They were all for it and headed for the bow while talking about how they'll walk after each meal to digest their food. They definitely need to exercise after eating.

Out on the deck, there was plenty of room to walk around and also stop at a rail and look out at the beautiful ocean and that's what Sebastian and Katherine are doing. He has his arm around her as they look out at the ocean. They soon looked at each other passionately and then slowly kissed. After that, they continued to look out at the ocean.

Oliver held Elaina's hand as they walked around on the deck. She stopped and they faced each other and kissed. She's 35 years old and he's 60 and they like each other a lot. They strolled over to the salon that had two sofas where you could sit and look out at the ocean. She leaned back into his arms on the sofa and said, "Thank you for taking me on this cruise, Oliver." He hugged her and said, "Even though I'm much older than you, I'm crazy about you, Elaina."

Before long, it was time for lunch. Sebastian made the cheeseburgers and Katherine made the potato salad while Oliver got the beverages and Elaina set the dining table. Everything looked yummy. After they ate, they all walked the deck to digest their lunch. The crew was also told about their lunch and they thanked their guests for making it.

Sebastian wants to be private with Katherine now so they left the deck and went into their master cabin and shut the door.

They first took a shower, then they put clothes on and went to lie on top of the bedspread with a pillow behind them to talk a little. They soon were embraced, kissing and getting very passionate. This is the most passion Katherine has ever felt with Sebastian. She paused and said, "Sebastian, I can't do this. It's too soon." He said, "Okay." They kissed a little more and got off the bed. She then said, "I want you and Oliver to dive off the swim platform now." He agreed to. They then went and got Oliver and Elaina in the salon.

Sebastian asked Captain Carlos to stop the yacht for awhile so there would be access to the water. After he did, Katherine and Elaina went and sat on the swim platform waiting for Oliver and Sebastian to dive into the ocean. They soon did and dove in at the same time and splashed water all over their women. While they swam around awhile, Sebastian yelled, "It feels so good!" They then came out of the water.

Later in the afternoon, Oliver and Elaina went to their VIP cabin. Sebastian and Katherine were in the salon sitting on the sofa looking out at the ocean while talking, having champagne and then laughing a lot. It was almost dinner time so they went to the galley to prepare white rice, chicken, shrimp and salads. Peach ice cream will be the dessert. They then went back to the salon for awhile. Oliver and Elaina joined them later at dinner time.

At the dining table, Sebastian asked his father Oliver about his jewelry business. He said, "It's going great! I'm doing well because I work at it." Elaina said, "He has given me some beautiful jewelry." Sebastian said, "I bet he did." They all laughed. Katherine asked Sebastian how he's doing with his book and he told her he has plenty to write about. He told her he has seen two ghosts. She looked at him in surprise and asked, "You've seen ghosts?" He told her he has seen Jenny's ghost twice and saw her mother Shannon's ghost. They were pale lifelike ghostly apparitions and spoke to him and he heard them because of his power. He went on and told her that spirits are different. You don't see them or hear them, you sense their message. After a few moments of everyone's silence, Sebastian said, "Look, I have a goal and it's to find out who murdered three people and then write my book about it. You all know I'm a criminal psychologist with a master's degree, and I'm a psychic medium and clairvoyant. Now, if you all don't mind, let's talk about something else."

Later, while Sebastian, Katherine, Oliver and Elaina were walking the deck to digest their food, Sebastian and Katherine stopped walking and just looked over the rail out at the ocean. She asked, "Sebastian, is everything alright with you since you've seen Jenny's ghost and Shannon's ghost?" He said, "Well, Katherine, it's getting complicated." He then stopped talking and she told him not to hesitate to tell her anything about the ghosts and that she'll keep it private. She also asked him what Jenny's ghost said to him and what did she look like. Sebastian told Katherine that he'd tell her later.

Sebastian continued walking the deck with Katherine. Captain Carlos went to him and said, "We'll be heading back to Marblehead in an hour." Sebastian told him he'd tell the other guests. He then asked Katherine, "Can we go to our cabin for awhile?" She agreed to and they left holding hands.

In the master cabin, Sebastian and Katherine were fully clothed as they went to lie on top of the bedspread with a pillow behind them to talk. While on the bed, they embraced and kissed passionately. He soon said, "Katherine, I never felt so strong about a woman as I do with you and I want a committed relationship with you." She responded, "I think I want that too, Sebastian, but I'm afraid to fall for the wrong man." He said, "Time will tell." She was okay with that. They then started getting ready to leave for Marblehead.

In the salon, near the galley, Oliver and Elaina were sitting around because they were all packed. Katherine and Sebastian finished packing and went and joined them and they all decided to have some champagne until they arrive in Marblehead.

Around 9:30 p.m. the yacht arrived at the Marblehead side of the inner harbor. Carlos and Harvey came over to their guests and they all shook hands and said goodbye while the guests thanked the crew for a nice ocean cruise.

After Sebastian walked Katherine to her car, they kissed very passionately and embraced and he told her he'd call her tomorrow. Oliver and Elaina hugged her and said goodbye and then they headed to Sebastian's rented car.

After arriving at the mansion, Sebastian, Oliver and Elaina were happy to be back and thought it was a nice cruise but it's always good to be back home. They all got settled and met in the Victorian burgundy living room for night caps of red wine. Oliver told Sebastian that he and Elaina loved spending time with him in the mansion and enjoyed the yachting cruise so much that they should do it again. He agreed to that and they soon went to bed. Early tomorrow morning, Oliver and Elaina will head back to New York.

5

CHARLIE THE GARDENER

A couple of weeks after the yachting cruise, Sebastian called his father Oliver to see how he and Elaina were doing and they were fine. He then followed that up with a call to Katherine who is back at work at her real estate office and is happy to hear from him. They talked a bit about the yacht and then she said, "I'm looking forward to seeing you again, Sebastian." He assured her they'll meet soon and told her he just called to say hello and now wants to get back to work on his book. In a few moments, they hung up.

While it's still September, Sebastian went outside the mansion to look at the lawn and just walk around for awhile. He saw Charlie, the gardener, who was tending to the shrubs and looked as though he was enjoying it. He still has not lost his gentle personality after working at the mansion for 40 years. Sebastian went to him and asked, "Charlie, how is your day going?" He told Sebastian he's having a good day. Sebastian paused and then asked, "Do you mind if I ask you a few questions about Jenny?" He didn't mind so Sebastian asked him if he ever saw violence around the mansion. Charlie answered, "There's definitely something scary going on in this mansion because I heard screaming before Jenny lived here." Charlie then stopped talking. Sebastian asked, "When Jenny and her mother Shannon moved here, did you ever hear arguments?" Charlie told him that when Jenny and her mother moved into the mansion, Jenny was a little girl and when she was 23 she was murdered. But before she was murdered, he heard her arguing a few times with a man. Sebastian asked him what he heard but Charlie told him he couldn't make it out. He heard them yelling near an open window and it sounded bad and he never saw who the man was that was arguing with Jenny. Sebastian thanked him.

While Charlie went on with his gardening, Sebastian went back in the mansion and documented the information in his book. He sensed Charlie knew more than what he said.

Sebastian soon prepared his dinner of fried haddock with fried potatoes and salad, and while he was eating it in the cozy kitchen, he was thinking about Katherine. He knows she doesn't want a committed relationship with him so he's thinking of calling Samantha who he's not in love with but is attracted to her beauty, she's a writer and they are friends so there is a lot to converse about.

Later on in the evening, Sebastian was in his living room sitting on one of his beautiful armchairs while in deep thought. He was having a soft drink and sipping it and he suddenly had the desire to call Samantha.

The Ghost And Sebastian

While Sebastian was on his cell phone talking with Samantha, she was so happy to hear from him and invited him to her condo in Marblehead tomorrow night but wants him to stay overnight. He told her he wasn't sure he'd stay overnight but he'd be there tomorrow in the early evening.

When Sebastian arrived at Samantha's condo the next evening, she opened the door wearing a short red negligee which looked stunning on her with her shoulder length dark brown hair and magnetic blue eyes. They immediately kissed and soon Sebastian went to lie on her bed on top of the bedspread with his clothes on and a pillow behind his head. She got on the bed next to him. He said, "Your negligee's enticing but let's talk for awhile about your romance novel." She didn't want to. He told her his murder mystery story was getting intense. Samantha stroked his chest with her fingers and asked, "What can you tell me about it?" He told her he can tell her a little about the ghosts. But before she let him, she wanted to know something else. She wanted to know if she's just his play toy. He said, "I'm not going to lie to you, Samantha. I'm fond of you but we're just friends." He started to kiss her neck while he still had his clothes on and then she slowly kissed his and that made him passionate.

Sebastian and Samantha's clothes were soon on the floor and they were in bed partially covered with a sheet making love. She said, "Sebastian, tell me we're more than just friends." He responded, "Just enjoy the love making, Samantha." She quickly sat up in bed, put her negligee on and stomped around the room throwing a fit. He sat up in bed watching her as she yelled, "No! I can't enjoy making love unless you tell me you have deep feelings for me!" He said, "Oh come on, Samantha, calm down." She picked up a small vase and threw it at him while yelling, "Get out of here, Sebastian! Get out now!" He got off the bed quite fast and grabbed his clothes and put them on while she yelled, "I never want to see you again, Sebastian! Never!" He was soon gone.

The next day, in mid-afternoon, Sebastian was in his mansion at his desk writing in his red hardcover book. While he was talking out loud to himself, he said, "I wonder what Jenny's boyfriend Pierce was like. Mrs. North said he had a temper but his mother, Mrs. Marlow, didn't say that." Just then, he felt a chill and the presence of a spirit in the room. He looked around but saw nothing so he started looking again. As he glanced at the fireplace, which was eight feet away, he encountered a pale lifelike ghostly apparition of Pierce. Sebastian was shocked and almost fell off his chair as he recognized him from a photograph. It was Pierce's ghost just before he was murdered at age 27 wearing jeans and a black shirt. He was tall, average build, brown hair and was standing still staring at Sebastian with wild eyes.

Pierce's ghost then became very angry as he started to pace a small area of the floor while swinging his arms. While still staring at Sebastian, he yelled out, "Stay away! Jenny is mine! Stay away or I'll kill you! Jenny is my love! We were murdered! Help! We were murdered!" Sebastian said, "I know you're Pierce. Who murdered you and Jenny?" As Sebastian remained silent waiting for an answer, Pierce yelled, "Yes, I'm Pierce! I'm Pierce! Don't touch my Jenny! She's my love! She's mine!" Pierce's ghost suddenly disappeared. Sebastian called out, "Don't go, Pierce! Come back! Who murdered you and Jenny?" Pierce didn't return. Sebastian said out loud, "Mrs. North was right about Pierce having a bad temper. I hope he never hurt Jenny."

While Sebastian's sitting down, he's thinking of how he has seen three ghosts and knows it's partially because he's living in the mansion where the murders occurred.

The next day at the police station, Sebastian was sitting with Officer Martin who said, "We officers listened to the tape you gave us of your interview with Alfred and liked the information but it's not enough evidence for us to arrest him for a robbery or murder." Sebastian asked Officer Martin if he thought there were two separate murders and the officer told him that he's not sure but it sounds like Alfred maybe did one. He also thanked Sebastian for his help. Sebastian is happy he was able to help the police. He then told Officer Martin he was on his way to his friend Alan's mansion in Marblehead who is a movie producer in Hollywood. Officer Martin wished him a good day and Sebastian left.

Sebastian was soon in the foyer of Alan's mansion and being greeted by him with a handshake and a hug as he said, "Sebastian! It's good to see you. Let's go into my office to talk." As they walked to it, Sebastian said, "It's good to see you again, Alan. I've been so busy with this murder mystery story." They got to Alan's office and Sebastian immediately sat on one of the dark red leather chairs. Alan sat at his desk and said, "I know you've been working on your book so how's it coming along?" Sebastian told him that the murder mystery is spooky and interesting. After pausing, he said, "Alan, I've met three ghosts and they were lifelike ghostly apparitions right in front of me. And because of my unusual power, they talk to me and I hear them." Alan said, "Ghosts! Tell me more!" Sebastian wanted to tell him about a particular ghost. He told him that the young lady who was murdered at age 23 was Jenny, and, one time, her pale lifelike ghostly apparition was in front of him wearing a sheer nightgown and she was beautiful and made love to him. He then added that he could feel her making love to him. Alan looks shocked while asking, "Are you kidding me? Go on! Keep talking!"

Sebastian went on and told Alan about the bathroom incident. He told him that when he got out of the shower one day and had a towel around him, he noticed the scent of gardenias which always precedes Jenny's apparitions. She then was right in front of him and her pale lifelike ghostly apparition was stunning as she was wearing a very sheer light green long nightgown. Alan is so stimulated by this story, he said, "Wow! Keep going! What happened next?" Sebastian told him he was in shock and couldn't move. Jenny then put her arms around him and slowly put her body against his trying to seduce him. While she continued, he suddenly was able to put his arms around her and it felt like she was alive. Alan got anxious and asked, "Then what?" Sebastian said, "We slowly slid onto the floor and made love and it was strange love pleasure, Alan! It was like nothing I ever felt before! Her spiritual power made my mind and body feel like I was floating. And sometimes Jenny talks and I hear her." Alan looked mystified as he stared at Sebastian.

Alan suddenly said, "Oh wow! Get me a ghost! It's hard to believe but I've read about that stuff in ghost stories. I wish I could experience strange love pleasure with a ghost!" Sebastian told him he knows it's hard to believe. Alan is so excited about this story that he suddenly said to Sebastian, "Let's get a contract started now! I want to make a movie about this story!" Sebastian told him that it sounds like it has a good chance to become a blockbuster movie. Alan went on and told him that when he's finished writing his story, he's going to have a big party in his honor whether or not he solves the triple homicide case. He also told him that this ghost stuff excites him! Sebastian thanked him and told him his book may be ready by the end of the year. Alan asked, "How are you doing with Samantha?" Sebastian told him he still sees her once in awhile and she still has a bad temper.

Alan has just pulled a contract out of his draw and is reading a little of it. He then handed it to Sebastian and said, "Take this contract home and look at it. There's plenty of time before you have to sign it and I'm the producer who wants to buy the rights to this story. I can already tell this is going to be big!" Sebastian told him he feels the same about the story and it's an important goal he wants to reach. Alan said, "It'll happen, Sebastian." After talking awhile longer, they stood up and Alan told him to keep in touch. Sebastian told him that he would as they shook hands goodbye. They have been good friends for a long time.

Sebastian is back in his mansion and his cell phone keeps ringing. He quickly went and sat on a chair and answered it and said, "Hello!" There was no answer so he again said, "Hello!" There was no answer so he ended the call. Within seconds, the phone rang again and he quickly answered it and said, "Hello!" This time, there was a lot of static and mumbling and he thought there was a bad connection so he ended the call. A few minutes later, his phone rang again and he answered it and said, "Hello!" There was no answer so he said, "Hello! Hello!" There was no one there at all so he ended the call and headed to his kitchen to make coffee and have a bagel with cream cheese. When he got to the kitchen, his cell phone rang again and he answered and said, "Hello!" This time there were weird spooky sounds. He soon hung up and said, "I wouldn't be surprised if the ghosts are calling me." Sebastian made his coffee and had a bagel in the kitchen while thinking of the weird calls he just received. He then took a second cup of coffee into the living room and placed it on a table and sat down next to it looking puzzled. He seriously thinks it was a ghost calling him up.

By late evening, Sebastian was in Jenny's bed sound asleep while naked and partially covered with the sheet. After several hours, he was in a deep sleep, then he awakened to the scent of gardenias which filled the air. With his eyes barely open, he saw Jenny's ghost sitting at her dressing table in front of the mirror and looking in it while she was brushing her hair. Her pale lifelike ghostly apparition was wearing a sheer aquamarine long nightgown. Sebastian called out, "Jenny, you surprised me by sitting at your dressing table. I'm so happy to see you!" She turned to look at him and smiled but didn't speak. He quickly got out of bed and put his pants on and went over to her and leaned over and kissed her cheek. She looked up at him and said, "Oh Sebastian, I love being with you. Thank you for trying to find my murderer and Pierce's." He told her he will continue to look for the murder. Jenny stood up and embraced him and kissed him on the lips and he told her she makes him very happy and wants to see her as often as he can. While they were still standing near her dressing table and embraced, he kissed her and then stroked her long light brown hair.

While Jenny's ghost and Sebastian remained standing and embraced, she suddenly sounded desperate as she said, "I was murdered! Please help me! I love you, Sebastian! Help me!" He looked at her and said, "Jenny, tell me who murdered you." Just then, while they are still embraced, he was stunned as he noticed Pierce's lifelike ghostly apparition across the room from them and he was wearing jeans and a black shirt. Sebastian knew this was going to be a power-play! Pierce kept moving around in anger while swinging his arms and watching Jenny's ghost in Sebastian's arms. Pierce's ghost, with wild eyes, stared into Sebastian's eyes showing anger as he swung his arms. He yelled, "Sebastian! Get away from my Jenny! I'll kill you!" Pierce's ghost took a lamp and threw it at Sebastian but missed him. Jenny was silent standing next to Sebastian but suddenly disappeared from being next to him and was now standing next to Pierce's ghost across the room. Sebastian was puzzled about that.

While both ghosts stayed next to each other as they moved around in the bedroom, Pierce yelled, Sebastian, "Stay away from Jenny! Jenny's my love! We were murdered! We were murdered!" Pierce's ghost suddenly disappeared and then Jenny's ghost disappeared and so did her gardenia scent.

After Sebastian's shocking ghostly encounters with Pierce and Jenny, he took a shower and then went to his kitchen and made some strong coffee and sat at the kitchen table having a couple of cups of it. He kept thinking about Jenny and Pierce's ghost. He soon made himself a healthy breakfast of ham and eggs and whole wheat toast with grape jelly, and when he finishes eating, he plans to work on his book. He later was at his desk documenting news but having a hard time to concentrate due to his last ghostly encounters in Jenny's bedroom that were powerful!

In late afternoon, Sebastian was finished working on his book for the day and was ready to relax on the sofa. He often has water in the afternoon or a soft drink but doesn't want either today. In awhile, he got up and paced the floor from room to room.

One early evening in mid-October, around 7:00 p.m., Sebastian was at his desk working on his computer when his cell phone rang. He had left it on the table next to an armchair so he got up and looked at it and saw it was his father's girlfriend Elaina calling from New York. He quickly said, "Hello." She sadly said, "Hi, Sebastian, it's Elaina. I have bad news for you. Your father just died." She then sobbed. Sebastian loudly asked, "What? Did you say my father just died?" She gently told him yes. She then went on and told him that today, around 4:00 p.m., she was in his home with him while he was standing and drinking some scotch when he suddenly fell onto the floor and had a seizure and then a convulsion and became unconscious and died. She began to sob a lot. Sebastian suddenly yelled, "Oh no! My father's dead! No! Not my father!" While he got choked up trying to hold back from crying, Elaina went on and told him how she immediately called 911 and they arrived within minutes and she rode in the ambulance with him. When they got to the hospital, his dad was pronounced dead on arrival. Elaina was sobbing as Sebastian started crying. She said, "I'm so sorry for you, Sebastian, and I'll be here for you in New York when you come to your dad's home to take care of this. Let me know if you need me for anything." He thanked her for her kindness and told her he'd get back to her shortly after he clears his head a little so he can make arrangements to go to New York to take care of everything. He's was very much in shock from this news and they were both quite emotional and choked up while saying goodbye.

After Sebastian hung up from the devastating phone call he just received, he sat down on a chair and cried. He loved his father so much. He then poured himself a glass of red wine and sat back down again and called Katherine. When she answered, he yelled, "Katherine, my father is dead! He's dead!" She said, "Sebastian, I'll be right over! Try to calm down." She then hung up fast.

Katherine was soon at Sebastian's door and when he opened it they immediately hugged while he sobbed. She felt so bad for him. She put her arms around him and then walked him into the living room where they sat on a sofa. Sebastian lost his calm. He put his hands on his face while sobbing and suddenly yelled, "My dad is dead!" Katherine quickly got up and poured herself a glass of red wine and went back and sat next to him on the sofa. She put her hand on his back and then asked him how he died. After he told her how it happened, she put her arms around him and tried to console him and said, "The pain is bad now, Sebastian, but each day it will lessen." He thanked her for her sympathy and then told her she is his soul mate and she loved hearing that. After they talked for awhile, she asked if she could sleep overnight in the guest bedroom upstairs. She didn't want him to be alone after hearing that devastating news about his father's death. He appreciated her sympathy and it wasn't long before they went to separate bedrooms upstairs.

The next morning, Sebastian and Katherine were in the dining room having breakfast which consisted of grape juice, doughnuts and coffee. He started talking about his mother. He has already told Katherine the whole story of how she helped the police by identifying a murdered who later had her killed by someone outside the prison. He likes to remember his mother

The Ghost And Sebastian

as a registered nurse and a psychic medium who worked for the police and solved a murder case for them. He doesn't like to think of how terrible it ended. He told Katherine that his mother was a good mom to him and he loves her and misses her so much. He was seven years old when she was murdered so his father raised him alone. Katherine then said, "That's a sad story, Sebastian. But you were so lucky you had such a great dad." She got up from the table and gave him a hug as they both had tears in their eyes.

In awhile, Sebastian walked Katherine to the door so she could go to work but she wants him to call her if he needs to talk. He watched her go to her car and then he closed his door. She certainly made him feel better as he began to make arrangements to go to New York and take care of business. His father will be cremated as he wished.

Sebastian, later, was on the phone with Elaina in New York and telling her he's flying out there in a few hours and may stay for three weeks. She said, "My heart is with you, Sebastian. I loved your father too." He thanked her for being so kind to him and told her he'd call her when he arrives at his dad's home in New York which he has the keys to. They soon said goodbye.

Sebastian called Officer Martin and told him what happened to his father and that he'd be away for three weeks. Officer Martin was sympathetic and said, "I'm so sorry to hear that but time will heal your sorrow. If you keep busy on your book you'll start to feel better, and in the meantime, if you want to talk, just give me a call." Sebastian thanked him for caring and they hung up. He then called his friend Alan and told him the awful news. Alan was kind and told him to come over to visit him and talk about it if he wants to. Sebastian thanked him and told him he'd call him when he gets back from New York in about three weeks. He needs to take care of all his dad's business. They then hung up.

Plans were made for Sebastian to leave today and he's all packed and going out the door to Logan Airport in Boston. He later arrived in New York and took care of business and had his father cremated, and after the ashes were put in an urn, he placed it on the mantel in his dad's house while Elaina was with him. He decided to live in his dad's house and continue leasing out his house nearby. He then did a lot of paper work at an attorney's office and the bank and found out his father left him everything because he was his only child.

Sebastian's inheritance from his dad was quite huge. It consisted of cash, stocks, investments, his home and a large amount of jewels in a safe. Within three weeks, everything was taken care of. Sebastian had some of his furniture from his house brought over to his dad's which will now be his permanent home. He and Elaina took time to eat in a deli in New York City which they love doing. It was then time for him to return to Marblehead Neck, Massachusetts to try and reach his goal of helping to solve the triple homicide that happened in 2006 in the mansion he's living in.

While Sebastian is back at his mansion in Marblehead Neck, he is feeling better now that he's back and unpacked and making some fresh perked coffee. Katherine was his first call and he invited her over and she'll be coming over after she finishes work at 5:00 p.m. Sebastian did a little work on his book but was quite restless because he could hardly wait to see Katherine. He paced the floor while thinking of her and his dad. Before long, she was at the door and they hugged and he was a lot calmer.

Katherine and Sebastian went into the dining room and sat next to each other while having tea with crackers and cheese. He thanked her again for being so kind to him at his time of need and she told him she feels so bad that he lost his father. He told her he's going to continue to lease his house in New York because he moved into his father's house. She thought it was

The Ghost And Sebastian

a very good idea. He then said, "Katherine, I was forewarned in a dream the day before my father died that something sad was about to happen to him. I didn't want to believe it." She said, "That is so interesting that you're also clairvoyant through dreams." He went on and told her that clairvoyant moments can prepare you for what's about to happen. If bad news is coming, you can sometimes prevent it. She finds it interesting that he gets forewarned about the future. They soon left the dining room and went into the living room and sat on a sofa for awhile and talked. It was getting late and Katherine wanted to leave because she has to work tomorrow so Sebastian walked her to the door and they kissed, but not passionately, and then she left.

The next day, Sebastian went near the edge of the cliff in front of his mansion and sat on the grass and looked out at the ocean while thinking about his father. He suddenly felt the presence of his spirit next to him which made him feel so peaceful. He later went to his mansion and sat at his desk.

In late afternoon, Sebastian thought to give his friend Samantha, the novelist, a call and tell her about his father. He likes staying in touch with her because they're in the same line of work which is writing. He called her and told her that his father died and she was sympathetic and told him if he needs her to be sure to call her. He thanked her and she suddenly apologized for being so short fused at times. After he told her she needs anger management, she told him that he needs a shrink because of the spooky mansion he's living in and seeing ghosts. He became silent and then she said, "Let's make appointments to see a shrink!" He said, "That's good for releasing tension." In awhile, they said goodbye.

A few days later, at the library, Sebastian was going to a computer to do research again on Alfred who has had trouble with the law. Flamboyant Sam, who is Sebastian's rival, was also there looking through homicide books and bringing them to a table. He spotted Sebastian so he walked over to him and made his peace and then told him the triple homicide case isn't over yet and believes he will solve it and be the hero. Sebastian ignored him and started walking away. Sam snapped and raised his voice in the library and said, "You're a washed-up writer, Sebastian! Get out of town!" The librarian came over and asked Sam to leave and he wouldn't so she called the police. They arrived within minutes and ordered Sam out of the library and so he left while giving Sebastian sign language as he raised one hand and pointed the first two fingers to his own eyes, then pointed them to Sebastian's, meaning, "I'm watching you." Sebastian has sensed how nutty Sam can be and ignored him.

It's now late October and Halloween eve. Katherine is still not ready to commit to a relationship with Sebastian so he's calling his friend Samantha. He invited her to come over tonight to have fun for Halloween eve and she agreed to. When it was 6:00 p.m., four children, in Halloween costumes, started to approach Sebastian's mansion with their trick or treat bags while looking scared. When they got close to the door, one child yelled, "Ah! This house is scary! Let's get out of here!" Another child said, "Let's stay close together and go to the door. Come on kids."

The children reached Sebastian's door and knocked a few times and he answered it and asked, "Oh! What have we got here? Hungry goblins?" The children all yelled, "Trick or treat! Trick or treat!" Sebastian told them to stay where they were and he'd go and get some treats for them. He left for a moment leaving his door open. The children peeked in the house and one child said, "Oh! It's scary in there!" Just then, Sebastian returned to the door where the children were with their bags and he started putting treats in all of them as they looked happy. He said, "This is all for you hungry goblins. Now be careful but have fun tonight." They all thanked him. As they were leaving, one child blurted out to Sebastian, "My mother told me there were people murdered in your mansion a long time ago!" He said, "That's right but everything is okay now. You all run along and have fun. Bye, kids!" The children left and still looked scared as they ran and yelled, "Ah! Ah! Let's get out of here!" Sebastian smiled as he watched them leave.

Samantha arrived a couple of hours later. As she walked towards Sebastian's front door, she couldn't help but notice how the winds picked up and swayed the bare tree branches and swirled the leaves around. It made the mansion look mysterious. Once inside, she sat on the living room sofa with a glass of wine while dressed all in black for Halloween. She had her dark brown hair bushed out to look scary and wore black eyeliner around her magnetic blue eyes and then added bright red lipstick. For fun, Sebastian dressed all in black and drew a black thin mustache on himself and walked around the mansion lighting black candles he bought. He said, "I'm surprised I'm making the mansion even more scary. It's already spooked with ghosts!" She got a kick out of it and laughed but then asked, "Where are the ghosts? I don't see any! I only know a little of what you told me. I believe in them but I've never seen one." He told her she may never see a ghost anywhere but some people do. And just because he sees them in his mansion, he's not sure if they'll come out while she's there but they may.

Sebastian went to the sofa and sat next to Samantha and started kissing her lightly on her neck and said, "Let's make spooky love tonight." She pulled away from him and stood up and started pacing the floor while angry and told him that unless he's serious about her, she doesn't want him close to her anymore.

He quickly got up from the sofa and went over to her and put his arms around her. While they were standing in the middle of the room, he said, "I care for you, Samantha, but don't take it out of context. We're writers and friends. I never said I love you." She didn't comment. They just looked into each other's eyes and then she kissed him passionately. As they were kissing, there was suddenly the scent of gardenias she noticed and so did he and he knew where it was coming from. They stopped kissing and he was speechless and not saying a word yet. She inhaled and asked, "Where's that scent coming from?" While there was no ghost in sight, suddenly a nearby heavy crystal candy dish came flying across the living room and headed right for Samantha's head.

Sebastian swiftly pulled Samantha out of the way holding her and yelling, "Watch out, Samantha! It's Jenny's spirit! She doesn't want me with you!" Samantha was stunned and speechless. Within seconds, the gardenia scent left the room which meant her spirit was gone. Samantha asked, "Do you mean that was Jenny?" He told her it was Jenny's spirit who was angry that he was with another woman.

Samantha is looking confused because of what just happened. She quickly rushed to the foyer and put the wall light switch on and then grabbed her coat from the closet and put it on. She said, "Sebastian, let's go to my condo! I believe you about this place being spooked! But how did you know that was Jenny's spirit?" He told her that the gardenia scent always precedes her apparitions except this time her pale lifelike ghost didn't show up. Samantha didn't comment and remained in deep thought. Sebastian started putting out all the candles while he said, "Samantha, I've seen several ghosts here." While she was waiting for him to put the candles out and get his coat, he saw the computer go on by itself and show a picture of a witch. He stared at it as he called Samantha to come and look at it but it quickly shut off. He said, "I think a spirit just pulled a Halloween prank! The paranormal activity here is becoming too much." Samantha asked him if Jenny turned the computer on and he told her no because there was no scent of gardenias.

The Ghost And Sebastian

She said, "You must love knowing when she's around." He said, "Exactly!"

The candles have all been put out and only the foyer light is on. Sebastian went to the closet in the foyer and got his coat and put it on. While they were near the door ready to leave, Samantha opened it wide before he put the wall light switch off. As he did, the door suddenly and forcefully slammed shut by itself. They looked alarmed as they stood there in the dim lighting. He said, "This is just what I mean.

That was the presence of an angry spirit. I find ghost more fascinating because I can see them. They're either pale and shadowy or pale and lifelike." He found the wall light switch and put it back on and then tried to open the door and it wouldn't open She was speechless. He said, "It won't open! What the hell is going on with these spirits!" He finally got the door open and they left for Samantha's condo.

While Sebastian and Samantha were in her living room, he had water and she had wine. She asked, "How can you stand to live in your mansion, Sebastian?" He told her it's only temporary and he's getting use to it. She told him she heard about a psychiatrist who knows a lot about ghosts and he should make an appointment just to talk about them. Even though Sebastian's a criminal psychologist, a psychic medium and clairvoyant, they might like telling each other about ghostly encounters. It would just be a conversation between a psychiatrist and a psychic medium and clairvoyant about their knowledge of ghosts. Sebastian didn't think it was a bad idea. She also told him she might want to make an appointment for her anger management. He liked that idea and told her she should do that. She then told him the psychiatrist's name was Dr. Louis and he use to have an office in Boston and later moved it to Marblehead. After pausing, she asked, "Are you interested in seeing him, Sebastian?" "I might be. What about you?" She told him she might make an appointment for anger management. She then gave Sebastian Dr. Louis' address and phone number in case he decides to see him.

While Samantha and Sebastian were still in her living room, they were not in the mood for love because Jenny's spirit was too much for them tonight. She soon walked him to the door and had a short kiss and then he left.

6

LOUIS THE PSYCHIATRIST

In early November, Sebastian and Katherine were in the mansion living room at the bar area while he poured them some champagne. After they took a sip of it, he looked at her and said, "Katherine, I invited you here tonight to ask you to have Thanksgiving dinner with me at a wonderful restaurant." "Sebastian, I'm very attracted to you but I don't want to get too involved with you yet because it may lead to a passionate affair and I'm not ready for that. I need to be sure about us." He looked so disappointed and then told her, until she wants to commit to a relationship, he will be seeing other women. She told him that would be fair and went on telling him she's planning to go to Los Angeles and spend Thanksgiving with a girlfriend. While they looked into each other's eyes, he sadly said, "I'll miss you."

After Katherine and Sebastian went and sat on the sofa next to each other, he asked her if she wanted to go to the attic to see if they'll have a ghostly encounter. She was all for it. They took their glasses of champagne with them and first went into the dining room to look in the china cabinet at all the fine bone china and lead crystal stemware. She said, "It's so beautiful but so breakable." He agreed and wondered why people spend thousands of dollars on it. They looked in the mirror in the china cabinet and this time Sebastian didn't see anything in back of his reflection. He knows that ghosts and spirits are unpredictable as to when and where they'll show up and no one will ever know why.

Katherine and Sebastian continued their tour and went to Jenny's bedroom which she thinks it's so pretty. Sebastian pointed to Jenny's bed and told her he's still sleeping in her bed. She asked him if he found that a little scary and he told her no and that he's use to it and loves the closeness he feels with Jenny. Katherine didn't say a word and just stared into his eyes for a moment and thought it was strange that he said that. She then suggested they go to the second floor.

On the second floor, the four bedrooms looked the same and so did the sewing room. While Sebastian and Katherine were on their way up to the attic, he said, "This attic is definitely eerie." She agreed. Once they were up there, he looked to his right where the mannequin had been and it was not there. He was surprised for a moment. He slowly scanned the attic and saw it in another area. He quickly said, "Katherine, I wonder how it moved there!" He went close to it and noticed that the mannequin's right arm was in a different position. Her black hair was still bushy, but, to him, her large haunting pale blue eyes looked stranger than before. He looked puzzled for a few moments and left the mannequin where it was to see if it gets moved again.

The Ghost And Sebastian

Sebastian has suddenly noticed that the rocking chair in the attic is now near a window and doesn't remember seeing it there. He said, "Katherine, this attic is so spooky! Maybe a ghost sits in this rocking chair and looks out the window." She said, "Let's get out of here until we know more." "You're right, Katherine, let's get out of here."

Sebastian and Katherine went to the kitchen and put their empty champagne glasses on the counter and then sat down at the table for awhile. He told her that his friend Samantha told him about Dr. Louis, a psychiatrist, who knows quite a bit about ghosts and he may want to talk with him for awhile just to see how much he knows about them. Katherine is very concerned and said, "Well, it wouldn't hurt you to see a psychiatrist because venting is a good thing for anyone." He thanked her for her concern and thinks he may make an appointment with him. He also told her that Samantha might want an appointment for her uncontrollable temper. Katherine said, "That's a good idea!" They soon called it a night and he walked her to the door where they kissed passionately and then she left.

A week later, Sebastian was sitting on a chair in Dr. Louis' office in Marblehead. After Sebastian introduced himself as a mystery writer, criminal psychologist, psychic medium and clairvoyant, the doctor told him that he has heard of him. He told the doctor that he was informed about his knowledge of ghosts and that's why he's there. He then told him that he's presently renting the Victorian mansion where the 2006 triple homicide happened in Marblehead Neck to write a book about it. He added that it's spooky there, and, although he has never seen ghosts in his past, he has now seen several in the mansion, hears them speak and communicates with them. And that he made love with a particular ghost who seduced him once and it felt real but was strange. Then last of all, he told the doctor he wants his thoughts about the ghosts. Dr. Louis, the well respected psychiatrist, told him to lie on his couch so he could hear more about his life first. He went and sat near him with a pad and pen.

While Sebastian was relaxing on the couch, Dr. Louis asked him what his childhood was like and how his relations were with his mother and father. Sebastian told him that he had a happy childhood until his mother was murdered when he was seven years old and it made him very sad. She was a psychic medium who worked for the police and helped them. He also told him that his father raised him and he loved him and he recently died. Dr. Louis kept writing notes. He then asked Sebastian to tell him more about the ghosts he has seen. Sebastian told him he knows that he's able to see, hear and communicate with ghosts because of his unusual psychic power. On the other hand, some psychic mediums don't see ghost and just communicate with spirits by sensing their messages. Dr. Louis told him he's aware that some people claim they have seen ghosts and maybe they have but he's skeptical because he hasn't seen any.

Dr. Louis and Sebastian soon went and sat on chairs. The doctor told him that he most likely will already be aware of some things he's going to tell him. He first told him how too much alcohol can create illusions. He then told him, to hear ghosts speak to him is unusual and he may really be seeing and hearing them because he's a powerful psychic medium. But, taking it a step further and believing that he's making love with a ghost, well, there are people who claim that has happened to them and it could be true. He also told Sebastian that it's good for people to vent their emotions because it makes things sound clearer or it can be just for therapy. He paused and then said, "Sebastian, your strong emotional control makes you successful in all that you do."

When Sebastian's appointment was about to end, Dr. Louis went to his desk and Sebastian sat across from him and told him he liked discussing the ghosts. He also thanked him and told him he'd call if he wants to see him again. He then left in a peaceful mood and is anxious to tell Samantha how he liked the doctor because she may want to see him for her temper outbursts which she can't control.

In awhile, Sebastian arrived at his mansion and went into his kitchen and made coffee. He thought about Dr. Louis and thinks he may visit him again, especially since the doctor thinks some people may see ghosts. Sebastian then started to think about his dad Oliver and Elaina who slept in the second floor bedroom when they visited him. He's wondering if they went up to the attic and touched the mannequin or moved it. He called Elaina and first asked her how she is and she told him she's fine and then asked how he is. He told her he's okay and called to ask a question. He asked her if she and his dad went to the attic when they slept over. She said, "Yes we did, Sebastian. and we touched the mannequin and moved her arm but we didn't move her. We also saw an old rocking chair behind boxes and pulled it out and sat on it. I hope it was okay." He told her it was and he was just wondering how the arm got bent on the mannequin and how it got moved. He thought a ghost moved it and obviously it did. He also thought the rocking chair got moved. After talking awhile, he told her they'll meet again soon and then they hung up.

Sebastian made a call to Katherine to tell her the news of how Elaina and his dad were in the attic when they slept over for the yachting day and that's how the mannequin's arm got bent. They didn't move it which means a ghost did it. They also spotted the rocking chair and sat on it. He then told her he saw a psychiatrist and she wants to hear about it but she's busy now so they ended the call.

Thanksgiving day arrived and Sebastian and Samantha were having dinner in the beautiful dining room in the Ultimate Inn where he knows Chef André and Bruce, the waiter. He also knows the food will be good. They're sitting in a warm and cozy spot and having champagne in a room that is filled with people. Samantha looks stunning in a short and pretty blue dress with her dark brown hair and magnetic blue eyes. Sebastian looks handsome and classy.

While Sebastian and Samantha were enjoying their delicious turkey dinner, he said, "It looks like we're going to have a peaceful Thanksgiving." She said, "Yes, I'll try to control my temper today." He thanked her and then they laughed. Their dinner is roast turkey with gravy, bread stuffing, cranberry sauce, mashed potatoes, butternut squash and date nut bread and they love their dinner.

Sebastian told Samantha that he's sorry Jenny's spirit scared her from wanting to make love the last time they were together. She told him that there are other places to make love, and, she usually doesn't scare easily, especially when she's angry. He then just stared at her.

Sebastian went on and asked Samantha how her new romance novel was coming along. She told him it's a good story but she's still angry about the person who may have stolen her manuscript copy of an old story she wrote which she left at the copy center. He told her to take care of it later. She said, "Well, I have an idea for this new romance novel." He asked her to tell him about it and she said, "It's about a love addict. That's all I'm going to tell you." He said, "Oh, that sounds steamy!" She responded, "It's very steamy!" She then made eye contact with him while having a sinister look in her eyes. After taking their time eating, it was time for dessert of warm mincemeat pie with fresh whipped cream and hazelnut coffee. He didn't look happy now because of a few things she said and her evil eye contact she gave him. He didn't even want conversation. He sensed something which gave him a bad feeling about her but he didn't know exactly what it was. Somehow, they enjoyed their dessert.

Last of all, before Sebastian and Samantha left the restaurant, Bruce, the waiter came out with the check and said, "It was nice seeing you again, Sebastian." He said, "Thank you and tell Chef André that the turkey dinner was delicious." Bruce thanked Sebastian for his tip and left. He went into the kitchen and went over to Chef André and gave him Sebastian's message. Chef André then smiled.

After Sebastian and Samantha left the restaurant and he was driving her home, she wanted to know more about how his father died. He told her that he had a seizure. She said, "I'm really sorry to hear that." He thanked her for her sympathy and then told her that he went to see Dr. Louis, the psychiatrist, and liked him. The doctor told him that many people claim to have seen ghosts and it's probably true but he is skeptical because he has never seen any. Samantha was happy that he went to see the doctor. They soon reached her condo in Marblehead and he parked the car for a moment and told her he didn't want to go in her condo tonight. She kissed him but he wasn't in the mood to kiss so they said goodnight. Sebastian didn't like an evil look she had at the restaurant.

Back at the mansion, Sebastian wanted to relax for the rest of the day and read his manuscript to see how it sounded and if he covered everything so far. He did that and then took a shower in Jenny's bathroom. After that, he just wanted to lie on Jenny's bed and think about what brought on the three unnecessary murders. A young lady, a young man and a mother murdered in the same mansion on the same day.

Early the next morning, the aroma of coffee perking in Sebastian's kitchen was heavenly. There was also some raisin cinnamon toast on the kitchen table with butter and extra cinnamon that he sprinkled on it. He sat down and slowly enjoyed himself before going to work on his book. He has the mansion's first tenant's name, Oscar, and the names of the previous tenants, before Jenny and her mother moved in, Claude and Josh. He wants to start looking into them after he finishes breakfast. Jenny and her mother moved in when Jenny was only two years old and she was later murdered at the young age of 23 and her mother was murdered at age 50.

Sebastian finished his breakfast. He then started doing a search on his computer of the previous mansion owner and found his name on police records under domestic violence. It read that Claude was the owner and lived there since the early 1930s and was murdered at age 51 in his mansion by his son Josh who was age 30 and lived with him. They had numerous altercations but their last one was deadly. Claude was having a clandestine love affair with his son Josh's girlfriend. Out of anger, Josh murdered his father and was convicted and given a life sentence and he was later murdered in prison.

After reading about Claude's death, Sebastian thought how awful it was. He started documenting the information in his red book at his desk, and, as he wrote the name Claude, there were suddenly strong winds in his living room blowing papers all over the room. Sebastian stood up and could hardly believe the wind because the windows were closed. As he looked around the room, to his surprise, not far from his desk, he encountered a pale lifelike ghostly apparition in a rage screaming and swinging his arms. He assumed it was Claude wearing blue jeans and a blue shirt and at the age of 51 when he was murdered. Sebastian heard Claude yell out, "He Murdered me! My son murdered me! Help me! Help!"

Sebastian had no picture of Claude so he quickly asked, "Who are you?" He saw his mouth move and heard him yell, "I'm Claude! I'm Claude! Help! My son murdered me!" Claude's ghost suddenly disappeared and Sebastian yelled, "Claude, don't go! Claude, come back!" Claude's ghost was gone and Sebastian was disappointed.

The living room was a mess with papers all over the place and objects were scattered all over the room from the wind. After Sebastian picked up a lot of papers and then straightened the room out, he went to the sofa to relax and think about what he just saw. He found Claude's ghost to be so strange.

While Sebastian is walking around, he said out loud, "How many damn ghosts are going to show up! That was Claude! He was murdered here 27 years ago! I just wrote his name and he appeared in this room! He appeared here because this is where he was murdered! This is amazing!" Sebastian is through writing for the day, that's for sure, and he knows he'll be lucky if he gets a good night sleep tonight. He had dinner with a glass of wine and then rested on the sofa again, only this time, with his hands behind his head. While thinking out loud, he said, "I can't believe what's happening in this place. How many ghosts am I going to see? So far, it's four! What a haunted mansion this is!"

It was days later, in the afternoon, Sebastian had just answered his door and he was so surprised to see Katherine standing there. It was early December and cold out so she was wearing a warm red coat, and after she entered the mansion, he hung it up and then they hugged. She was in a pretty blue suit that looked good with her shoulder length blonde hair and green eyes. She recently returned from Los Angeles where she spent Thanksgiving with a girlfriend.

Sebastian and Katherine walked to the living room and sat on the sofa and held hands and told each other how happy they are to be back together. They embraced as he said, "We're soul mates." She said, "I'm convinced we are." He then asked her how her trip to Los Angeles was and she told him she had a good time but missed him. They smiled at each other and then Sebastian went on and told her how she just missed a ghostly encounter that came in like a hurricane. She wanted to know more about it. He first asked her if she wanted anything to eat or drink and she said, "I'd like tea with crackers and cheese?" He told her, "Stay where you are and I'll heat the water." While the water was heating, he went back in the living room and sat with her and they looked so happy as they talked.

Katherine asked Sebastian how his Thanksgiving was and he told her it was okay and that he took Samantha, his novelist friend, to dinner. While Katherine looked into his eyes, he said, "When you're not near me, I always miss you, Katherine." Suddenly the tea kettle whistled and they both got up and went and made their tea. They decided to have their tea with crackers and Swiss cheese in the white and blue cozy kitchen.

While Katherine was sitting, she looked around the kitchen and at the butler's swinging door and said, "I love this Victorian kitchen." He said, "I love this place too but it's spooky! I've seen a total of four ghosts so far and they all talk to me!" She looked amazed as she asked him if he was scared to live there now because of all the ghosts. He answered, "I can handle it, although, after living here seven and a half months, I thought I'd be further along solving this murder." She told him to keep working on it and he may suddenly get a lead as to who committed them. He loves how she is concerned and so inspirational.

Katherine said, "You know what? We should visit the cellar some day and take a good look around." He said, "That sounds like something I want to do. Should we do it now?" She told him no because she's in her suit and wants to do it with her jeans on because cellars are dusty.

Sebastian started talking about the ghosts. He told Katherine, the reason the ghosts keep coming out is because the mansion is where they were murdered and they're angry that someone killed them and they want justice. He went on and told her how he just saw Claude's pale lifelike ghostly apparition and he wants justice because his son Josh killed him in the mansion before Jenny lived in it. And Claude might think his son Josh is still alive and doesn't know he was convicted for murdering him and given a life sentence, then someone murdered him in prison. Some ghosts keep showing up even if their murderer is dead or alive because they're angry that someone took their life. Sebastian also told Katherine, if Jenny's murderer is found, it's possible that she may never show up again or she may just because someone took her life. Some people get murdered and never come back as ghosts or spirits. They just pass on to the other side.

Katherine said, "That's a good explanation of ghosts." Sebastian thinks it's fascinating how some people come back as ghosts. He told her that he wishes he could tell her more but he has to keep some things confidential until his book comes out. She told him she understands. She also told him she'd be scared to see a ghost in front of her. He told her, when he first saw Jenny's pale lifelike ghostly apparition, he thought she was so beautiful. She was thin with long light brown hair and brown eyes and spoke messages to him. He also told Katherine that he has seen her three times but he doesn't want to tell the details of what happened yet. Katherine's eyes opened wide as she said, "I'm very interested in all this ghost stuff. Oh wow! What a story this will be! And maybe a movie!" He said, "That's the idea!"

As Sebastian and Katherine started leaving the kitchen, he gently kissed the side of her face and said, "You smell wonderful." She told him it was a new perfume, and since he loves it, she'll wear it more often. They then wanted to go in Jenny's room so they held hands as they walked into her bedroom just to look around. Katherine sat at her dressing table for a moment and got a strange feeling that she didn't like so she quickly got up from it. She said, "I almost think that Jenny's spirit was in the room and saw me sitting there and didn't like it." He told her there was no gardenia scent in the room, therefore, Jenny's spirit didn't see her at her dressing table. Katherine said, "It still felt eerie." He then gave her a hug and she smiled.

Bernice Carstens

While Sebastian and Katherine were still standing in Jenny's bedroom, they were facing each other when he gently put his hands on the upper part of her arms. They then looked deep into each other's eyes as he said, "Katherine, there's something about you. I'm feeling such intense chemistry between us and it feels so right. You're the woman I want in my life. You're beautiful in and out." She said, "Thank you for saying those wonderful words to me, Sebastian. I'm very attracted to you and you know it, but how long will it take for me to commit to a relationship, I don't know." He paused and then gave her a kiss on the lips and then they left the room while he had his arm around her and they headed back to the living room and sat on the sofa. They immediately embraced and felt so passionate and wanted to lie on the sofa so Katherine did with a pillow behind her head.

While Sebastian and Katherine were still on the sofa kissing, she almost gave in to making love with him. She sat up quickly to stop the passion and said, "Sebastian, I have to leave now." He knew why she wanted to leave. It was because she almost gave in to making love with him. He got up and walked her to the door. They kissed passionately again, and when they stopped, she looked like she was in a whirlwind heading for Oz. He was extremely heated up and wanting more as he watched her leave and go to her car.

Sebastian felt lonely now as he walked back to his living room and headed to the sofa. With a pillow behind his head, he then thought about Katherine and how badly he wants her. Not just for a night, for a lifetime. She is the first woman he ever wanted to spend his life with.

The following weekend, on Saturday night, Katherine and Sebastian were in a dine and dance place and were sitting at a table having champagne with appetizers and talking. She looked gorgeous wearing a silver dress and her blonde hair was pulled to one side showing off her eyes. She was wearing the same perfume Sebastian loved on her a few days ago. He looked dashing in a blue suit with a classy tie and shirt and his brown wavy hair had a strand of it on his forehead. They were making passionate eye contact while romantic music was playing in the background. He then asked, "Katherine, I'm not much of a dancer but do you want to try it?" After she smiled at him, she answered, "Yes. I've been waiting for you to ask me that question." They got up and danced very close while she put her head against his face and they looked like they were so in love. When the song ended, a Salsa started and they laughed. He then said, "Oh no! You're not going to get me to do that!" After she laughed, she said, "Come on! I'm willing to try it!" They tried to do the Salsa but stopped and went back to their table laughing. She then said, "We're so compatible." After several hours in the dine and dance place, they left.

Back at the mansion, there was a very romantic Latin song playing while Sebastian and Katherine were dancing in the living room. They love how the Latin beat makes them feel so passionate when they're dancing close and their bodies touch each other. He's wondering how long the ladylike Katherine will be able to hold off before she gives in to making love. He's also always wondering when she'll commit to a relationship so they can explore their love making.

When the dance ended, Katherine said, "Play another song like that. I never want to lose the feeling it gave me." He played another romantic Latin song and they danced with their bodies against each other except when he sometimes slowly twirled her around. They were having a wonderful time. When the song ended, he went to pour them some champagne but she didn't want any so he didn't either. They stood close and embraced as she said, "What a wonderful fun night we had and I want to do it again." He said, "I promise you we'll dance to the Latin beat again." They then had a long and passionate kiss.

7

EAVESDROPPING - ULTIMATE INN

In early December, on a sunny morning, Sebastian was driving his car down the main street in Marblehead and saw Samantha walking on the sidewalk. Her shoulder length dark brown hair with the black winter coat she was wearing made her look mysterious and more so with her magnetic blue eyes. While he was in the middle of traffic, he blew his horn at her and she looked at him and waved and ran to his car. He stopped and rolled down his window and she screamed at him, "Why haven't you called me up!" While he was holding up traffic, he suddenly had a clairvoyant moment of her scratching his car with her keys. Then, it ended.

Sebastian then answered Samantha's question and told her he did not want to discuss anything while in the middle of traffic.

While horns kept on blowing for Sebastian to start driving his car, he said, "I've been busy, Samantha. As a matter of fact, I've been dating someone else and I'll call you later to explain it." He started driving away and she yelled, "Wait!" He kept driving and could hear her yell out that she never ever wants to see him again and he's a creep like all the rest. As he continued to drive, her voice started to fade out yet he could still see her in his rear view mirror standing in the street. He then thought about the clairvoyant moment he just had that forewarned him to drive away from her and he's glad he did because she would have scratched his car.

While Sebastian was driving, he said, "What a temper Samantha has and can't seem to control it but she does eventually calm down." When he got to his mansion and parked, he was quite happy to be back. He went into his foyer and hung his jacket up and then went to his kitchen and got a soft drink. As he paced the floor with it, he thought about Samantha's temper problem again and feels sorry for her and knows psychotherapy and medication could help her.

Sebastian soon went to his desk to work on his book. By late afternoon, he prepared his dinner and then sat on a chair with a bottle of water to think about his book. Of the two wing armchairs and two sofas all in burgundy velvet, he favors a particular wing armchair. He feels like a king sitting on it and he looks like he could be a king. He is charismatic and has a classy presence no matter what he is wearing. He's also highly intelligent and has a wonderful personality.

Before long, Sebastian was in his dining room having a delicious roast lamb dinner with gravy, roasted potatoes, peas, a salad and a glass of red wine as he relaxed. After he finished his dinner and was on his way to the kitchen with the dishes, he took a look in the mirror that is in the china cabinet and spotted a pale shadowy ghost of someone in back of his reflection that swiftly moved across the room. He got surprised and dropped his dishes onto the floor and quickly turned around and there was no one there. He doesn't know what to think other than it could have been Oscar's ghost, the first tenant. Sometimes he wonders how the ghosts decide when and where they're going to show up. He picked the dishes up off of the floor and went into the kitchen with them through the butler's swinging door. He then made a strong cup of coffee and sat in the kitchen with it to think of what he just saw. While sipping his coffee, he also thought about all the ghosts in his mansion that he has seen so far and somehow likes seeing them visit him.

A few nights later, Sebastian was on his way to the Ultimate Inn cocktail lounge for a change of scenery and to see Saul, the bartender. He's also wondering what's new in the coffee shop and if Sam, the trouble maker, has been around lately. When Sebastian arrived at the Ultimate Inn lounge, it was packed with people at the bar, at tables and in booths. Sebastian went and sat at the bar and talked with his friend Saul a few minutes and then ordered a soft drink. Saul brought him his drink and told him that he's lucky he doesn't have an alcohol problem. Sebastian agreed with him and then told him so many lives get messed up from alcohol. A person says and does things they normally wouldn't say or do sober. Saul totally agreed with him and told him that he rarely ever drank alcohol his whole life. Danny, the piano player, suddenly started playing a tune on the keyboard with his hat on while pretty faced Phoebe was right next to him singing along with the music. She is so happy singing and entertaining the audience. As Sebastian watched her, she suddenly danced around and then started spinning around the dance floor while everyone applauded her. Someone yelled, "Go for it, Phoebe!" When the song ended, everyone kept on applauding her. She yelled out, "Thanks, everybody!" Danny started to tickle the ivories and sang a song that people loved. When he finished, there was a thunderous applause.

Although there were two bartenders, Saul was still very busy so he and Sebastian could only talk when he got the chance. Sebastian started to eavesdrop on two guys sitting close by him in a booth that was next to the end of the bar. He couldn't help but hear them because they were drunk and talking loud. As Sebastian listened, one was telling the other that the famous writer from New York was now living in Marblehead Neck trying to find the murderer who killed the three people at their mansion in 2006. And then he's going to write a book about it. Just then, Sebastian carefully turned his head to see who said that. It looked like, Alfred, the person who he recently interviewed at his home about the murders. Alfred is age 45, thin, dark, and wears glasses. It was him, for sure. He was talking with his friend Dex who is age 31, obese and also frumpy. Sebastian listened to Alfred tell Dex that he wished Dex hadn't told him about the mansion with the antiques and that it would be an easy place to rob. He went on and told Dex that he ended up having to shoot the old lady. In awhile, Saul came over to Sebastian to see if he wanted another soft drink and he didn't. Sebastian then softly told him to listen to the two guys next to the bar. He told him one of them was Alfred who robbed the mansion and shot the mother and he just heard him confess it to his friend Dex.

Saul pretended to be talking to Sebastian and listened in on the two guys as Dex said, "Hey, Alfred! I didn't make you rob the mansion! I just told you about it!" Alfred said, "I got caught and had to shoot the old lady so she couldn't identify me and then I got the hell out of there fast with a few antiques." Saul looked at Sebastian and said, "You have me for a witness." Sebastian thanked him and then they carried on with the evening without Alfred and Dex ever knowing someone was listening to Alfred confess to a robbery and murder.

Sebastian stayed at the bar and decided to have another soft drink which is his second one and will be his last one because that's enough for him. However, he likes drinking water anytime and he always feels fortunate that he is not an alcoholic. Saul went back to Sebastian with his drink and quietly said to him, "That was lucky how you overheard Alfred confess to the mansion murder." Sebastian agreed and told him he can't wait to give that information to the police. He also told him he'd be leaving the Ultimate Inn after the two thieves leave so they don't recognize him. Within fifteen minutes, the two thieves left the Ultimate Inn while staggering out the door. Sebastian stayed another fifteen minutes to make sure he wouldn't run into them anywhere.

Saul and Sebastian were soon shaking hands goodbye as Sebastian said, "I'll keep you posted with the news we heard tonight." Saul said, "I'll see you later, Sebastian." Sebastian was driving back to his mansion and very happy how he got so lucky to eavesdrop on something so important to tell the police. While driving, he thought of how there's one murderer that will be arrested for one of the three shootings. Now, if he could only find out who shot Jenny and Pierce, he'd have a blockbuster book and movie.

When Sebastian arrived at his mansion, he went to his kitchen and made toast with peanut butter and poured a glass of cold milk and then took it through the butler's swinging door into the dining room and sat there and enjoyed it. After that, he took a shower and then went to Jenny's bed hoping to have a dream about her tonight and maybe get some answers from her that he wants so badly.

The next morning, Sebastian was sitting at his desk with his T-shirt and pajama bottoms on having coffee while reading some of his notes in his red hardcover book. In awhile, he took a shower and then got casually dressed, as he usually does, and went to his desk to document some important news that he just got. He has all the news from Alfred, the thief and murderer, who was talking with his friend Dex when he eavesdropped on them last night at the Ultimate Inn. He also has Saul for a witness. Sebastian wants to go to the police tomorrow afternoon because he needs time to document all his news that he has for them.

In the late afternoon, Sebastian was still working on his computer as shadows of bare tree branches were moving on the wall. He stopped again to look at them a few seconds and noticed how spooky the shadows look when they're just bare tree branches.

While Sebastian was still at his desk, he decided to go and sit on an armchair to read, in doing that, he suddenly fell asleep and his book fell onto the floor. He was sound asleep when a sudden loud noise awakened him. He immediately saw two pale lifelike ghosts right in front of him having an altercation that became violent. He could hear them and was surprised and curious while watching them. He recognized one of the ghosts as being Claude who has already appeared in front of him. He was a man in his 50s wearing a blue shirt with rolled-up sleeves with jeans. The other ghost looked like a younger man in his 30s wearing a white shirt with rolled-up sleeves with jeans and kept hitting Claude over the head with a poker. Sebastian found it very difficult to watch. While Claude tried to dodge from being hit on the head, he yelled out, "Stop him! Someone help me! My son Josh is killing me! My son's killing me!" Sebastian was momentarily frozen in time.

While Sebastian is still sitting on the armchair, he is now sitting on the edge of his seat watching and wishing he could help Claude. While Josh kept hitting his father over the head with a poker, Claude yelled out again, "Help me! Help!" Sebastian heard him, as he does all the ghosts, and then saw him fall to the floor. Josh was still standing over his father as he kept hitting him over the head with a poker while he appeared to be dead.

Josh yelled out to his father, "I hate you, father! I hate you! You slept with my girlfriend! I saw you! You went and stole my girlfriend!" At that moment, Claude and Josh's ghost swiftly disappeared together and Sebastian didn't call them back.

Sebastian is so shocked at what he just witnessed and felt sad that no one could help Claude. He rested his head on the back of the armchair and then suddenly sat up straight and yelled, "This mansion is so haunted! I just witnessed the murder of Claude which was committed by his son Josh about 27 years ago in this mansion! I saw his son murder him! Oh hell!" Sebastian remembers reading about this murder and started thinking of how unnecessary it was. It was all over a girlfriend that the father stole from his son. He knows Claude's ghost came back because his son Josh killed him and he couldn't rest because of that. Sebastian then yelled, "This makes six different ghosts I've seen! How the hell many are there?" He went to lie on the burgundy velvet sofa and put a pillow behind his head to think this through. He's anxious to document this news in his hardcover book and the computer.

Sebastian soon got up from the sofa and made himself a cup of tea and a sandwich and sat in the kitchen to eat it. He was thinking of the ghostly apparition he saw of Claude being murdered by his son Josh which was 27 years ago. He's amazed he witnessed it right in front of him, and, exactly where it happened! It was a flashback of the actual murder!

After seeing a powerful apparition of Claude being murdered, Sebastian feels his special power is giving him the ability to see ghostly murders actually taking place, not just hearing gunshots. He then went to lie on Jenny's bed to try to think of who could have murdered her and Pierce.

Later that evening, Sebastian was still on Jenny's bed with a pillow in back of his head just trying to make sense of all these ghosts he has seen. After awhile, he tried to put it out of his mind so he could get some sleep but he couldn't. He tossed and turned all night. In the middle of the night he got up and sat in the kitchen snacking on cold meatballs and crackers and then went back to bed to see if he could sleep. When it was 4:00 a. m., he fell asleep.

The same day, in the late morning, Sebastian woke up and took a long shower, got dressed and then made fresh perked coffee. After a couple of cups of coffee, he made himself a breakfast of French toast and had it with a glass of milk. After that, he decided to take his third cup of coffee into the living room while he reviews his notes. He started to document all his new information in his red book and then updated it in his computer and is planning on giving his new information to the police in the afternoon. After spending about three hours on his book, he decided that he wanted to go out for awhile to clear his head from all the ghosts so he put on a warm jacket and left the mansion. He needed a change of scenery. He went to Crocker Park and walked around for awhile and saw all the boats docked and tied up for the winter. He soon left the area and went to a tea room nearby who has a tea leaf reader there. She is a large woman named Annabel but better known as "the tea leave reader." After he drank his tea, she proceeded to read his tea leaves left in his cup as he was quite fascinated watching her because this was his first time.

The tea leaf reader first told Sebastian that he's now involved with something that will change his life. He smiled at that. She went on and told him to expect some rocky times which won't be easy to deal with. She paused and then told him she saw two women in his life but warned him to be careful with one who has a troubled past. She then didn't want to tell him anymore. He smiled at her and gave her a generous tip. She thanked him and he left the tea room feeling skeptical about it but enjoyed it. Annabel has drawn a lot of business for the quaint and attractive little tea room which also has delicious muffins and pastries, and, you can get your tea leaves read, if you'd like. It was something to take Sebastian's mind off of the ghosts for awhile and it did.

After riding around for awhile, it was soon mid-afternoon and Sebastian was back at his mansion and feels better now that he had a change of scenery. In his kitchen, he made a ham and Swiss cheese sandwich on some crusty bread and is at the table having it with a glass of cold milk while thinking about all his notes he has for the police. When he finishes eating, he plans on going to the outsource police station to give them his latest earthshaking news which really is big news.

Sebastian soon left his mansion with a large manila envelope full of information for the police. When he arrived at the station, he saw Officer Martin and went over to him and sat down. They both smiled at each other and then Sebastian handed him the envelope with information and said, "Oh do I have news for you and it's all in this envelope. I went to the Ultimate Inn the night before last and got very lucky. I eavesdropped on Alfred who was sitting near me." Officer Martin said, "I'll read it later and show the chief and then get back to you." Sebastian couldn't resist telling Officer Martin a little about what happened. He told him how Alfred and his friend Dex were drunk and shooting their mouths off about the mansion murder which was in 2006 and how Alfred robbed it and shot the mother and got away with it. Sebastian added that he called the bartender Saul over just in time to hear what they were saying about the murder, therefore, he can testify to Alfred and Dex's confession. Officer Martin is surprised and said, "Thanks, Sebastian!"

Sebastian then wanted to tell the officer about Claude and Josh who were the previous tenants that lived in the mansion before Jenny. He said, "Officer Martin, you're going to be shocked when I tell you this. I just witnessed a 27 year old murder!" The officer stared at him. Sebastian told him how Claude and his son Josh's pale lifelike ghost appeared together in front of him, in his living room, while having an altercation which turned violent. He saw Josh hit his father Claude over the head with a poker until he fell to the floor and then kept hitting him. Officer Martin said, "I know about Claude and his son Josh. Claude was 51 and his son was 30 when he killed him for stealing his girlfriend. Now, in 2010, you witnessed the actual murder that happened 27 years ago in your mansion. I'm amazed."

Sebastian told Officer Martin that most people won't believe his ghost stories. The officer said, "I know you recently saw a psychiatrist so what did he say about your ghostly encounters?" Sebastian told him the doctor believes some psychic mediums experience ghostly encounters, but, to hear a ghost speak is unusual and he's hearing them speak because of his extraordinary psychic ability. Some psychic mediums just communicate with spirits and sense their messages and never see ghosts. The doctor also told him that psychic mediums are sensitive to power beyond the physical world. Sebastian paused and then said, "Officer Martin, the psychiatrist I went to is skeptical about ghosts because he has never seen one but because so many people claimed they have seen ghosts, he believes they may have. The doctor also told him that his encounters with ghosts are unusual because they are pale lifelike apparitions and not pale shadowy ones, and, he also hears them talk. Therefore, there will always be skeptics who will question whether or not there are ghosts. The officer said, "That was well put, Sebastian."

Officer Martin switched gears and told Sebastian that after he and the other officers go over all the information he gave them, they may take Alfred in for questioning. The officer likes the fact that Sebastian was the first one to hear this confession from Alfred. He also added that his prints were nowhere in that mansion, however, he could have worn gloves and murdered all three of them. He also wonders, if there is another murderer, will the other murderer ever be caught. Sebastian said, "I don't think Alfred shot Jenny and Pierce because he would have confessed to that too while he was talking about how he shot the mother." Officer Martin said, "Exactly. It sounds like he didn't shoot all three of them. We'll just have to wait and see." After a few more minutes talking, Officer Martin stood up to say goodbye to Sebastian and thanked him for his help. Sebastian told him he is happy to help the police and wants to continue working with them on this case. He thinks it looks like they are one step closer to solving the murder mystery and the officer agreed. Sebastian then left the police station.

While Sebastian was on his way back to his mansion, he was thinking about dinner and how he was going to spend his evening. He wants to do some writing and then check the attic and the sewing room again.

After a short ride, Sebastian arrived at his mansion and parked in his driveway which he doesn't always do. He often parks on the street in front of his mansion. Some houses are far apart which gives those homeowners a lot of privacy. Mrs. North's house is the only close neighbor to Sebastian.

Sebastian opened his mansion door and entered the rose foyer and, shockingly, there was the scent of gardenias and Jenny's ghost standing a few feet in front of him. Her pale lifelike ghostly apparition was wearing a sheer lavender blue nightgown which was long and loose-fitting and looked ethereal. Sebastian was stunned and couldn't move or take his jacket off because he hasn't seen her for awhile. She was as beautiful as ever with her long light brown hair, hypnotic brown eyes, beautiful face and pale rose lips. While he stood in the foyer near the door, they stared at each other as she softly said, "I've been waiting for you, Sebastian. I love you. Please help me! I was murdered!"

Sebastian was still standing in the foyer with his jacket on and not moving. While he was thinking of how he has made love with Jenny's ghost, she walked close to him and slowly removed his jacket and dropped it on the floor. She put her arms around him and kissed his lips passionately and he was suddenly able to move his arms around and actually feel her. His mind then went into a whirlwind as he felt her against his body. He then said, "Jenny, I miss you so much. Why did you take so long to come back? I've been wanting to ask you if we can take a shower together? Can ghosts do that?" Jenny's ghost looked into his eyes and said, "Yes, Sebastian." She gently kissed his neck and then took his hand and slowly led him to the bathroom where they passionately kissed. In a moment, his clothes and her sheer lavender blue nightgown were on the floor and they were in the shower. He was in a trance because the power and charm of Jenny's ghost was so overwhelming to his soul. He felt like he was physically and mentally transported to the world of ghosts.

While Jenny's ghost and Sebastian stood in the shower, they could be seen as slow moving shadows behind the glass shower door and glass wall which was covered with steam, and, as the water poured over the naked and lifelike ghost of Jenny, it didn't change her ghostly appearance. She almost looked alive but he knew she was a ghost that gave him a spiritual journey that he never felt in the world of the living.

While still standing in the shower, Sebastian caressed Jenny's ghost and then moved his hands all over her and she did likewise to him. They soon decided to lie on the shower mat as the water pulsated down on them. Jenny used her power to give him strange love pleasure while he was living in the world of ghosts.

Sebastian and Jenny's ghost soon sat up in the shower and he held her in his arms as she looked at him and said, "Sebastian, please find my murderer." He said, "Jenny, I will but I need a name or description of the murderer." While they were embraced and in her world, she swiftly disappeared along with her gardenia scent.

Sebastian was now left alone sitting on the floor in the shower with empty arms. He was almost devastated that she left. He yelled, "Jenny! Jenny! Don't leave me!" Sebastian got out of the shower, covered himself with a towel and went into the foyer and couldn't see her anywhere. He went back to the bathroom where they left their clothes and saw that his were still on the floor but was shocked when he saw her sheer lavender blue nightgown there. He thought, "It's surreal that Jenny's ghost disappeared and left her nightgown!" He picked it up and it felt like real material and then he smelled it and it had a gardenia scent. He held it close to his body and said, "It's a keepsake from Jenny. I'll put it her drawer." He then thought of Alan who will want this scene in his movie.

About a week later, Sebastian was in Dr. Louis' office sitting on a chair across from the doctor who was at his desk. Sebastian first said, "Dr. Louis, I want to discuss the ghosts again." The doctor responded, "Yes, let's do that." Sebastian then told him that he has never been in a Victorian mansion before and believes that's why he's now seeing ghosts for the first time, and, the ghosts or spirits are present because it's where they were murdered. But he also knows ghosts don't just appear in mansions. He asked the doctor's thoughts on why he thinks he's only seeing them in the mansion. Dr. Louis told him that he believes there is no set time of when or where a person will see a ghost. He most likely needed to be in a mansion where the murders occurred to see his first ghost and now he might see them outside of the mansion.

Dr. Louis and Sebastian started discussing mental health. The doctor told him that he believes Sebastian is seeing ghosts and hearing them speak because he's a gifted, powerful psychic medium. Otherwise, if he were not a powerful psychic medium, it would mean it was all in his imagination. Sebastian said, "Being a psychic means beyond known physical processes. It's a person who's sensitive to non-physical power and I have unusual power."

Dr. Louis told Sebastian he's a psychic medium like his mother was and able to help police solve murders and he is able to do the same, and, because he's clairvoyant and is a criminal psychologist, that also helps him solve murders.

Sebastian then thanked Dr. Louis. They agree that because he was in a mansion where the murders occurred and saw ghosts, it opened the door for him to see ghosts somewhere else. Sebastian wants to see where and why other people were murdered. He feels it would be rewarding if he could help their restless spirits go to the other side.

8

THE ATTIC AND THE CELLAR

Sebastian has invited Katherine to come over and spend the evening with him tomorrow and she accepted the invitation. He hasn't seen much of her lately because she doesn't want to rush into a serious relationship, and, he feels very passionate when he's near her. This is the woman he wants to share his life with and he will never get over the beautiful Katherine who rented him the mansion.

The next evening, in the living room, while soft music was playing, Katherine was sitting on the burgundy velvet sofa having a mild after-dinner drink on the rocks while Sebastian had the same but pacing the floor with his while he was meditating about something. Katherine asked him what he was thinking about but he wouldn't tell her.

Sebastian then sat down next to Katherine and started kissing her face and she loved it and soon she had to succumb to his passionate kisses. As he held her close to him, she fell back on the sofa with him on top of her. They were so passionate at this time that she suddenly said, "Oh no, Sebastian, we're not going to make love here." "I'll never stop trying, Katherine. When I'm next to you, I want to make love. You're the love of my life." After she allowed him to stay on top of her for awhile, she suddenly told him she wanted to sit up and so they did.

While sipping their mild after-dinner drinks, Sebastian suggested that he and Katherine go to the attic and check to see if there's anything unusual going on with the mannequin. She agreed so they put their drinks down and headed for the staircase. On their way up to the attic, they looked in the four bedrooms and sewing room which had no ghostly findings.

Katherine and Sebastian proceeded up to the attic. When they arrived at the entrance, he immediately noticed the mannequin was back in its original place and was shocked that it wasn't naked and went over to it. It was wearing the sheer lavender blue nightgown that Jenny's ghost recently left in the bathroom when she and Sebastian made love in her shower. He's thinking to himself that he's positive he put the gown in Jenny's bedroom drawer. He also doesn't want Katherine to know, at this time, that he made love with Jenny's ghost because he's afraid of what she'll think so he's putting it off. Therefore, he said, "Katherine, do you like the nightgown on the mannequin?" "She told him yes and asked him where it came from. He told her a ghost had moved it and must have put the nightgown on it. He then noticed that everything else was normal on the mannequin. She had the bushy black hair, red lipstick and large haunting pale blue eyes. Then Katherine just stared at Sebastian and wondered what was going on in the attic. He quickly said, "Come on, let's get out of here." But she didn't want to leave yet.

While Katherine and Sebastian are still in the attic, they're now looking in boxes but not seeing anything very interesting other than some old household decorations. He suddenly came across a framed picture of Pierce and Jenny that he didn't see the last time he looked in boxes. As they both stared at the picture, Sebastian said, "Katherine, Pierce was so in love with Jenny." She responded, "He must be a very angry spirit now that someone killed the both of them." Sebastian definitely thinks that's true. They went on to look in trunks and found old clothes, blankets and a hat. She tried the hat on and they laughed. Sebastian then started thinking to himself again about Jenny's sheer lavender blue long nightgown that's on the mannequin and believes Jenny's ghost must have put it on it and moved it to its original place.

Katherine went over to the rocking chair that has arms and sat on it and smiled at Sebastian. He told her he hasn't sat on it yet. She went to get off the rocking chair so he could try it but it wouldn't stop rocking. She yelled, "Sebastian, it won't stop rocking!" He tried to stop it by grabbing it's arms and in a few seconds he was able to stop it. Katherine said, "Sebastian, there's something going on here. Something was forcing the rocking chair to keep rocking. Let's get out of this attic!" He told her he feels the presence of a spirit who must have done that and the whole place is haunted. When they started to leave the attic, Sebastian was suddenly shoved by something in back of him. He said, "Katherine, I just felt someone put their hand on my back and shove me. That was an angry spirit who did that." They're both wide-eyed and silent for a moment while wondering whose spirit is doing this. Katherine said, "We just felt the presence and power of an angry spirit here, Sebastian. First it was me in the rocking chair and then it was you being shoved." He told her it could be Jenny and Pierce because he and Katherine came across their picture and stared at it. He wants to get out of there so they left the attic and headed down the staircase.

At the dining room table, Katherine and Sebastian are having some tea and pastries she brought while they're discussing what just happened to them in the attic. He said, "Katherine, a spirit has never pushed me before and that rocking chair has never done what it just did to you." They are wondering if this mansion is going to have any more surprises. She said, "It's getting too spooky for me, Sebastian. I don't know how you can stand to live here." They tried to eat the pastries but it wasn't easy because of what just happened in the attic. He told her that there's nothing they can do if the mansion is haunted. It's coming from distressed souls who can't rest because of the way they died so they come back as spirits and sometimes ghosts and they want help. She told him that maybe he should move but he doesn't want to. He let Katherine know that he can handle it and he wants to see the murder mystery solved and also so he can finish writing his book about this unsolved murder of 2006. She told him that she understands why he wants to reach his goal. They smiled at each other and he got up from the table and went over to her and leaned over and kissed her lips. She lit up because she is very attracted to him.

Katherine and Sebastian walked into the living room and soon embraced and kissed passionately for awhile. She suddenly stopped him because it was making her feel too passionate. She loved it but she just wasn't ready to commit to a serious relationship. He wonders if she ever will. She changed the subject and asked him to show her his red hardcover book that he writes in and some of his computer documents about the murder case. While they were looking at the computer, there suddenly was a loud noise coming from the cellar that startled them. They kept listening as the loud noise wouldn't stop. He said, "Let's go to the cellar." There are two doors to the entrance and they both know that. One leads to the outside of the mansion and one is off the kitchen.

After Sebastian opened the kitchen door, he continued to hear the noise which got louder. He immediately called out from the top of the cellar stairs, "Whose there?" A voice answered, "It's just Charlie." Sebastian didn't respond to Charlie, instead, he called out, "Katherine, come on! Let's go!" They quickly headed down the stairs to the cellar to see what was going on and then the noise stopped.

While in the cellar, Sebastian asked, "Charlie what are you doing down here at this time of night?" The 62 year old Charlie told him he was putting things away and something fell over. Sebastian asked him what fell over, so Charlie felt obligated to tell him about the book he has been keeping in the cellar for decades and that an old tenant before Jenny gave it to him. He told him he accidentally knocked over an old chair then picture frames and other things fell when he went to get his book. Sebastian asked to see it. Charlie went to a dark spot where the book was hidden and pulled it out and handed it to him. It was a very old thick brown hardcover book. He opened it and read a little of it which read it was from the 1800s. Sebastian wanted to read more. He asked Charlie if he could take it upstairs for awhile and Charlie agreed to let him but wants it back. Sebastian thanked him and told him he'd definitely get it back. He asked Charlie if his job was going okay. He answered, "Oh yes, Sebastian, but because it's winter, there's not much to do so I organize the cellar and sometimes read my book." Sebastian and Katherine soon said goodbye to Charlie as he left by the cellar door that took him outside where his car was parked.

Katherine and Sebastian have already started to read the old 1800s book at the dining room table. The cover is brown, very worn, faded and the pages are old and brittle so he's carefully turning them while Katherine watches. After turning a few pages in the book, Sebastian suddenly saw some writing that interested him so he read it to Katherine. "The first tenants: In 1850 a wealthy man had a mansion built in Marblehead

Neck and named it Paradise and he, his wife and their son Oscar occupied it. The father and mother soon died and the son became the owner with his wife. She later became a suspect in his murder when he was age 60. It was said that she caught him having sexual affairs and then brutally murdered him with an ax. While she was awaiting trial, she died in the mansion at age 50. Then a man named Claude and his son Josh became the second tenants in Paradise mansion and the son eventually murdered the father for stealing his girlfriend." The book then read, "This book only documents the first and second tenants in Paradise mansion. It's believed that this mansion is haunted."

Sebastian paused and then continued reading. "It is also believed by some people that when a person dies, the soul enters the flesh of a living person which is called reincarnation. And if the soul was that of a murderer that entered the flesh of a living person, then that living person may be a murderer." Sebastian stopped reading and looked at Katherine and asked, "Well, what do you think about that?" She answered, "That's a lot to absorb for now."

After Katherine and Sebastian walked into the living and she sat on the sofa and he sat on a chair, they sipped red wine. He told her how he wants to do more research on Claude and Josh who were the previous tenants to Jenny and Shannon. She wants to read more of the book too but thinks it's so scary. He soon went and sat next to her.

While Sebastian and Katherine were still on the sofa, he was kissing her neck and she gently went down on the sofa and he put his body against hers and she loved it as she sighed. He unbuttoned a few of her buttons on her blouse and she let him. He then started kissing the top part of her breast which set her on fire like he is. He was so passionate that he took his shirt off as she softly said, "Sebastian, I'm not ready for a serious love relationship right now. When and if I'm ever ready, it won't be on this sofa. It must be a bed." He softly said, "I want us on a bed too, Katherine, so I won't take my pants off here." She smiled at him and then wanted to sit back up and so they did. He buttoned her blouse and put his shirt back on and they kissed again. She said, "Sebastian, I think about you all the time." He said, "I never stop thinking about you either."

Sebastian asked Katherine if she wanted anything to eat or drink but she didn't so he didn't either. He got up and paced the floor and soon sat on a chair while conversing with her. He said, "I'm showing you that I can love you from a distance too and that I don't have to be on top of you to tell you how much I care about you." She said, "Oh Sebastian, it's so nice that you're saying that. I feel the same as you. I'm so passionate about you whether you're near or far from me." While they sat across from each other, they looked into each other's eyes and one could see and feel their passion they had for each other. All of a sudden there was a crashing noise.

Sebastian and Katherine quickly went and looked through the window and saw the strong wind blowing which was whipping things around. It's December, yet, instead of snow, there was suddenly wind-swept torrential downpours of rain. Within seconds, there was howling wind and crashing noise that was so powerful and unusual that it frightened Katherine. This was not a normal storm and Sebastian knew it. While the howling wind continued, the crashing sounds got worse and more frequent.

While Sebastian and Katherine kept walking around and looking out the windows, the strange sounding wind continued and it suddenly sounded like the mansion was going to be demolished. They looked puzzled because they never experienced anything like this. The hurricane force wind and the crashing noise blew in two windows in the living room along with broken glass as the rain poured into the mansion.

The hurricane wind also blew the window draperies all over and tossed candlesticks and picture frames around the room. Katherine and Sebastian were cold from two windows blown in so they quickly went and got their coat and jacket. Sebastian quickly went and found cardboard he nailed up on the window frames and picked up broken glass.

While the storm's strange crashing sounds continued, Katherine yelled, "Oh no! Sebastian, what can we do?" He went and put his arms around her while telling her to try and be calm. As he was still holding her, the strong howling wind kept blowing and the strange crashing sounds suddenly became more frightening and wouldn't stop. That's when Sebastian told Katherine he could feel the presence of an angry spirit that was trying to torment them. She asked, "Whose?" He said, "Maybe it's coming from the first tenant's son, Oscar, who lived here and his wife murdered him, or, maybe it's coming from Shannon or Claude or Josh! Maybe it's coming from Pierce who is angry that someone murdered him! But the spirit is not Jenny's that I'm sensing because there's no gardenia scent! It's someone who wants us to know he or she was murdered." After he released her from his arms and they walked around, he told her that sometimes, even after justice has been served, spirits and ghosts just never leave. They just never make it to the other side.

While Katherine and Sebastian are in the middle of the living room, all of a sudden the wind and strange crashing noise stopped along with the rain. They were surprised they didn't lose electrical power during that storm.

Sebastian soon started looking for something more to block the two windows with no panes which the wind blew in. He found blankets and more cardboard and tacked it on the window frames and plans to call the window repairman in the morning. Meanwhile, he asked Katherine if she wanted to sleep over because it was late but she declined because she finds the mansion too scary. They made some tea and had ham and egg sandwiches and ate them while they sat in the kitchen talking. She told Sebastian she wanted to go home after she finished her sandwich because it was late.

Around 1:00 a.m., Sebastian was walking Katherine to the door. They kissed and then embraced as she told him she's worried about him living in the mansion. He comforted her by telling her he can handle it and not to worry. She then left and he watched her get in her car and leave. He went and took a shower and then went to Jenny's bed to try to sleep. He tossed and turned all night because of so much on his mind. He's trying to find the out who murdered Jenny and Pierce and he has to keep working on his book.

After a bad night sleep, Sebastian was in his kitchen at the table the next morning sipping fresh perked coffee. He called the window repairman on his cell phone, and by noontime he showed up and repaired the windows. He told Sebastian there was no storm where he lives which is nearby. Sebastian paid him and thanked him and he left. He's anxious to call Katherine now to tell her what the repairman said.

It's was soon early afternoon and Sebastian was sitting on a chair while talking with Katherine and telling her what the window repairman told him about the storm they just experienced. He said, "Katherine! There was no storm like the one we experienced last night, according to the window repairman!" She asked, "What did you say?" He told her the repairman told him that there was no storm, just light rain and no noise and it didn't last long. He also told him that his mansion is known to be spooked.

Katherine then said, "Sebastian, you need to get out of that mansion." He told her he will not leave until he finishes his book because persistence often leads to success. He also doesn't think that ghosts can hurt anyone. She told him to be very careful while living in there. He then changed the subject and asked Katherine if she would join him at the mansion for Christmas which is only a week away. She told him she would think about it and let him know and then they soon hung up. After that call, Sebastian went into his living room and cleaned it up since the storm made a mess of it and then he sat at his desk and worked on his book.

Meanwhile, in the psychiatrist's office, Samantha, the writer and beautiful brunette, was on the couch and being evaluated by Dr. Louis for the first time. She was telling him she has an uncontrollable temper. He asked her what her childhood was like. She told him she hated it, she came from an ignorant family of verbal and physical abuse and she had no bonding. Her parents gave her no attention or praise, and if she asked a simple question, they'd yelled at her. When she was silent, her mother would verbally attack her with hurtful derogatory comments, She paused and then said, "My mother told me that I was an unwanted pregnancy and her husband came first in her life, not her children." The doctor said, "They had bad psychology, Samantha, but there's more in your past that I need to know." He waited for her response.

Samantha then told Dr. Louis, when she's angry, she screams and yells and sometimes physically attacks people. She seeks revenge in some way. She went on and told the doctor that there were traumatic things that happened to her in her past that she doesn't want to tell him because she's afraid he won't understand. Dr. Louis told her everything between them will be confidential and he will understand. He needs to know specifically about any trauma or violence in her past. After an hour on the couch, he told her she could sit up on a chair and so she did and sat across from him while he was at his desk writing information down. He told her he wanted to see her again and he also prescribed a sedative.

Bernice Carstens

After Dr. Louis made an appointment for Samantha, she thanked him and they said goodbye. While she slowly walked out of the doctor's office, with a swing to her hips, he stared at her until she was out the door. After that, he said out loud, "What an attractive woman. Dark brown hair, magnetic blue eyes that look violet, and such a curvaceous body."

Samantha went back to her condo and called Sebastian on her cell phone while she was having coffee. When he answered, she said, "Sebastian, I just got back from the psychiatrist's office." He said, "I'm glad you went, Samantha. How did it go?" She told him it was a good session but she drew the line as to how much she was going to tell him. She also told Sebastian that she has another appointment with Dr. Louis and he gave her an anxiety medication. Sebastian said, "I'm anxious to see if it controls your temper, but, you also need to tell Dr. Louis everything so he can help you."

After chatting awhile, Samantha changed the subject and asked Sebastian what he has been doing besides working on his book. He said, "I've been seeing a woman off and on for awhile. What have you been doing?" She told him she's going to get a novel published soon and she's excited about that. She then asked Sebastian if the woman he's off and on with is someone he seriously wants. He avoided the question and changed the subject and told Samantha he can't stay on the phone long now because there's something he has to do. She told him to call her when he's not on with that other woman. He didn't respond to that comment so they soon hung up as friends do. Even though she has temper tantrums, they stay in touch with each other because they're both writers and like to talk about their books.

It was late afternoon when Sebastian went to his dining room table and started reading Charlie's very old book that contains information about the mansion. He knows about the first and second tenants before Jenny and Shannon. He has read and knows about reincarnation. He's now reading the definition of a spirit and a ghost which he already knows about. It read, "Spirits can move objects. A psychic medium can send a message to a spirit and the spirit can return one but only through a psychic medium who then senses what the message is about. The message cannot be heard unless the psychic has unusual power." The ghost definition read, "A ghost is a disembodied spirit of a dead person that appears as a shadowy apparition and sometimes a pale lifelike ghostly apparition which happens if the psychic has unusual power. Ghosts often appear because they are angry and want help. The same applies if you feel the presence of a spirit."

Sebastian suddenly wanted to go up to the second floor and look in the sewing room. He went there and saw several boxes and opened one with Jenny's memorabilia. He started to read letters and one was from Pierce that he gave her when they first met. It read, "My dear Jenny, I love you with all my heart and cannot live without you " It went on and it was very emotional.

After a couple of hours in the sewing room reading letters and other things that Jenny saved, Sebastian left the room feeling relieved that he didn't find anything eerie in there. He wanted to see if there were any clues to the murders that might help him.

Sebastian soon went to the kitchen and thought about what he was in the mood to do. He decided to go to the cellar and look around so he did and pondered over many antiques. He suddenly saw a black cat running around and tried to let it go out the door but the cat wouldn't go. It looked at him and showed its teeth as though it was ready to attack him. Sebastian remained silent and the cat finally went outside. He then left the cellar and went back upstairs in a happy mood.

Later, in the kitchen, Sebastian opened a bottle of red wine and poured himself a glass and then remembered he needed to buy more for his guests and himself. He wrote it down on a piece of paper in the kitchen and plans to get the wine later on. Meanwhile, Sebastian is still a little restless from the awful storm that happened last night in his mansion and he and Katherine got a little stressed out from. The best thing he can do for awhile is to stay active so he's thinking about going to the Ultimate Inn and talking with Saul, the bartender, later on. If he were at his home in New York, he'd have plenty of places to go to. He then went to lie on the living room sofa for awhile listening to soft music.

In the evening, Sebastian decided to go to the Ultimate Inn coffee shop for a salad and French fried potatoes. He likes it there because it's very cozy and he sometimes sees Veronica who is a nice young waitress who is in her 20s. He thinks she's so pretty with her long red hair and bubbly personality and chews gum. After he arrived there and sat in a booth, Veronica soon came over and she hasn't seen him for some time. She approached him and said, "Hi, Sebastian. I haven't seen you for awhile." He said, "It's nice to see you again, Veronica. How have you been?" She told him she was fine and asked him for his order and while waiting for it she chewed her gum. He told her he wanted a garden salad with a creamy dressing and some fries and coffee. She wrote it down and told him she'd be back shortly with his order. She smiled at him and then left chewing her gum. He gets a kick out of her and thinks she's adorable.

In awhile, Sebastian was served his salad, fries and coffee and enjoyed it. He then went to the lounge and sat at the bar and ordered a soft drink from Saul, the bartender. After Saul served it to him, Sebastian told him how he turned in the information on Alfred, the confessed murderer, that they heard the night of the Ultimate Inn party. Just then, Inspector Bradford, who is the Ultimate Inn's Hotel Security, suddenly came over to Sebastian and shook hands with him. They talked about the party night how flamboyant Sam, the drunken trouble maker, got arrested

The Ghost And Sebastian

for punching Sebastian in the face. Gerard, the Ultimate Inn's manager, came over and shook hands with Sebastian and all four of them conversed and asked Sebastian how his book was coming along. He told them that he still needs to find out who murdered Jenny and Pierce. They all wished him luck and told him to come back again. Sebastian soon left.

While Sebastian was driving back to his mansion and thinking of the nice people he has met in Marblehead and Marblehead Neck which he feels good about, he soon arrived at his mansion and parked in his driveway. He then entered the rose foyer which looked normal considering all that has happened in it since he's been living in it. He hung his coat up in the foyer closet and proceeded to the living room and flopped down onto an armchair and rested.

A couple of days later, Sebastian was at his desk reading some notes in his red hardcover book and comparing them with his computer notes. He decided he wanted a bottle of water. When he stood up to go get it, he felt a strong breeze and was suddenly shocked when he saw Shannon's ghost sitting at the piano and playing it! The piano was located several feet from his desk in the living room and he recognized her right away. Her pale lifelike ghostly apparition had some gray hair and she was dressed in house clothes. Her fingers were going up and down the piano keyboard and Sebastian was able to hear the music as she played a sad song. He was so fascinated and curious that he couldn't take his eyes off of her and the piano keys as he enjoyed watching and listening to her.

Sebastian went close to Shannon at the piano and said, "Shannon, I haven't seen you for awhile and I didn't know you played the piano." She stopped playing it and looked up at Sebastian in distress and yelled, "I'm Shannon! I'm Shannon! Help me! Where's Jenny?" He didn't want to tell her yet that Jenny was murdered so he didn't answer that question. Shannon then continued to play the piano. This time, she was singing loudly in a trembling voice while playing another sad song. As he stayed next to her watching and listening to her, she suddenly disappeared right in the middle of the song. He looked around the room and yelled out, "Shannon! Shannon! Don't go!" She was gone.

Sebastian is amazed how he saw Shannon's ghost again and heard her play the piano and sing. He then fell onto one of the wing armchairs and put his head back trying to figure out how these ghosts keep appearing. He does know they're restless souls because of their untimely deaths. And now that he knows Alfred murdered Shannon, he so much wants to know who murdered Jenny and Pierce.

While it was the same day, but late in the afternoon, Sebastian was not in the mood to continue working on his book. However, he went to his desk and forced himself to document the unexpected visit of Shannon's ghost playing the piano and singing in his living room. He loves the fact that he hears ghosts speak as though they were alive. He said out loud, "What's next? These ghosts are unpredictable!"

After Sebastian left the desk, he went right over to one of the armchairs and started thinking about having a nice lamb dinner tonight which he rarely has. And he also wishes Katherine could join him. He suddenly remembered that she was suppose to call and let him know if she was going to spend Christmas with him. He then said out loud, "I'll have to call her because Christmas is around the corner and I need to get her a few nice gifts."

While Sebastian was preparing his lamb dinner, he decided to call Katherine and get her answer about whether or not she'll spend Christmas with him. While he was in the kitchen, he called her on his cell phone and asked her about it. She said, "Yes, I'll join you, Sebastian, although that haunted mansion doesn't make me feel comfortable." He was so happy with her answer and told her they can talk about it later. In awhile, they hung up and he smiled because Katherine will be coming to Christmas dinner.

Meanwhile, Sebastian was soon at his dining room table having red wine with his delicious lamb dinner while music played softly. All he can think of is Katherine as he eats his delicious dinner. He took his time finishing his main course of lamb with gravy, mashed potatoes and asparagus. He didn't want dessert. He cleaned up the dining table and then migrated into the living room to lie on the plush velvet sofa and put his head on a big pillow. He started thinking of Christmas with Katherine which is a little more than a week away, therefore, he suddenly decided that he wants to go shopping tomorrow and start buying her some beautiful presents. He stayed on the sofa awhile and soon dozed off. About an hour later, he took a shower and then planned to go to sleep in Jenny's bed.

The next day, when Sebastian got his mail, he was so surprised and happy he received a Christmas card from Elaina in New York. He's happy she was his father's girlfriend before he died a few months ago. Her card read, "I hope you and Katherine have a happy Christmas. Your friend Elaina." He loved the card and decided to call her. When she answered the phone, he said, "Elaina, thank you for the beautiful Christmas card and I'll show it to Katherine. What are you doing for Christmas?" She told him she will spend time with her sister who is married. They talked for awhile and Sebastian told her to call him anytime and they will meet again when he gets through his book. He will then leave Marblehead Neck and move back to New York. She said, "I can hardly wait." After talking awhile, they said goodbye.

Sebastian then wanted to call his friend Alan, the movie producer with a mansion in Marblehead. When he called him, the phone rang and rang and then he answered his phone and said, "Alan speaking." "Alan, it's Sebastian. How are you?" Alan said, "I'm fine, Sebastian! Listen, we have to get together. I miss your company and want to know how the book is coming and I want to hear more about the ghosts!" They both laughed and then Sebastian told him he had a lot of news to tell him and he'll visit him soon. He then told Alan that he called to wish him happy holidays. Alan appreciated that and wished Sebastian the same. They are truly good friends who like to visit each other whenever they can, but, right now, Alan was very busy so they had to shorten the call.

After they hung up, Sebastian momentarily thought of how Alan is planning on making a big movie of his story.

It was afternoon and Sebastian was out shopping for Christmas gifts for Katherine. He saw several things he liked but couldn't decide. He finally decided on some emerald earrings and necklace he thought that would look beautiful on her with her green eyes and blonde hair. He had the jeweler wrap the gift in beautiful paper with a big bow on it. He walked out of the jewelry store very happy carrying a gift bag and heading back to his mansion. He wants to hide it until they get a Christmas tree to put it under and he also wants to get her a couple of more gifts. He's going to have to get a tree fast because Christmas is only days away and he wants Katherine to decorate it with him.

The next day, Sebastian went and bought Katherine two more gifts which he hopes she'll like. He then went to a department store to buy tree trimmings and then he went and bought a real Christmas tree and had it tied to his car. When he got back to the mansion, he spent time standing the tree up in his huge living room and it filled the air with the scent of fresh pine. He later called Katherine to tell her about the Christmas tree and she told him she'd be over to decorate it with him.

Meanwhile, Sebastian decided to call Samantha before the holidays to say hello so he went and sat on a chair and got on his cell phone. When she answered, he wished her a Merry Christmas and then asked her if she would like to get together after the holidays to discuss her novel she's going to have published. She wished him a Merry Christmas and told him she would love to discuss her novel with him. She also told him that she'll be going to Los Angeles for Christmas because she has a few friends there that she has not seen since she left there a couple of years ago. Sebastian wished her a safe trip and told her to call him when she gets back and then the call ended.

At the police station the following morning, Sebastian was standing with Chief Brooks and Lt. Darwin wishing them a Merry Christmas. The chief said, "Good information you gave us about Alfred murdering Jenny's mother Shannon." Sebastian thanked him and then Lt. Darwin said, "Your rival Sam's here today." Sebastian looked around and then saw flamboyant Sam in another area. The police know he's a wannabe writer trying to solve the triple homicide before Sebastian does so he can be the hero. Sebastian told Chief Brooks and Lt. Darwin he was going to Officer Martin now.

After Sebastian sat down with Officer Martin, the officer said, "Sam's here and wants to talk to me about Alfred robbing and killing Jenny's mother Shannon. I told him I'd bring him over here in a few minutes." Sebastian shook his head and said, "Here comes trouble." Officer Martin went and got Sam and brought him over to sit next to Sebastian. Sam looked a little inebriated. The officer asked Sam, "Okay, when did you get the news about Alfred?" Sam blurted out that he heard Alfred confess Shannon's murder last night while he was on his cell phone talking to someone and telling the person to be quiet about it because it happened four years ago and he was cleared. Officer Martin told Sam, "You're too late because Sebastian saw and heard Alfred confess that news to someone two weeks ago and turned it in to us." Sam quickly stood up and said, "Well, maybe I'll have better luck next time." He left without saying bye.

Officer Martin said to Sebastian, "That Sam can't seem to stay out of trouble." Sebastian agreed and told the officer that he just stopped in the station to wish the officers a Merry Christmas and little did he know he'd run into Sam. They talked a little longer and then Sebastian shook hands with Officer Martin and left.

While Sebastian was driving back to his mansion, he decided to stop at a bookstore so he parked in a large parking lot. When he got out of his car, Sam was suddenly in his face and definitely inebriated as he punched Sebastian in the eye and staggered away trying to run. He evidently stalked Sebastian after he left the station. Sebastian couldn't see where he ran to so he headed back to the police station and went over to Officer Martin who was at his desk. When Sebastian sat down, Officer Martin took one look at him and saw he just got punched in the eye because his eye and face were swollen and red. Sebastian told Officer Martin what just happened and the officer said, "Sebastian, you need to press charges against Sam for assault and battery so we can take this trouble maker to court to wake him up and give him a warning." Sebastian agreed to do that so he signed a written statement about the attack. He then proceeded to leave again while Officer Martin said, "I'll talk to you later about this in case you decide to drop charges." Sebastian called out as he left, "Thanks, Officer Martin and Merry Christmas."

Sebastian was soon home in his mansion and on the velvet sofa with his head on a pillow holding an ice-pack on his eye to keep the swelling down. In the evening, he had something to eat and then showered and went to Jenny's bed to relax and think of nasty Sam. He wished he could have punched him back. Sebastian soon snapped out of his anger and became his normal understanding self again knowing there will always be conflicting times in the world. He knows everyone needs to learn how to deal with obstacles and never lose sight of their goals and spend very little time with the negative and continue with the positive.

9

BOMBSHELL IN PARADISE

It's two days before Christmas and Sebastian's eye is still sore and discolored from intoxicated Sam's punch he received in the bookstore parking lot. That didn't stop him and Katherine from decorating the Christmas tree in his living room which they are doing now. After Sebastian went up high on a ladder and put the lights on the tree while she hung the ornaments, he turned on the lights and they thought the tree looked beautiful. They stared at it and smiled and then Sebastian hugged Katherine and said, "You did a great job decorating." After she thanked him, she told him that being with him and seeing the Christmas lights makes her feel so warm inside. He told her he always loves being with her and then they kissed passionately while their hands slowly moved up and down each other's backside.

The Ghost And Sebastian

While Katherine is in Sebastian's arms and they're still standing, she said, "Sebastian, how did all this happen with us? I only wanted to rent you the mansion." Before he could answer, bulbs started falling off the tree and the tree lights went off. Sebastian was puzzled as to what caused that and couldn't seem to fix the problem so he unplugged the tree. Meanwhile, Katherine went home to sleep although she'll be back tomorrow night because it's Christmas eve. Sebastian sat on a chair wondering if there was paranormal activity in the room that caused the bulbs to fall and lights to go off.

It's the next evening and it's Christmas Eve and the tree is lit with several gifts under it wrapped in Christmas paper and have bows. Katherine is looking beautiful in white and having white wine in the living room looking at the tree as the lights seem to be working now. He's wearing a lavender shirt and black pants and his brown wavy hair and good looks gives him charisma. He is also having white wine while telling her he thinks there was paranormal activity in the room that caused the bulbs to fall and lights to go out last night. Katherine said, "I think that's what happened!" They then stared at each other for a few moments.

Sebastian has just opened his gifts from Katherine and is excited that she gave him a beautiful blue sweater and a beautiful pink silk tie and blue shirt. She also gave him some cologne and a gold neck chain. He thanked her and hugged her and then handed her the gifts from him. As she opened them, there was a very pretty peach colored sweater and she loved it and can't wait to wear it. Another gift was perfume with an exotic scent that she loved. When she opened her last gift, her eyes opened wide as she saw emerald earrings and a necklace to match. She tried the set on and it looked beautiful on her with her blonde hair and green eyes and pretty face. She hugged Sebastian and thanked him so much.

Katherine went into the kitchen to prepare some appetizers for Christmas Eve such as grain crackers, imported Swiss cheese and mini-meatballs in a spicy sauce. Sebastian helped her bring everything to the living room coffee table and then they sat on the plush velvet sofa. While they sipped their white wine, music played softly as they munched on the appetizers and talked. She's sleeping in the mansion tonight and it will be her first time sleeping with Sebastian. One can imagine how anxious he is because he waited a long time to be intimate with Katherine. Of course, who knows what she will do once she gets in bed with him. She's in her early 30s and has only been intimate with one man in her past.

When it got late, Katherine insisted that she and Sebastian sleep in Jenny's bedroom because it's so pretty and she loves that room. He agreed to, knowing it might upset Jenny. Katherine then took a shower alone as she thought about how she's about to be naked with Sebastian for the first time. When she finished her shower, she came into the bedroom in a light blue very short negligee that was very pretty as the room was dimly lit coming from two lamps nearby. She said, "It's your turn, Sebastian." While he went and took a shower, she sat at the dressing table combing her hair for awhile and then sat on a chair waiting for Sebastian. He soon came out with a towel tied around his waist and they embraced and kissed and were soon in bed naked but partially covered up with the sheet. He kissed her passionately which threw her into a trance because of his surprising kissing technique tonight and this is the first time they are both naked together. While they are on the beautiful rose colored sheets, she faced Sebastian and said, "I love you and this is why I'm in bed with you." He said, "I love you so much, Katherine." They then agreed to be in a committed relationship.

Sebastian slowly started to make love to Katherine by tenderly moving his hand around her body and she did likewise to him. When he gently kept kissing her breast area, it set her

The Ghost And Sebastian

on fire and she wanted more. She said, "Oh, I'm so happy we're in bed together." He almost couldn't contain himself because he waited so long for this moment. While they continued to make love, she responded with sighs and so did he.

Katherine and Sebastian were so content as they told each other how much they love each other. While they were still making love and wanting to explore what they've never explored together, suddenly the scent of gardenias filled the air. They immediately stopped making love before they ever went into ecstasy.

While Sebastian and Katherine sat up in bed, she covered her breast with the sheet and they inhaled the gardenia scent while looking around the room. Then the dresser drawers started opening and slamming shut with a loud noise they both could hear. Katherine asked, "What's causing all that? And that scent smells like gardenias! Is it from Jenny?" Sebastian answered, "Yes. Exactly. Jenny's spirit is in this room right now." Katherine looked frightened as she watched on. He told her that Jenny's spirit is causing the drawers to open and shut because she's very angry that he's in her bed with another woman. He also told her he has had encounters with her pale lifelike ghostly apparitions several times and this is only the second time that just her spirit has been present. Katherine was silent while listening intensely. Sebastian then said, "I hate to have to tell you this, but, she used her power to seduce me two times and she was successful." Katherine, while still silent, just stared at him in shock as he looked deep into her eyes and said, "I've made love with Jenny's ghost." Katherine was speechless as the drawers continued to open and shut with a bang.

While Sebastian and Katherine were still sitting up in bed, the drawers suddenly stopped opening and slamming shut. Within seconds, Jenny's pale lifelike ghostly apparition was at the foot of the bed which once was hers. She was wearing a sheer white nightgown which was long and loose-fitting. She looked angry as she kept moving and causing her light brown hair to fly around. She and Sebastian stared at each other as she yelled, "Sebastian! I love you! How could you? A woman in my bed! How could you?"

Sebastian has his arms around Katherine while she is frightened and clinging to him as she yelled out, "Sebastian! I've never seen a ghost! I heard her yell! What's happening? Let me out of here!" He said, "Calm down, Katherine. I'll take care of this." Jenny's ghost continued to swish around the room and she looked like she was floating while grabbing things like mirrors, brushes and vases and throwing them at Sebastian and Katherine while they were sitting in bed dodging them. Sebastian yelled, "Jenny, stop it! You can't do this to me! You can't control me!" Jenny yelled, "I can! Yes I can, Sebastian! You'll see! I love you!" Jenny's ghost then went over to her vanity and got a letter opener and held it up in the air like a dagger and slowly headed for Katherine. Sebastian shielded Katherine's body with his and yelled, "Stop! Stop it, Jenny!" Jenny stopped with the letter opener in her hand that she was aiming at Katherine. She then dropped it and swiftly disappeared with the gardenia scent.

Sebastian and Katherine looked somewhat relieved as they continued to look around the room while sitting up in bed. He put his arms around her as she trembled and he tenderly said to her, "I'm sorry you had to witness this, Katherine. You never would have seen her or heard her speak if you weren't with me." She asked, "How can you live here, Sebastian? It's too spooky!"

Sebastian and Katherine were not able to make love now or even sleep in Jenny's room. They went upstairs to a bedroom and finished the night with no love and no ghost.

The next morning, Sebastian and Katherine woke up late and had a light Christmas breakfast and then sat around talking

The Ghost And Sebastian

about the surprising visit of Jenny's spirit and then her ghost last night. He told her that he was use to it. By late afternoon, snowflakes were falling while they were at the dining room table enjoying a delicious roast duck dinner with gravy, apple stuffing, mashed potatoes and peas and having white wine. Katherine told Sebastian she doesn't know how he can live in the mansion because of the ghosts. He told her he might extend his lease until late July or August because he needs the time to find out who murdered Jenny and Pierce. Katherine said, "Well, maybe it will be worth it." Dinner finished with warm mincemeat pie, ice cream and coffee.

Later on, in the living room, Katherine was sitting on the sofa and Sebastian was sitting on a chair while talking. She told him she's not going to see him until New Year's Eve because she needs to rest her mind from Jenny's ghostly apparition last night. He was okay with that and said, "I understand how shocking it was for you to witness the presence of Jenny's spirit and then see her ghost for the first time and hear her speak. I promise you we'll have a nice New Year's Eve in a hotel where she won't appear." Katherine was relieved to hear that. He told her that angry ghosts sometimes appear because they were murdered. She responded, "Well, I'm sure getting educated on the spiritual world."

The evening ended with Katherine and Sebastian on the sofa feeling passionate but there was no love making. While she had a pillow behind her head, there was just closeness and kissing, and when it got late, Katherine wanted to leave so Sebastian walked her to the door and then he held her in his arms and said, "I love you so much, Katherine." She said, "I love you too, Sebastian, and maybe New Year's Eve will be better." He said, "I know just what you mean." They had one last kiss and then he opened the door and it was snowing lightly as he watched her go to her car and drive off.

During the week, between Christmas and New Year's Eve, Sebastian sat at his desk documenting information from Christmas Eve into his red hardcover book and the computer. He stopped to think of how his and Katherine's first night in bed together was interrupted by Jenny's spirit, then her ghost while they were making love for the first time. He knew there was a chance Jenny may show up but he wanted Katherine to get use to it. He then continued to write about how he plans to continue his stay at the mansion a little longer to see if he can find out who murdered Jenny and Pierce. He knows persistence is needed to reach a goal.

Five days before New Year's Eve, Sebastian finished writing early and then called Charlie who was at his home and asked him if he could come over and get his old book about the mansion. In a couple of hours, Charlie arrived and Sebastian invited him in for coffee but he declined as he was a little shy about staying for coffee so he waited in the foyer near the door. Sebastian asked, "How is the winter going for you?" Charlie told him there's not much to do and he's anxious for spring to plant flowers and take care of the bushes. Sebastian excused himself for a minute while he went to get the book. He returned to Charlie who was standing in the foyer near the door and handed him the book and thanked him. He then handed him an envelope and said, "Happy holidays, Charlie!" Charlie took it and said, "Thank you, Sebastian. Happy holidays to you." Charlie then opened the envelope in front of him and saw a very beautiful card and a check for one thousand dollars. Charlie read the card and said, "Thank you so much, Sebastian." He then started to leave while holding his old book and his envelope. They both said goodbye to each other and then Sebastian shut the door as he felt good about giving Charlie a one thousand dollar check for Christmas.

Sebastian then tried to think of things to do while he takes a short break from his writing, but because it's winter, he doesn't care to go out much in the cold. He plans to visit Jenny's grave

The Ghost And Sebastian

at the cemetery when it gets warmer and also look at the harbor boats again. His cell phone suddenly rang and he took the call while sitting on a chair. He said, "Hello!" Katherine answered and sadly said, "Sebastian, I'm in the hospital." He asked, "What? What are you doing there?" She told him she fell in the shower and hit her head and then took a taxi to the emergency room at her hospital. After they did some test, they wanted to keep her overnight so they could do more tests. He asked her what hospital and she told him and then he quickly hung up. He was very upset. He quickly went to his car and got in it and started speeding to get to Katherine's hospital.

Sebastian arrived at the hospital and was told what room Katherine was in. He walked quite fast to get to her and soon found her room and there she was in a hospital bed sitting up and looking very pale. He went to her and gave her a kiss and then sat down next to her. He said, "I hope you'll be alright. Does your head hurt much where you hit it?" She told him her head doesn't feel right and by tomorrow they'll know what's wrong. Somehow, she doesn't believe they'll be going to a hotel on New Year's Eve like they planned. He told her it's best she gets well first because that's more important and he wants her to call him with any news. After staying awhile by her bedside, he kissed her gently on the lips and then said, "I love you." With tears in her eyes, she said, "I love you too, Sebastian." He left the hospital very sad and worried and thought about her as he drove home.

When Sebastian arrived back at his mansion, he was still worried about Katherine. He was restless and thinking that the best thing to take his mind off of her would be to write some more so he wrote at his desk. He suddenly felt cold breezes that continued for awhile. He got up and looked around the rooms and saw the dining room window open about six inches which he doesn't remember opening. He then closed it. He wondered if it was an omen that something bad was going to happen to

Katherine. In awhile, Sebastian went into the kitchen and made a cup of tea and a slice of toast to have before going to bed. He doesn't have much of an appetite because he's worried about Katherine. After taking his time eating and thinking of her, he took a shower and went to bed and knew he'd have a hard time to sleep. He was right. He tossed and turned all night.

The next morning arrived and it was only three days before New Year's Eve. Sebastian got up and couldn't wait to hear about Katherine's tests' results. He waited and waited for the phone to ring and by noontime the phone rang and it was Katherine. She said, "Sebastian, the tests' results show that I had a mild concussion and I should take it easy for awhile but I can go home now." He made a big sigh and then said, "Oh, Katherine, I was so worried about you. I'll be there to pick you up in an hour." He quickly hung up and said, "This means, she most likely will not be able to go out New Year's Eve which is in three days."

Within an hour, Sebastian was at the hospital to get Katherine. After she was wheeled outside, he walked next to her and then helped her into his car.

After a short ride from the hospital, Katherine was propped up with pillows on the sofa in Sebastian's living room while he was getting her something to eat and drink. He finished making her scrambled eggs and toast and poured her some orange juice. He also had some applesauce that came in a container from the market. Sebastian sat on a chair as she ate at the coffee table. After taking a few bites of scrambled eggs and toast, she smiled at him and then said, "This is so good." He pampered her and she loved it. She has a slight headache from the fall but has medication if she needs it and she'll get checked again in ten days. He told her he doesn't want her to go out New Year's Eve unless she really thinks she can do it. Her health is more important to him because he wants her and needs her in his life. She said, "Oh I'll know by tomorrow noontime if I can go out

New Year's Eve. I'll still have time to recover a little and go to the hotel like we planned to." He said, "Only if you feel up to it." He paused and then told her to take a nap after she eats and she can sleep overnight in a bedroom upstairs, or, if she would rather go home, then she can do that. She finished eating and stayed on the sofa and put her head on a pillow and soon feel asleep. Sebastian remained quiet so he wouldn't wake her up.

By early evening, Katherine was feeling better and decided to go home and get in bed and will call Sebastian in the morning to tell him how she feels. He told her that would be fine so he drove her home and hopes she feels better tomorrow because in two days it will be New Year's Eve.

The next day, Katherine called Sebastian and told him she felt okay except she still has mild headaches off and on. He told her to keep resting and to let him know if she needs him to help her with anything. This day seems long for Sebastian because tomorrow morning he'll get Katherine's answer whether or not she will go out New Year's Eve.

The next morning, Katherine was on the phone with Sebastian as she said, "I feel better today and tomorrow is New Year's Eve and we're going to the hotel to celebrate!" "That's great, Katherine, if you're sure you're well enough to go out." She told him she just checked with her doctor and he thinks she'll be okay but not to have alcohol at all. Sebastian told her, "I won't have any either." This means they have to start preparing for tomorrow night as to what they're going to wear. They talked a bit and decided to leave at 7:00 p.m., have dinner in the dining room at the hotel and then go to the lounge if she wants to listen to music or they can just go to their room. Katherine and Sebastian kept busy all day getting ready for tomorrow's New Year's Eve celebration.

The next evening arrived and Katherine and Sebastian have just checked into a luxury hotel with one small suit case and are now checking the bedroom out and they love the décor. They threw themselves on top of the bedspread to see if they liked the mattress and they did as they laughed. They then got up and went to the dining room which was classy with white tablecloths and small lamps lighting each table making it look romantic while the room was filled with people. Katherine looked beautiful wearing a pale yellow dress with her new emerald earrings and necklace and her shoulder length blonde hair was slightly pulled to one side. Sebastian was wearing a dark blue suit with his new blue shirt and deep pink silk tie and his hair always adds to his good looks. She was wearing the perfume he gave her for Christmas and he was wearing the cologne she gave him. They have just been served their dinner and their spirits are high. They're having filet mignon with baked potato and sour cream and asparagus and they're having a soft drink. They plan on having soft drinks or water throughout the evening.

Sebastian said, "I'm so happy you are going to be okay, Katherine. That was a bad fall you had in the shower." She said, "It was and it was the first time I have ever fallen in a shower so I need to be careful in the future." Before long, they were having their dessert of strawberry ice cream with coffee while still deciding what to do when they're finished. They either want to walk around the hotel lobby or go to a gift shop for awhile to digest their dinner or go to the lounge and listen to music. They soon decided on walking around awhile and then going to the lounge to listen to music.

Later on, Katherine and Sebastian entered their hotel bedroom about 10:00 p.m. and the minute they got in the room, soft romantic music played. She leaned against a wall as Sebastian put his body close to hers and they passionately kissed and it wasn't long before they were in the large shower. Their

The Ghost And Sebastian

shadowy bodies could be seen through the glass shower door and glass wall which was covered with steam as warm water poured down on them. They passionately kissed and embraced and then went on to suds themselves.

Later, after Sebastian and Katherine got in bed and partially covered up with the sheet, he caressed her and said, "Don't worry, Katherine, no ghost will bother us here." She said, "I hope not, Sebastian." She kissed him on his neck for awhile and then he kissed her where it stepped up her anxiety and made her say, "Oh, I'm so crazy about you, Sebastian. You're thrilling me." She then sighed. They were so full of passion that it seemed like it wouldn't end so they continued to make love. He told her how he's is so happy she went back with him and he never wants to be separated from her again. She told him that she wants their love to last forever. They soon went into ecstasy which was as good as it gets in the real world. After they slowly came back from being dazed from making love, he softly said, "I never want to lose you, Katherine." She said to him, "I want you to know that you do thrill me." They kissed and then she said, "Sebastian, I'm not sorry at all that we finally made love." He told her they'll have a great future together and he'll always protect her and he's looking forward to having children. They then embraced for awhile.

It was almost midnight and time to ring in the New Year of 2011 so Katherine and Sebastian first put the TV on, showered again because of their perspiring while making love and then returned to the bed to talk while their heads were on pillows. There soon was a sign on TV that read, "Happy New Year!" People were yelling out, "Happy New Year!" After Katherine and Sebastian wished each other a Happy New Year, they kissed and then turned the TV sound down so they could talk. Katherine said, "Sebastian, I never would have believed in ghosts if I hadn't seen one. And we can't go in Jenny's bedroom again. Our first night together in her bed and it was interrupted by her spirit and then her ghost! Who would ever believe that?" He told her he was not surprised.

Katherine went on and asked Sebastian how is it that Jenny's ghost is in love with him. He told her he doesn't know everything but she loves the fact that he's trying to find her murderer which he hopes he can. He swiftly changed the subject and told her he has seen six ghosts and they're all angry. Sebastian started naming them and said, "Well, there's Jenny, her boyfriend Pierce, her mother Shannon, Claude, Josh and Oscar." He told her that Claude is an older man who was murdered when he was 51 by his own son Josh who was 30. She asked, "How can you live in that mansion with all those ghosts?" He answered, "I'm not scared because they haven't hurt me. And, well, Jenny is seductive." He paused and didn't want to talk about her anymore. Katherine said, "Go on and tell me more about your love making with Jenny."

He would not answer so they just stared into each other's eyes and it wasn't pleasant and it didn't take a psychic to sense that there was a storm coming. They eventually fell asleep.

The next morning, Sebastian and Katherine checked out of the hotel and headed for her home because that's what she wanted. When they got there, they kissed in the car and he then said, "I love you, Katherine, and I'll call you later." "I love you too, Sebastian, and Happy New Year!" She got out of the car and went inside her home as he watched her and then he drove off to his mansion. While driving, he thought to himself how he hopes Katherine can get over Jenny. He then blew it off because it's out of his control.

During the following week as Sebastian and Katherine talked on the phone, they decided to meet for lunch at the Ultimate Inn coffee shop at the end of the week. He was happy about that and so he went to his desk and got right back into his story trying to find the murderer of Jenny and Pierce and he knows he may never but there's always the chance. Besides talent, people can get lucky if they're persistent until they have tried everything they can think of and Sebastian knows that very well.

Sebastian called a few people to wish them a Happy New Year and they wished him the same. Then he called Elaina in New York, his late father Oliver's girlfriend. She was happy he called and wished him a successful 2011. He thanked her and told her he'll be staying in Marblehead Neck until late July or August, and, if there's a special occasion in his honor while he's in Marblehead Neck, he'll invite her. He told her his producer friend, Alan, wants to celebrate his book before he leaves and thinks she would enjoy meeting him, producers, directors and writers. And Katherine will be also there. Elaina told him it sounds wonderful and she'd like that. They chatted a bit more and then hung up.

On January 5, 2011, Katherine and Sebastian took their own car and drove to the Ultimate Inn and are now sitting in the coffee shop waiting to order lunch. Veronica, the young waitress, suddenly spotted Sebastian and came over to him. She still has her long red hair and loves to chew gum and still has a bubbly personality. She said, "Sebastian, I haven't seen you for awhile! Happy New Year!" He said, "Happy New Year to you, Veronica!" He introduced her to Katherine and they said hello to each other and then Veronica asked, "What would you both like to order?" They ordered cheeseburgers with fries and coffee. After she wrote everything down, she smiled and then left chewing her gum.

Katherine said to Sebastian, "Veronica is so pleasant." He responded, "Yes she is. That's why I enjoy eating here. It's relaxing when you have a good waitress." While waiting for their lunch, Katherine suddenly stared into Sebastian's eyes with a serious look as she said, "Listen to me, Sebastian. I have something important to tell you. I have decided that I can't stay with you any longer because the ghosts frighten me. Especially Jenny's!" He is stunned that she's telling him she's leaving him after they finally made love about five days ago. He said, "Katherine, trust me. I've seen the ghosts time and again and they've never hurt me. They may end up helping me! They can't rest because they've been murdered!" While her hand is on the table, he put his hand on hers and said, "Please, Katherine, don't do this to me. I love you." She got excited and said, "I know you do but I've decided not stay with you! Mainly because you made love with Jenny's ghost and who knows how many times you have and how many more times you will! When will it end! You're the only man I have ever loved and it's over!" She quickly walked out of the restaurant and got in her car and drove off speeding.

Veronica soon arrived with Sebastian and Katherine's cheeseburgers, fries and coffees. Sebastian sadly said to her, "Katherine left so give these cheeseburgers and fries to someone else or you have them." She stared at him as he paid her and tipped her and then got up and headed for the lounge.

Sebastian is at the bar in the Ultimate Inn lounge now and talking with his friend, Saul, who he always talks with. He ordered a soft drink and Saul served it to him. Sebastian then told him that life is all ups and downs and he just hit another downer and what a huge one. Saul was sympathetic and said, "You're right about life being up and down. But time heals sadness and then you feel better again." Sebastian agreed with him. Saul then asked him if he wanted to tell him what happened and maybe it would help him feel better. Sebastian said, "Thank you, Saul, but it's nothing I want to discuss with anyone." He soon said goodbye while looking quite sad and left the Ultimate Inn lounge and drove off.

After Sebastian arrived back at his mansion, the first thing he did was lie on the sofa and meditate about Katherine. He then got up and paced the floor. He feels devastated because Katherine left him and this is the only woman he has ever loved and wanted to marry. He can't believe how fast she left him after they both waited so long to make love together. Then, after the first time they finally make love, she decides to leave him because he has made love with Jenny's ghost and she doesn't know if it will ever end.

Katherine obviously thought about this a lot and then suddenly exploded. She's hurt and very angry that Sebastian has made love more than one time with Jenny's ghost and wonders what kind of love he could possibly make with a ghost. What does she do to him. Katherine is almost out of her mind with hurt and fury and can't go on knowing that he makes love with a ghost.

Now that things are bad for Sebastian in the romance department, to make matters worse, a major snowstorm was just predicted to hit Marblehead and surrounding cities. They've been pretty lucky so far with very little snow but they're about to get plenty overnight.

Sebastian is in a local market stocking up with a few things in case he's snowbound for awhile. While he's in there with a shopping cart, he spotted flamboyant Sam, his rival writer. He tried to dodge him but Sam saw him and threw something in front of Sebastian's shopping cart to cause him to go into a wall of can goods which came tumbling down. Sebastian saw Sam nearby laughing. He ignored his child-like mind, knowing something went wrong in his childhood.

Back at the mansion, Sebastian put all his food away and then was in the mood to have a workout with weights in a room upstairs so he did that before his dinner. Life sure took a turn for him but life is full of surprises and life still goes on.

While Sebastian was in one of the bedrooms upstairs working out with weights, he thought he'd look at more of the notes and letters Jenny was saving in the sewing room. In about an hour he went in that sewing room and sat on a chair and looked in a box where Jenny kept notes. There were so many that he planned on gradually reading them. He wants to read all of them because he may find clues. After awhile, he stopped reading because there wasn't anything significant.

Later on, in the kitchen, Sebastian was preparing his dinner and was not in the mood to cook much so he made a grilled cheese sandwich. His spirits were down so he ate in the kitchen while reading a newspaper. He soon finished and just wanted to lie on the sofa and meditate about how fast your life can change and you have to get over it.

The next morning, Sebastian looked out the window and there was a couple of feet of snow but it wasn't snowing anymore. He also noticed that Charlie had already shoveled a path from his door to the sidewalk and to his driveway. He then thought about what he could do in the snow rather than just stay in. He decided to go to the library later and do more research.

By afternoon, Sebastian was at the library and ran into Katherine and was so surprised. She was dressed warmly wearing a turtleneck sweater and slacks and reading a book at a table. He went over to her and kissed her cheek and she got so surprised and said, "Oh, Sebastian! I didn't expect to see you out in all this snow." He sat next to her and asked her how she was doing and she told him she has been having a hard time to control her emotions over their breakup. He told her he wants her to know, because of their breakup, he's going to see other women and she should see other men. It's the only way he knows how to lessen his pain. They both agree with that and both feel very sad how fast things can change. She then didn't want to talk about it anymore and wanted to be alone so he gave her a little kiss on the cheek and then left. He went to get some books on a shelf regarding ghosts and sat down and browsed through them. After awhile, he left the library feeling terrible.

10

PLEASURE

Sebastian is ready for a change of life all because Katherine called off their committed relationship which just began. He's trying to get over it so he called his friend Samantha, the beautiful brunette novelist, and they're at a museum looking at beautiful paintings while they're casually dressed. Sebastian said, "Samantha, I'm happy we reconciled and I noticed your anxiety medication from Dr. Louis is working." She responded, "It has calmed me down."

While Sebastian and Samantha viewed the art, he put one arm around her and said, "Samantha, you know I value our friendship, and you know I'm not in love with you, but somehow, your charisma fascinates me." She didn't comment and they went on to look at a nude painting of lovers.

The Ghost And Sebastian

While no one was in the particular room they were viewing art in, they faced each other and embraced. He suddenly had a clairvoyant moment of the two of them in a small room with the door locked. She was out of control forcefully trying to take his clothes off to make love while he was fighting her off with a struggle. This was telling him to beware! Samantha noticed he was silent for a few seconds so she told him they should go to the museum's sickroom because he doesn't look well and she needs to lie on the couch. He told her he was okay but agreed to go with her to the sickroom. They walked around and found it and went in and saw there was a couch in it so she locked the door. She immediately kissed him passionately on the lips and he was okay with that. She then forcefully tried to unbutton his shirt while he tried to stop her. He finally got control of her arms and held them down. He said, "Samantha, don't ever try to force me to make love!" She apologized. He said, "Let's go. Don't ever do this again!" She told him she wouldn't. He went on and told her that she has a serious anxiety disorder and needs professional therapy beyond what she's getting now. She remained silent and looking sad.

While Samantha and Sebastian were at the door and ready to leave, he got angry again and said, "You can't do this in a museum, Samantha." She told him she wanted to make love in an unusual place. He snapped and said, "Making love in the museum's sickroom is crazy! You need to be more intelligent." She told him she thought it would be exciting. He said, "Oh no, Samantha. I know better than that."

Samantha and Sebastian then left the museum's sickroom and walked around the museum while she looked sad and he was unhappy with her behavior. However, she apologized to him and they decided to go to her condo just to talk for awhile because she promised to stay calm.

Later, while at Samantha's condo, Sebastian is sitting down on the sofa with a soft drink while she's taking a cold shower. He's thinking of Katherine who's still on his mind because she broke off with him because he made love with a ghost. However, Samantha has told him she's glad Katherine broke off with him because it's just what she wanted and maybe they can become lovers.

Samantha finished her shower and asked Sebastian if he wanted to go skiing now. He agreed to and within an hour, they were on the slopes having a great time. She suddenly fell and he went over to her and asked her if she was alright and she was. She stayed sitting on the snow and wanted him to kiss her but he wasn't in the mood so she stood up and made snowballs and threw them at him. He then threw some at her as they laughed and after awhile they left.

Hours later, Samantha and Sebastian were ice skating. They loved it until she knocked him down on the ice which caused him to crack and chip two teeth. He got angry and said, "What the hell is wrong with you? You just knocked me down!" She claimed it was an accident. He told her she needs another kind of medication because she turned the day into a disaster. He drove her back to her condo and wouldn't let her kiss him goodbye. While getting out of the car, she told him she was sorry she broke his teeth but he didn't think she felt that bad about it. He yelled out, "Don't call me for a long time!" She then left looking sad.

Sebastian's back at his mansion and knows he has to see a dentist tomorrow and he's also thinking of what a day he had and regrets spending it with Samantha. It didn't help him get over Katherine breaking up with him. However, he feels like calling Katherine now so he tried to but her number was changed. He was so surprised and then tried to get it from the operator but couldn't. He's going through an unsettled and unhappy time. He had some red wine and then called it a day.

The next morning, Sebastian went to a dentist and found out that he needs to get his two front teeth replaced so an appointment was made. In the mean time, he has to walk around for awhile with two cracked and chipped teeth.

In the afternoon, Sebastian was at his desk working on his book. He started thinking about how he could get some answers from Jenny or Pierce's ghost as to who murdered them. Every time he has asked them who murdered them, they dodged the question yet he's anxious to see them again so he can continue to ask them. His persistence may pay off in time. He went on his computer and started setting up his story with a different ending, in case he never finds out who murdered Jenny and Pierce. That ending would not make him totally happy. To find their murderer would mean he reached his goal. He worked on his story into the late evening hours.

About a week later, Samantha was at the psychiatrist's office who just asked her to lie on the couch and she did and was wearing a very short skirt while talking with him. Dr. Louis asked her how her medication was working and she told him it helped a little but she still gets evil thoughts. He told her she needs to tell him more about herself and then she may not need medication. She couldn't tell him anymore. She only told him that she can be a very cruel person if she's angry at someone. He asked her what she did that was cruel. She said, "I'd rather not say, Dr. Louis. I just try to forget the bad things I've done." He told her, "You will feel better if you talk about it, otherwise, it will cause you to have anxiety forever." She didn't want to tell him all of her past. She asked him if she could have another mediation to take the mean spirit out of her that sometimes can make her so violent and uncontrollable. When doctor Louis told her she can't have another medication, she looked disappointed. He went on and questioned her about her past for awhile.

Dr. Louis then asked Samantha to sit up on a chair across from him while he sits at his desk. She quickly did and crossed her legs while her short skirt went up quite high and then she gave him a passionate look with her eyes. The doctor said, "Samantha, you need to get your thoughts together and be more serious right now. You're in the doctor's office trying to seduce me. Stop it or I will not see you again!" She apologized and uncrossed her legs but her skirt was so short it almost showed her underwear. He looked at her and didn't look too pleased and went on and told her she may have a childhood hang-up. She agreed and then went on and told him when she was a child something very bad happened to her but she couldn't tell him about it because it hurts her too much. He said, "It's okay, Samantha. Let's make another appointment." They made one and then she thanked him very much for his help and started to leave. He watched her walk to the door as she swung her hips. When she was gone, he said to himself, "Something is seriously wrong with that woman." The doctor then took a bottle of pills out of his drawer and opened it and threw a couple of them in his mouth and swallowed them with bottled water.

After a couple of weeks went by, it was late January and Sebastian got his new teeth and felt better about that. He has also been pacing the living room floor a lot while thinking of how he can get information that will lead him to Jenny and Pierce's murderer.

The next day, Sebastian got an idea and sat at his desk to write it in his red hardcover book. He was energized as he began to write about a new strategy that might work and solve the murder. He wrote fast and then stopped to think and then continued. All of a sudden, the scent of gardenias filled the air which made him look happy as he inhaled. He stood up and looked around the living room for Jenny's ghost but she wasn't there so he called out, "Jenny! Jenny!" She was nowhere to be seen yet the gardenia scent remained in the air. He went into the dining room and kitchen and she wasn't there so he went into her bedroom and bathroom and she wasn't there. He doesn't know what to think so he went and sat on a wing armchair to figure this out.

While Sebastian was sitting on a large wing armchair and thinking of Jenny, he felt the presence of her spirit close to him and almost as if she was hovering over him. He turned his head to look in back of his chair and she popped her head up from behind it. Her pale lifelike ghostly apparition was smiling at him. He looked shocked as he stayed on the chair with his head still turned looking at her. She suddenly came around to the front of his chair wearing a sheer raspberry nightgown which was long and loose-fitting and she was mesmerizing. Her face was beautiful and so were her hypnotic brown eyes and her long flowing light brown hair.

Sebastian is thrilled while watching Jenny's ghost that is standing in front of him yet she hasn't spoken. She then sat on his lap facing him after she placed her legs just so, then she put her arms around him and started kissing his neck. When she stopped, he gently felt her pale lifelike ghostly body. He's aware that this is the fourth nightgown she has worn that he has been able to feel the material. They soon kissed passionately on the lips and it made him feel like he was entering her world of ghosts. According to Sebastian, it's a world of strange love pleasure that can only be felt from a ghost because of their spiritual power. Love is satisfying in the world of the living but not like in the world of ghosts.

While Sebastian and Jenny's ghost are still on the wing armchair, he looked at her and asked, "Jenny, where have you been? I need to see you more." She responded by kissing him on the lips and then his neck. He kissed her neck and then gently moved his hands around on her body and noticed she was in ecstasy. After awhile, she kissed his neck again and then looked at him and said, "Sebastian, I love you so much. Please help me. Pierce and I have been murdered!" He said, "I know that, Jenny, and I will help you but I need information from you to help me find the murderer." He asked her if it was a man or a woman but she didn't answer.

Sebastian was feeling so passionate but tried to keep it together so he could get more information from Jenny's ghost. He asked, "Jenny, can you please tell me who murdered you and Pierce? I need to know this so I can help you." Sebastian waited a moment for her response. She then said, "We know the murderer! We do know the murderer! Where is the murderer?" Even though she didn't answer his question, Sebastian was still happy. It's like he thought. She knows who murdered her and Pierce and that leads him to think, if she sees the murderer, she may point him or her out to Sebastian. He wishes he knew if it was a woman or a man.

Sebastian and Jenny's ghost are still on the wing armchair feeling very passionate. He asked her if she loved Pierce. He waited for her response and soon she said, "He's gone. Please find our murderer, Sebastian?" He told her he's trying to find the murderer and won't stop. She slowly got off his lap and stood in front of him. He then stood up close to her and they embraced and then his deep passion for Jenny's ghost had escalated and made his face flushed. While they looked into each other's eyes, she softly said, "I want to make love to you, Sebastian." While he is silent, he is thinking that she must have been a very passionate lover in the real world.

Sebastian then asked Jenny's ghost if she'd like to make love in her bed and she said, "Oh yes, Sebastian, yes!" His clothes and her light raspberry nightgown were soon on the floor in her bedroom and they were in bed partially covered with the sheet. He stared at her for a moment and then put his arms around her and said, "Jenny, you're so beautiful and I love you." Jenny just smiled as he went on and told her that he never in his wildest dreams thought that someday he'd be talking or making love with a ghost. He also told her that he loves her spiritual power that gives him strange love pleasure and he knows how difficult it will be for him to give up living in her world of ghosts.

While Sebastian and Jenny were making love in her bed, she continued to thrill him and he didn't want her to stop. After awhile, he said, "Jenny, it's hard for me to control my love for you and I don't like being away from you. The sensation of our love making is so wonderful and intense and it lingers awhile." He sighed and then said, "Oh Jenny, I'm in ecstasy and I want to stay there." She then gently told him that this is their first time together that he has told her he loves her. She also told him to never leave her because she loves him so much. He soon heard her sigh and then they continued making love. He then said, "Jenny, don't ever stop making love to me! Don't ever stop." She then kissed him until he became unconscious.

Sebastian slowly recovered from being unconscious from Jenny's love making and is in bed looking fatigued while Jenny's ghost is still next to him and staring at him. He looked at her and softly said, "Jenny, I know how fast you disappear, but please don't leave until you tell me the name of the person who murdered you. Was it a man or a woman?" She said, "I know who murdered me! Help me!" He then embraced her and remained quiet with still no answer.

While Sebastian and Jenny's ghost were still next to each other in bed and his arm was around her, he asked her again if the murderer was a male or female but she was silent. He then told her he's sorry about the time that she saw him in her bed with Katherine who is in the world of the living.

While Sebastian still had his arm around Jenny's ghost in bed, he gently told her that he's thinking of moving out of his mansion soon and he needs her help before he does. He told her he needs the name of the person who murdered her and Pierce. He also told her she's interfering with his personal affairs. She looked at him and sadly said, "Please don't move out of the mansion, Sebastian! Today you told me you loved me!" While they were close and now face to face, he said, "I told you I love you but I meant I love you in your world." He paused and then told her that she left her lavender blue nightgown at the mansion and he wants to know if she put it on the mannequin in the attic but she didn't respond. While he kept waiting for an answer, Jenny's ghost swiftly disappeared from her bed with her gardenia scent. He yelled, "Jenny! Who murdered you and Pierce?"

Now that Jenny's ghost has left her bed, Sebastian stayed there awhile and is sad because he doesn't know when he'll see her again. This was the first time they slept in her bed together. He also knows when he mentions Katherine's name, she's silent. He soon got out of bed and noticed that Jenny's ghost left her light raspberry nightgown on the floor. This is the second one. She left the first one in the bathroom. He thought again how surreal it is that a ghost can do that! He held it close to him and smelled it and it had a gardenia scent and he then put it in her drawer. Aside from that, he wishes she could give him a description of the murderer although information from a ghost may not be reliable. Maybe the murderer was wearing dark clothes and glasses.

The next day, in late afternoon, Sebastian was sitting on his sofa having a glass of wine and feeling better. He's actually celebrating a bit of good news from Jenny's ghost, yet, on the other hand, he's still suffering from Katherine breaking up with him because he made love with Jenny's ghost and doesn't know if it will end.

The Ghost And Sebastian

As Sebastian continued to sip his wine and eat chips which were in front of him on the coffee table, he soon got tired and fell asleep on the sofa. In awhile, he was suddenly awakened by pounding on the walls over and over again and then it stopped. He felt the presence of a spirit in the room. While still half asleep, he stood up and stayed in one spot while looking around. He yelled out, "Well, that's different! I have never heard pounding on the walls before!" The pounding started up again and continued, so he yelled, "I know someone's doing this. It's one of you ghosts! Who's there?" The pounding stopped again and there was no message and he's very curious as to who is causing it.

Within moments, the pounding on the walls started again. While Sebastian was still standing, he looked at the walls and yelled, "Who the hell are you this time? Is that you Claude? What's your problem, Claude?" There was no response from any ghosts until suddenly an object flew across the room and Sebastian watched it and heard it as it crashed into a wall mirror and broke it. Sebastian is furious and yelled, "Was that you, Josh? Don't play rough with me! What in the hell are you doing, whoever you are?" Sebastian kept turning around in circles looking everywhere waiting to hear pounding. He yelled, "Come out you ghost, wherever you are! Come out, I said! You're ruining my life! You've chased Katherine away! She's the love of my life!" He went over to the sofa and fell asleep for the night and never got to find out whose angry spirit was pounding on the walls.

The next morning, around 11:00 a.m., Sebastian was at the table in the dining room having ham, eggs, juice and toast and two cups of strong coffee. Then, suddenly, Shannon's ghost was sitting on a chair across the table from him. He was stunned and dropped his cup of coffee. Her apparition, again, was of a pale lifelike ghost of an older woman with gray hair wearing a housedress and sobbing. He stared at her and said, "What's going on? You ghosts are coming out of the woodwork almost daily! I know you're Jenny's mother Shannon and I haven't heard from you for awhile nor Pierce." As Shannon stared at Sebastian, she cried out, "Yes! I'm Shannon! Where's Jenny? Help me!" Sebastian continued to engage in conversation with her as best as the living can with a ghost. He said, "I know who killed you, Shannon, and it has been taken care of. I don't know who killed Jenny and Pierce. Do you know who killed them?" Shannon's ghost didn't respond to his question. She got up and slowly started walking out of the dining room as her pale lifelike ghost faded as she sobbed and then called out, "Help me! Help!"

Sebastian was silent for a few moments after Shannon left. In awhile, he said out loud, "Hell, it's hard to believe this place is so haunted!" Then, with a little humor, he said, "And Shannon didn't even stay for coffee! It's best I keep a sense of humor in this place." While Sebastian went on and ate his breakfast, he thought about seeing the psychiatrist, Dr. Louis, again to update him on what's been going on in his life and mainly to discuss ghosts with a professional who knows a lot about them and they really enjoy talking about ghosts.

This day, Sebastian is not in the mood to write in his book. Because of all the paranormal activity that has been going on, he wants to think about it and wants to think about Katherine. He also wants to get a lot of rest today and maybe call Dr. Louis for an appointment.

A week later, Dr. Louis was sitting at his desk and Sebastian was sitting across from him and telling him what's going on with his life. He first told him how the breakup with the love of his life, Katherine, has hurt him so much. She was the only woman he ever wanted to marry and she left him because he made love with Jenny's ghost and she's scared of the other ghosts. Then Sebastian told the doctor how he still sees the ghosts, all six of them, but he only sees them once in awhile and never knows when they'll show up. He still asks them questions and he hears them answer, except Oscar's ghost who just flies around. He went on and told the doctor that his book is coming along although it's frustrating that he can't find out the information that he wants but he does get other information. He also told the doctor that he finds the ghosts fascinating because he never knows from day to day when they'll come out or what they'll do or say.

Dr. Louis then told Sebastian he was sorry to hear about his romantic breakup with Katherine but maybe they'll get back together again. Life changes every day. And if they don't get back together, life goes on and what's the use of fighting something that can't be changed. There's nothing you can do about it if the other person doesn't want you. And why would you want someone who doesn't want you? Sebastian told him he knows all that is true but it still hurts him when he thinks of Katherine.

Dr. Louis told Sebastian that life is always full of ups and downs. The thing about breaking up is, it's hard to get over, but if you analyze the situation, you will get over it and maybe it was never meant to be. If it is meant to be, you'll get back together. There could also be someone else who will come into your life in the future. Sebastian agreed. After talking for awhile longer, he thanked Dr. Louis for their conversation and told him he may call again. He then left.

It's early February and there hasn't been much snow lately. Sebastian is feeling better since he saw Dr. Louis and they discussed his breakup with Katherine. He now has the desire to call her and ask her if they can get together for Valentine's Day but he's afraid of her rejection so he changed his mind and didn't make the call.

Sebastian was soon at his desk writing notes in his red hardcover book. He then went on his computer to document all the new information he discovered about Jenny's ghost and how she knows who murdered her and Pierce. However, information coming from a ghost is not necessarily reliable. Who knows? He certainly needs more proof and information to solve this murder case. He's planning to move out of the mansion in late July or August and it's already the beginning of February. He knows it's not the end of the world if he doesn't find the murderer but it means so much to him to write a blockbuster book and it would mean a lot to the police too. The afternoon went well for Sebastian as he worked on his book for several hours. He then decided to lie on the sofa and rest for awhile.

In the evening, while Sebastian ate his delicious pork chop dinner in the dining room, he thought about the ghost he once saw in the china cabinet mirror. He wants to look today to see if he sees anything strange. When he finished eating, he got up and took his dishes with him, and on the way to the kitchen with the butler's swinging door, he stopped and looked in the china cabinet mirror. He saw something in back of his reflection. Only this time, he's sure he saw a pale shadowy ghost of a man that swiftly went by him. When he saw it, he dropped his dishes and turned around fast to look at it but it was gone. Even though it went by so fast, he believes it was Oscar's ghost. He still doesn't fear paranormal activity because the spirits and ghosts haven't harmed him.

The next day, Sebastian went to the second floor and checked out the four bedrooms to see if anything had been disturbed by the ghosts but nothing was. He went into the sewing room and nothing looked changed. He then sat on a chair in there and thought about Jenny's letters she saved over the years. He has already read them and there was nothing earth shattering in them so he left the sewing room.

Sebastian then went up to the attic to look around and saw the mannequin hadn't changed her location and she was still wearing the sheer lavender blue nightgown. Her hair was still black and bushy and her large haunting pale blue eyes were still quite scary. He went and looked at the rocking chair and debated on whether or not to sit on it because the last time Katherine sat on it, it wouldn't stop rocking. But because he is so brave about these spirits, he just went and sat on the rocking chair and rocked for several moments. He suddenly sensed the presence of a spirit. When he went to get off of it, it started rocking fast and wouldn't stop. He yelled, "Stop it! Whoever you are, stop it!" It continued to rock fast so he pressed his feet firmly on the floor and was soon able to stop it. He said to himself, "That was definitely an angry spirit who did that." He then yelled, "It's time for some of you spirits to leave this mansion!" There was no message sent back to him and he sensed the spirit left so he left the attic and wasn't worried about what just happened.

In the evening, Sebastian was in his kitchen having tea with toast and trying to enjoy it. When he finished his snack, he wanted to take a shower and was hopeful that he would get a good night sleep, even though there has been so much paranormal activity in the mansion.

Sebastian later went to bed with Katherine on his mind for awhile and eventually fell into a deep sleep.

11

VALENTINE'S DAY

Valentine's Day is approaching and cupid's arrow is pointing to lovers all over the world. The stores are decorated and beautiful Valentine's Day cards are plentiful and are being bought as fast as they're put out.

Katherine is feeling sentimental and wants to call Sebastian to say hello. She thought about it and then called him. While his cell phone rang on his desk, he was there documenting information in his red book. He answered it and was so happy when he heard Katherine's voice. She softly said, "Hi, Sebastian. How are you?" "Oh, I'm better now that you called, Katherine. I tried to call you one day but your number was changed and I couldn't get it from the operator." She told him she changed it because she was angry at him.

Katherine then gave Sebastian her new phone number. He told her, since she broke off with him, he has been quite sad. She expressed how important it is that he stops feeling sad because whatever is meant to be will be. He agreed and then asked her, "How do you feel about us getting together at a coffee shop some day?" "Oh, Sebastian, I'd love to. You just made my heart beat faster. I miss you so much." He told her he can't wait to see her again so they made arrangements to meet at the Ultimate Inn coffee shop. She also told him she won't walk out on him this time. He said, "I didn't know if this day was ever going to come and it must be cupid's arrow that caused it." She told him that it might have played a part in it. She then told him she had to get off the phone and they could talk later. They chatted a bit longer and were so happy they were going to meet at a coffee shop.

A week later, Sebastian was in the Ultimate Inn's coffee shop sitting in the waiting area waiting for Katherine. She soon entered and looked as pretty as ever with her shoulder length blonde hair and green eyes. They first hugged and he gave her a little kiss on the lips which she accepted. After they went and hung up their coats, they sat in a booth and had warm apple pie with coffee while they sometimes looked at each other with love in their eyes and talked. They know they're soul mates and very much in love.

While Katherine and Sebastian are still at the coffee shop, he asked her if she would consider getting together for Valentine's Day. He stared into her eyes as he waited for her answer. In a few moments, she said, "I'd love to, Sebastian, but it's the ghosts that scare me. And the thoughts of you making love with Jenny's ghost stunned me. I don't want to share you." Her eyes watered up. He told her he was sorry that he hurt her but he is in a situation where he can't move out of the mansion because Jenny's ghost really may lead him to the murderer. He then told her he's waiting for answers so he can solve the murder mystery and how it is so important to him and the police. They'd be able to close a case that has been unsolved for four and a half years to-date. After talking awhile, Katherine and Sebastian decided to go to his mansion.

In Sebastian's living room, later on, he and Katherine were standing while having champagne to celebrate the fact that they're talking again. In fact, they are so happy about it, it caused them to laugh a lot and the champagne contributed to some of it. They put their glasses down on the coffee table and then went and sat on the burgundy velvet sofa. As they looked at each other, he couldn't resist putting his arms around her and just holding her for a few moments. She put her arms around him and then her hand stroked his hair as she smiled at him. They then had a passionate kiss that showed the passion they had for each other never ended.

In awhile, Sebastian and Katherine left the sofa and took their champagne to the dining room table and sat next to each other while he told her his new information for his book. She loves hearing about the ghosts but finds it scary to see them. And she's furious that Sebastian slept with a ghost. To her, it's not only weird, she doesn't want him to share his love with another woman whether she's dead or alive. He told her he's in a tough situation with Jenny's ghost. She may be his chance to solve the murder mystery, therefore, he can't cut her off, plus, she's so in love with him. He then thought how he doesn't want to hurt Katherine. He's torn between two lovers and feels sad about it. Jenny is dead, although her spirit isn't, and Katherine is alive. They're both in love with Sebastian.

While Katherine's hand is on the dining room table, Sebastian put his hand on hers and asked, "Can can you sleep at the mansion the night before Valentine's Day?" She took a moment to think about it and then said, "Okay, I will." They smiled at each other and then leaned towards each other and had a little kiss on the lips.

Sebastian kept his hand on top of Katherine's while telling her he's so happy she'll be sleeping at the mansion Valentine's Day eve. He went on and told her that they can sleep on the second floor where Jenny's ghost doesn't appear and her spirit won't bother them either. But they don't want to sleep in Shannon's room nor the housekeeper's so they'll sleep in one of the guest bedrooms.

Katherine then commented about her sleeping over at the mansion. She told Sebastian that she'll be taking a chance and hoping she won't see any ghosts on the second floor, especially Jenny's. He told her she won't because her bedroom is downstairs. They both stood up and embraced and then kissed. He said, "Katherine, you just made me so happy. I love you so much." She responded, "I love you too, Sebastian, and that's why I'm going to sleep over. However, you have to get information from Jenny's ghost without sleeping with her anymore." He just smiled at her.

In a week, Sebastian hired his regular cleaning staff to clean the entire mansion. After that was done, he decorated the first and second floor with a Valentine's Day theme and it was so warm and romantic even though it still had an eerie edge. He placed paper heart designs several places and strung up a Valentine's banner along the fireplace. Later, he put fresh long stemmed red roses on the mantel in the living room, on the dining room table and in the guest bedroom that they'll be sleeping in. The place was smelling roses no matter where you were in the mansion. He even has many crystal candy dishes filled with chocolates wrapped in red foil. He planned a special menu and a special surprise.

The day before Valentine's Day arrived and it was around 7:00 p.m. Sebastian was wearing a red sweater and black pants with dark red designer slippers. He loves them because they're classy looking. Seeing he's in the mansion for the evening, why not slippers? While Sebastian is waiting for Katherine, he went to his bar area and got beautiful lead crystal champagne flutes and wine glasses ready. He stays stocked with champagne, different kinds of wine and after dinner drinks. He hasn't had any of the above so far today but will when Katherine arrives. He doesn't keep hard alcohol around because he knows how bad it can change a person.

Sebastian then went and put romantic music on to set the mood. There was soon a knock on the door and when he answered it, Katherine was standing there smiling while wearing a pretty black coat and carrying an overnight case. They smiled at each other as she stepped into the rose foyer. After he put her case aside, he embraced her and kissed her and then said, "I'm so happy you are here." "I'm happy too, Sebastian." He hung up her coat and she was wearing a white sweater with a red heart. She then looked at the Valentine's Day decorations on the stairway banister and the roses on the foyer table. She said, "Oh, I love the décor!" He told her he did it all for them because they're back together. He thinks Katherine is very pretty and has class which is one of the things he especially loves about her.

Sebastian showed Katherine the dining room with roses on the table and then the living room filled with roses. She loved it and said, "Oh, the roses smell so wonderful!" They went upstairs while he carried her overnight case and went into the guest bedroom where they're going to sleep. To her surprise, the bedspread had rose petals strewn all over it and she smiled. They went in the bathroom and the claw foot tub had rose petals in it. She was quite happy at what he did so she gave him a big hug. He told her they're going to have a wonderful evening and a wonderful day tomorrow.

Back in the living room, he said, "Katherine, I thought you might want to start out the evening with champagne and we could switch to pinot noir later." She told him she agrees with him but doesn't want too much wine because they'll wake up tomorrow not feeling so well and it'll ruin their Valentine's Day and he agreed.

Sebastian and Katherine went into the kitchen and prepared different kinds of appetizers that would go well with their champagne. They plan to have different appetizers to go with their pinot noir they will have later. They spent the evening walking around with their drinks and sometimes sitting on the velvet sofa talking and then laughing, and, of course, getting pretty frisky on the sofa as they reclined on it. He said, "I can't wait for us to get in bed on the second floor." She said, "I am too but I hope we don't see any ghosts." He told her not to worry because he sees them often and they don't harm him. She then reminded him that she won't tolerate him making love with Jenny's ghost. He didn't say a word and just stared at her for a few moments.

When it was around midnight, Katherine and Sebastian wanted to shower and go to bed so they cleaned up the dishes and decided to take some pinot noir upstairs.

A little after midnight, on the second floor, Katherine and Sebastian were in the bathroom that goes to the guest bedroom and kissing passionately for awhile. Then, they got into the large shower. Through the glass shower door and glass wall, which was covered with steam, their shadows could be seen kissing and embracing. They soon lathered themselves with suds all over because it felt so good and they loved it and didn't want the feeling to stop. Katherine has never had a love affair like she's having with Sebastian because she only had one other lover in her life and it wasn't good with that person.

Bernice Carstens

After awhile, Katherine and Sebastian started rinsing the suds off of their body and they took their time doing it. He told her he's so happy that he is with the woman he wants to spend his life with and she is everything he ever wanted. She told him she thought this day would never happen to her in her lifetime.

The bedroom was dimly lit with soft pink bulbs while Sebastian and Katherine were now in bed and partially covered up with a sheet. After their embracing and kissing and rolling around on the bed for awhile, she softly said, "I've never felt this passionate before and I don't want it to end." He responded, "It won't end. I'll give you that pleasure the rest of your life."

While Sebastian and Katherine continued to make love, he used his special technique. She sighed and was soon in ecstasy and so was he. When they eventually became conscious, Sebastian said, "Katherine, making love to you is wonderful." She told him that he just sent her to the moon. They laughed. He then said, "And, there were no ghosts, how about that?" She said, "I'm very surprised. I really thought that there was a good chance we might see Jenny's ghost."

Then, the scent of gardenias filled the air. Katherine and Sebastian's eyes opened wide as they sat up and looked around. In seconds, Jenny's pale lifelike ghostly apparition was in front of their bed wearing a sheer peach nightgown which was long and loose-fitting. She looked angry while moving around as her hair was flying around. Katherine was shocked as she was clinging to Sebastian and he was silent staring at Jenny. Then, Jenny's ghost shouted out, "Sebastian! Sebastian! Don't do this to me! I love you! You're with another woman! No! No! And where's my murderer? Help! Help!" Sebastian gently said, "Jenny, this is the same woman that you saw me with in your bed previously and her name is Katherine, and, you're interfering with my life." He paused and waited for her response. In a few moments, he heard her sob and then she swiftly disappeared and so did the gardenia scent. He told Katherine that he was surprised she went to the guest bedroom.

Sebastian was happy that Katherine saw more of Jenny's ghost and she didn't freak out over it. He held her in his arms and asked, "That wasn't so bad, was it?" She paused and then answered, "Well, it's still scary to me but it didn't frighten me as much as the first time and I don't want you making love with Jenny's ghost or we are through!" He didn't respond to that comment. After awhile, they managed to get some sleep.

The next morning, Katherine and Sebastian were in the kitchen. The aroma of fresh perked vanilla flavored coffee was in the air while they walked around talking and preparing their breakfast of orange juice, soft-boiled eggs and whole grain toast. When it was ready, they took their breakfast through the butler's swinging door that led to the dining room. Katherine loved the looks of the table with the huge vase of red roses in the center and their wonderful scent.

Sebastian and Katherine sat across from each other eating their breakfast and looking happy. She got up for a moment and said, "I'll be back in a minute. I have to get something." She went back upstairs where her overnight case was and got something and then went back to the dining room table. While Sebastian was still sitting there, she stood next to him and gave him his gift which was in a small square box wrapped in red paper and gave him a card in a pink envelope. She said, "Happy Valentine's Day!" She kissed his cheek and then sat down. He first said, "Happy Valentine's Day to you too. I didn't forget to say it." He proceeded to open his card first and it was a very beautiful valentine. He read the verse to himself and told her the card was beautiful and then he opened his gift and it was a stunning pair of cufflinks and tie pin. He loved it and said, "Katherine, you have good taste! I love these cufflinks and tie pin! Oh, and I didn't forget to get you a gift but you're not getting it until dinner time but I'll give you a card now." He went and got it out of the buffet draw right in the dining room and handed it to her. She opened it and read it and then said, "This is a beautiful card, Sebastian. I love the verse and I love you." He got up and kissed her while she was still sitting and he then went and got them more coffee.

After Sebastian brought Katherine and himself another coffee and they were still sitting across the table from each other, she suddenly looked at him and said, "I'm feeling so passionate, Sebastian. I don't know what's causing it but I want to make love right now!" He said, "I feeling the same. It must be the carryover from last night so let's make love. And where would you like to?" She told him she wanted to go back upstairs in the same bed and he told her he was all for it. They got up from the table and embraced and then kissed on the lips and he kept kissing her neck and then their hands were all over each other's body. They went upstairs and were soon naked in the same bed as they were in last night and partially covered up with a sheet. They were still just as passionate as they were last night and it didn't take long for them to go into ecstasy. They now think there's something special about making love on the second floor in that bed.

After Sebastian and Katherine's romantic Valentine's Day morning, they were energized for the day. They went and showered again and are happy as can be walking around this morning. She's looking at the Valentine's Day banner he strung up along the fireplace. He liked the colorful pictures on them so much that he bought a bunch and hung them around the fireplace and a few other places.

In awhile, Sebastian suggested that he and Katherine should get some fresh air and walk around outside the mansion because there's no snow on the ground and it's not very cold out even though it's February. They put their coats on and went outside

The Ghost And Sebastian

and looked at the bushes and trees. He said, "Before long, Charlie will be planting flowers." She told him she's so much looking forward to spring because she doesn't like winter. He doesn't like it either but makes the best of it. After they circled the mansion, they strolled over near the edge of the cliff and looked out at the ocean. She said, "Oh, look at the view of the ocean." He looked out at it and told her it makes him feel so peaceful. It also brings back memories of how he and his father use to fish together. She said, "That's a wonderful memory. You must really miss him. Come on. Let's go back in the mansion because it's getting cold." They both left the cliff area.

Katherine and Sebastian went to the second floor of the mansion in the sewing room where there were some weights and a mirror. She watched him do a few curls and squats with the weights. He asked her to try it but she didn't want to. They soon went back downstairs and she sat on one of the mahogany wing armchairs while he sat on the other one. While looking at the mahogany, she commented, "These chairs are gorgeous." He told her he really likes the Victorian style except it can give an eerie feeling unless the room is made a little cheery. He suddenly said, "I think I'll go prepare our dinner and then I'll just have to cook it." She said, "And I want to help, Sebastian." The both got up and went into the kitchen.

She asked what they were going to have for dinner and he answered, "What you love, filet mignon." They looked at each other with eyes wide open and smiled. She then asked what was for vegetables and he told her he knows what she likes so there will be au gratin potatoes with peas and salad. Dessert will be strawberry shortcake with fresh whipped cream. She said, "Oh, I can hardly wait! It sounds so good!" She hugged him and then they started preparing the meal by cutting onions and garlic for the filet mignon and then preparing the potatoes au gratin and salad.

After preparing the dinner, Katherine and Sebastian went into the living room and had champagne in lead crystal flute glasses. For dinner, they'll switch to pinot noir with their filet mignon which sounds good to them. Katherine strolled over to the piano and sat down and tickled the ivories a little and it didn't sound too bad. He went over to her and said, "You didn't tell me you knew how to play the piano!" She said, "I took piano lessons when I was young but never kept it up although I never forgot what I learned." He told her to keep playing so she did but in awhile stopped. She told him she was limited to how many songs she could play.

The potatoes au gratin were in the oven for awhile and are now smelling wonderful and almost finished and the filet mignons will only take about 7 or 8 minutes on each side. Meanwhile, Katherine set the table for dinner and took a moment to smell the roses on the table. She's also thinking of the Valentine's Day surprise Sebastian has for her and she will soon find out. In a short time, they put everything out on the table and sat down to a delicious dinner.

While Sebastian and Katherine are tasting their food, she said, "Oh, the filet mignon is delicious." He said, "I like the potatoes au gratin. I don't often make them." They sipped their pinot noir as they ate and sometimes talked about his book and he told her how he wonders if he'll actually find out who murdered Jenny and her boyfriend Pierce. She told him not to worry to much about it. If it doesn't happen, it won't be the end of the world. He thanked her for her support and told her, if he doesn't find the murderer, he'll still have a good story because the ghosts have added interest to it. And that's why his friend Alan, the movie producer, wants to make a movie of it. She got excited and said, "Oh, that will be so wonderful! How lucky you are that Alan is your friend." He then told her he's going to visit him soon to let him know the latest news. He's such a swell guy and she will meet him when he throws a big party for him at his mansion. Alan also told him he's going to have the party a short time before he leaves Marblehead Neck. Katherine is so happy for him and looking forward to meeting Alan.

The main course was finished and it was time to clear the table for dessert and Katherine and Sebastian were doing just that. She started the fresh perked coffee which was chocolate cherry kiss for Valentine's Day. She offered to whip the cream for the strawberry shortcake and started doing that. Katherine wanted to use the fancy china for their dessert that had raspberry roses on them which will match the roses in the middle of the table and add beauty to the table setting.

It was soon time for dessert with coffee. Katherine sat down and Sebastian stepped over to the buffet and took a small present from the draw and put it on her dish. It was wrapped in pink paper and had a red bow. He then sat down and watched her look at the present as she smiled. She then looked at him and said, "Oh, I wonder what's in that present."

He said, "Go ahead and open it up." Her face lit up as she unwrapped the present and then her eyes opened wide because she was amazed at what she saw. It was a huge gorgeous diamond engagement ring set in platinum. The diamond was flanked with baguettes. She was stunned for a moment and then said, "Oh, Sebastian, I never would have dreamed you'd be giving this to me today!" While she was sitting and the ring was still in the box, he went over to her and took the ring out of the box and got on one knee and held her hand and asked, "Katherine, will you marry me?" She was overwhelmed as she looked into his eyes and said, "Yes." He put the ring on her left hand ring finger and then they stood up and kissed. She is ecstatic she just got engaged and he's so happy they're going to be married. What a Valentine's Day it is for Katherine and what a day it is for Sebastian who wondered if she'd accept the engagement ring.

They had a hard time to sit and have their dessert but they did while she kept looking at the sparkling diamond ring on her left hand ring finger. He kept looking at her while smiling because she was so happy about the engagement.

Back in the living room, later on in the evening, they again toasted their engagement with champagne. They then talked about when they were going to get married. He said, "Before I leave Marblehead Neck in late July or August." She got excited and can't believe this is happening and she agreed to it which is only five or six months away. She wants a church wedding and wants to wear a beautiful wedding gown. They even went into a conversation about whether or not they want children and they agreed they want at least two. It soon got late and the night was ending for Katherine and Sebastian because she planned to go home tonight. They stood at the doorway having a passionate kiss goodnight. As soon as she left, he was already feeling lonely without her.

The next day, Sebastian and Katherine were on the phone talking about how happy they were that they got engaged to be married. They continued to talk to each other every day on the phone or she would go over to the mansion and they'd make love in the same bed on the second floor.

About two weeks later, Sebastian and Katherine were at a classy restaurant celebrating his 35th birthday. They were dressed attractive as usual and they were having a lamb dinner while they were talking about how they're engaged to be married. He said, "Katherine, I'm in shock just as much as you. I wasn't sure you'd accept the proposal." She said, "Oh, I knew I wanted to marry you a long time ago." All of a sudden, he spotted the waiter coming out with a birthday cake lit with candles and put it in front of him and he looked so surprised. She told him she wanted to surprise him with a cake so she secretly told the waiter about it. After he blew out the candles, she handed him a small present gift wrapped in birthday paper and also a card attached. He read the card first, then leaned over a gave her a kiss on the lips. He opened the present and it was a beautiful and unusual high quality watch with diamonds. He thanked her again with a kiss.

In a couple of days, Sebastian was at Katherine's real estate office to sign papers to extend his lease at the mansion to the end of August 2011 which will give him more time to try and help solve the 2006 murder mystery. He read everything he needed to and signed the papers and Katherine gave him a copy for himself. Then, they sat and talked for awhile. She asked him if it was worth him renting the mansion. He asked her, "What do you think?" They both looked at each other and smiled with love in their eyes.

12

SHOCKING POLICE NEWS

Today, at the outsource police service station, Sam, the wannabe writer who is Sebastian's rival, is outrageously dressed in bright colored clothes sitting and talking with Lieutenant Darwin at his desk. Sam just told him he now knows who murdered Jenny and Pierce four years ago. It was Alfred. The same person who murdered Jenny's mother Shannon hours earlier on the same day in their mansion. The lieutenant told him he was making a strong allegation. Sam told him that he knows he is.

Lieutenant Darwin listened while Sam went on and told him he overheard drunken Alfred in a booth again talking to his friend Dex about the 2006 murders he got away with. He told Dex, he wished he hadn't gone back to the mansion to break

The Ghost And Sebastian

in a second time for antiques because Jenny and Pierce were home and saw him. He didn't want them to identify him so he shot both of them while they were in her bedroom. He also stole a few antiques and took off. Sam paused and then said, "Lt. Darwin, Alfred murdered all three people."

Lieutenant Darwin is quite surprised at what Sam is alleging. He said, "Sam, you need to put this in writing now. Do you mind?" "No! I don't mind at all lieutenant." The lieutenant handed him a form to fill out and write down what he just told him but to wait a few minutes.

Lieutenant Darwin went and talked with Chief Brooks and Officer Martin about Sam's information he just gave. He explained how a jury could find it interesting that they have proof it was a 22 caliber that shot all three people. It could have been Alfred. And they have two reports about Alfred who was in a drunken state awhile back. He was sitting in a booth with his friend Dex and was overheard by Sebastian and Saul, the bartender, at the Ultimate Inn. Alfred confessed to Dex about the mother's murder he did. He could have come back within hours and shot the other two. Chief Brooks and Officer Martin think there's something more to Alfred.

Lt. Darwin, Chief Brooks and Officer Martin then went back and sat with Sam and stared at him. Sam said, "I hope I'll be honored for this when you police arrest and find Alfred guilty." The lieutenant already knew he was an obnoxious egomaniac only concerned about being the hero for solving the triple homicide. The lieutenant told him they know who to honor and when to. He then asked Sam if he would sign an affidavit now and he agreed to as the three officers watched. Lt. Darwin then thanked him for his information and told him the police will get in touch with him if they need to. Sam got up and said goodbye to the officers.

He also drew a lot of attention with his outrageously bright colored clothes he was wearing as he walked out the door smiling and looking wacky.

It's now early March and today Sebastian is at the Ultimate Inn bar in the late afternoon talking with his friend Saul and having a soft drink. There was no Danny the piano player present because it was still afternoon. Saul told Sebastian he noticed that Phoebe has been sad lately. He knows she's self-conscious about her overweight but doesn't know why she would be sad about that because she's a pretty brunette who loves to sing with Danny. Sebastian said, "I've heard how she loves to sing with him while he plays the piano. I wonder what's wrong with her?" Saul told him that no one knows and she won't tell anyone why she won't sing anymore. She sits in a booth alone and cries sometimes. She probably needs a shrink. Sebastian said, "I'm sorry to hear that. She's usually singing, laughing and dancing around while Danny plays tunes. Something's bothering her."

Out of the blue, Phoebe walked into the lounge area while looking sad. She was wearing blue jeans and a jacket as she headed over to a booth and sat in it. Saul called out to her, "Phoebe, come on over here and talk to us! Let me introduce you to the renowned mystery writer, Sebastian, who is from New York." While still looking sad, she slowly walked over to them and sat down on a captain style bar stool while she was being introduced to Sebastian. He told her he's happy to meet her and offered her a drink of her choice. In a sad voice, she told him she wanted a rum and coke. While Saul made her one, Sebastian asked her, "I hear you're not your happy self anymore. What happened?" She slowly answered, "I wish I could find a nice boyfriend. I'm so lonely." Sebastian asked, "Is that all that's wrong?" She told him yes and that it's making her so depressed. Sebastian told her about Dr. Louis, the psychiatrist, and that she should make an appointment to see him. He also added that he's a terrific doctor and he can help her get over her loneliness. He wrote the doctor's phone number down and handed it to Phoebe. As she took it, she thanked him and seemed to look content now. Saul brought her the rum and coke and left. As she sipped it, she suddenly looked at Sebastian and said, "Thanks for the delicious drink." He told her it was his pleasure. After awhile, Saul came back and told Phoebe that he noticed she and Sebastian have become Ultimate Inn friends." She smiled and then said, "I think so." After a couple of hours talking, Sebastian had to leave so he said goodbye to Saul and Phoebe who were still at the bar.

Back at the mansion, Sebastian is in the cellar looking at a lot of antique frames which he loves. There are also so many cobwebs there and lots of dust that's making the cellar look spooky. While he was looking at one particular frame, he suddenly heard a door slam. He turned to look at the cellar door that led to the outdoors and it was closed. He stared at it for a moment and then it slowly opened by itself and then slammed shut. He went and looked at it and couldn't figure out what was making it open and slam shut. For a second, he paused and then thought out loud, "Could that be a spirit doing that? If not, I'll have to tell Charlie about it and maybe he'll be able to fix it."

While Sebastian continued to look at antique frames, he soon heard something crash. He stopped to listen for a moment and then something else crashed. He looked around and finally saw a big black cat which looked like the same one he once saw in there before. He let the cat outside and he stayed in the cellar to see if he could find out where the noise was coming from. He didn't think the cat did it. He then heard some banging over and over again and he believes he is feeling the presence of a spirit in the cellar nearby him. Somehow, today, he doesn't like the feeling he's getting and thinks he's being forewarned to get out of the cellar. He went back up the stairs that led to his kitchen.

When Sebastian got in his kitchen, a tremendous wind suddenly whipped through the mansion and it seemed to be in every room and he couldn't figure out what suddenly was causing it. It was blowing so many things around and he thought the windows were closed. He said, "Well, here we go again." He looked around and things were getting knocked over, such as candle holders, vases and picture frames and the curtains in the windows were blowing as though the windows were all open. He immediately thought there was paranormal activity in the mansion causing it yet he still wanted to check the windows in every room. As he did so, he heard the piano suddenly and loudly playing sad songs When he looked at the piano, no one was sitting there yet the keys were going up and down. Shannon's ghost wasn't there like it once was. He went to every window and found one that was open halfway in Jenny's bedroom. The curtains were blowing a lot and he didn't think he left it open. As soon as he shut the window, the wind stopped in the entire mansion and so did the piano playing. He also knew that one window couldn't have made all that wind. He's still thinking of how the piano started playing and how he heard the music with no one sitting there. He knows spirits can get very spooky and that's for sure.

Sebastian then decided to have a cup of coffee and so he heated up some water in the kettle. This is a very strange day. He also doesn't know if he should tell Katherine about this because it might scare her. He'll be calling her in awhile so they can discuss how she wants to celebrate her 34th birthday in a few days. He wants to know where she wants to have dinner and what else she wants to do to celebrate.

Meanwhile, now that the crazy wind stopped blowing and the piano stopped playing, Sebastian knows he has to have dinner. He chose to have rigatoni pasta tonight to go with his salad. He grated some cheese and put that aside and started to make a marina sauce with onion, garlic, salt, sugar, black pepper and a little red wine. After he cooked it, he put it aside. He'll only have to heat it up and boil the water for pasta when he's ready to eat and it sure sounds like he's going to have comfort food for dinner.

Back in the living room, Sebastian is at his desk and reviewing the data in his computer because he wants to update information. He likes documenting everything in his red book too because then he knows he can access it from two places. And sometimes he's not in the mood to go on the computer and would rather write it in his red book which he thinks is easier. After working on his computer for quite awhile, he thought about his dinner and was feeling hungry and wanted to eat.

Sebastian was soon sitting at the dining room table having a bowl of rigatoni with his homemade marina sauce topped with fresh grated cheese and having red wine and crusty bread with it. He would love to have Katherine with him now but she can't always be there. Aside from that, they'll be married in about four months and that will change things. They now have to make a lot of arrangements relating to their wedding and her job as a real estate agent.

When dinner was over, Sebastian wanted to recline on the burgundy velvet sofa and rest a bit and think about his book. He still doesn't know who murdered Jenny and Pierce. In late July or August, after he gets married, he will move out of the mansion and then he and Katherine will leave Marblehead Neck and move to his home in New York.

Within a few days, Officer Martin called Sebastian and asked him if he could come into the station to see him and of course Sebastian told him he could. He was soon at the officer's desk and they were engaged in conversation. Officer Martin told him his rival Sam was in a few days ago and wrote and signed a document. He claimed he overheard intoxicated Alfred again in the Ultimate Inn telling his friend Dex he was sorry he went back to the mansion later to rob again because Jenny and Pierce were there and saw him so he shot them. He went and robbed a few more antiques and then ran out the door. Alfred also told his friend Dex that he was lucky he never got caught for the three murders. The officer waited to see Sebastian's reaction so he stared at him.

Sebastian was a little surprised at what Officer Martin just told him. He said, "I'm surprised but then again I'm not because that news comes from troublemaker Sam, my rival." The officer said, "I understand your point." Sebastian asked the officer if Sam had any proof that he heard Alfred saying all that. The officer told him that Sam was alone and it's just his word. Sebastian then told Officer Martin that Sam wants to be the hero for solving the triple homicide. He then added that Sam is envious of his renowned fame as a mystery writer from New York and wants him out of the picture because he knows he plans to write a book about this murder mystery. Officer Martin said, "We police know all that because Sam asked us if he'd be honored after they arrest Alfred for all three murders and sentence him." Sebastian shook his head and said, "He is pathetic." He paused and then told the officer that even though a 22 caliber was used to shoot all three people, hours apart, he's not convinced one person shot all three of them because Sam has no proof. He only has his own word.

Officer Martin agreed with Sebastian, but told him that police have to keep a record of all news even though it's not enough to interrogate Alfred yet. As Sebastian was ready to leave the station, he told the officer he'd be in touch with him if he gets any news about the murderer. They then said goodbye and Sebastian left with a somewhat unsettled feeling just hearing what the officer told him. He went back to his mansion and continued to think about troublemaker Sam. He worked on his book but it was a little difficult to keep his mind off of the latest police news.

The Ghost And Sebastian

Meanwhile, it didn't take long for Phoebe to see Dr. Louis, the psychiatrist, whose office is in Marblehead. She is sitting across from him as he sits at his desk. Her dark eyes and short dark brown hair looked nice as she was wearing red lipstick and a short red dress. The doctor asked her, "How can I help you, Phoebe?" She was shy as she answered the doctor's question and said, "Well, I'm not myself anymore. I'm no more fun." Dr. Louis asked her to lie on the couch and she did as he helped her onto it because she's short and overweight. He then sat on a chair near her with a pad and pen. He said to her, "Phoebe, I want you to tell me about your childhood. Was it good or was it sad? Did anything terrible happen to you that you never revealed to anyone?" Phoebe said, "I liked my childhood until kids made fun of me being overweight and I never revealed to anyone how much it hurt me." The doctor stopped her and said, "You must not let anyone upset you because of that. Children and adults can be cruel. What you can do is to ignore them or go on a diet."

Phoebe went on and told Dr. Louis that it is difficult to ignore hurtful comments people make about her weight so she'll try to go on a diet. The doctor asked her to go on and tell him what makes her happy. She told him she use to be a regular at the Ultimate Inn lounge for a long time where she would sometimes sing with Danny, the piano player, and also dance and it made her happy except when someone made fun of her. He asked her, "What else happened that made you unhappy?" She told the doctor that she can't get a date and wants a boyfriend badly because she's lonely. While her eyes suddenly looked passionate, she slowly moved around on the couch in seductive ways as her short red dress was moving up and she softly said, "I want sex in my life." Dr. Louis got angry and told Phoebe to stop moving around like she was and so she stopped. He told her, if it's meant to be, she'll have a boyfriend and there'll be sex because it's a part of nature and her weight will have nothing to do with it. Some men prefer heavy women and it's the personality that matters.

Dr. Louis then told Phoebe, if she can't get over hurtful comments, she should go on a diet which is not that difficult to do. Either way, a man may come to her and fall in love and he may be overweight or too thin. He reminded her that it's her personality that matters. After pausing, he said, "You have a weight complex. My advice to you is, it would be healthy for you to lose some weight but also keep it in mind, it's your personality that's going to keep a lover around you."

The doctor soon helped Phoebe off of the couch and she went and sat on a chair across from him while he was at his desk. He said, "You don't need any medication, all you need is to get over your weight criticism or go on a diet. The decision is up to you, Phoebe." He was finished talking and she said, "I'm so happy I came to see you, Dr. Louis. I feel better already." He told her to call and make another appointment if she needs to and she agreed. She got up from her chair and thanked him and they said goodbye. While she headed over to the door, the doctor watched her waddle out of the office. He then said, "She has such a pretty face. She wants to be sexually active and that's okay. But she needs to lose weight or it will interfere with her health in the future."

On this day, Sebastian and Katherine are in a classy restaurant dining room celebrating her 34th birthday with champagne and dinner. He looks sharp wearing blue and she is all in pink with her shoulder length blonde hair brushed to one side. Her diamond engagement ring is beautiful as it sparkles so much. She sometimes looks at it and then looks at Sebastian and they smile. They are in the middle of their dinner which is roast prime rib of beef with Julian style green beans with almonds and baked potatoes with sour cream. He said, "I hope you're enjoying your birthday so far." She responded, "Oh course I am. As long as I'm with you." He smiled at her and told her he loves her more than she loves him but she disagreed with that.

When it was time for dessert, Jacque, the young waiter, brought out the chocolate ice cream Katherine and Sebastian ordered. He then came back with a birthday cake with white frosting and candles all lit and put it in front of Katherine as she looked surprised. Sebastian said, "Happy Birthday!" The people around them watched. She blew out the candles and said, "Oh, the cake is so beautiful. What a shame we have to cut it" He said, "The good part is, they'll be plenty left for us to take back to the mansion." She cut into the cake which was white with a berry filling and they loved it. Sebastian told her that the best part of her birthday is when they get back to the mansion because he has a gift for her. She asked, "What? I can hardly wait to see what it is." They soon finished their cake with ice cream and coffee and were ready to leave with the leftover birthday cake. Sebastian left Jacque, the waiter, a generous tip and he thanked him.

Back at the mansion, Sebastian and Katherine are in the living room having champagne while sitting on the sofa. Her birthday roses are in front of them on the coffee table which she occasionally smells. He got up for a moment and then came back with her present that was in a jewelry box wrapped in pink paper with a white bow on it and he had a card for her. He handed it to her and she immediately opened the card first and read it to herself. When she finished, she leaned over and gave him a little kiss on his lips. She then unwrapped her present and her eyes popped as she saw a gorgeous diamond bracelet. She said, "Oh, this is stunning, Sebastian! It's unusual and that's what I like." She thanked him and they leaned over to each other and had a little kiss. He said, "Happy Birthday, Katherine." She said, "Thank you so much for such a wonderful birthday, Sebastian. I love you." He responded, "I'm so in love with you, Katherine."

Sebastian put the diamond bracelet on Katherine's right wrist and she adored it as she kept looking at it. It had so much sparkle to it. The rest of the night was filled with romance. Sebastian and

Katherine went on and talked about their marriage for awhile and how she'll have to quit her job because they will be moving to New York the end of July or August after they're married. She told him she will miss selling real estate in Marblehead although it will be exciting moving to New York. They embraced and kissed and then he said, "I'm so happy we're getting married." She responded, "Sebastian, I must be crazy about you for me to leave my job. Oh, and I have to find a wedding dress!" He smiled at her and then said, "What will I wear?" They agreed that whatever they wear they'll look gorgeous together. Their wedding date at church has already been set.

Katherine couldn't sleep over tonight because she had to get up early tomorrow morning for a real estate meeting and would rather sleep home to insure she gets a good night sleep. Therefore, when it was near midnight, Katherine left the mansion hating to leave Sebastian but it's only for tonight. There will be plenty of other nights they'll sleep together.

The next day, while Sebastian was sitting on one of the mahogany wing armchairs, he called his good friend Alan, the Hollywood movie producer, and they're talking about health. After hearing Alan was okay, Sebastian told him he misses seeing him and has been planning on going to visit him at his mansion in a few weeks. He then asked him if he was going to be around? Alan told him he'll be going to Hollywood to his other mansion for awhile to take care of some business but he should be back in early May. He wanted to know if Sebastian had something urgent he needed to see him about. Sebastian told him he just wanted to see him and tell him about many new things that have been happening to him. Alan asked, "You mean with the ghosts?" Sebastian laughed and then answered, "That and other news." Alan told him he's anxious to see him again and after talking a little longer, the phone call ended because Alan was very busy. He's always flying back and forth to Hollywood, California.

Sebastian felt good after talking with Alan and now knows he can look forward to seeing him at his Marblehead mansion in early May. He can hardly wait to tell him about Jenny's ghost and how he is engaged to be married to Katherine. He and Alan love talking about personal matters.

While Sebastian spent the rest of the afternoon on his book, he kept thinking about the fact that he's getting married. He never in his life ever wanted to marry anyone until he met Katherine. She's the love of his life. He loves her beauty, inspiration, intelligence and she has class. She has everything he wants and feels lucky that he has found her and she feels the same about him. He wonders how she will like living in New York in his beautiful home that was once his father's. And she doesn't have to be a real estate agent anymore if she doesn't want to. They have discussed having children and he thinks it would be a blessing to be a father.

Sebastian soon stopped daydreaming about himself and Katherine of how life will be when they're married. He went back to his writing, but as he started to write, he started dwelling on troublemaker Sam who just went to the police station with news about Alfred which could be a hoax as far as Sebastian's concerned.

Sebastian didn't have much desire to work on his book today. He decided to check the attic to see if anything crazy has happened up there and if the mannequin is still wearing Jenny's sheer lavender blue nightgown. He doesn't know how it got on it. When he rented the mansion, the mannequin was naked until Jenny's ghost left her lavender blue nightgown on the floor in the bathroom. That's when he stripped naked and she took off her nightgown and they got in the shower. He thought of how they sat down in the shower and he had his arms around her, then, she suddenly disappeared from his arms and never took her lavender blue nightgown with her that she left on the floor. He put it in her drawer but someone later put it on the mannequin. He recently put her raspberry nightgown in her drawer. She left that one on her bed room floor after they made love in her bed.

In the attic, awhile later, Sebastian was stunned to find the mannequin missing. He was looking all over for it and it was gone. He can see the rocking chair but he wonders what happened to the mannequin. He sat on the rocking chair to think about it. While he slowly rocked, the chair started to rock fast. He yelled, "Stop it! Stop it whoever is doing this!" He tried to stop the rocking chair so he could get off but he couldn't stop it this time. He felt the presence of a spirit hovering over him. He yelled, "Get out of the mansion!" The chair suddenly stopped rocking and he no longer felt the presence of a spirit but he still wants to know where the mannequin is. He wonders if someone broke in and stole it.

He looked in back of many boxes and suddenly saw the mannequin on the floor as though someone knocked it over. At first, he didn't know what to believe. The mannequin still had the lavender blue nightgown on, bushy black hair, red lipstick and large haunting pale blue eyes. He stood it up and stared at it and wondered how it fell over. He paused and then came to the conclusion that an angry spirit was there and knocked it over. He said to himself, "That's it. There's a lot of paranormal activity in this attic as well as throughout this mansion. This place is totally haunted!"

While still in the attic, Sebastian sat down on a box for awhile thinking of why an angry spirit would have a problem with the mannequin or the rocking chair.

Regarding the mannequin, Sebastian thinks that maybe a female spirit thought the mannequin was the woman who stole her lover when they were alive so she knocked her over. He paused and then wondered if it was a male spirit who thought the mannequin was the female who gave him trouble when they were alive so he knocked her over.

Sebastian was full of scenarios. He was trying to envision what spirits might do. He then said, "They seek revenge like some people in the real world do." Today, he hated to leave the attic because he's so interested in what angry spirit knocked the mannequin over and why. He senses a spirit did it, for sure.

After awhile, Sebastian left the attic and went down to his kitchen and made a cup of tea and sat in the dining room with it just to meditate on what just happened in the attic.

13

COMPANY IS COMING

It was a sunny day in April and you could feel that spring had arrived. Sebastian had breakfast and then headed out to the market to buy a few things but instead he returned back to his mansion with many bags of food. After entering the rose foyer, he hung up his spring jacket in the closet and then carried the bags into the kitchen and started putting the food away as he sensed someone was in the mansion.

In a short while, Sebastian went into Jenny's bedroom for a minute and immediately heard the shower running. As he stood still and inhaled, he was puzzled because there was no gardenia scent in the air. He said to himself, "There's no gardenia scent so that's not Jenny's ghost in that shower." He entered the bathroom and saw a shadow of a woman taking a shower. He yelled,

The Ghost And Sebastian

"Who's in there?" No one answered. Then the shower stopped. Within seconds, the sliding shower door opened a little and a hand reached down for a towel outside the door. Then you could see the woman's shadow behind the glass wrapping the towel around herself. The shower door slowly opened wide and she stepped out. It was Samantha! She smiled as she and Sebastian made eye contact. While her shoulder length dark hair was wet, she still looked beautiful as she went and stood in front of him smiling. He was stunned as to how she got in the mansion.

While Samantha was still in front of Sebastian, she suddenly said, "Surprise, surprise!" He was furious as to how she got in the mansion without an invitation. He asked, "How did you get in here?" She took her finger and slowly stroked his chest and then said, "I copied your mansion key when you were at my condo one day taking a nap. You left your keys on the dresser and I thought it would be nice if I had my own key to the mansion so I could surprise you."

Sebastian was so angry he didn't care about losing his temper so he yelled, ""You had no right to copy my key! Are you crazy?" Samantha was startled at his anger and didn't answer. Her towel almost fell off as she quickly backed off and was now against the wall. Her anger was under control since Dr. Louis gave her new sedatives.

While Samantha was standing near the wall with the towel partially around her, she said, "Sebastian, calm down. Don't I make you feel sexy standing here with just a towel around me?" He was not interested. He hated the fact that she copied his key and got in the mansion and knows that's breaking the law. He was outraged that she did such a thing so he started yelling, "Who the hell do you think you are? I want you out of here now!" She didn't respond and let him vent while she stayed away from him while covered with just a towel. He then yelled even louder, "Who the hell wants you after you claimed you accidently knocked me down while ice skating which caused me to bust my teeth! And then you steal my house key and make a copy of it and use it to break in my mansion! Get out of here now! I care about you as a friend but get some professional mental help!"

Samantha said, "Give me a few minutes to get dressed and I'll leave." Sebastian saw her set of keys on the bathroom dressing table and grabbed them fast as she saw him do it. He went into the living room and removed two mansion keys from her key ring. He then went back into the bathroom and said, "Here are your keys. I removed two mansion keys. One for my front door and one for my back door. Now get out!" In a short while, he saw Samantha leave out the foyer door while yelling, "Bye, Sebastian!" He didn't answer. He thinks she may have another set of keys which she probably does.

Sebastian is in Jenny's bathroom looking around to see if Samantha did anything unusual but she didn't. He got rid of the towels she used and put fresh ones out. He then went into the kitchen and finished putting the food away and made a cup of tea and took it into the living room. He presently can't stand Samantha's behavior even though he knows she has a mental disorder and sometimes needs help.

While sitting on an armchair with his tea next to him on a table, Sebastian continued to think about Samantha's shocking intrusion onto his property. He will get over it eventually because life goes on. After he finished his tea, he went to the sofa to relax and get his mind off of her. Then he started to think of what he wanted for dinner and he soon decided on having just soup and a good sandwich with milk.

Later, after Sebastian had his soup and sandwich for dinner, he felt relaxed. He cleaned up the dishes and went to his desk to try and think about his book. He looked at his red book and then went on the computer and somehow he worked well into the evening hours. He later got tired and wanted to take a shower. When he got in the bathroom, he hated the fact that Samantha was just in there so he cleaned the shower area and sink and anything he thought she might have touched. He knows what she did would have angered anyone. He wants to get her to tell Dr. Louis her deeply troubled past so he can help her. Before long, Sebastian was in Jenny's bed and restless for awhile but eventually fell asleep.

One afternoon in April, Charlie was in the backyard looking around at the landscape. Sebastian saw him through the window and went out and talked with him. He asked, "Charlie, how have you been?" He answered, "Good, now that spring is here." Sebastian asked him if he remembered anything else about Jenny when she lived in the mansion with her mother Shannon. Charlie said, "All I can tell you is that it's a spooky mansion but I have no problem working here." Sebastian asked him if he ever saw a ghost around the mansion and he told him he never has but believes there are ghosts in it. Sebastian told him it's because too many people who lived in the mansion were murdered in it and died angry. Charlie looked deep in thought as though he knew something but was hiding it.

Sebastian soon said goodbye to Charlie who quickly responded by saying, "Have a good day, Sebastian." Charlie carried on with his landscaping and flower gardening as he was preparing what kind of flowers he was going to plant and what bushes he was going to move. Sebastian went back into his living room and really felt better now and went to his desk to work on his book. He feels, this was quite a day.

A few days later, Samantha was on the couch in the psychiatrist's office venting to Dr. Louis who sat nearby with a pad and pen. He asked, "Samantha, is the medication working?" She told him yes and how she was recently able to control her temper when otherwise she would have been violent. She then told him she came to see him today for something else. Dr. Louis said, "I'm happy the medication's controlling your anxiety so why are you here today?" She paused and then suddenly told him she changed her mind as to what she was just going to tell him. He told her she needs to tell him more if she wants to get well.

Samantha suddenly yelled out, "What makes me do things that some people wouldn't do?" The doctor told her it's because she's not telling him her traumatic experiences. She then told the doctor how she recently copied a friend's house keys without him knowing it and entered his home when he wasn't there. She wanted to surprise him when he came home but instead he was outraged. Dr. Louis told her that was breaking the law. And something in her past that she is concealing is causing her to act out in crazy ways, such as, copying someone's house keys without their permission. She needs to discuss her painful past with him to end her madness. She said, "I can't." He said, "I told you that you need to release something that's bothering you. Tell me what it is. I know something's causing your strange behavior."

Samantha thought for a few moments and then said, "I can't tell you everything but I wish I could, Dr. Louis." He told her that maybe she will in time when she feels she can trust him. He asked her to sit on a chair and he went to his desk. He looked at her and said, "I'd like to see you again in a few months. She agreed to another appointment. After they said goodbye, he watched her leave and then said, "She's a beautiful woman with a serious mental problem."

One early morning, Sebastian sat on a wing armchair with his cell phone while calling his friend Alan, the movie producer. He wants to see if he's back from his business trip in Hollywood where his other mansion is located. Alan's phone kept ringing and ringing and he didn't answer it so Sebastian left him a message to call him back because he wants to visit him.

Sebastian later became restless so he immediately decided to go to the harbor and look at the sailboats and yachts. With the warm weather approaching, there'll soon be a lot of activity going on with people renting boats or yachts for their vacation. The harbor is a beautiful site, if you like boats. And seeing the sailboats with their sails against the sunny blue sky makes great souvenir photographs.

After putting on spring clothes and a light jacket, Sebastian was ready to go to the harbor so he headed out to his car that was parked in his driveway. After he got to it and sat behind the steering wheel and was ready to turn the ignition on, he noticed the air was suddenly filled with the scent of gardenias. His eyes opened wide while he looked alarmed and speechless. In a few seconds he said, "This can't be happening! Jenny's ghost in my car!"

Sebastian looked in his back car seat and Jenny's ghost wasn't there. As he remained still, he felt the presence of her spirit and knew something was about to happen. Within seconds, Jenny's pale lifelike ghostly apparition was sitting next to him in the front seat looking at him and smiling. He was amazed while remaining silent and staring at her. She was beautiful to look at as she was wearing a sheer light blue nightgown which was long, loose-fitting and looked ethereal. Because it was sheer, it revealed her being naked and a mesmerizing sight. Her pretty long light brown hair, was her crowning beauty, was flowing over her shoulders and also showing off her beautiful face with hypnotic brown eyes and pale rose lips.

Sebastian looked at Jenny's ghost and said, "Jenny, you surprised me! You've only appeared in front of me in the mansion!" She kissed him passionately on the lips and then embraced him. Sebastian loves his unusual power that allows him to communicate with spirits or ghosts and live in their world temporarily, but sometimes he's unable to move his arms for a few moments when she first appears. That's when he can't stop her from seducing him because she overpowers a living person. However, he wants the strange sensation he gets from making love with Jenny's ghost. It's nothing like he has felt in the real world although it's satisfying there.

While Jenny's ghost and Sebastian were in the front seat of the his car and he was still behind the steering wheel, she started kissing him passionately on the lips again, then his neck and then stopped and just smiled at him. He got the impression that she just wanted to cuddle and talk. He moved away from the steering wheel so he would be more comfortable and she moved with him. Then he said, "Jenny! I'm so happy to see you but more surprised that you are in my car waiting for me." She said, "I wanted to be near you just to talk, Sebastian." He told her he understands and why don't they get in the back seat where there's more room. She suddenly disappeared and he looked in the back seat of the car and there she was waiting for him.

Sebastian got in the large back seat of his car and they kissed and then talked because that was what Jenny wanted this time. She told him how she misses him and loves being with him and is so happy he's helping to find her murderer. He told her that he will never stop and then they embraced as he told her she can show up anytime and anywhere to be with him. They kissed passionately but that's as far as she wanted to go and he wasn't about to pressure her into making love.

Sebastian and Jenny's ghost are enjoying being with each other, even if it's just to cuddle and talk. He stroked her hair and told her how pretty she is and she thanked him and told him she loves him very much. He responded and told her he loves her, and he can't believe he's telling a ghost that he loves her, because they're in two different worlds. He also told her he keeps thinking of ways to find who murdered her and Pierce but he needs her help. He asked her if she knew the murderer's name. After pausing, she said, "Pierce and I know the murderer. We know our murderer! Help me, Sebastian!" He told her he's happy she knows her murderer, but, she needs to tell him the murderer's name and anything else that might lead him to the murderer. While he waited for her response, she suddenly disappeared from his arms and the gardenia scent followed. He yelled, "Jenny! Wait!"

Sebastian remained in the back seat of his car just thinking and stunned that this is the second time Jenny told him that she knows her murderer and that Pierce does also. But she doesn't give Sebastian a name or tell him if it's a male or female. He keeps it in mind that Jenny's ghost lives in another world and that's why no one knows why they act like they do. However, he loves being with her and wishes he could help her. While he's ready to go back in his mansion, he's thinking of this unusual car visit and no love making, although she has appeared before just to talk, but he wants the murderer's name. It's the reason he came from New York and moved in the mansion so he could help solve this triple homicide. He rested his head on the back of the car seat for a moment and said, "What a surprise this car visit was and that was the fifth nightgown I was able to feel the material."

Now that Jenny's ghost was gone, Sebastian left his car and went back into his mansion. He first made some coffee and sat in the kitchen to sip it while he meditated about this first time car visit from Jenny's ghost. He already knows that she doesn't always want to make love but she does like to talk and cuddle. His day has totally been rearranged because of the car visit. It just about shocked him. He never got to the harbor to see the boats like he planned to do today but knows he can always do that another day. He loved being with Jenny's ghost and this time he made progress because she told him again that she and Pierce knew their murderer. That's good news for Sebastian.

After awhile, Sebastian went and took a shower and then went to the sofa to relax and do nothing but think of Jenny. While he was on his velvet sofa with a pillow behind his head, he started thinking about all this new information he can put in his book. And especially Jenny's ghost meeting him in his car which she has never done. And, again, she didn't want to make love, she just wanted to talk and cuddle. He also thinks, if he wrote the details of his love making with Jenny's ghost, it would shock the living.

Sebastian wonders if Jenny's ghost would mind if he told all the details about her in his book. He wouldn't want to make her angry because of her spiritual power and also because he came to love her soul. He wants to contact her living friends and Pierce's and their acquaintances again to help find their murderer. He may stay at the mansion longer than he planned to, especially if he is making progress. He also needs to visit the police to give them his latest news that Jenny's ghost told him again that she knows her murderer and he also believes she does.

While Sebastian stayed on the sofa meditating, he then noticed the gardenia scent. He sat up and inhaled and looked around the room and called out, "Jenny! Jenny!" There was no response. He can feel the presence of her spirit yet he doesn't see Jenny's ghost. He walked around and soon the gardenia scent was gone which he thought was strange. He asked himself, "Did she come back to say hello and leave?"

The next day, Sebastian went to the harbor to see the boats. While he sat down looking at them, he thought of how Jenny's ghost has repeated to him that she and Pierce know their murderer. She waited long before telling him that but he always believed she knew the murderer. Sebastian thought of Pierce's body that was shot near the door which means he was awake when he was shot. While she was in bed, she heard gunshots, then quickly looked and saw the murderer who then shot her. Sebastian soon left the harbor.

One evening, in early May, Sebastian's phone kept ringing. After her answered it, his friend Alan said, "Hi, "Sebastian, I just got back from my office in Hollywood and got your message. When would you like to come over to visit and tell me the latest news? And let's have lunch together!" Sebastian said, "It's good to hear from you, Alan. How about getting together this weekend?" Alan agreed but wants to be called the night before. After chatting awhile, they hung up.

When the weekend arrived, Sebastian was seated with Alan, the movie producer, in his office at his mansion. Sebastian was sitting on a large dark red leather chair while Alan was sitting at his desk. Alan said, "I can't wait to hear all your news!" Sebastian started out by telling him, on Valentine's Day, he and Katherine got engaged to be married. He proposed and she accepted and he put a diamond ring on her finger. Alan was so surprised. He immediately shook hands with Sebastian and congratulated him and then asked when the wedding will be. Sebastian told him, in late July which is a few months away. Alan was thrilled for them.

Sebastian then said, "I know you're anxious to hear more ghost news." Alan said, "Oh yes! I'm very anxious." Sebastian told him how the love making has continued with Jenny's ghost and she keeps surprising him. While Alan just stared at him, Sebastian told him that he went to his car a few days ago, and after he got in it and sat behind the steering wheel, the scent of gardenias suddenly filled the air. Within seconds, Jenny's pale lifelike ghostly apparition was sitting next to him. This time, she was wearing a sheer light blue nightgown. Alan said, "Oh wow!" Sebastian told him she just wanted to kiss and cuddle while he was behind the steering wheel so he moved away from it a little. She continued to kiss and cuddle. He then told her they needed to get in the back seat where there was more room to stretch out. She then disappeared. When he looked in the back seat, there she was waiting for him. Alan said, "She's fascinating." Sebastian stared at Alan and said, "She didn't want to make love this time, she wanted to talk, Alan!" He said, "Wow! Tell me more! Then what happened?"

Sebastian continued telling Alan about the car talk Jenny's ghost wanted and sometimes they kissed and cuddled and he'd stroke her hair. Alan asked, "How did she look?" Sebastian told him he could see through her sheer nightgown that she was naked and beautiful and mesmerizing. Alan said, "Oh that makes me feel so romantic." Sebastian went on and told him that while they sometimes kissed and cuddled, he became very passionate and he could tell she was also but she wanted to talk more than anything else. She told him she loves being with him. Alan said, "Tell me more." Sebastian told him, he told Jenny's ghost she can be with him whenever she desires, then, while they were embraced, she disappeared.

Alan told Sebastian that this is such a nice story about a ghost and a living person. Sebastian told him how he loves Jenny's spiritual power which gives him strange love making pleasure and lingers awhile. Alan said, "Oh, wow! I want a ghost! How can I get one?" Sebastian told him he'd have to be in a haunted house and encounter a romantic ghost that wants to make love. Sebastian added, "Not in my wildest dreams did I ever think I'd be making love with a ghost."

Alan suddenly said, "Let's have a drink. What do you want?" Sebastian wants a glass of red wine and Alan wants scotch on the rocks. While Alan was still at his desk, he called up the butler and asked him to bring them their drinks to his office. Alan went on and said, "Sebastian, what a book and movie this story will make. I told you I'm making you a big party right here in my mansion, most likely in late July before you leave Marblehead Neck in August."

The butler soon arrived with the drinks and Alan thanked him. Sebastian told Alan he really appreciates him wanting to make a party for him. Alan told him he thinks he's special and so happy they're friends. Sebastian said, "After Katherine and I get married and then move to New York, I want you to visit us and stay for awhile. I moved into my father's large house that he left me when he died and it has three guest rooms. I then leased my house I had been living in." Alan thanked him and told him he will visit him.

As Sebastian and Alan sipped their drinks, Alan said, "When we finish our drinks, let me show you around the mansion again because I have some new sculptures I recently bought." Sebastian told him he'd love to see them, in fact, he needs to buy one for his home in New York. Alan went on and told him that he just finished the production of a movie that took two years because of many different locations it was shot in. Sebastian told him he hopes it does well at the cinemas. They soon finished their drinks and Alan took Sebastian on a tour of his mansion showing him his new original sculptures created by famous artists.

Sebastian loved the sculptures, some were of love goddesses. He kept telling Alan how beautiful his mansion is and everything in it is so impressive. The huge grand room where he has his pitch sessions is where Sebastian's party will be held. Alan told him that the room will be filled with authors, producers, directors and friends. It will be a wonderful night to celebrate his book and a future movie of it. Sebastian said, "And you're the producer. I couldn't ask for a better one, Alan." Alan thanked him for the compliment.

It's late afternoon now and Alan suggested that he and Sebastian go out to eat. They thought of a restaurant near the harbor where they could see the boats through the window while they eat. They took their own cars because they'll leave separately when they finish dinner.

At the restaurant, Alan and Sebastian each ordered a seafood plate and drinks and they laughed and then talked about old stories. Alan isn't that much older than Sebastian. He's in his late 40s and Sebastian is 35. After a couple of hours, it was time for them to leave so they gave each other a pat on the back and then went their separate ways.

Back at the mansion, Sebastian feels so good that he saw his friend Alan and spent quality time with him. He's just relaxing now on the sofa and plans to take a shower shortly. He also wants to go to bed early so he can get up early and document new information in his red book and the computer. While he's on the sofa, he suddenly noticed that a crystal candy dish isn't in the same place he put it in, but he is not getting too alarmed about it because he is use to the ghosts making sounds, showing up whenever and wherever they want to. However, he became curious and got up and moved the crystal candy dish to a different location and wants to see if it will get moved by a ghost in the future.

Later on, in Jenny's shower, Sebastian's shadowy image could be seen through the glass shower door and glass wall which was covered with steam. The hot water felt wonderful to him as he began to lather his body. In awhile, he felt so refreshed as the hot water poured down on him washing away the lather. Shortly after his shower, he anticipated a good night sleep as he went into the kitchen and sat down and had a glass of milk. He then went straight to Jenny's bed to think for awhile about how his life was going. He'll be seeing his future wife, Katherine, tomorrow which he hasn't seen for a few days because of her work schedule although they talk to each other a little each day.

Before long, Sebastian was fast asleep and it looked like it was going to be a long and peaceful night.

During Sebastian's deep sleep, he had a clairvoyant dream of Alfred, the alleged thief and murderer, rushing around on the first floor of his mansion and then showed Alfred at the police station with an officer. Then the dream ended.

14

A SURPRISE ARREST

Officer Martin has just arrived at the outsource police station with Alfred, a thin 40 year old dark haired man with glasses, who has his hands already handcuffed in back of him. After the officer signed him in, he was fingerprinted and then taken to the interrogation room for questioning.

Present in the interrogation room is Officer Martin, Lieutenant Darwin and Alfred. Officer Martin looked at Alfred and said, "You're being held for the speed chase you were just in with me. I eventually stopped you, you argued, you took a swing at me and resisted arrest." Alfred asked if that was all he was being held for. Officer Martin told him he was also being held for the 2006 robbery and triple homicide in Marblehead Neck. Alfred's eyes opened wide as he looked stunned to hear what he was charged with. In anger, he said, "Now wait a minute! What do mean, triple homicide?"

Officer Martin told Alfred they have witnesses who will testify to a grand jury that in 2006 he robbed a mansion and shot at least one person, or, shot all three people in it on the same day. Therefore, he may want to confess to it now or plea-bargain later to shorten a death sentence that could be in his future. He added that his case will be going to court.

While Alfred was still stunned and staring at Officer Martin because he has that information about him, he said, "It never happened! Half of that's lies!" Officer Martin told him it's up to him whether or not he wants to make a confession now or plea-bargain later. Right now, he's being held without bail. Alfred said, "I can confess to some of this stuff but not a triple homicide!" Alfred is now sweating and asking for water so the lieutenant went and got him some.

Alfred was silent for awhile as Officer Martin told him he was in trouble and lucky he wasn't arrested four years ago. Alfred refused to talk anymore other than telling Officer Martin that he needed a court appointed attorney because he doesn't have any money. The interrogation was soon over.

Alfred was taken to a holding cell. Officer Martin and Lieutenant Darwin left the room while the lieutenant talked about how he was on that triple homicide case and remembers it well. He hopes it will get solved so they can close the books on it. Officer Martin told the lieutenant how Sam, the trouble maker who is Sebastian's rival, has been reporting news about Alfred. He also added how the renowned mystery writer, Sebastian, has been reporting news and is waiting for a major break to come from Jenny's ghost who knows who murdered her and Pierce. The lieutenant just shook his head.

At the mansion, Sebastian is at his desk and has his red hardcover book out. He's documenting a message he recently received from Jenny's ghost telling him that she and Pierce know who killed them. He feels this is important because Jenny has told him more than once she knows who killed her and Pierce so it must be true. It's big news!

By late afternoon, Sebastian was still working on his book. He looked up for a moment and noticed a silhouette on the wall of tree branches moving around. It's the time of the day when the windows allow sunlight to spill into his living room and casts shadows on one wall. He kept looking at it and noticed the branches had many leaves because it's spring. And in the fall, the shadows take on an entirely different look of the bare tree branches making the shadows look quite spooky but perfect for Halloween.

The book work finally ended for the day and Sebastian had his dinner and then went to get ready to go out to the Ultimate Inn lounge to say hello to Saul, the bartender. Within a couple of hours, Sebastian was sitting at the bar having a soft drink and talking with his friend Saul. The lounge had a good crowd tonight and Danny, the piano player, had his hat on while playing a variety of songs and singing. While Sebastian enjoyed watching and listening to him, he noticed Phoebe sitting at a table alone. He went over to her and said, "Hi, Phoebe. Do you remember me?" In a shy way, she answered, "Of course I do, Sebastian. You gave me a psychiatrist's number and I made an appointment and saw him." Sebastian was happy to hear that and asked if it helped her. She told him it did a little and she's going back to him. Sebastian told her he's sitting at the bar if she wants to talk. He then left. Back at the bar, Sebastian told Saul about Phoebe whose making progress seeing a psychiatrist. Saul said, "I'm happy to hear that."

After an hour or so, Phoebe was up at the piano telling Danny, the piano player, something. When she finished, she stood by the piano and started belting out a tune while looking at the audience. Everybody stopped to watch and applauded her because she hasn't been singing for awhile. Saul said to Sebastian, "That proves, seeing the psychiatrist helped. Psychotherapy is a good thing."

Inspector Bradford, the hotel security officer, just approached Sebastian and said, "It's good to see you again." Sebastian told him likewise and they shook hands and talked a bit. He then asked Inspector Bradford how Gerard, the manager of the Ultimate Inn, was doing. The inspector told him he's doing well and he's around the Inn somewhere tonight. The inspector then called Gerard on his cell phone and told him Sebastian was at the bar. After that call, Gerard was soon on his way over to see him. He spotted Sebastian and went over to him and said, "I haven't seen you in awhile." They shook hands and Sebastian asked, "Who was the manager here before you, Gerard?" He said, "It was the 27 year old Pierce who was murdered." Sebastian then asked him if he ever heard of Pierce spending a lot of time talking with anyone in the Inn or dating them. Gerard told Sebastian that he heard about Pierce dating several women and Officer Martin investigated them and other people who knew Pierce and they were all cleared. Sebastian said, "Well, somebody somewhere does know who murdered Jenny and Pierce."

Sebastian was happy to see Gerard and Inspector Bradford but they soon said goodbye and went about their business. Saul then asked Sebastian if he wanted another drink. He answered, "No. I have to leave now." Phoebe suddenly approached Sebastian and said, "I can't believe I'm singing again! Thanks to you, Sebastian." He told her he's happy she is back singing but now he's just about to leave and he'll see her another time when he drops in the Ultimate Inn lounge. She then left smiling.

Sebastian got up to leave and said, "I'll see you later, Saul." "See you next time, Sebastian."

A few days later, Sebastian was at the police station and had just started talking with Officer Martin who was at his desk. The officer said, "I have good news, Sebastian. We are holding Alfred for the alleged robbery and for the triple homicide because your rival Sam came in recently with more news and signed an affidavit." Sebastian said, "Oh." The officer then told him that Sam claims he recently overheard Alfred, who was drunk again, telling his friend Dex that he wished he hadn't gone back to the mansion a second time to rob because Jenny and Pierce were home and caught him so he had to shoot them. Sebastian was shocked at that news. He said, "Officer Martin, I just came here to tell you the latest news I just received from Jenny's ghost telling me, again, she knows who murdered her and Pierce! That's big news!"

Sebastian told Officer Martin that he senses it was someone close to Jenny and Pierce who murdered them. The officer told him that news from Jenny's ghost is interesting but he needs more proof. Alfred will be going to court to answer for robberies and murders. He added that Alfred most likely murdered Jenny's mother Shannon and robbed her. They're going to see if they can get him to confess to all three murders, if not, they'll get him on one. He has been arraigned and is being held without bail. Sebastian remained silent.

Officer Martin told Sebastian that he would be the one to be honored because he was first to report the news of how he overheard Alfred telling his friend Dex he had to murder Shannon because she saw him, and then he robbed the mansion. Sebastian told him he just doesn't feel it was Alfred that committed all three murders.

As Officer Martin went on, he told Sebastian that they have three witnesses and they'll offer Alfred a plea-bargain to get him to confess. He also thanked Sebastian for his new information. When they were finished talking, they stood up and said goodbye and Sebastian left looking pensive.

Later on, at the mansion, Sebastian called the love of his life, Katherine, and asked her to come over for awhile tonight to cheer him up. They can have dinner together and talk about their future more. She agreed to and will definitely be there for dinner to see her man.

It was soon early evening and Katherine and Sebastian were in the dining room eating homemade salmon pie with a homemade crust which Katherine made. It was his first time having it and he loved it. He said, "I hope there's some left over for me to have another day." She smiled at him as she looked lovely today with her shoulder length blonde hair and nice eyes. He always wears something sharp and his good looks and brown wavy hair gives him charisma.

While Katherine and Sebastian are still eating, he said, "I miss you, Katherine. I can't wait until we get married and live together." She responded, "I feel the same way as you, Sebastian. I have everything ready for the wedding and I hope you'll like my gown." He told her he knows she'll look beautiful. He then told her he'll be wearing a tuxedo with a vest that he has purchased and it is being altered to fit him. She said, "Oh, I know you'll look handsome." They're not going on a honeymoon until after they move to his home in New York and she can hardly wait for that day.

Sebastian and Katherine were finished their salmon pie and are having a large salad. They're not having dessert because they just want fresh fruit with wine later.

Later on, in the living room, Katherine and Sebastian were standing while embraced and kissing passionately. Within seconds, they were on the burgundy velvet sofa and moving around a lot wanting the ultimate thrill but it wasn't going to happen on the sofa. She said, "Let's play a game just like when we were kids. It's called hide and seek." He laughed and then said, "Okay, let's." Sebastian first went to the bathroom and when he came back into the living room, Katherine was gone. He knew the game had started.

Sebastian was looking all over the first floor for Katherine and calling out, "Katherine! Katherine!" She wouldn't answer. He looked in the laundry area, then in the butler's quarters, then in the extra bathroom but there was no Katherine. In the living room, he went and looked behind both Victorian mahogany wing armchairs and she wasn't there. It is a huge living room so he even looked in back of both burgundy velvet sofas and there was no Katherine. He looked in Jenny's bedroom closet and still no Katherine.

Sebastian then went to the second floor looking for Katherine. He checked all three bathrooms first. He went into the sewing room, the maid's quarters and then Shannon's bedroom and saw no Katherine. There were two guest bedrooms left to look in so he figured she must be in one of them unless she's in the attic or cellar.

While slowly heading towards one of the bedrooms, Sebastian heard something moving around. He didn't know if it was a ghost or Katherine. He went into the bedroom and looked around and there was no Katherine so he left. While he headed for the last bedroom, he thought out loud and said, "I hope she didn't go up into the attic alone." He walked into this last bedroom and there she was propped up with a big pillow and smiling at him. He smiled and then joined her and they started taking their clothes off. Within seconds, they were under the sheets making love and heading to ecstasy.

It was still May and Charlie, the gardener, was in the yard daily enjoying himself planting and taking care of the bushes. He also mows the lawn and there's a lot of it. Sebastian went outside to talk with him and Charlie seemed to like that. He told Sebastian he needs to trim some branches on a few trees and Sebastian said, "I don't know anything about that. Why don't you show me how to do that" Charlie gladly showed him. Sebastian was suddenly up on a ladder trimming a few tree branches and got a kick out of it. It was such a nice sunny day to be gardening or landscaping.

Sebastian asked Charlie if he'd like some bottled water or a beverage but he didn't want any. Charlie then asked, "How did you like that old book you borrowed from me referencing the first tenants in this mansion?" Sebastian told him he found it interesting how the first tenant's son, Oscar, was murdered by his wife for having sexual affairs behind her back. She was a suspect but died awaiting trial. Charlie said, "That's what I mean. This place is definitely spooky and that first murder might have something to do with it." Sebastian told him he has a good point. They soon said goodbye.

Back at the mansion, Sebastian was in the kitchen making a cup of tea and going to have it with Katherine's cookies she left. He suddenly stopped what he was doing because he was startled. Jenny's mother Shannon's pale lifelike ghostly apparition was three feet in front of him near the stove. She's in her 50s, has gray hair and is wearing a housedress and is staring at Sebastian. He said, "Shannon, I know you're looking for your daughter Jenny but someone murdered her and I'm sorry your spirit is not in touch with hers but it will someday." Shannon cried out, "Jenny! Jenny! Oh Jenny! I miss you!" She started sobbing and then she suddenly and swiftly disappeared right in front of his eyes. He yelled, "Shannon! Come back!" She was gone. He is so amazed at how these ghosts communicate with him.

In the evening, Sebastian was at his desk reading his red book and worked into the late evening hours documenting news his rival Sam gave to the police about Alfred being the sole murderer of the triple homicide.

While Sebastian continued reading his red book, he suddenly heard a lot of racket coming from the attic so he quickly went up there. When he opened the door, there was a fierce wind along with a shrill noise and he felt the presence of a spirit. Small boxes were blowing all around with some things flying in the air as though a cyclone hit the attic. While the wind kept blowing, the mannequin was knocked down and he could see it on the floor with only its feet showing from behind a box. He then saw a window open so he went to it and noticed there was no wind outside yet there was wind in the attic. He closed it but the wind continued in the attic for awhile, then stopped and he sensed the spirit was gone. He also knows he never left the window open and wonders if spirits will ever stop haunting the mansion.

He cleaned up the attic and stood the mannequin back up and it looked the same while still wearing Jenny's lavender blue nightgown. He looked at the nightgown which brought back memories to him of the bathroom where she left it, then they went into the shower and made love. He looked at the rocking chair but didn't sit on it because he knows a spirit may come back and rock it fast. He then left the attic.

Sebastian was soon in bed with his hands behind his head thinking of when he'll get more information from Jenny.

The next day, Sebastian went to his desk to document the latest news of how the presence of a spirit caused a windstorm in the attic. His red book is quite full now.

While still at his desk, Sebastian meditated on the friends and acquaintances that Jenny and Pierce had when they were alive. He started with Vicki, the redhead masseuse, who was engaged to Pierce before he met Jenny. She was cleared by police and soon moved with her mother and father to Los Angeles where they planned to retire. At that time, Vicki thought it was an opportunity for her to chase her dream of becoming a cosmetologist. She and her family haven't been heard from since they moved from Revere, MA.

Saul, the bartender, has already told Sebastian that a blonde woman spent a lot of time talking with Pierce and sometimes would leave with him. He had a few women who frequented the Ultimate Inn when he was manager and dated them. When he blew them off, maybe one sought revenge.

Sebastian then thought of the bookstore where Jenny worked and wondered if she had an admirer there that she wasn't interested in and it evolved into a jealous rage of revenge. He thinks that could have happened. For the second time, he went to the bookstore where she worked and asked management about the employees they had while Jenny worked there. He was told she had regular customers she talked with but no one noticed her having a romance with any except Pierce. She could have had a stalker who watched her come and go to work, and, in his sick mind, broke in her mansion when he knew she was there with Pierce.

Sebastian has checked out every scenario he could think of. He knows information from Jenny or Pierce is his only hope to solve this murder mystery.

The long afternoon at the desk ended for Sebastian and he went and sat on an armchair with a soft drink before dinner. He suddenly thought of something that might be helpful in finding Jenny and Pierce's murderer. He thought to himself about Pierce's long lost brother who was living in Florida and broke. Could his envy of Pierce being a manager of the Ultimate Inn and having a girlfriend who lives in a mansion cause him to go to Marblehead Neck to murder him. And Jenny happened to be in the same room with him so he shot them both. It's possible. He needs to know where the brother is now so he can be tracked down. He looked into it and found the brother died before Pierce as murdered.

Sebastian was soon eating his delicious lamb dinner in the dining room and having some red wine with it. He kept thinking about Pierce's long lost and down-and-out brother in Florida all through his meal and wondered how he died.

After dinner and well into the evening, Sebastian was on the burgundy velvet sofa with a pillow behind his head and thinking of other possible suspects. Right now, he can't come up with anyone else other than Pierce's brother who maybe, before he died, hired someone to kill Pierce. He soon took a shower in Jenny's bathroom and then went to her bed early. He likes to call it her bed and her shower even though she's not alive anymore and only there in spirit. It was hard for him to get to sleep tonight as he tossed and turned right into the morning hours. When he fell asleep, it was time to get up.

The next day, Sebastian was at the cemetery where Jenny, her boyfriend Pierce and her mother were laid to rest. He is sitting in front of Jenny's gravestone and hoping for a bit of news. He thought of how beautiful she is when he sees her as a ghost and how gentle she is. He knows she must have been a beautiful person in life, physically and spiritually.

While Sebastian continued to think of Jenny, he had a strong sense that this was going to be a special day. As he kept staring at her gravestone, the scent of gardenias suddenly filled the air and he said, "She going to appear here." Within several seconds, Jenny's pale lifelike ghostly apparition was in front of her gravestone and was as beautiful as ever as she stared at him. This time, she was wearing a sheer white nightgown which was long and loose-fitting. A light breeze was blowing her gown around along with her long light brown hair as she looked angelical.

Sebastian is almost speechless because she never leaves the mansion other than her last appearance which was in his car. He suddenly said, "Jenny! Oh Jenny, I'm so happy to see you. Tell me the name of your murderer. You told me you knew who murdered you and Pierce." He waited for her response. While staring at him, she softly said, "I love you, Sebastian." He suddenly heard three gunshots and Jenny immediately bent over slightly while gasping. He then saw blood coming from the gunshot wounds to her chest as she faintly mumbled, "The murderer is, unh, unh, unh." As he stared at her, she swiftly disappeared with the gardenia scent. He knows it was a flashback of when she was murdered and she didn't have the chance to give him the murderer's name.

Sebastian has made more progress again. Jenny's ghost started to tell him who it was that murdered her and Pierce but her message became a flashback of her actually being murdered. But where was Pierce?

Another appearance of Pierce might help but Sebastian hasn't seen his ghost for awhile and he doesn't know when or where any of these ghosts will appear. He's going back to the mansion feeling deeply moved because he witnessed Jenny being shot. That's very big news!

Back at the mansion, Sebastian kept thinking about the shocking apparition he just saw at the cemetery of Jenny getting shot. It made him sad. Her ghost appeared in front of her gravestone which surprised him and he almost got the murderer's name. To him, he thinks there's more to come from Jenny's ghost and it may happen like he initially sensed it would. He knows it's not just because he's a powerful psychic medium and clairvoyant, it's also his persistence.

Sebastian is at his desk now documenting all the new cemetery news in his red hardcover book and also on the computer. This means more news to give to Officer Martin who is kind of skeptical about believing in ghosts.

After pausing for a moment, Sebastian looked at the shadows on the wall of tree branches he often sees caused by sunlight coming through the windows. He loves looking at them when the branches have leaves on them. It's a beautiful sight and it gives him a nice little break from his writing.

While still at his desk, Sebastian thought about what it takes to reach a goal. He knows the goal must be reasonable, you need to have faith in it 100% even though another person doesn't agree, you need to be very knowledgeable of the work you're doing, persistent, being in the right place at the right time with your idea, and, have it in the hands of someone who is interested. Most of all, he knows from experience that persistence can make a major change in anyone's life.

After a full day at his desk, it was time for Sebastian to relax so he got a bottle of water and sat on a chair thinking of his day's accomplishment. He can't wait to tell Katherine the latest news about Jenny's ghost at the cemetery so he decided to call her. After letting her phone ring over and over again with no answer, he left her a message to call him.

While Sebastian was in the middle of making himself a cup of coffee, his cell phone rang and it was Katherine, the love of his life. He answered it and said, "Hi, sweetheart!" Katherine softly said, "Hi, darling. Aren't we being romantic with pet names?" He told her he loves romantic name calling and that he also misses her. He also told her about his new progress he made while talking with Jenny's ghost at the cemetery. Katherine said, "Wow! That's different! That reminds me, Sebastian, I want to talk about a few things with you. I'll tell you what they are when I see you. Maybe this weekend." He told her the suspense will be on his mind until he knows what she wants to talk about. Then, in a humorous way, he said, "Psychics don't know everything!" "That's true, Sebastian." After they chatted a little longer and told each other I love you, they called it a night.

15

EARTHQUAKE

While it's still May and the flowers are blooming in front of the mansion and other areas, it makes the gardener happy. Sebastian went outside to look at the flowers and heard the lawnmower so he looked for Charlie in the back of the mansion. He saw him and yelled, "Charlie!" Charlie stopped the lawnmower for a few seconds and asked, "How are you, Sebastian?" "I'm fine and I like the flowers. You did a good job." Charlie smiled and then went on with his lawn-mowing as Sebastian walked around looking at the landscape.

In awhile, Sebastian went inside the mansion and made himself a cup of coffee and sat in the kitchen sipping it. He suddenly heard some noise in the dining room as though someone was in there. He left his coffee and rushed into the dining room and there was a ghost floating around the room fast while the chandelier was swinging. Sebastian stood still and watched it but couldn't tell who it was because this ghost sighting was pale and shadowy. The other ghosts he has seen, in another rooms, were not shadowy. They were pale lifelike ghostly apparitions. He also noticed the china cabinet door was open. He then thought the ghost must have flown out of the china cabinet and maybe that's the one he sees in back of his reflection when he looks in the mirror in the china cabinet. He thinks it might be the first tenant, Oscar.

While the ghost continued to move around the dining room table and hit the chandelier which made it swing back and forth, Sebastian stared at it and yelled, "Who are you?" There was no response so he asked again, "Who are you? Are you Oscar?" The ghost didn't answer and kept moving around. All of a sudden, it swiftly flew back into the china cabinet and disappeared as the door shut by itself. Sebastian looked in the china cabinet and couldn't see any ghost in it. He then looked in the mirror in the cabinet and he couldn't see a ghost in back of his reflection like he has in the past. This is the sixth ghost and he thinks it might be, Oscar, the first tenant who lived in this mansion with his parents who had it built in 1850. They later died, then Oscar married and lived in it with his wife who murdered him in 1934. He hopes that this ghost returns with clues to all the mansion murders.

Back at his desk, Sebastian documented the latest ghost sighting in the dining room. He wants it known what happened at the mansion while he lived in it for over a year writing about the 2006 triple homicide in Marblehead Neck.

When it was time for Sebastian to end his day of work, he got a bottle of water and sat on a chair and had crackers, cheese and grapes. He'll be seeing Katherine tomorrow.

It's Saturday evening and Katherine is at Sebastian's mansion for the weekend and they're casually dressed and staying in. She always looks good with her shoulder length blonde hair and her beautiful eyes, and Sebastian's hair adds to his good looks. It's brown and wavy and there's often a strand or two on his forehead which gives him sex appeal. Tonight, he knows she has something she wants to talk about.

While Sebastian and Katherine are standing in the living room holding lead crystal glasses filled with soft drinks, she said, "We need to talk, Sebastian. Let's sit on the sofa." He responded, "Okay, lets. I know you had something you wanted to talk about and I want to hear it."

Katherine and Sebastian went over to the coffee table and put their glasses on it and then sat on the burgundy velvet sofa next to each other. He said, "Tell me what's on your mind, Katherine." She looked deep into his eyes and said, "Sebastian, I'm going to get to the point. When was the last time you made love with Jenny's ghost?" He didn't expect her to ask that question so he paused and then told her she has to understand that he doesn't try to make love with Jenny's ghost, she suddenly appears and seduces him to make love with her. And even though he has unusual power, she overpowers him when she wants to make love and she wins. Katherine yelled, "What!" He then told her he found out that making love with a ghost is equally as satisfying as in the world of the living, except, in the world of ghosts, it is strange love pleasure because of the spiritual power that ghosts have. He added that he wants Katherine to know all this because she and lots of other people will be reading it in his book someday. He wants the living people to know what he experienced with a ghost and the powers they have that the living people don't have. He then paused and stared at Katherine as she was speechless.

The Ghost And Sebastian

Sebastian stunned Katherine by telling her about his love making with Jenny's ghost and knew it made her feel sad but wanted her to know about it. He didn't mention that there wouldn't be any more love making with Jenny's ghost once he moves out of the mansion. At the moment, they are silent.

Katherine is so angry and steaming because Sebastian told her that making love with a ghost is equally as satisfying as on earth but it's strange with a ghost and he likes it. While they're still sitting, she started questioning him on a few things. She loudly asked, "When was the last time that you made love with Jenny's ghost?" He quickly blurted out, "Near late January." She became more angry as she went on and asked him, "And when was the last time you were with her?" He blurted out again, "In April in my car but we didn't make love." Katherine went wild and quickly got up from the sofa and started pacing the floor. He got off the sofa and stood still watching her. He asked her, "Do you want me to lie to you?" She paced the floor while her face was quite red.

While Sebastian waited for Katherine to talk, she soon stopped pacing the floor and went up close to his face and yelled, "Just before you got engaged to me you had made love with Jenny's ghost! And after we were engaged you were with her in your car! We had only been engaged two months, and, during that time, you were in your car with Jenny's ghost and most likely made love! Are you crazy?" Sebastian put his arms around her but she pushed his arms away. She pulled her engagement ring off and threw it across the living room. He grabbed her and held her arms and yelled, "Katherine! No! don't do this!" She then sat on a wing armchair and he sat on the other one.

Katherine was suddenly silent but looking angry and steaming while she stared at Sebastian who was sitting across from her. He tried to explain that he's not a liar. She appreciated that but doesn't like what he said because it hurts. She suddenly blurred out, "I don't want a man who tells me that making love with a ghost is equally as satisfying as in the real world, except, with a ghost, it's also strange and he likes it! You're a fool, Sebastian!" She quickly got off of the wing armchair and he got off of his and grabbed her arms and embraced her. She pulled away yelling, "This engagement and wedding is off!" She stormed out of the mansion.

Sebastian hurried and caught up with Katherine but she quickly got in her car and started speeding away. He was unable to talk to her again. He stood there watching her speed down the street and then he slowly walked back into the mansion with his head down feeling and looking sad. He's thinking of what a night it was for him and Katherine and what will they do now, after they have made all those wedding plans. While in the living room, he's looking all over the floor for the expensive diamond ring she threw across the room. He is presently unable to find it and plans on looking for it again tomorrow.

Sebastian then started thinking as he paced the floor to see if he could calm down after this awful evening. Besides him having a problem trying to find Jenny and Pierce's murderer, he now has this problem, the wedding is called off! He then said out loud, "What a bad night this was."

Sebastian soon went to the sofa and put a pillow behind his head. He kept on thinking of how the night turned out so bad and the wedding is now off. This is the love of his life and he lost her. He's almost devastated and is wondering how he'll get over this. He got up again to pace the floor awhile and then he went back to the sofa. This time, he fell asleep on the sofa and slept there all night.

The next morning, Sebastian was not happy. He was feeling very bad knowing that Katherine broke off their engagement and their wedding which was about to take place in two and a half months. He's wondering what he can do about it. He said out loud, "And now I know what kind of temper Katherine has." Sebastian went and made his breakfast of just coffee and toast and had it in the kitchen while thinking of her. He slowly forced the toast down as he didn't have much appetite.

After his breakfast, Sebastian just had to go out somewhere, anywhere, just to feel better. He's already thinking of calling Katherine later today to see if she is still through with him but he wants to give her a chance to think about their breakup. He headed out to his car to drive around Marblehead Neck with no particular place in mind. He ended up at Crocker Park and then went and sat down and looked at the sailboats. They did look beautiful with their huge sails slightly blowing in the wind and it took his mind off of Katherine for a few seconds.

Sebastian then strolled over to the tea room to see the tea leaf reader. He is desperate. He's sitting at a small table with tea in front of him and sipping it fast so he can have his tea leaves read. The large female tea leaf reader, Annabel, came over to him and sat down and read Sebastian's tea leaves. She told him that he's heading for deep water and needs to be strong. The reader was silent for a few seconds while reading his tea leaves. She then told Sebastian that he may find peace eventually but has a long road ahead of him to sort many things out and make the right decisions. She finished reading his tea leaves and he found the reading to be pretty much like the way his life was going but he's taking the reading lightly. He thanked Annabel and gave her a generous tip and then ordered a cup of tea and a muffin.

On the same day Sebastian had his tea leaves read, Katherine was at her office trying to concentrate on her real estate work but she couldn't. She left work early because she kept getting teary eyed. When she got home in Marblehead, she cried and cried and her eyes were all red.

Katherine went to lie on her sofa and think how she has to return her wedding gown and hoping they'll accept it back. All the wedding plans have to be canceled, such as, the church where the wedding ceremony was to take place, the place of the reception, the invitations, the wedding cake and the food catering service. After she cried a little, she said out loud, "Sebastian, how could you have done this to me? You were the love of my life. For the first time in my life, I fell in love!" She cried again. She thought of seeing Dr. Louis, the psychiatrist, to get over this awful feeling.

Sebastian soon arrived at his mansion after having his tea leaf reading and parked in his driveway. He got out of his car and walked slowly towards his front door with his head down looking sad. Charlie was working on the garden and saw him and yelled, "Hi, Sebastian!" Sebastian looked at him and sadly said, "Hi, Charlie." He then continued walking slowly to his door. Charlie knew something wasn't right with him so he paused while looking concerned.

Inside the mansion, Sebastian was not in the mood to work on his book because he couldn't get his mind off of how Katherine broke up with him and canceled their wedding plans. He's just moping around like it was the end of the world. He took a cold shower to see if he could snap out of it but it didn't work. He's thinking of calling his good friend Alan, the movie producer. He recently told Alan he was getting married and now he has to tell him Katherine broke up with him. He thinks Alan may be able to cheer him up.

While Sebastian is sitting on a chair, he is on his cell phone talking to his good friend Alan and telling him about Katherine breaking up with him. Alan said, "I'm sorry to hear that, Sebastian, but your life isn't over! Sometimes awful things happen in life but we find the strength to go on. And I know you can do it! You're strong!" Sebastian told Alan he appreciates his words of comfort and is glad he called him. Alan told him to call him anytime because they're good friends and he hates to see anyone in sad situations. Sebastian thanked him again for his kind words and told him he's a special person. In awhile, they ended the call.

Sebastian still wasn't able to work on his book. He appreciated what Alan said to him but he's thinking of also seeing the psychiatrist again. He knows that venting his emotions to someone in the field of psychiatry is the best therapy for anyone, even though a friend may be comforting.

A week later, Sebastian was on the couch in Dr. Louis' office in Marblehead. The doctor sat nearby with his pad and pen. Sebastian said, "Dr. Louis, the terrible breakup with my fiancée, Katherine, is killing me inside. She asked me when I made love with Jenny's ghost, and, when I told her, she almost went berserk." Sebastian paused and the doctor said, "Go on." Sebastian then told the doctor that he wanted to be honest with Katherine so he told her how Jenny's ghost surprises him and seduces him and her force is unstoppable. And, from experience, he now knows making love with a ghost is the best love a man can ever have because it's so powerful and strange. It is nothing like it is in the real world. He paused while noticing Dr. Louis' eyes pop. He then went on and told the doctor that after Katherine heard that, she snapped and broke off with him. She threw her engagement ring across the room and stormed out of the mansion and he has been so sad ever since because she was his only love.

Dr. Louis said, "Yes, you have a problem, Sebastian. And that's quite interesting about love making with a ghost." Sebastian told the doctor that he is only being truthful. The doctor told him that he should try calling her every once in awhile. She may be able to get over the love making he had with Jenny's ghost. He went on and told Sebastian to let Katherine know that he won't be living in the mansion much longer and what happened was in another world and not in the real world. The doctor offered him sedatives but he refused them. They're both aware that time heals pain with or without medication for some people. He then got off the couch.

Dr. Louis went and sat at his desk while Sebastian sat on a chair across from him. The doctor asked him if he wanted to make another appointment but Sebastian told him he'd call him if he feels he needs one. He thanked Dr. Louis and they both said goodbye and shook hands.

A few days went by and Sebastian decided to call Katherine to see if she would talk to him but he waited until evening when he was relaxed. He later sat on a chair and called her. She answered her phone and softly said, "Hello." He said, "Hi, Katherine, I'm surprised you took my call. How are you?" She sadly said, "I'm not well. I'm having a hard time getting over this breakup and wedding cancellation." He asked her if she might change her mind and get back with. She said, "I'm afraid not, Sebastian." She then was silent and he was shocked that she said that. He thought maybe she'd change her mind but she didn't. He then asked her if he could call her once in awhile and she said, "No, Sebastian. This is too hard for me. You were my life and it's over." He told her he was sorry for hurting her. He wanted to be honest with her. She asked and he told her the truth. He told her that the ghosts are in another world and it'll be over soon because he'll be moving out of the mansion in just a couple of months. She remained silent for a few moments and then said, "I'm hanging up now, Sebastian." She did and he was stunned at that too. He now knows how stubborn Katherine is besides having a bad temper, but nothing like Samantha's.

The next day, Sebastian thought it would be good if Katherine saw Dr. Louis, the psychiatrist. He may be able to help her see things another way. That evening he called her but she wouldn't answer her phone so he left a message telling her he doesn't mean to bother her but he thought maybe she might want to see his psychiatrist that he occasionally sees. He told her that Dr. Louis is very good and then left his number and hung up. Somehow, Sebastian feels better now that he has left a message on Katherine's answering machine. He said to himself, "Who knows, maybe she'll go and see Dr. Louis."

The day dragged on for Sebastian. When it got late in the afternoon, he suddenly got in the mood to work on his story so he went to his desk and started reading his hardcover book. He then went on his computer and looked up different information about ghosts because he keeps wishing he could make them give more clues. He spent awhile on that subject and then started typing in some notes from his red hardcover book. All of a sudden, his cell phone rang and he quickly jumped up and ran across the room to answer it. He said, "Hello!" There was no answer. He was disappointed because he thought maybe it was Katherine. He went back to his desk and worked on his book.

It was soon 6:00 p.m. and time for Sebastian to stop working. He got a bottle of water and some crackers and cheese and then sat on a wing armchair to relax after working on his book all day. He finds this chair is one of the best places to relax other than a sofa or bed.

A few days later, Katherine was in Dr. Louis' office. He was sitting at his desk while she sat across from him looking lovely wearing a pink suit. He was so pleased to meet her because he knew she was Sebastian's ex-fiancée. He asked, "How can I help you today, Katherine?" She said, "I know Sebastian comes to see you and he suggested I see you. I thought about it and so here I am." He asked her to lie on the couch and she did and he sat in his usual place nearby.

The doctor asked Katherine if she had a happy life and she told him she was sad when she lost her mother and father years ago, then she had a serious boyfriend and it didn't work out. Then things changed when she rented the mansion to Sebastian who turned out to be the love of her life. But while living in the mansion, he was making love with Jenny's ghost while they were engaged and she couldn't handle that.

Dr. Louis never mentioned his conversations he had with Sebastian because it's confidential. He went on and told Katherine that ghosts are in another world, therefore, Sebastian making love with one is not as bad as she thinks it is. She and Sebastian live in the real world and that's all that matters. And making love with Jenny's ghost will soon be over and then they can go on with their future. He paused while waiting for Katherine's response. She said, "Dr. Louis, I wish I could accept your explanation but I can't. The mere thought of Sebastian sleeping with someone else almost devastates me, let alone a ghost." He told her that ghosts don't count because they're not in the real world. They're disembodied spirits who appear as ghosts and they do all sorts of things. Some are romantic and some are violent. He told her not to worry about Jenny's ghost because it will end soon.

Katherine then told Dr. Louis she'll try to get over Sebastian making love with a ghost. He said, "Good, you can sit up now." She did and went to a chair across from his desk. He was at his desk writing and stopped for a moment and said, "Katherine, if you and Sebastian are meant to be, it will be." He stared at her and then she said, "Thank you, Dr. Louis, and I'm glad I came to see you." He asked if she wanted to see him again but she told him she'd call him if she needs to. She got up to leave and he watched her walk towards the door. After she left, he thought out loud, "What a lovely lady. She would be a wonderful wife for Sebastian."

The Ghost And Sebastian

While Katherine was driving home, she looked relaxed as she said to herself, "I'm happy I went to see Dr. Louis but there will still be no reconciling with Sebastian. I just want to get over him." She continued on driving home. Once there, she made herself a cup of tea with no desire to eat and has no intentions of calling Sebastian to tell him this doctor news at the present time. She feels he'll sooner or later call her. If he doesn't, she'll call him to tell him about her Dr. Louis visit.

At the mansion, Sebastian's on Jenny's bed thinking about so many things and especially Katherine. He's having a rough time getting over how she broke off their engagement and he can't help but hope they'll get back together. His thoughts then shifted to dinner.

Sebastian's planning on sitting in the dining room to have his dinner today. He loves the atmosphere there and in the entire mansion because he likes the Victorian style. He soon went to his kitchen and prepared his dinner, after it was in the oven for awhile, the aroma coming from the kitchen was heavenly. He was roasting prime rib of beef with au gratin potatoes and will have fresh string beans to go with it. It looks like his appetite is back so he put the music on and that seemed to help him feel a little better. It also looks like he may survive the breakup.

Sebastian went and got a bottle of water before dinner, which he often does, and then walked around the mansion with it while looking at the paintings on the wall in the foyer. They're beautiful old oil paintings. Some are just landscapes and some are of women and children. When he finished looking at them for awhile, he went and looked at the paintings in the living room. While looking at them, the timer went off in the kitchen telling Sebastian his prime rib of beef and au gratin potatoes were ready. He went to the kitchen and opened the oven door and it smelled wonderful.

Before long, all the food was on the table. When Sebastian entered the dining room to eat, he couldn't resist looking in that china cabinet to see if he could see a ghost. Especially after he recently saw the china cabinet door open and a ghost was in the dining room floating around fast and hitting the chandelier. The ghost then flew back into the china cabinet and disappeared. Today, he didn't see any ghost so he'll probably enjoy his meal more. While slow music played softly, he sat down and relaxed having his delicious dinner of beef with vegetables and a glass of red wine. When he finished eating, he didn't want dessert.

Later that evening, Sebastian went outside and walked around the yard for awhile. He then went to the second floor of the mansion that leads to one of the outside wrap-around porches and sat down on a rocking chair. He's still trying to get over the awful breakup he and Katherine had. He thought of her and wondered if they'd ever get back together. On the other hand, Sebastian is strong and knows he will accept the painful fact because life goes on. He knows lots of people have been disappointed over relationships who break up before they get married. Then they go on with their life and find someone else and get married and find out that they married the right person. It was the better choice.

It's almost June and there has been no phone call from Katherine. Sebastian is working on his book and hopes to see Jenny's ghost soon to see if he can get some information from her. He would even like to see Pierce if he could because he also knows the murderer. Sebastian feels, if he doesn't get help from those two ghosts, he'll have to write his book without solving the triple homicide of 2006. But he'll still have a good book. Especially since he has had so many ghostly encounters and twist and turns in the search to find the murderer. He was so close to getting the murderer's name from Jenny's ghost when he saw her at the cemetery recently.

While writing in his red hardcover book, Sebastian was in deep thought when his cell phone rang which was on his desk next to him. He answered it and it was Katherine. He was surprised and told her he was so happy to hear from her. She told him that she decided to call him to tell him that she saw Dr. Louis, the psychiatrist. He said, "Katherine, I'm so happy you did that. How did you like him?" "Oh, I liked him and I would go back to him if I needed to." Sebastian told her that he hopes they can get back together again because he still wants to marry her. She said, "That won't happen, Sebastian. I'm sorry but that's how I feel." He was sad to hear that but then asked her to please call him once in awhile and she agreed to and soon they hung up.

Sebastian started thinking of Katherine and what she just said, therefore, he couldn't get back in the mood to work on his book. He decided to end his writing for the day. While he was on the sofa, he dozed off and had a clairvoyant dream of a lot of noise in the mansion, and, a terrifying storm was approaching. Then, the dream ended.

16

SOMETHING IS BREWING

This morning, after Sebastian was awakened by his dream, he got out of bed and put his pants on and went into the bathroom. He suddenly heard crashing sounds that were coming from the cellar. His clairvoyant dream from last night was unfolding.

On his way down to the cellar by the kitchen door, Sebastian felt negative energy around him as the crashing sounds continued. When he got to the bottom of the stairs, there was silence. Everything had been thrown from one end of the cellar to the other. He stood still while looking around to see if he could see a ghost or to feel the presence of a spirit that was causing the turmoil. Then, an apparition of a pale lifelike ghost was swiftly moving around throwing objects.

The Ghost And Sebastian

Sebastian took a good look at the ghost and saw that it was Pierce. He was tall, average build, about age 27 and wearing jeans and a blue striped shirt like he was wearing in his last apparition. Pierce's ghost now keeps throwing things in Sebastian's direction. While Sebastian dodged wooden objects, chairs and boxes that were flying, he continued to watch him swiftly moving around. Sebastian asked, "Pierce! What's the problem?" He then waited for his answer. Pierce's ghost stopped moving around momentarily as he stared at Sebastian and yelled, "I was murdered! Jenny and I were murdered! She was my love!" He then continued to move around. Sebastian yelled, "I know, Pierce! Tell me who murdered you and Jenny? Could it have been your redheaded ex-girlfriend Vicki who you were engaged to before you met Jenny, even though she was cleared?" Pierce's ghost stopped moving around and threw something heavy at Sebastian which hit him on his forehead and then stared at him and yelled, "It wasn't him! Help!" Pierce's ghost suddenly disappeared.

Sebastian is wondering if it was a man or woman who murdered Pierce and Jenny because Pierce's ghost just yelled to him, "It wasn't him!" Maybe he was trying to say it was a man. Messages from a ghost can be confusing. And, even though the murderer might be a man, he still doesn't have his name. Sebastian thought about the wreck in the cellar he has to clean up. His forehead hurts from Pierce's ghost throwing something at him and it's bleeding. Sebastian went upstairs and planned to have his cleaning service clean the cellar.

Sebastian walked around his mansion with a band-aid on his forehead and then went and sat down at his desk to document his latest encounter with Pierce's ghost.

Later on, Sebastian went outside and walked all around the mansion to get some fresh air and clear his head and to also have a change of scenery. The weather is warm now and it will get hot soon. He just had a thought that maybe he needs another yachting cruise but doesn't want to waste time.

Later on in the day, in the mansion kitchen, Sebastian prepared a light dinner which he will have later. It will be a salad with shrimp, tomato, peas and lettuce. He'll also have some crusty bread and red wine. After he finished preparing and refrigerating it, he got a bottle of water and went into the living room and sat on a chair to relax and be quiet so he can concentrate on the cellar event that just happened. He likes to meditate on events that have recently happened.

Sebastian soon could hear a lot of rumbling noise which sounded like a storm approaching. He looked out the window and the sky was gray and there were several threatening clouds that he could see. The other part of his clairvoyant dream of last night was coming true. He soon heard thunder and the wind picked up and then the rain began to pour down. He suddenly remembered that all the windows were open on the first floor so he hurried to the first one, and, while trying to close it, it wouldn't close. He also noticed how the strong winds were blowing everything around in the room. When he got to the second window, he couldn't close it. He went to another one and couldn't close it. He then said, "There's negative energy in this mansion that's causing this and I wonder whose."

Sebastian and everything else in the mansion's first floor was getting soaked from the rain coming in. After trying to shut the windows for a second time, they still wouldn't shut. He's positive this is the work of a very angry spirit. There is no ghost in sight so whose spirit is doing this, he'd like to know. The mansion soon looked like a hurricane hit it.

The candlesticks blew off of the mantel and several pictures had blown over. Even Jenny's bedroom was a wreck from wind and rain and her lamps were knocked over. It also looked like a cyclone hit the first floor.

To make matters worse, Sebastian just heard noise in the dining room so he quickly went to check on it. When he got there, he didn't see a ghost in the room but the china cabinet door was open. He now wonders if this spirit is a new strange one that he knows nothing about and if the ghost he once saw flying around in the dining room and hitting the chandelier was Oscar's, or, are they both Oscar's spirit and ghost. They could be because they show up at separate times. Oscar lived in the mansion in the late 1800s until 1934 when he was murdered by his wife with an ax.

While the bad storm continues outside and inside the mansion, Sebastian is still in the dining room and feeling the presence of a spirit. The cabinet door is still open so he's waiting for the spirit to go back in it. Sebastian suddenly felt a breeze and then all of a sudden the cabinet door slammed shut. However, he's a little uncomfortable with this spirit and the ghost he once saw in here. He doesn't know what they are up to other than coming out and going in the china cabinet and slamming the door. And when the ghost floats around the dining room and hits the chandelier, Sebastian senses that chaos is coming. He then left the dining room.

The entire first floor of the mansion is a mess because of the storm which hasn't stopped yet and the windows can't be closed. Sebastian then went upstairs to see if those windows were closed because that's the way he left them, and, when he got there, they were. He then went up to the attic and saw those windows were closed like he left them. It was only the first floor that an angry spirit wrecked. He is so restless because he's waiting for the storm to stop so he can see if he can close the windows on the first floor.

Sebastian looked out of his living room window and saw the storm was ending as the wind subsided, however, it was still windy in the mansion. While he stood still in the living room looking puzzled and his hair was blowing around, the wind gradually stopped in the mansion. He quickly went to each window on the first floor and was able to close every one of them. He said out loud, "That sure was caused by an angry spirit." He then went into the kitchen and poured himself a soft drink and sipped it while sitting on a chair. In awhile, he went into the dining room and had his light dinner which consisted of a large salad, crusty bread and wine, not knowing if Oscar's spirit or ghost would be coming out of the china cabinet while he eats.

Early the next day, Sebastian looked out the window and saw that it was a nice sunny day. He decided to hire his cleaning service to come in and clean the mess up on the first floor of the mansion that was caused by the storm. He's also having them clean up the cellar which Pierce's ghost wrecked earlier. He thinks it might take two or three days to clean up everything.

Within a few days, the first floor of the mansion and the cellar were in tip top shape, thanks to Sebastian's cleaning service. Today, he's in the mood to get out so he's planning to go to the library which he hasn't done for awhile. He loves being surrounded by books because knowledge is power and he also likes the quietness of the library. When he got there, he went and looked for books on the shelf that referenced stories of people who have had paranormal activity in their homes. He took a few books to a table and read for a couple of hours. When he finished, he wanted to drive around.

It was soon late afternoon and Sebastian was at his desk doing what he planned to do. He was taking a fresh look at his story from the beginning and up to his last entry.

While concentrating on his story, Sebastian's tea kettle was whistling. He got up and made a cup of tea and took it to his desk to sip while he read his story. After reading for several hours, he stopped but wants to continue reading tomorrow. He knows that sometimes you need to step back from something you're working on and get a change of scenery and then go back to it.

Later on, Sebastian called Katherine on his cell phone while he paced the living room floor. Her phone rang and rang and she finally answered it. Sebastian said, "I hope you don't mind if I call you once in awhile, Katherine." "No I don't mind but nothing has changed with the way I feel about us." He told her, if she's still firm about them not getting back together again, he still plans on dating someone because it's a way to get over a romantic breakup or anything. You can't go on depressed over something that's out of your control. A person needs to get over sadness. That means, out of sight, out of mind.

While Katherine and Sebastian continued the phone call, she agreed with his philosophy, of out of sight, out of mind. He told her it's how you get over pain. She snapped and said, "But I can't believe you're planning to sleep with someone else so soon! We've only been broken up a couple of weeks!" He said, "Katherine, you said it was permanent! How do I know if you'll ever change your mind! Meanwhile, I have to snap out of it! I can't go on feeling so hurt!" She told him that she hurts too. He then told her that you don't keep high fat foods in the house if you're trying to lose weight. And you also cut calories and workout. She became silent for a few moments and then slammed her cell phone down on a table and shut it off. He then said to himself, "I'm going to do what I have to do to get over her."

Sebastian then called Samantha, his friend and writer, who he often has trouble with because of her temper but then they reconcile. He told her he and Katherine are still broken up and asked if she wanted to get together and she accepted.

Within a few days, Sebastian and Samantha were in the Ultimate Inn coffee shop having coffee and a fig square with vanilla ice cream. They were sitting in a booth and both wearing jeans with colorful tops and Sebastian's gorgeous brown wavy hair had a strand of it on his forehead. Samantha is as beautiful as ever. Her shoulder length dark brown hair always looks good and her gorgeous blue eyes can only be described as hypnotic or magnetic. She draws you in with her eyes alone and then you notice all her other beauty which includes her curvaceous body. Her teeth are beautiful and she has confessed to Sebastian that they're porcelain. Sebastian sometimes thinks about their bad arguments. One was when she broke in his home with a key she secretly made from his key ring and he found her in his shower. He was outraged and threw her out. One of their other arguments was over her breaking his front teeth when she, allegedly, pushed him down while they were ice skating. Samantha's an alcoholic with a bad temper and Sebastian doesn't have those problems.

Veronica, the waitress, came over to Samantha and Sebastian's booth and she knows them from previous times when she served them. She's still attractive with long red hair and a bubbly personality and chews gum. She asked, "Is there anything else I can get you?" Sebastian said, "Just two more coffees," Veronica smiled at Sebastian, then started chewing her gum and left with her happy and bubbly spirit.

While Samantha and Sebastian sipped their coffee, she stopped and stared into his eyes and said, "I'm surprised you called me after your last explosion. You threw me out of your mansion because I got in with a key that I copied from your key chain." He told her that you can't blame anyone for having a fit over that and she better not ever do that again. What she did was breaking in and entering and you can get arrested for that. She said, "Okay, I know." He then asked, "Seriously, how did you get the key from my key chain?" She told him, while he was napping at her condo one time, she took his keys and copied the mansion's back door and front door key. He looked at her and thought of how much she needs help He then said, "That's breaking in a home! Don't ever do it again if you ever want to see me again!" She said, "Alright! Alright! Don't get so excited over it! It's a thing of the past! It won't happen again!" He told her that no one will associate with her if she breaks in their home.

Samantha and Sebastian soon left the coffee shop and were on their way to her condo for a change and it didn't take long for them to get there. They then sat out in her backyard for awhile at a table. While they each had their own chair, she suddenly got up and sat on his lap and started kissing him passionately on the lips and he didn't mind that. She then stood up and pulled him out of his chair and held him close and felt his body. But this time, he was not interested. He removed her hands from his body and started leaving her backyard without saying a word. As she stood at the table watching him leave, she had a menacing look in her eyes. She then made a fist with one hand and banged it on the table top because he rejected her.

Sebastian thought that making love with Samantha might help him get over his recent and painful breakup with Katherine but now realizes it won't. He can't get in the mood to make love with Samantha because he's thinking of how Katherine broke up with him and canceled their wedding.

Back at the mansion, on another day, Sebastian was in the sewing room on the second floor to see if anything looked different and suddenly noticed an envelope sticking out from behind a cabinet. He quickly pulled it out and saw it was addressed to Jenny and it was typed out. Before he sat on a chair to read it, he said out loud, "If I could only find some clue to who murdered Jenny and her boyfriend Pierce."

He opened the envelope and it consisted of a few lines that were typed out. He was surprised because it was a threat. The top of the page read, "2006." There was no month nor day. Down further, there were a few lines that were all in capital letters threatening Jenny. One read, "STAY AWAY FROM PIERCE OR YOUR DEAD!" There was no signature, although the envelope showed it was mailed in Marblehead. Sebastian thought he was getting somewhere now and is anxious to give this to the police. He took the letter downstairs and put it on his desk and then went to the kitchen and made tea and toast. He then sat in the kitchen having it while thinking of the letter he just read in the sewing room that threatened Jenny. He was thinking that it could have been a man or woman who murdered Jenny and Pierce. He then thought of scenario one. Maybe it was a woman who wanted Jenny dead and shot her so she could have Pierce but he got in the way and she accidentally shot him too. He thought of scenario two. Maybe it was a man who wanted Jenny to himself, and when he pointed his gun into the bedroom to shoot Pierce, he accidently shot Jenny and then quickly shot Pierce. While Sebastian thought about it, he finished his tea.

Sebastian then thought of Pierce's ex-girlfriend Vicki but she was cleared and she is now living on the west coast. He then thought that Pierce maybe had another girlfriend or Jenny had a secret admirer who stalked her and Pierce. Sebastian brought his dishes to the sink and left the kitchen and went to his desk to document the threatening short letter to Jenny. He now knows that the letter he just found may eliminate Alfred from being the murderer of Jenny and Pierce and their murders were maybe over a love triangle. Alfred was a thief who broke in the mansion to rob but Shannon caught him so he shot her. Also, the person who wrote the threatening letter may not have even been the murderer. It could have been someone else.

Sebastian is now so full of scenarios that he can't imagine there being anymore. He's thinking of taking a little break from all this and maybe go to the Ultimate Inn lounge for a change of scenery. Just then, there was a loud noise coming from the second floor so he left his desk immediately.

While Sebastian was walking upstairs to the second floor, the noise continued. When he got there, the noise was coming from the sewing room so he rushed into it and the room was a wreck with Jenny's letters scattered all around the room. Sebastian immediately felt the presence of a spirit in the sewing room. He sat on a chair and thought for a moment that the spirit may be trying to tell him something. Maybe the threatening letter he just found addressed to Jenny was from the actual murderer and not just the threat from someone else. Sebastian believes the spirit in the room with him knows he was looking through Jenny's letters.

Sebastian cleaned up the sewing room and put all the letters back in the box where they were. He's glad he already took the threatening letter to his desk which he will show the police. He doesn't feel paranormal activity in the room now.

A few days later, on a beautiful sunny day, Sebastian went to the harbor to walk around and maybe stop in the tea room for just something to eat and drink. It's a quaint little tea room with a warm and friendly atmosphere that has delicious homemade muffins and good coffee and tea. You can also have your tea leaves read. All around the harbor, there seems to be friendly people.

When Sebastian had enough of watching the harbor boats, he went to Crocker Park nearby which was having a flea market in one area of the park. It had many tables selling lamps, dishes, picture frames, a bronze bust of Beethoven and old memorabilia of artists. There were many people there and even a popcorn vender nearby. Sebastian slowly walked around and suddenly spotted Katherine. He was surprised to see her there alone. He went up in back of her and surprised her with a kiss on her cheek. She quickly turned to look at him and then asked, "What are you doing here?" He answered, "The same thing you're doing here. Just walking around." He immediately asked her if she changed her mind about them reconciling and she told him she will not change her mind. She also told him she wants to be alone now. She then walked away from Sebastian. He can't believe how she is so stubborn. He went on his way and walked around and soon left the park.

While driving back to his mansion, Sebastian thought of how strange it was to run into Katherine at the flea market and how they were both alone. He seems to be happy that they saw each other, even though she hasn't changed her mind about getting back with him. He also knows he's going to eventually have to date someone because Katherine might be serious about them never getting back together again. It has painfully sunk in to Sebastian that Katherine ended their affair because he made love with Jenny's ghost.

It's the next morning and Sebastian is on his way to the police station with more information for them. He seems to be getting bits and pieces of news every so often. It's like putting a jigsaw puzzle together.

After Sebastian arrived at the police station, he sat across from Officer Martin who is at his desk. The officer said, "It's good to see you again, Sebastian." Sebastian responded, "It's good to see you too." He then handed the officer Jenny's letter while saying, "Wait until you read this news and then tell me your thoughts.

Officer Martin read the letter Sebastian handed him and then said, "This is interesting information. I wonder why Jenny

The Ghost And Sebastian

didn't ever report this threatening letter that was sent to her with no signature when she was alive." Sebastian said, "I guess she didn't take it too seriously. Even though it's typed and has no signature, it's a bit of a clue." Sebastian then handed the officer the envelope the letter came in. He looked it over and said, "The envelope shows Jenny's name and address was typed on it so that's no help. But the envelope also shows it was mailed from Marblehead." Sebastian said, "Exactly." The officer told him he's aware that Alfred was from Marblehead and after the murders, he moved to Swampscott. Vicki, who was Pierce's ex-girlfriend, was from Revere and after the murders she moved to the west coast. However, this letter could have also come from any man or woman that had a romantic interest in Jenny or Pierce. Sebastian was in total agreement with Officer Martin.

The officer told Sebastian that the police have enough evidence to believe Alfred is responsible for Jenny's mother Shannon's murder and they have enough information to convict him. It's also possible he did the three murders. After pausing, he asked Sebastian, "Do you have any other news?"

Sebastian went on and told Officer Martin that he has important news from Jenny's ghost. While he was recently at the cemetery, he saw a lifelike ghostly apparition of her in front of him and he asked her who murdered her and Pierce. While he stared at her and she started to talk, he suddenly heard three gunshots and Jenny's ghost immediately bent over and mumbled, "Unh, unh." Her upper torso was full of blood while she was gasping and then she swiftly disappeared. The officer said, "You saw a flashback of her being murdered."

Officer Martin finds Sebastian's information startling and told him he believes in ghosts now. Sebastian went on and told the officer that almost the same thing happened when Pierce's apparition was in front of him and he asked him who murdered him and Jenny. He didn't hear gunshots, he just saw Pierce trying to tell him the murderer's name, then gasped over and over while he was slightly bent over. Officer Martin said, "It's sounds like you might get the name of the murderer out of Jenny or Pierce." Sebastian said, "Yes. My persistence is often the key to my success." The officer told him to continue asking them the same question. Sebastian said, "I intend to, as long as I'm living in the mansion which turned out to be a spooky one." Officer Martin smiled.

Sebastian went on and told Officer Martin how there has been several storms in the mansion caused by angry spirits. They've trashed the mansion so bad at times that he has had to have his cleaning service restore it back to normal. Officer Martin said, "You're a strong person to live in that mansion with all the paranormal activity you're telling me about." Sebastian told the officer that the paranormal activity is not harmful except for one time in the cellar when Pierce's ghost threw a board at him and it cut his forehead. The officer asked, "You got hit by a ghost? How can you live there?" Sebastian told the officer that he's not afraid.

It was time for Sebastian to leave the police station so Officer Martin wished him luck at his mansion and told him to be careful. Sebastian said, "Spirits or ghosts don't scare me." He smiled at the officer who smiled back and then he left the police station.

Back at the mansion, Sebastian feels good that he told the police officer his latest news and he now wants to go out tonight to relax at the Ultimate Inn lounge and have a good time. He likes saying hello to his friends there, such as Saul, Phoebe, Danny, Inspector Bradford and Gerard who is the Ultimate Inn's manager. Sometimes Sebastian sees Bruce, the waiter, and Chef André, if he's having dinner there. And he never forgets the waitress Veronica who is usually in the coffee shop but sometimes in the lounge.

It was soon late afternoon and Sebastian was planning to have his dinner, take a shower and then dress up in casual clothes and go to the Ultimate Inn. His dark brown wavy hair and good looks attract attention, especially women. And he's not only good looking, he's a warm person, an extrovert and the kind of guy that is comfortable in his own skin and everyone wants to be around him.

17

CALLING DR. LOUIS!

At the Ultimate Inn lounge, Danny, the piano player was wearing a small hat while playing a song and people were dancing and laughing. Sebastian had arrived and was sitting at the bar and looking comfortable with a soft drink full of ice. His friend Saul, the bartender, came over to him and asked, "How's your book coming along?" Sebastian told him he still doesn't have the murderer yet and hoping he will soon. Saul then told him that Phoebe has been singing a lot since she has seen Dr. Louis, the psychiatrist. Sebastian told him, if he ever needs a shrink, he's the doctor to see. He's very helpful and likeable. Saul said, "I'll keep that in mind." He then went and waited on someone else at the bar.

Phoebe suddenly came over to Sebastian and said, "Hi, Sebastian! How are you?" He told her he was just fine and asked her how she was. While standing, she told him she has been happy yet sad because she still doesn't have a boyfriend and she knows that being in her 30s is not the problem in finding one.

Sebastian told Phoebe to go back and see Dr. Louis and talk with him. She told him she intends to because his psychology may help her get a boyfriend and what good is life without love. Sebastian told her she has a good point but if it doesn't happen, life goes one. Maybe she'll get involved with some kind of work that will take her mind off of a boyfriend. Phoebe started to tear-up when she heard that so Sebastian invited her to sit next to him at the bar. She got up on the bar stool and he told her to order her favorite drink so she ordered a rum and coke with ice from Saul.

After Phoebe got her rum and coke with ice, she drank it rather fast and wanted another one. Sebastian told her she needs to wait awhile because she just drank her beverage too fast which will make her intoxicated. She told him not to worry about that because she can hold a lot of alcohol and food. He told her he still wants her to wait awhile. She said, "Okay, I will." She then smiled at him and he smiled back. He asked? "Are you okay?" She said, "Yes I am. And I want you to know that you're my type, Sebastian." He said, "Oh no, you can't have me. I'm too busy with life." She started to cry because of what he said and also because she was intoxicated. She suddenly fell off the bar stool. Sebastian quickly got up and slowly picked her up off the floor while she was very dizzy. He then slowly walked her over to a booth close by.

While Sebastian and Phoebe were sitting in a booth, he said, "Listen to me, Phoebe. I want you to go to Dr. Louis as soon as possible. You have a serious problem with alcohol and men it seems. Will you call Dr. Louis?" In a drunken-like state, she yelled, "Yes! Okay, I'll see him!" Sebastian asked her if she'd like to go to the sickroom and lie on the sofa for awhile and she yelled, "Okay!" He escorted her to the sickroom in the Ultimate Inn. He made sure that she did lie on the sofa and then he shut the door.

Sebastian was back at the bar now and telling Saul about Phoebe how she only had one rum and coke with ice and fell off the bar stool. Saul told him that he's not going to serve her any more drinks that have hard alcohol in them.

The Ultimate Inn lounge was packed now and Danny had his hat on while playing another tune and singing along with it. Some people were dancing and some were just sitting down drinking, talking and then laughing a lot.

It was soon getting near midnight and no Phoebe was in sight. Sebastian spotted the waitress, Veronica, who he loves talking with because of her bubbly personality and also finds her attractive. He went to her and told her about Phoebe in the sickroom and asked if she could check on her. Veronica did and came back and said to Sebastian, "She's out cold." He thanked her and went back to his seat at the bar where he told Saul about Phoebe.

Sebastian forgot to ask Veronica how Phoebe was going to get home so he called Veronica over and asked her about that. She offered to give her a ride home when she gets out of work in a couple of hours. Sebastian said, "Thanks so much, Veronica." She responded, "No problem, Sebastian." He then put $100 in her hand. She said, "You don't have to do that." He insisted that she take it and so she did and said, "Thank you very much." She smiled at him and then left.

About an hour later, the Ultimate Inn lounge was still full of people but Sebastian was tired so he said goodbye to his friend

The Ghost And Sebastian

Saul. He also went over to Veronica while she was at a table waiting on customers. He said, "Excuse me for interrupting you, Veronica, but I'm leaving now and I wanted to thank you again for taking care of Phoebe." She smiled at Sebastian and then said, "Okay, I'll see you the next time you stop in." He then left. Veronica looked at her customers and said, "Excuse me for the interruption. Can I take your orders?" After the customers gave their orders for drinks and lots of fries, Veronica walked away chewing gum.

Sebastian carefully drove back to his mansion with his radio on listening to love songs. He's not over the breakup yet with Katherine and he also knows playing love songs won't help him get over it but tonight he's playing them.

After arriving at his mansion, Sebastian parked in the driveway and then entered his rose foyer. He suddenly couldn't walk and just stood there and had a flashback of Jenny's ghost. He was thinking of when she met him in the foyer and they embraced and kissed passionately and she led him to the bathroom where he removed his clothes. She then removed her sheer lavender blue nightgown and escorted him into the shower for an erotic time. It was his third encounter making love with her. Her power makes him feel mentally and physically transported to her world, the world of ghosts.

Sebastian suddenly snapped out of it and made it through the foyer after having a flashback of Jenny's ghost. He went to his kitchen because he wants a sandwich before bed, maybe ham and Swiss cheese on a crusty bread with a little mayo and also a glass of cold milk. He prepared his night snack and had it in the kitchen. In awhile, it was time for him to get a good night sleep in Jenny's bed.

Days later, in Dr. Louis's office, Samantha was sitting on a chair across from the doctor while he was at his desk. She was wearing a hot-pink dress that was short and she had her legs crossed which made her dress look daringly short. She was still curvaceous with shoulder length dark brown hair and her beautiful blue eyes drew you in like a magnet. Dr. Louis asked, "Why are you here today, Samantha?" She said, "I can't seem to control my temper and sinister thoughts. The medication isn't working now." He asked her to lie on his couch so she did and he sat near her with his pad and pen.

While Samantha was on the doctor's couch, he looked at her and her hot-pink dress because she kept posing her legs in seductive ways. He said, "Samantha, I want you to keep your legs down straight." She said, "Oh come on, Dr. Louis. Can't you control yourself? Ha ha ha!" He got angry and reminded her she was in a doctor's office and this was serious business. And if she didn't stop posing her legs, he was going to stop having her for a patient. She got angry and jumped up off the couch and stood in front of him while dramatically moving her arms around and yelling, "You're what? I need help and you're going to throw me out?" The doctor got up and went to his desk and took out a bottle of pills and gave her two with some water and said, "Take these right away to calm down." She quieted down after she took the medication. He told her to get back up on the couch and she did.

After Samantha remained quiet, the psychiatrist then continued his analysis while Samantha kept her legs straight down. He told her he knows she's hiding something terrible that happened to her in her past and it mentally traumatized her. He paused as they looked at each other. He then went on and said, "Because you didn't get therapy, it caused you to be psychologically damaged. You can be cured to some extent if you tell me what happened to you in your past that upset you so much." She told him she couldn't tell him because it was too painful and there were also revengeful things she has done in her past. He said, "I want you to tell me everything, Samantha, so I can help you." She stared into space and it looked like her mind was far away.

Dr. Louis asked Samantha to get off of the couch and sit on a chair if she was not going to tell him about her painful past. She got off the couch and sat on a chair in front of his desk while he sat there staring at her a few moments. He started writing down a new prescription for her and he also told her he needs to see her in six weeks. She then stood up and took the prescription and said, "Thank you, Dr. Louis. I'm sorry I'm like this but I've been this way practically my whole life." He was sympathetic and told her he'd continue to help her. She suddenly winked at him and then gave him a smile. He said, "Samantha, you need to stop that! I'm a doctor and you're a patient!" She just stared at him. After he told her she could leave, she smiled at him again and then strutted out of his office swinging her hips while he watched her. After she left, he said out loud, "She's so beautiful. What a shame she is psychologically damaged." He opened his draw and reached in for a bottle of pills and took a couple with water nearby.

Samantha took a taxi back to her condo in Marblehead and soon arrived there and then called Sebastian. His phone kept ringing and ringing and there was no answer so she left a message saying, "Sebastian, it's Samantha. Call me because it's urgent." After that, she made herself some coffee and sipped it while she sat on her sofa and thought.

While still in deep thought, Samantha's phone rang and she quickly answered it and it was Sebastian. He asked her what was wrong and she told him she needs to see him.

It didn't take very long for Sebastian to arrive at Samantha's condo. While they're standing in her living room and facing each other, she said, "I just got back from seeing the psychiatrist and he explained what's wrong with me but he can't help me if

I don't tell him the terrible things in my past." Sebastian was sympathetic and put his arms around her and told her she should tell him. It's strictly confidential. He paused while noticing how drowsy she looked. He asked, "What medications are you on?" She told him it's something stronger than what she was taking. Dr. Louis told her she needs it to avoid getting physically out of control. She went on and told Sebastian how she lost it and jumped off of the couch and stood in front of the doctor and went into a rage. Sebastian told her she better take her medication and don't skip any and she thanked him for his comforting support.

Sebastian and Samantha went and sat on her sofa next to each other. He asked, "Why did you call and tell me it was urgent?" She embrace him and he pulled away and got off of the sofa and said, "Oh no, Samantha. We're not making love. I'm still trying to get over Katherine who is emotionally upset because I told her I made love with Jenny's ghost." Samantha got off the sofa and stood in front of him and asked, "Why did you tell her that? What do you mean, you made love with a ghost?" Sebastian told her that Katherine wanted to know more about his making love with Jenny's ghost and he wanted to be honest with her. Katherine got upset and broke off their engagement so now there won't be a wedding.

Samantha was staring at Sebastian and said, "I can't believe you made love with a ghost. How can that happen?" He answered, "It can happen and it did happen." They were both silent while staring at each other. He told her he was leaving and she can call him if it's urgent. She tried to give him a hug but he pushed her away and said goodbye.

On Sebastian's way back to his mansion, he thought about visiting some of Castle Rock Park that has castle-like homes which are near his Victorian mansion. He hasn't done that yet. He loves spending time at Crocker Park which has good views of the harbor and boats and so does Fort Sewall.

After visiting some of Castle Rock Park, Sebastian went to his mansion. He arrived there and saw Charlie near the backyard doing garden work and he looked like he was enjoying himself. When Sebastian walked towards him, Charlie said, "Hi, Sebastian. I have something to tell you." "What is it, Charlie?" While Charlie was digging in the soil, he stopped and said, "When Jenny was alive, she told me that she was afraid of someone who was threatening her. I just thought of that now." Sebastian asked him if he got the person's name but Charlie told him he didn't. He just told Jenny to report it to the police and then she walked away. Sebastian told Charlie to let him know if he thinks of anything else and then he left.

Sebastian headed over to his doorway while thinking of what Charlie said about hearing Jenny being threatened and wonders why Charlie just thought of that now. Sebastian thinks it's related to the threatening letter he just found to Jenny. He then went into the mansion and sat at his desk and documented more information.

It's time for Sebastian to end his day on the computer so he got a soft drink and poured it in a lead crystal glass and added ice to it. He thought of all of the fine bone china, flatware and stemware that was left in the mansion and it goes with the rental or purchase of the mansion. Of course, if anything gets broken, the tenant is responsible and must pay for all of it. So far, Sebastian hasn't broken anything yet. However, a spirit threw a candy dish across the room once at Samantha but it missed her and hit a mirror which broke along with the candy dish. Sebastian then paid for the damage and replacement even though a spirit caused it.

Sebastian went and sat on an armchair and thought about Katherine while he sipped his soft drink. He wishes she would call and tell him she wants him back. While thinking of her, his cell phone rang and rang while it was next to him on the table.

He finally answered it and it was his friend Alan. Sebastian said hello to him and asked him what was new. Alan said, "Sebastian, I just had a mild heart attack." Sebastian was alarmed and said, "Oh! Are you going to be alright?" Alan told him he's now on medication so he should be alright if he eats right and exercises. Sebastian asked if he was at his mansion in Marblehead because he'd like to visit him. Alan said, "Yes, I'm in Marblehead and I'd love to see you. I want you to know that I'm still making a party for you before you leave Marblehead Neck and move to New York." Sebastian told him not to worry about the party and to take care of himself.

After talking to his friend Alan for awhile, Sebastian told him he'd call him back. Alan said, "Nice talking with you, Sebastian." They then hung up. Sebastian was shocked that Alan had a mild heart attack so he's dwelling on that. It made him realize that he needs to walk on a regular basis to keep his circulation in check. He also has to watch his nutrition and not have too much fat or salt. He's presently controlling that himself so he doesn't have to take medication for it. He paused and then said out loud, "That's enough health talk today."

Sebastian went to his kitchen and did inventory of the groceries he needs to stock up on. He really doesn't like this part of living alone but he has to do it.

The next afternoon, Sebastian surprised his friend Alan by visiting him at his mansion in Marblehead. The butler let him in and took him over to Alan who was at his desk in his office. When Sebastian peeked in the doorway and knocked on his door, Alan quickly looked up and said, "Sebastian, I'm happy you came to see me!" Sebastian walked in and said, "You're my friend, Alan. How can I not visit you after you had a heart attack?" Alan stood up and they both hugged and then sat down. Sebastian asked him all about his heart attack and Alan told him he was at his desk when he got it and pressed the emergency buzzer on his desk and the butler came in and called 911. He stayed with him until the ambulance arrived and then he rode with him to the hospital.

Sebastian said, "I'm so sorry that happened. You need to take good care of yourself. I know you don't smoke now." Alan told him that he is exercising regularly and eating low salt and low fat foods. He also told Sebastian that heart trouble runs in his family so he needs to be very careful. Sebastian said, "And you're only in your late 40s, Alan. I want you to be around for a long time."

Alan asked Sebastian if he had any new ghost news. Sebastian told him that the ghosts are coming out often and sometimes raising hell. But he hasn't seen Jenny's ghost since her cemetery apparition of her getting shot. Alan looked shocked. Sebastian told him it was a flashback of when she was murdered. He then told him how he and Katherine are still not together which means the engagement is off because he told her he made love with Jenny's ghost. Katherine wanted the truth and he told her and then she got hysterical.

Alan said, "Sebastian, if it's meant to be, she'll be back so don't get stressed out over it." Sebastian told him he's having a hard time to get over her but appreciates his concern.

He then asked him if he wanted to go over to his haunted mansion again sometime. Alan answered, "Yes, another time I will definitely go."

Then, Alan and Sebastian walked around the mansion and Sebastian asked him if he had any new sculptures in his collection but Alan didn't. He took him to his kitchen and showed him around and took him to his dining room which he loves. It is elegant and he uses it only for special occasions. They then went to the grand room where the pitch party was held when

Sebastian first got to Marblehead. Alan said, "This is where your party will be held before you move, Sebastian." Sebastian told him it's a beautiful room and he feels honored that Alan is going to do that for him. Alan said, "It's my pleasure. You're my good friend and I think you might have a blockbuster book and movie. I'm so looking forward to it." They smiled at each other and then Sebastian said, "If you don't mind, Alan, I'm going to leave now. I wanted to pay a visit to you to see how you're still doing since your heart attack." Alan thanked him for coming over to see him and he then walked him to the door and they said goodbye.

On the way back to his mansion, Sebastian thought he'd stop in the Ultimate Inn lounge and ask how Phoebe is since she fell off the bar stool after drinking a rum and coke. He's wondering if she's okay and wonders if Veronica gave her a ride home like she said she would.

At the Ultimate Inn lounge, Sebastian went right over to his friend Saul but he did not sit down at the bar. He asked him about Phoebe and Saul told him Veronica did give her a ride home. Sebastian said, "Good. Have you seen her since?" Saul said, "No I haven't." Sebastian told Saul he just stopped in to inquire about Phoebe. After talking a little longer, they then said goodbye.

Sebastian was finally going back to his mansion and he was happy he went to see his friend Alan and also happy he checked up on Phoebe. While his radio played love songs as he drove, he started to think of Katherine so he shut it off and thought of a way to run into her again. He knows she goes to flea markets but doesn't know if it's always the same one.

After arriving at his mansion and parking in the driveway, Sebastian planned to look at the sewing room to see if any paranormal activity took place in there again which previously wrecked the room with Jenny's letters. He then wants to check the attic which he finds fascinating, mainly because of that mysterious mannequin. He doesn't trust it.

He first went into his kitchen and made a cup of coffee to have with some crackers and peanut butter at the kitchen table. When he finished, he went upstairs to the second floor and looked in the sewing room and everything was normal so he proceeded up to the attic. When he got there, he noticed something was not right. The mannequin was not in its usual place, it was in a different area in the attic and he immediately thought a spirit must have moved it. He went over to it and it still had Jenny's sheer lavender blue nightgown on, had black bushy hair, red lipstick and large haunting pale blue eyes that looked the same. He decided to leave the mannequin there to see if it gets moved again.

Sebastian then looked for the rocking chair and noticed it was also in a different place and a spirit must have moved it. Right now, he doesn't feel any energy in the attic although there could be at any moment. He then decided to try the rocking chair out to see if it would rock normally and it did, simply because there was no paranormal activity there right now. He's also ready to leave the attic and feels lucky that he doesn't fear spirits or ghosts.

Sebastian was soon in his living room sitting at the piano. Just for fun, he tickled the ivories a little and wished he could play it. He remembers one time that Jenny's mother Shannon's ghost was sitting there playing it.

It's close to dinner time now and before Sebastian prepares it, he wants to look in the china cabinet mirror to see if there will be someone standing in back of his reflection. He went into the dining room and immediately felt the presence of a spirit. He opened the cabinet door and stared into the mirror and suddenly a ghost appeared in back of his reflection. It was a pale shadowy ghostly apparition moving back and forth and he couldn't tell who it was. He quickly turned around and saw the ghost swiftly disappear which left him wondering if it was Oscar or a different ghost. The last ghost he saw in the dining room was also pale and shadowy.

Sebastian closed the china cabinet door and went into the kitchen to prepare his dinner. The menu tonight was red beans and rice with salad. He just cooked the rice for 40 minutes and opened a can of red kidney beans. When the rice was ready, he fried an onion and added it to the rice along with the red beans. It's a comforting meal.

Later, at the dining room table, Sebastian was enjoying a delicious serving of red beans and rice and he will follow it up with his salad that will have an oil and vinegar dressing. He usually waits to have his dessert later in the living room and tonight it will be frozen coffee yogurt.

The dining room table was soon cleared and the dishes were done. Sebastian then went into the living room to lie on the plush velvet sofa with a pillow behind his head to rest for awhile and think about the dining room ghost. He's planning on spending a part of his evening going over his red book.

A couple of days later, early in the morning, someone was knocking on the front door of the mansion. Sebastian went and answered it and it was Charlie. He said, "I'm sorry to bother you, Sebastian, but I need to take the rest of the day off and maybe a couple more. I just got a call on my cell phone that a family member has died." Sebastian said, "I'm sorry to hear that and of course you can take time off." Charlie went on and told him that it was his aunt who raised him that died. Sebastian told him he was sorry to hear the bad news and asked if he'd be alright. Charlie said, "I feel very sad." Sebastian told him to come and talk to him about it anytime, if he needs to. Charlie thanked him and then said goodbye and slowly walked away with his head down. Sebastian said, "Bye, Charlie." He watched him get in his car and drive away.

Sebastian went and took a long shower after hearing Charlie's bad news. While showering, the news reminded him of how sad he was when he lost his dad Oliver who was a highly respected jeweler in New York. He then thought about the good time he had with his dad when he came to his mansion to visit him with his girlfriend Elaina and they went on a yachting cruise for a day. Katherine also joined them. That memory suddenly reminded him to call Elaina and tell her how he'll soon be moving back to New York close to where she lives and they'll be able to visit often. Sebastian also wants to invite Elaina to his party that his producer friend Alan will be making for him before he moves back to New York.

18

EMOTIONS RUN WILD

Emotions are running wild with Sebastian. He won't give up on trying to see Katherine and persuading her to go back with him and get married like they planned. Even though she doesn't want to see him again, he's thinking of how he can run into her. He knows she likes flea markets because he saw her at one and remembers where and when.

After looking in the newspaper and on the computer, Sebastian noticed a flea market day ad at Crocker Park which is where he last saw Katherine. He's going to proceed with his plan and go there around the same time he last saw her there and hopes to get lucky.

The Ghost And Sebastian

The next day, Sebastian was feeling quite happy as he got dressed for the flea market. He sensed that he will run into Katherine today although there will be a disagreement between them.

While driving to the flea market at Crocker Park, the silence in the car allowed Sebastian to concentrate on what he was going to say to Katherine to convince her that they should get back together and follow through with their wedding plans. Who knows? Someday she may change her mind and get back with him.

After a short drive to Crocker Park, Sebastian arrived at the flea market and there was a huge crowd of people and a popcorn vender there again. While he slowly walked around looking for Katherine, he knew he was going to have a hard time finding her, if she was there. He kept on walking around and looking through the crowd of people but he didn't see her. He was keeping in mind that she may not even be there today.

Sebastian went and bought some popcorn from the vendor and then sat on a bench nearby and watched the crowd from a distance. After awhile, he got up and walked around again looking through the crowd of people. He suddenly saw the back of a woman nearby that looked like Katherine so he hurried over and got right in front of her and saw that it wasn't her. He said to the woman, "I'm sorry. I thought you were someone I was looking for." He went on and continued looking for Katherine.

It was about an hour later, while still walking around the flea market, Sebastian thought he saw Katherine again. He rushed through the crowd of people and there she was! It was Katherine! He went and faced her and smiled and then said, "Katherine, I'm so happy I found you." She was so shocked that he seemed to be stalking her. She couldn't even smile, instead, she just stared at him. He said, "Katherine, we have to talk." She yelled, "Why are you stalking me! I don't want you anymore!" The crowd nearby heard her yell and they started watching them argue.

Sebastian put his arms around her but she pushed him away and told him to leave. But because the people nearby were watching them, in a soft voice, he said, "Not until we have a talk." Katherine snapped and yelled, "If you don't leave me right now, I'm going to call for help!" He stared at her a moment and then walked away looking sad.

While Sebastian was back sitting on the bench nearby, he was still sad that his plan didn't seem to be working. He waited about a half an hour and then returned to the crowd of people and continued his search for Katherine.

Sebastian knows that his persistence to achieve what he sets out to do is usually what makes him a winner and that's why he's staying at the mansion so long. He keeps on inquiring about Jenny and Pierce to everyone who knew them because he may get an answer as to who murdered them.

It's now late afternoon and Sebastian is still going through the crowd of people and eventually he saw Katherine again buying a small lamp at one of the flea market tables. He quickly went up to the sales person and said, "I'll pay for that." He pulled out a hundred dollar bill and handed it to the sales person who looked at Katherine to get her approval. She told the sales person to let him pay for the lamp. He felt relieved and thought he was making progress with Katherine. While the sales woman made change, Katherine said, "Look, let's go sit on the bench and talk." He said, "Yes, let's." They looked at each other and smiled a little and then slowly walked over to the bench nearby while he carried her lamp.

While Katherine and Sebastian were sitting on the bench with the lamp next to them, they faced each other and then he said, "Please listen to me, Katherine. I want you more than anything. Let's get married like we planned." He waited for her response. She said, "Sebastian, I will never go back with you because you continue to sleep with Jenny's ghost!" She was getting excited so he tried to calm her down telling her that making love with a ghost was okay because it wasn't in the real world. She got angry and yelled, "You think it's okay?" He said, "Look, ghosts are not in the real world so making love with them is in their world. The world that ghosts live in! Think about it." She got more angry and screamed out, "I hate you, Sebastian! I hate you! I hate you!" She then broke down and cried so much she couldn't stop. Sebastian put his arms around her and tried to comfort her.

Sebastian continued to hold Katherine while trying to console her as she sobbed. He then went on and explained that he wants to tell her the truth about Jenny's ghost before it comes out and gets published in his book, newspapers and magazines for millions of people to read. He paused and then looked into her eyes and said, "This might end up being a blockbuster movie that my friend Alan, the movie producer, is going to make, based on my book."

While waiting for Katherine's response, Sebastian asked, "Do you get my point, Katherine?" She got hysterical and yelled, "I can't take it! I can't take it!" She started crying loudly again. Sebastian said, "I want to take you to Dr. Louis. Will you let me?" She screamed, "No! Leave me alone!" She jumped up from the bench and then he did. She started running to the crowd of people so he couldn't find her. He sat back down on the bench and noticed she left her lamp there. While thinking, he said out loud, "She's going to have a nervous breakdown if she doesn't get in control of herself."

Sebastian soon got up from his bench and went to the crowd while carrying Katherine's lamp. He wanted to make sure she was going to be okay after her outburst she just had with him. He went to the table where he bought the lamp for her and asked the saleslady if she remembered him. She did remember him and told him Katherine was just at her table again and left. Sebastian asked if Katherine was crying and the saleslady told him she wasn't. Knowing that, Sebastian feels it's okay if he leaves now. He wants to give her some space before calling her up again, even though he's worried about her mental health. And when he does call her, he knows she may not answer her phone. For some reason, Sebastian left Katherine's lamp on the flea market table.

Back at the mansion, Sebastian was having a bottle of water while pacing the living room floor and thinking about Katherine. He thinks her mind is in a fragile state right now and wishes she'd go to the psychiatrist again. She went one time to see Dr Louis and needs to go again. He plans to try and get her to go.

After Sebastian had a difficult night trying to sleep, he was soon at his kitchen table having breakfast and thinking it might be alright to call Katherine later in the morning just to see how she is, even though she might hang up on him. He made a second cup of coffee and took that one into the living room and put it down on the table next to a chair. He sat there for awhile and then felt like it might be a good time to call her so he did. Her phone rang and rang and after awhile she answered it. He asked, "Katherine, are you alright?" She yelled, "Yes I am and don't call again!" She slammed her cell phone down on something that made a loud noise. He was not too happy but happy that she said she was okay. He knows he has to get his mind off of her today and fast so he decided to get out of the mansion and get a change of scenery.

While sitting on a chair near the edge of the cliff near his mansion, Sebastian was looking out at the Atlantic ocean which looked so peaceful. He has been sitting there for awhile now and enjoying the view. Once in awhile he sees a boat or ship go by and looks through his binocular glasses to get a closer look. Sebastian was relaxed as his mind was taking a fresh look at life. He knows he's a strong character, intelligent and has tenacity. He soon was ready to leave.

Back at his mansion, Sebastian went to his desk and started writing in his red book and then went on his computer documenting more information. He suddenly noticed the sun spilled into the living room from nearby windows casting shadows on the wall of the tree branches with leaves so he stopped to look at it and enjoyed it for a moment.

A few days later, Sebastian called Samantha up and asked her how she was and how her new anxiety medication was working. She told him she was feeling better due to the new medication but she worries that she may become more violent than ever if she forgets to take it. Simply because it's stronger than the last one she was taking. He said to her, "I think we should see each other once in awhile just as friends and talk about our writing." She agreed to that, however, she's very attracted to his sexual charisma. She told him she's going to be publishing her new novel soon and it's called, The Stolen Manuscript. He inspired her and told her he likes the title and is looking forward to her first publication.

While they were still on the phone, Sebastian asked, "When will your book be published?" She told him probably the end of this year and he told her that was good. They chatted a bit more and he told her he'd call her again and maybe they can go for coffee. She told him she's looking forward to them getting together and then they said goodbye.

The next morning, Sebastian was at the police station talking with Officer Martin about the 2006 unsolved triple homicide that happened at his mansion. Sebastian asked, "Any more news from flamboyant Sam who is my rival?" Officer Martin said, "No. We haven't heard from him since the last time he was here and signed an affidavit with more news." Sebastian said, "Tell me about it." Officer Martin told him that it was big news that Sam gave to the police. He told them how he recently heard Alfred, the thief, confess to his friend Dex that while he was robbing the mansion in the morning, the mother caught him so he shot her. Within hours, he went back to rob the mansion but didn't know Jenny and Pierce were in her bedroom. Pierce heard noise and went to the bedroom doorway. He and Alfred looked at each other in surprise and that's when Alfred shot Pierce and then shot Jenny who was on the bed. The officer was finished talking. Sebastian told him he doesn't believe Alfred shot all three. He thinks Jenny and Pierce may have been shot because of a love triangle. He heard that Pierce had women chasing him.

Sebastian asked Officer Martin when Alfred will go to court and stand trial. The officer told him that it will be soon. Sebastian said, "Sam may have lied about overhearing Alfred confess that he was Jenny, Pierce and Shannon's murderer?" The officer said, "Then he would be charged with perjury." Sebastian went on to say that he thinks Sam lied just for the sake of being called a hero. After the officer finished talking, Sebastian told him he'd be in touch with him if he has anymore news. They said goodbye to each other and Sebastian left the station.

Sebastian went back to his mansion for a cup of tea and toast and had it at the dining room table. He doesn't have much time left at the mansion to get the answer he so desperately wants which is who murdered Jenny and Pierce.

On the weekend, Sebastian and Samantha went out to the Ultimate Inn coffee shop and are sitting in one of their booths. They are casually dressed and she looks as beautiful as ever with her magnetic blue eyes, silky brown hair and her light rose lipstick today. She's still curvaceous. Sebastian is happy being with her today while having coffee and key lime pie but he's noticing her personality is not quite the same. She is wound up too tight.

Samantha asked Sebastian if he was able to get back with Katherine yet and he told her he wasn't and that the affair is most likely over because that's what she wants. Just then, Samantha yelled at him, "Why the hell do you keep trying to see her! Don't you get it? She doesn't want you!" Sebastian was startled that her personality snapped as much as it did. He told her to calm down and then asked her if she was still taking her medication. She said, "No! I should be able to live without taking anxiety mediation!" He told her she needs to continue with her medication because it's the only thing that will control her temper. She then yelled out, "Katherine! Katherine! That's all you want to talk about! I want you! She doesn't want you! Go to hell, Sebastian!" She jumped up off of her seat and yelled, "I'd rather take a taxi home than ride with you!" He stayed calm while sitting and watching her storm out the door of the Ultimate Inn coffee shop. He then lingered for awhile and thought to himself, "Why do women get so darn emotional? However, there are men that do too because I know a few."

Veronica, the young waitress, came over and asked, "Are you okay, Sebastian?" He looked at her and said, "I'm okay, Veronica, but thanks for asking." She smiled at him then chewed her gum and walked away with her long red hair and bubbly spirit. As he watched her, he thought, "What a lovely person she is."

Sebastian was ready to leave the Ultimate Inn coffee shop but decided to stop and say hello to his friend Saul, the bartender, in the lounge. Before he got to the lounge, he ran into Phoebe, the customer and sometimes lounge singer, who was leaving so they stopped and talked a little. Sebastian asked, "How are you, Phoebe?" She answered, "I'm okay, Sebastian. I just can't have hard alcohol anymore. Ha ha ha! Oh, and I'm going on a diet!" He smiled at her and then said, "I'm happy to hear you're okay." They both said goodbye. As he was on his way to the lounge, he thought about how Phoebe loves to sing and desperately wants a boyfriend and cries at the thought of not having one someday. She also has an appointment with Dr. Louis, the psychiatrist. Sebastian started thinking about how he recently sat with Phoebe at the bar while she drank a rum and coke too fast and suddenly toppled off the stool and onto the floor. He picked her up and took her to the sickroom and Veronica the waitress gave her a ride home and now all is well, it seems.

Sebastian arrived at the bar to say hello to his friend Saul. He told him how he was just having coffee in the coffee shop with a writer friend and she snapped because she wasn't taking her anxiety medication. Saul said, "Women are so much more emotional than men are." Sebastian said, "I agree with that. Lately, I have been around people with so much emotional anxiety but they are mostly females." Saul asked, "Do you want anything to drink, Sebastian?" He told him he didn't want anything and that he just stopped in to say hello. After talking a few minutes, they said goodbye.

Sebastian drove back to his mansion with his radio on playing love songs. He suddenly snapped the radio off and said, "I'm going to try to get over Katherine by maybe seeing more of Samantha and helping her with her problems and that might help the both of us."

The Ghost And Sebastian

When Sebastian got to his mansion, he felt good because he had a change of scenery, although he's concerned about Samantha's mental health. His cell phone soon started ringing which he left on a table near a chair like he usually does. He hurried to answer it, but when he did, the ringing stopped and there was no message left. He was hoping that it was Katherine.

While later pacing the floor, Sebastian started thinking about his late father's girlfriend, Elaina, in New York. He decided to call her to see how she is and because he's planning on inviting her to his party that his friend Alan will be making for him. He got comfortable on a chair and made the call and she answered. He first asked her how she was and she was okay and happy to hear from him. She asked him what was new. He first reminded her of the big party that his friend Alan, the movie producer, will be making for him. It will be to honor him for his new murder mystery story that will be published in the near future. He went on and told her that Alan is going to produce a movie of it after it's adapted to a screenplay. She said, "That's wonderful! I'm so happy for you!" He then reminded her he's inviting her to that party which he now knows will definitely be at the end of July. After that, he'll be moving back to New York.

While Elaina and Sebastian continued talking, she told him how she's looking forward to reading his book and wishes him the best of luck with it. He thanked her. She then said, "Sebastian, I'll be in Europe for most of July and August and unfortunately I won't be able to go to your party." He was disappointed but then wished her a wonderful time in Europe. He then told her what was going on with him and Katherine. Elaina expressed how sorry she was to hear about his breakup and that he'll be okay because he's a strong person. He thanked her for her support. She then said, "On the other hand, I'm so happy you're moving back to New York and we'll be able to see each other often and go to our favorite deli and have bagels." He agreed that he loves doing that and going to different restaurants.

After they chatted for awhile, Elaina told Sebastian how proud she is of him and that he reminds her so much of his dad and how she truly loved him. Sebastian liked hearing that and soon their phone call ended.

The call to Elaina made Sebastian's day. He is very anxious to see her at the end of the summer when he moves back to New York. They'll have so much to talk about and he can hardly wait to introduce her to his friend Alan when he visits him later on at his home in New York and stays with him for awhile.

Sebastian started reminiscing about how he, Elaina, his father and Katherine went on a one-day yachting cruise together. Elaina is quite a knock-out to look at. She's in her 30s, pretty, has long blonde hair, curvaceous and wears short and tight clothes. She's also very likeable.

Then Sebastian suddenly wanted to have a beverage so he went to his bar area and poured himself an after dinner drink with ice which was a mild drink. While sipping it, he started thinking about life and how fortunate he is to have some special friends. He still feels bad about his breakup with Katherine and still wants to marry her but he knows you can't make people do what they don't want to do. Therefore, life goes on. There's life after sadness. And he knows that there'll always be happy times and sad times which is the cycle of life. Some people regret what they've done in the past which can't be changed but they can change their future. We all have good times and sad times.

In order for Sebastian to go on with his future and get over his sadness about the breakup with Katherine, he knows he must socialize more with Samantha which will help her and him. He began recalling how he met Samantha at Alan's pitch party. She was a new writer who was intoxicated and causing a scene arguing with Brad, the producer, so Alan stepped in and stopped her and then introduced her to Sebastian. They became friends and their sexual chemistry led to intimacy a couple of times. It was hard for him to resist her silky dark brown hair and stunning magnetic blue eyes.

Sebastian's last time with Samantha at the Ultimate Inn coffee shop was unpleasant because she had stopped taking her anxiety mediation. He still thinks of how she got so angry over his love for Katherine. At the moment, he's questioning himself if he'll ever get over Katherine by getting more friendly with Samantha. He and Samantha are just friends and writers who like discussing books they're writing, although Samantha would like them to also be lovers. She's not someone he would marry because the chemistry isn't there, therefore, he doesn't want to get intimate with her.

Sebastian's past love making with Jenny's ghost that he experienced three times was strange, it was different from the real world. Her spiritual power made him mentally and physically feel like he had been transported to her world, the celestial world. However, he now knows his past strange love experience with Jenny's ghost is over because he's leaving the mansion and he's not planning on waiting for a ghost to show up somewhere else. He's aware that making love in the real world is satisfying and it also is in Jenny's world of ghosts. The difference is, ghostly love making is strange and he likes it. However, he has to settle for a woman in the real world so his choice is Katherine because she's someone he'd marry. Sadly, she broke up with him.

A couple of days later, Sebastian went to Marblehead harbor to sit and watch the boats because of the way they look and it's also a good way to relax. The harbor was full of sail boats today which was a beautiful sight. And because it's the month of June and it's summer time on the east coast, people love to go sailing and some just like to cruise around on a yacht for the day or for a longer time. There are so many people here on this hot and beautiful sunny day.

Marblehead is one of the premiere yachting centers on the east coast and it's coastal community is over 18,000 residents as of 2011. Sebastian's aware it's also the birth place of the United States Navy.

After spending several hours at Marblehead harbor, Sebastian is quite relaxed and ready to head back to his mansion that is perched on a cliff along the east coast of Marblehead Neck near Castle Rock Park. There are also other mansions there. He thinks it's an awesome place to live.

Sebastian soon arrived at his mansion and parked in his driveway. He entered his rose foyer and it felt good to be home after spending the day at the harbor. After being in the sun most of the day, he took a cold shower and then went into his kitchen and made a tall ice coffee. He took it into the living room and put it on the coffee table and then went to lie on the burgundy velvet sofa with a pillow behind his head. He occasionally sat up and drank some of his ice coffee that he found so refreshing after being out in the hot sun all day which made him tired.

While Sebastian was still on the sofa, his cell phone rang and rang and he wasn't in the mood to answer it and soon fell asleep and never finished his ice coffee. He even slept on the sofa the entire night.

The next morning, Sebastian was surprised he fell asleep on the sofa and slept there all night. It happened to him once before but it's rare that he does that. He got off the sofa and went and took a long shower. He then went to his kitchen and prepared himself a healthy breakfast of orange juice, scrambled eggs and a slice of low sodium ham along with whole wheat toast with grape jelly. He's also going to have fresh perked hazelnut coffee which is now perking.

In awhile, Sebastian was at the table in his dining room eating his delicious breakfast while thinking of how he plans to spend the day. He wants to work on his book which is soon to be finished whether or not he finds out who Jenny and Pierce's murderer is. He feels his story is still good enough to become a blockbuster book and movie because the ghosts have made the story so fascinating for people to read about.

After his breakfast was over, Sebastian cleared the table and washed the dishes in the sink. He then went back into the dining room and looked in the china cabinet mirror to see if there would be a ghost standing in back of his reflection again. He waited several moments and there was none. He also hasn't seen Jenny's ghost for awhile and so he stood there for a few moments thinking and wishing he could see her ghost again. He thought of her strange love making and also how he grew to love her gentle soul and now to think it's all coming to an end is overwhelmingly sad to him.

In the afternoon, Sebastian was at his desk thinking of how he has been at the mansion almost a year and three months, and if it's necessary, he'll stay longer. He's aware he may never get an answer from Jenny or Pierce's ghost telling him who murdered them but is still hoping he does. He also has sympathy for all of the ghosts he has met because they were once alive and something terrible happened to them.

19

BREAKING POLICE NEWS!

On this evening, classical music is playing softly in Sebastian's living room while he's with Samantha and their relationship is strictly platonic. She looks gorgeous while sitting on a wing armchair wearing a black short cocktail dress with her legs crossed. Her brown hair which is pulled to one side, and her magnetic blue eyes and lipstick are enhanced by her intoxicating perfume. However, Sebastian only likes Samantha as a friend.

While there are already chips and nuts on the coffee table, Sebastian told Samantha he has plenty of food in case she gets hungry and to make herself at home. She told him she may want something to eat later on. He then told her that he's happy she's visiting him tonight.

While Sebastian was at his bar area, he was pouring Samantha some white wine and he wanted red. He was wearing gray pants and a violet blue and white silk shirt with short sleeves, and with his good looks and brown wavy hair, he had charisma. His cologne had a wonderful scent.

Sebastian then brought Samantha's wine over to her and he sat across from her on the other wing armchair with his. She stared passionately into his eyes and he asked her what she thought of the wine. She took a sip of it and then looked into his eyes again and told him that it was perfect. After he smiled at her, they continued sipping their wine. Samantha suddenly said, "It's amazing how we're still talking to each other. And I promise I won't have a key made for your mansion." He said, "Good!" She added, "I guess I got lucky since Katherine broke up with you?" He told Samantha that she has the wrong idea. Just because Katherine broke up with him, he still loves her and will try to get back with her. Samantha then went on and told him how she's really sorry about the breakup. He was silent for a few seconds and then said, "Well, there's no reason why we can't stay friends, Samantha. That's all I want with you."

While Samantha and Sebastian continued talking, he got up to get her more white wine because she wanted it. While pouring it, she stood up and paced the floor and said, "I wonder what's in store for us this evening." He told her there would be nothing but food, beverages and conversation.

Samantha's wine was ready so Sebastian brought it to her and she sipped it while they were standing. He asked her about her novel she plans to publish this year and she told him it's ready and she's excited about it. He told her he loves the title. The Stolen Manuscript. She looked at him and was happy that he said that. She went on and asked him if his triple homicide mystery will be finished soon. He told her it will be. She then asked, "Did you find out who murdered Jenny and Pierce?"

He told her that he still doesn't know who murdered them, and, whether he does or doesn't find out, the book is still good because of the ghostly encounters he has had. Samantha told him she can hardly wait to read it, even if he doesn't find out who murdered Jenny and Pierce.

As Samantha and Sebastian were still standing and walking around in the room, he told her about the celebration party that their friend Alan is making for him in July before he moves back to his home in New York. She was sad to hear that he will be moving but then she got excited and asked, "Am I going to the party?" While he stood next to her holding his wine, he said, "Of course you'll be invited!" She stared into his eyes passionately and then gave him a kiss on the lips which he wasn't expecting and didn't want so he gently told her not to do that again.

Samantha then asked Sebastian, "What's so hard about you falling in love with me?" He told her she's not his type to fall in love with and any intimate times they had in the past were a mistake. He told her that he got intimate with her so he could try to forget Katherine but it didn't work. While Samantha was silent and looking sad, he said, "Look, you're a friend and I hope you're okay with that." She didn't respond so he then changed the subject and asked, "Remember how Jenny's spirit frightened you by hurling a candy dish at you? Well, imagine if you saw an actual ghost in front of you how that would really scare you." "Oh I'm not sure it would, Sebastian." All of a sudden, the room filled with the scent of gardenias and Sebastian told Samantha to remain quiet because it was Jenny's spirit. She's most likely angry because he's with another woman. In seconds, Jenny's spirit grabbed a bunch of Samantha's hair in back of her head and then yanked her backwards away from Sebastian causing her to almost fall down as she quickly screamed, "Ahhhh!"

While Sebastian was stunned that Jenny's spirit pulled Samantha's hair, the gardenia scent slowly left the room while dust, somehow, flew into Samantha's eyes. She now needs to remove her contact lenses to clean them so she and Sebastian went and sat on the sofa. As she started to take them out, she said, "Jenny's spirit scared me so much that my magnetic blue contact lenses almost fell out." He told her that he didn't know she wore them. When she took them out, he looked at her eyes and said, "Oh, you have very nice brown eyes." Samantha is so infatuated with Sebastian that she said, "Well in that case, I'll let you look at them for awhile and I'll put my magnetic blue lenses back in later." She left her magnetic blue contact lenses in a case on the end table.

Sebastian then said, "Samantha, I know you said you wouldn't be afraid of a ghost but a spirit was just here and you screamed." She told him it was because the hair pulling hurt and she was shocked it happened, and, she hopes she doesn't ever see a ghost because she now thinks it might frighten her. He asked her if she felt relaxed now that Jenny's spirit was gone and she told him she was a little. He put his arms around her to comfort her and knew she liked that because she has had romantic feelings for him for a long time.

Sebastian and Samantha were soon interrupted by the scent of gardenias again. He immediately looked around the room and said, "Oh no. Jenny's spirit or ghost is just about to show up again." Samantha quickly said, "Sebastian, I remember that scent in the room when Jenny's spirit hurled a candy dish at me but missed and hit a mirror." He didn't pay attention to her, instead he kept looking around the room for Jenny's ghost he thought might appear. Samantha was silent.

Sebastian stood up while he kept looking around the living room and so did Samantha. Then, Jenny's pale lifelike ghostly apparition was about five feet in front of them. She was wearing a sheer pale light red nightgown which was long and loose-fitting and blowing around along with her long light brown hair.

She was in a rage swinging her arms and staring at Sebastian. Samantha looked startled as she showed a slight uneasiness seeing her first ghost.

While Sebastian and Samantha were silent, Jenny's ghost yelled, "Sebastian! How could you? No! No!" Then Jenny just stared at Sebastian as her hair and gown kept blowing around. Samantha yelled, "I'm seeing Jenny's ghost for the first time! I heard her talk!" Sebastian said,. "You see her and hear her because I'm here." Samantha stared at Jenny and yelled, "That's Jenny's ghost! Oh no! It's really her!"

While Jenny's ghost was still in front of them moving around, Sebastian said to her, "Jenny, please leave us alone. You can't do this to me!" Jenny yelled, "Oh yes I can, Sebastian! It's her! It's her! Vicki! It's Vicki! Pierce's ex-girlfriend he was engaged to before he met me!"

Sebastian was momentarily stunned at what Jenny's ghost just yelled out. He then asked, "Jenny, what are you saying? What do you mean?" Within moments, she answered, "It's Vicki! It's Vicki! She murdered me and Pierce!" Sebastian is shocked at what Jenny is saying. He then said, "There's no Vicki here, Jenny! I know what Vicki looks like from police photos! She has red hair, brown eyes, wears glasses, was overweight and was in need of dental work!" He paused and waited for a message. Jenny's ghost then yelled, "Sebastian, "That's Vicki! That's Vicki who is with you in your living room! She murdered us! She murdered me and Pierce! Help, Sebastian! Help!"

Samantha quickly became fidgety while yelling out, "I'm getting out of here! This is a mad house! She's crazy!"

Jenny's ghost kept moving around while watching Sebastian and Samantha. He suddenly sensed something very suspicious about Samantha. He quickly grabbed a hold of her before she

The Ghost And Sebastian

could leave the living room. He held her two arms while shaking her and yelling at her, "You're not going anywhere! Who are you? Are you Vicki?" Samantha didn't answer so Sebastian shook her and yelled, "Are you Vicki?" Samantha wouldn't speak as her brown eyes stared at him.

Jenny's ghost suddenly yelled, "Yes, Sebastian! Yes! That's Vicki! She has red hair! See her hairline! She had facial surgery, lost weight and had dental work!" He looked at the hairline on the back of Samantha's neck, and, sure enough, red hair roots were visible. He asked Jenny how she knew Vicki was in disguise. She told him it's because she's a ghost and has been following her around and this was the time to expose her real identity. Sebastian's shocked by this.

Then, out of nowhere, Pierce's pale lifelike ghostly apparition was next to Jenny's ghost as he was swinging his arms in anger. He was wearing the clothes he had on when he was shot which were jeans and a blue striped shirt. Pierce yelled, "Sebastian, "I'm Pierce! It's her! It's Vicki! She murdered me and Jenny!" Jenny's ghost then yelled, "Sebastian! That's Vicki! It's Vicki!" Sebastian said to Jenny and Pierce's ghost, "I know it! I saw her red hair roots! And she has been wearing magnetic blue contact lenses for disguise and the dental work you mentioned she had done is correct. She now has porcelain teeth. I'm calling the police!" Then, Jenny's hair and gown stopped blowing around.

While Sebastian held onto Samantha, she suddenly got away but he grabbed her as she yelled out, "Get away from me! Let me go! You're all crazy! Get away!" Samantha suddenly broke loose from Sebastian's grip again but he quickly grabbed her and was able to stop her from getting out of the mansion. He yelled, "Oh no you don't, you're sick, Samantha! Your name was Vicki when you committed those murders! It was you all the time! But even though you're a murderer, I will always value our friendship. Those magnetic blue contact lenses drew me into your life and I'm not sorry. You just need psychiatric help so please get it, Samantha!"

Samantha a/k/a Vicki was still struggling to get away as Sebastian yelled, "You are Vicki, aren't you?" She didn't answer so he went on and said, "You dyed her hair dark brown, changed your name, had porcelain teeth put in, lost weight and most likely had plastic surgery on the west coast because I saw your pictures before you moved from Revere, Massachusetts to the west coast! The police have your photos and so does the masseuse place you worked at in Boston!"

Sebastian had to drag Samantha a/k/a Vicki to the kitchen to get his cell phone and some rope to tie her up. Jenny and Pierce's ghost followed them into the kitchen and saw Sebastian tie Samantha a/k/a Vicki to a chair and call the police. Officer Martin came to the phone and Sebastian said, "Officer Martin! This is Sebastian and do I have big news for you! I caught Jenny and Pierce's murderer! I'm holding her in my kitchen where I tied her to a chair. How fast can you get here and bring another officer with you?" Office Martin said, "Right away!" He quickly hung up. While waiting for the police, Sebastian sat on a chair staring at Samantha who was silent. He then looked at Jenny and Pierce's ghost who were watching and looking content. Within seconds, their ghosts suddenly disappeared but Jenny's spirit remained with her gardenia scent and Sebastian looked pleasantly surprised.

Sebastian continued to wait for the police while staring at Samantha a/k/a Vicki as she was tied to a chair. He soon heard the police at the door yell, ""It's the outsource police!" Sebastian yelled, "I'm in the kitchen!" Officer Martin and Lieutenant Darwin walked into the kitchen and saw Sebastian standing next to Samantha. Sebastian said, "Officers, this is Samantha a/k/a Vicki. Vicki murdered Jenny and Pierce and has been in disguise as Samantha." With controlled emotion, Officer Martin asked, "What's that scent?" Sebastian said, "It's from Jenny's spirit who is presently here watching us. Her ghost and Pierce's were here earlier and then left."

Sebastian told the officers that while he and Samantha were standing in his living room talking, the gardenia scent filled the air and then Jenny's spirit pulled the back of Samantha's hair and he saw her falling backwards. Jenny's scent soon left so they then sat on the sofa while Samantha told him Jenny's spirit almost knocked her contact lenses out. She then took the blue lenses out to clean them and that's when he saw she had brown eyes. He told her he liked them so she didn't put the blue lenses back in. Then the gardenia scent was back. Jenny and Pierce's ghost appeared and yelled to him that he was with Vicki, their murderer! Jenny's ghost told him Vicki's a redhead and dyed her hair dark brown. He looked at her neck hairline and saw red roots which were a disguise. The officers observed the red roots and brown eyes.

Officer Martin then read Samantha a/k/a Vicki her rights and told her he's taking her to the police station. She said, "Let's get it over with." Before the officer untied her, he asked, "Is Samantha your legal name?" After pausing, she said, "Yes. It use to be Vicki and I changed it to Samantha on the west coast." He asked her, "Did you shoot Jenny and Pierce in this mansion in 2006?" She wouldn't answer. Officer Martin untied her from the chair, then handcuffed her and walked her to the door with the lieutenant as Sebastian followed them. Then, Jenny's gardenia scent left. Samantha a/k/a Vicki soon had an arraignment and pleaded guilty and given a court-appointed attorney. The prosecution is seeking a life sentence and Samantha a/k/a Vicki is plea bargaining.

Later, at the outsource police station, Officer Martin told Sebastian that Samantha was showing bizarre behavior as she impulsively confessed to everything while her attorney and the police were present. They think she has a serious mental disorder. She confessed to the murders of Jenny and Pierce and it was over a love triangle. The "death threat letter" Sebastian found was from her because Pierce was dating her and Jenny at the same time. Samantha a/k/a Vicki also confessed she copied Jenny's mansion keys from Pierce and Sebastian's keys when they visited her and took naps. One day, Vicki was in a fury and went to the mansion when she knew Jenny and Pierce were there. She gained entry with her key through the back door and then heard a little noise in the bedroom with the door closed so she walked to the door. Pierce heard sounds and opened the bedroom door and Vicki was right in front of him and she shot him twice in the doorway. Jenny was on her bed and heard the noise and looked up and saw Vicki so Vicki shot her three times.

Officer Martin told Sebastian that Samantha a/k/a Vicki admitted to facial reconstruction she had done on the west coast plus other things. Cheek implants, chin implant, nose surgery, eyebrow lift, porcelain teeth, blue eye contact lenses, loss of weight, dyed her hair and changed her name. She also wanted a new image because she was pursuing a career in acting, writing or cosmetology but didn't succeed. She then met Alan, the movie producer, and was obsessed with him and he tried to get her connections at the writers' pitch sessions but competition was too stiff for her. She also disliked earthquakes. She and Alan became friends and she knew he had a mansion in Marblehead so she planned to move there because he was her friend and could help her further her career as a writer. She also had told Alan she was familiar with the east coast because she once lived there.

Officer Martin then told Sebastian that the police knew Samantha a/k/a Vicki was from Revere, MA and she lived with her parents as Vicki the redhead. After the murders, they moved out to the west coast because her parents planned to retire there. No one knew this was Vicki's chance to hide out from the murders she committed. Sadly, her parents were killed there in a car crash. Two years later, she came back to the east coast in disguise as Samantha and bought a condo in Marblehead with funds her parents gave her from the sale of their house in Revere, MA. She soon met up with Alan in Marblehead who wasn't aware she was in disguise. Officer Martin was finished and Sebastian asked him for a printout of the information so he gave it to him. Sebastian thanked him.

Officer Martin then told Sebastian that he's one of three heroes who helped solve the triple homicide which has been cold for five years. He moved from New York to Marblehead Neck to help solve the murders, then lived in the mansion for a year and three months, and he being a psychic medium and clairvoyant, soon led him to communicating with Jenny and Pierce's ghost. And one evening, while his friend Samantha was visiting him, Jenny and Pierce's ghost appeared identifying her as Vicki, their murderer, who was in disguise as Samantha. Therefore, there are three heroes. This mystery has ended. Officer Martin looked at Sebastian as they smiled and shook hands and then Sebastian left. When he got outside, the rain was pouring down and he didn't care as he stood still in it for a few seconds looking content. The 2006 unsolved triple homicide mystery was now solved.

While Sebastian drove back to his mansion, he thought of what it took to help solve the murder mystery. It was the progress with the police, his persistence, extending his lease, and by him inviting Samantha over for a friendly evening which resulted in a surprise visit by Jenny and Pierce's ghost who finally exposed her as their murderer. He then thought of how the murder mystery was quite a puzzle.

Sebastian was soon back at his mansion and was as happy as he could be. After making a cup of tea, sipping it and finishing it in the kitchen, he went to his desk to start documenting his news.

He first thought of what an ending he will have for his book, and, how his persistence paid off big time! The newspapers will come out with breaking news that the Marblehead Neck 2006 triple homicide is now solved!

While Sebastian was still working on his story at his desk, there was suddenly a gardenia scent that filled the air. He remained seated at his desk while inhaling the wonderful scent and looking around the room. He called out, "Jenny! I know you're here! I can smell gardenias!" He then remained silent looking around the room. When he looked at a wing armchair which was several feet from him, a pale lifelike ghostly apparition of just Jenny's head popped up from behind the chair and smiled at him. She then came out from behind the chair wearing a sheer pale pink nightgown which was long, loose-fitting and looked ethereal and her long light brown hair crowned her face. As she and Sebastian stared at each other, she slowly approached him at his desk and then smiled at him as she gently sat on his lap.

While Jenny's ghost was sitting on Sebastian's lap, he gently put his arms around her and she made him feel like he was in her world, the world of ghosts, and he loved it. She caressed his face with her hands and then passionately kissed his lips and he loved it. He's also aware this is the sixth nightgown he has been able to feel. She looked into his eyes and said, "Sebastian, I love you!" He said, "Jenny, you can rest now that we know who murdered you and Pierce." Jenny kissed his lips again which made his spirits soar. He thanked her for helping to solve the murder and told her that Vicki is going away forever to pay for murdering her and Pierce, and Alfred is going away for murdering her mother. She said, "I know, Sebastian." He then asked her how she felt seeing the police arrest Vicki. She said, "Justice has been done. Thank you for helping me, my mother and Pierce."

Sebastian then took Jenny's hand and held it and tried to comfort her as she sat on his lap. He said, "Jenny, there's something I have to tell you. I'm going to be moving out of the mansion and moving back to my home in New York."

After Sebastian told Jenny's ghost that he was soon moving out of the mansion, she suddenly and swiftly got off his lap and stood in front of him looking hurt and angry. This is when he noticed her pregnant! Through her sheer pale pink nightgown he saw she had a baby bump and she looked about five months pregnant, he thought. He became overwhelmed, confused and speechless. While she stood in front of him, she yelled, "No! You can't leave me, Sebastian! You can't!" He then heard her sob. He is so confused because she is pregnant and he can't figure out how it happened and if he's the father! He then wondered how he could have gotten a ghost pregnant because they're in a different world. A living person getting a ghost pregnant is not believable. He then wondered if maybe she was pregnant at one time when she was alive and maybe this was a flashback. While he was stunned and unable to ask her about her pregnancy, she swiftly disappeared and so did the gardenia scent. He quickly yelled, "Jenny!" He went and sat on the sofa looking shocked at what just happened.

Two days later, in a hall in Marblehead, Sebastian was with the outsource police service. Officer Martin was at a microphone ready to speak to a crowd of people who were earlier informed about breaking news. Also there was Chief Brooks, Lieutenant Darwin, other officers and Sebastian.

Some of the people who were in the crowd waiting to hear the news were Sebastian's friends: Alan, Dr. Louis, Mrs. North, Mr. and Mrs. Marlow, Jenny's Aunt Irene, Charlie and Jacque. The Ultimate Inn employees: Inspector Bradford, Manager Gerard, Saul, Veronica, Danny, Phoebe, Chef André, and Bruce. Katherine was there hiding in the crowd because she didn't want

Sebastian to see her although he is the love of her life. She's just there to see him get honored by the police. All the other people there were concerned citizens.

It was time for Officer Martin to start speaking and he first said, "We have breaking news! The 2006 unsolved triple homicide mystery that happened in Marblehead Neck has now been solved!" The crowd cheered. Officer Martin went on and told the crowd of people that the murder suspect of Jenny and Pierce has been found and identified as Samantha a/k/a Vicki who has confessed. The prosecution will be seeking a life sentence for her. The murderer of Jenny's mother Shannon has been found and identified as the well known Alfred who has confessed. The prosecution will be seeking a life sentence for him. Also, Sam, the flamboyant wannabe hero who was Sebastian's rival, has been arrested on perjury charges and waiting to be sentenced. The crowd cheered for Sebastian and yelled out, "Yes! Yes! Sebastian!"

Officer Martin then said, "It gives the outsource police service such a pleasure to honor Sebastian for his extreme dedication to help and solve the 2006 triple homicide mystery in Marblehead Neck." He turned to Sebastian who went and stood next to him at the microphone and then handed him a plaque honoring him as a Citizen's Hero. Sebastian thanked him as the people cheered. He said, "I'm honored and I want to thank Officer Martin, Chief Brooks and Lieutenant Darwin from the outsource police service for all their continued investigations to help solve these murders. I'm most thankful to an unearthly source, Jenny and Pierce's ghost." The crowd gasped. He then said, "As you know, I'm a psychic medium and clairvoyant, and somehow, Jenny and Pierce's ghost have appeared in front of me many times. They recently appeared while my friend Samantha was visiting me and they revealed her as their murderer who later confessed. Unfortunately, Jenny and Pierce's ghost are not here with us to celebrate but I'm sure they're watching us."

Just then, the wonderful scent of gardenias filled the air and the crowd suddenly looked stunned as they knew it was a sign from Jenny.

After a few moments, an old woman in the crowd waived and yelled out, "Sebastian!" He recognized it to be Mrs. North who was Jenny's neighbor. Another old woman was crying loudly and suddenly stopped and yelled out, "Sebastian! Sebastian!" He recognized her as Mrs. Marlow who was Pierce's mother and he waived to her. The crowd loved him and kept on cheering, "Sebastian! Sebastian!" Officer Martin stayed on stage as Chief Brooks went to the microphone and said a few words and Lieutenant Darwin did. The crowd cheered. Katherine ducked out of the hall so Sebastian wouldn't see her. She loves him but doesn't want him back because he kept making love with Jenny's ghost.

The next day, the newspapers had headlines that read, "Breaking News! The Marblehead Neck 2006 Unsolved Triple Homicide Is Solved!" A story followed and there was also a picture of Sebastian with the headline, "Our Hero!"

20

SEBASTIAN'S FATE

Now that the news is out in all of the newspapers honoring Sebastian as a hero, his phone kept ringing with people calling to congratulate him. After it stopped ringing for awhile, he got another call and it was Katherine and he was elated as he answered it and said, "Katherine! You surprised me! I didn't think you'd ever call!" She asked him if she could come over to see him today. He said, "Of course you can! What time will you be coming over?" She told him it would be in the early evening and he told her he could hardly wait to see her. She then said, "I miss not seeing you, Sebastian." "I miss you too, Katherine." Then the call ended.

Sebastian went to his desk and managed to get his mind back on his book. He had a lot of news to document and what an ending he's going to have for his story now.

The Ghost And Sebastian

In mid-afternoon, Sebastian kept thinking of Katherine who was coming over in the evening which totally surprised him. With that on his mind, he soon finished writing for the day. He went and sat on a chair while he was having a cup of tea and thinking of how he had doubts Katherine would ever call him or come over because she was so firm about their breakup. He's now wondering what's on her mind. Is this going to be just a visit because she read about him in the newspaper being a hero or is she going to rekindle their love affair and get engaged again. He then went and prepared his dinner while still thinking of Katherine.

Later on, music played softly while Sebastian was at the table in the dining room having his roast turkey dinner and a glass of dry white wine. Somehow, he didn't have much of an appetite as he kept thinking about all the paranormal activity that has occurred in the china cabinet in the past. He plans to look in it after his dinner. Meanwhile, his phone kept ringing and he didn't answer it.

After dinner, when the table was cleared and the dishes were done, Sebastian went and looked in the china cabinet while the doors were closed. As he looked in the mirror, through the glass door, he saw his reflection and didn't see a ghost standing in back of it. He started to leave but then he heard some noise coming from the china cabinet so he turned and stared at it and one door was now open. He suddenly had a clairvoyant moment of a dead man on the dining room floor in front of him, full of blood next to a bloody ax. He knew it was Oscar because he read how he was murdered by his wife with an ax. He then said, "Oh, this is horrific! This is the spot where Oscar was murdered."

Sebastian went and took a shower while he thought about what he just saw and got dressed while he kept thinking about the bloody body of the first tenant who was brutally murdered by his wife with an ax for having sexual affairs.

Sebastian is wearing tan pants with a white summer top and his mind is almost back to normal as he waits for Katherine. There was soon a knock on the door, and when he opened it, Katherine was there looking pretty with her blonde hair and green eyes. He said, "Katherine!" After she entered and they hugged, he told her she looked lovely. She said, "Congratulations on becoming a hero!" He thanked her. She was wearing a yellow cotton dress which was knee-length and loose-fitting and he noticed she put on some weight.

Katherine and Sebastian walked into the living room while classical music was playing. She said, "You look startled about something." He said, "I just had a clairvoyant moment of the first tenant dead on the dining room floor in a pool of blood with a bloody ax next to him." Katherine said, "Oh! That must have been a terrible sight." They were quiet for several seconds. He then asked her if she wanted a glass of wine and she said, "No." He asked her why and she didn't answer as she stared at him. He looked at her waistline and belly and then looked into her eyes and asked, "Are you?" She smiled as she looked into his eyes and nodded her head. He then asked, "Mine?" She nodded her head again and he hugged her and asked, "Oh, Katherine! How far are you?" She said, "I got pregnant on Valentine's Day and I'm four and a half months pregnant." He asked, "Why didn't you tell me?" She said, "I didn't want us to be together just for the sake of the baby." Then they hugged.

Sebastian suddenly went and sat on the sofa and put his head in his hands thinking while Katherine was watching him. He's overwhelmed again because he recently noticed that Jenny's ghost looked about five months pregnant. He is aware that he made love with Jenny's ghost three times and the last time was in late January when she popped up from behind his chair in the living room wearing a light raspberry nightgown and they made love in Jenny's bed. The next time he was with her was in April when she met him in his car wearing a sheer light blue nightgown but didn't look pregnant. And they didn't make love because she only wanted to kiss, embrace and talk. It would have been in late January that he impregnated her if it's possible to impregnate a ghost. He's thinking of how Jenny's ghost has taken him spiritually to her world where they made love and it felt real so maybe it can happen. He also physically felt transported there.

Katherine went and sat next to Sebastian on the sofa and asked, "Are you alright? You've been thinking and not talking. Aren't you happy about this pregnancy?" He said, "Of course I am. Are we still engaged to be married?" She said, "Yes, we're still engaged but I don't know when we'll get married. And I'm over the fact that you made love with Jenny's ghost several times." He told her he'll be moving out of the mansion and it won't happen again. Sebastian got up and went to the bedroom for a minute and then went to the kitchen and poured himself and Katherine some root beer and brought it to the living room. He then surprised her as he took her engagement ring out of his pocket and said, "I found your ring you threw across the room when you broke up with me." She was thrilled as he put the ring back on her finger.

Sebastian went on and told Katherine, that while they were broken up, he socialized with his friend Samantha in his living room and that led to solving the murder mystery. She said, "Oh, I read all about it in the newspaper, Sebastian, but go on." He went on and told her that when he and Samantha were talking, Jenny and Pierce's ghost appeared in front of them full of anger while telling him that Samantha was really Vicki, their murderer in disguise. He then found it to be true because he saw Samantha take out her blue contact lenses earlier and she had brown eyes. Jenny's ghost told him Vicki had red hair so he looked at her hair roots and saw red hair.

While sitting on the sofa, Sebastian then told Katherine that he had some bizarre news, but before he tells her what it is, he wants to tell her what led to it. He began by telling her that in the first week of January, while they were in a committed relationship, she told him she was afraid of ghosts and knew that he slept with Jenny's ghost so she broke off with him. After that, it just so happened that in late January he made love with Jenny's ghost again. Sebastian was now ready to tell Katherine the bizarre news. He paused and then dropped a bomb! He got excited and said, "Jenny's ghost recently appeared in front of me to talk and she looked about five months pregnant! I must have impregnated her in late January because it's early July now! Maybe I'm the father!" After pausing, he told Katherine that Jenny's ghost must have been about three months pregnant when they were in his car in April when they didn't make love and just kissed, embraced and talked. It was in late January in the mansion when he impregnated her, and, it was also when he and Katherine were broken up. Sebastian then told Katherine he was finished telling her the bizarre news. He then stared at her while waiting to hear her response. She was speechless.

While Katherine and Sebastian stared at each other, she yelled, "Why did you keep making love with Jenny's ghost!" He yelled, "It's in the past!" They calmed down and he said, "How can a living person get a ghost pregnant? In her recent apparition, she was pregnant. Maybe it was a flashback of her from a time when she was pregnant!" Katherine thought maybe that was it. However, their minds won't rest now.

Katherine and Sebastian are so overwhelmed about Jenny's ghost being pregnant and they can't figure it out. She's not in the real world so how could that have happened. He then stood up and yelled, "Whose baby is it? Could I have impregnated a ghost? That's impossible!" Katherine stood up with him and told him not to worry about it because Jenny's dead. He started to pace the floor then stopped and said, "I can't help but wonder whose baby is it! Who's the father?" Katherine went and embraced him. He then went and got two soft drinks and came back and gave one to Katherine and they sipped them while continuing to pace the floor. She said, "Sebastian, it's surreal to believe you impregnated a ghost, and, if it's true, it was a few weeks before you impregnated me when we were back together on Valentine's Day. It also might be like you said. Maybe it was a flashback at a time in her life when she was pregnant. But someone impregnated her!" He looked sad while deep in thought.

Katherine and Sebastian then went and sat at the table in the dining room while they were having tea and were quiet while thinking about Jenny's pregnant ghost. He's mainly wondering who the father is of her baby. Katherine tried to comfort Sebastian and said, "I know what you're thinking and you'll never know who the father is of Jenny's baby. You're not going to see her again because you're moving out of the mansion. You'll never know!" She got up from the table and stood in back of him and massaged his shoulders and told him to relax. He said, "Oh, that feels good, Katherine." It was getting late and he asked her if she wanted to sleep over but she didn't. He told her he never wants to be with another woman again. He wants her because she's the love of his life and is a true soul mate. She told him she's getting mixed feelings about a lot and he didn't comment although he knows what she meant. They were soon at the door and embraced while saying goodnight.

Katherine called Sebastian for the next few days to see how he was feeling. Then the weekend arrived and she was back visiting him. She looked as pretty as ever wearing a pink dress which was loose-fitting and he looked dashing wearing sharp looking sport clothes. While in his living room, they sat and talked about how it's only a week away from his big party at his friend Alan's mansion. Many people will be there to celebrate his new book that will be coming out and the movie Alan will later produce.

Later on, Katherine and Sebastian were standing and facing each other. He started kissing her and then stopped and asked, "How are you feeling?" She said, "I'm fine. How are you? Are you still thinking of Jenny's baby?" After he told her he's still thinking about it but tries to put it out of his mind, she tried to comfort him by telling him each day he'll feel better. He told her he's anxious to see his and Katherine's baby. She went and sat on a chair and he went to the kitchen and got them each a tall glass of root beer with ice. He continued to stand and occasionally pace the floor with his drink. All of a sudden, the scent of gardenias filled the air and Katherine and Sebastian looked at each other as she asked, "Oh, is that going to be Jenny's ghost?" He answered, "Maybe." He then put his root beer down on the coffee table.

Katherine got off her chair and stood next to Sebastian and she held his arm as they waited and hoped Jenny's ghost would appear. While the gardenia scent remained, it meant that Jenny's spirit was there and maybe they'll see her ghost. Within seconds, Jenny's pale lifelike ghostly apparition was about five feet in front of them and had a white aura. She was wearing a sheer medium blue nightgown and, yes, she was pregnant and looked about six months along. While her long light brown hair was flowing, she looked pretty but sad as tears rolled down her face while she was staring at Sebastian.

Sebastian immediately said, "Jenny, I'm so happy to see you but why are you crying? Please don't cry." She sadly said, "You can't leave, Sebastian! I love you! Please don't leave me!" He and Katherine are emotional because Jenny's ghost is in love with Sebastian and looks about six months pregnant. He said, "You're pregnant Jenny! Who is the father?" She didn't answer that, instead, she passionately cried out, "I don't want you to leave, Sebastian! I love you and I need you!" She then was silent as his question went unanswered. He's holding a lot of sad feelings inside but his eyes are showing emotion as he fights back tears. He yelled, "Jenny, if I'm the father, it could change my life!" Jenny didn't respond, so he tenderly said, "Jenny, maybe I'll stay. I can't go the rest of my life wondering if I'm the father of your baby." Jenny was silent as she stared at him with tears in her eyes and Katherine was shocked that he said that to her.

Then, lightening hit the living room! Sebastian and Katherine looked shocked as they encountered four powerful pale lifelike ghostly apparitions floating around near Jenny's ghost and they all had bright auras. One of the ghosts was Jenny's mother Shannon who was sobbing and had a golden yellow aura, and one was Jenny's boyfriend Pierce who was angry and had a bright red aura and they were the closest to Jenny's ghost. The other two ghosts were Claude and his son Josh who still looked angry and they each had a fiery reddish orange aura. As the four ghosts kept floating around, Jenny's ghost looked sad. Sebastian's eyes watered as he was standing near Jenny's ghost and watching her. But Katherine looked angry now because Sebastian told Jenny he might not move. While the ghosts kept floating in the air, Jenny's ghost stood still with tears in her eyes staring at Sebastian.

Claude's ghost started screaming when his son Josh's ghost got close to his which caused their auras to become aura of fiery reddish orange. Josh started bashing his father over the head with an instrument that was horrifying to watch.

Sebastian then looked at Jenny's ghost who now has tears running down her face while still staring at him. He sensed her pain and said, "Jenny, you'll be alright." She cried out, "No! Please don't leave me! Please! Don't leave the mansion!" Sebastian said, "Jenny, I told you I might not move!" With tears in her eyes, she asked, "Do you mean that, Sebastian?" He said, "Yes, Jenny." Katherine stayed silent while looking angry as she watched Sebastian tell Jenny he might not move. Then Jenny's ghost, with tears in her eyes, swiftly disappeared with her gardenia scent and her mother Shannon's ghost followed while sobbing. Then Pierce's ghost left angry. Claude and his son Josh's ghost became calm and had separate auras again which were fiery reddish orange. Then Claude's ghost left and Josh's ghost followed. All five ghosts had disappeared with Jenny's ghost leading the way. The sixth ghost, Oscar, from the china cabinet who was the first tenant to live in the mansion, never appeared. Sebastian thought of his recent clairvoyant moment of him dead on the dining room floor full of blood next to a bloody ax.

Now that the ghosts were gone, Sebastian embraced Katherine but sensed her coldness. He said, "I couldn't tell Jenny's ghost that I was in love with you, Katherine, because she was sad." Katherine pulled away from him and yelled, "You told her 'maybe' you'll stay in the mansion!" He said, "I'm not sure what to do. You're talking about a baby, Katherine, that might be mine!" She said, "What about me? Jenny's baby shouldn't change your life! I'm sick of hearing about Jenny!" After they calmed down, he told her that five ghosts came out and maybe it was because they know he might move. She yelled, "You 'might' move! I'm done with you, Sebastian!" She's supposed to sleep over so she stormed upstairs to sleep alone in a separate bedroom on the second floor because she's angry Sebastian told Jenny he might not move. Unknown to them, Jenny's ghost hovered over them all night going from bed to bed staring at them as they slept.

The next morning, Sebastian and Katherine woke up and neither one was pleasant while having breakfast. She said, "Regarding your uncertainty about moving, let's put that behind us for now." He agreed. As she planned, she'll shop today for

Alan's party that he's making for Sebastian in a few days. She needs a dress that'll look good with her baby bump.

A few days later, it was the day of Sebastian's party which his good friend Alan, the movie producer, arranged at his mansion that's not very far away. Sebastian and Katherine are all dressed and ready to leave for the party. While he is wearing a blue suit with a white striped shirt and a sharp tie, his unusual cologne smells wonderful and his good looks and wavy brown hair make him charismatic. Katherine is looking absolutely beautiful in a blue silk dress that shows her baby bump. Her shoulder length blonde hair is pinned to one side showing her pretty face and green eyes, and her light shade of lipstick is perfect. She's wearing perfume with an orient scent and is not wearing her diamond engagement ring because she has called off their engagement.

Around 7:00 p.m., Sebastian and Katherine entered Alan's mansion and were greeted by Butler Winston who is now escorting them to the grand room. When they got there, the grand room was filled with many guests and Katherine was in awe of the beauty and elegance everywhere. The room was sparkling from the glow of beautiful chandeliers that were slightly dimmed.

While some of the guests were mingling and laughing, others were engaged in serious conversations with producers, directors, writers and friends. Mostly everyone was holding a cocktail. Sebastian suddenly spotted his friend Alan and said, "Come on, Katherine. Follow me." They walked over to his good friend Alan. Then Sebastian approached him and gave him a hug and said, "Hi, Alan. How are you feeling?" He answered, "I'm good and taking better care of myself now." Sebastian introduced him to Katherine as his fiancée and Alan was pleased to meet her as they shook hands. Katherine said, "I've heard good things about you, Alan. But let me correct Sebastian.

We're not engaged anymore." Alan said, "Oh I'm sorry to hear that." He looked puzzled and then Sebastian whispered to him that she's pregnant and to excuse some of her comments.

Within moments, the young waiter, Wesley, went over to Alan, Sebastian and Katherine and asked, "What can I get all of you?" Sebastian ordered a soft drink and Katherine ordered the same. Alan ordered another scotch on the rocks. Alan then told Sebastian of what a shock it was to hear their writer friend Samantha a/k/a Vicki was a murderer. He went on and told Katherine and Sebastian of how he met her in Los Angeles as a new writer who found the competition too tough in Los Angeles and they became friends. She got obsessed with him thinking he could help her in Marblehead so she moved here. Sebastian said, "It sure was shocking." Alan added, "Little did we know she was a murderer yet I knew there was a psychological problem going on with her." Sebastian told him she was very mysterious.

Alan then told Sebastian and Katherine that there was plenty of food at the buffet whenever they want it. He also told Sebastian he was going to be giving a speech shortly to honor him. Sebastian said, "It's kind of you to make this party for me, Alan. I appreciate it." The waiter, Wesley, was back with their beverages and appetizers on a silver tray and served them and left.

Sebastian later said, "Alan, let's introduce Katherine to some producers, directors and writers." He agreed and they walked around meeting people. They went over to their friend Brad, the producer, and Sebastian shook hands with him and said, "I want you to meet my fiancée Katherine." Katherine snapped and said, "Sebastian, I told you we're not engaged anymore!" Sebastian just smiled as he blew off her comment and Brad shook hands with her as he sensed they had an argument. He then told Alan and Sebastian of what a shock it was to hear about Samantha a/k/a Vicki being a murderer. They all agreed that it was shocking.

Sebastian then asked Katherine if she was feeling alright and she told him she was. Just then, Alan left Brad, Sebastian and Katherine and went and stood on a platform that was provided for him so everyone could see him. He called Sebastian to come over and stand next to him with Katherine so they did. Alan spoke into the microphone and asked, "Can I have your attention, everyone?" The room became quiet as he said, "We're here tonight to honor the renowned mystery writer, Sebastian, who helped solve the 2006 triple homicide in Marblehead Neck." Everyone applauded and then Alan said, "He has written a book about it entitled Ghostly Murder Mystery! which will be published soon. After it's adapted to a screenplay, I'll make a movie of it. The outsource police have honored him with a plaque as a citizen's hero and I agree that he is a hero along with his ghostly connections Jenny and Pierce." Just then, the scent of gardenias filled the air in the grand room and everyone was stunned and in awe. This is a night they will all remember.

Alan and Katherine then watched Sebastian as he took the microphone and said, "That was Jenny's scent." He paused and smiled with the crowd. He then said, "To help solve this triple homicide, it took many investigations by police since 2006. I believe that my living in the mansion where the murders took place, stirred up the spirits to come out and help solve these murders through me and my psychic powers. It was also a visit by my friend Samantha one night at my mansion that led to Jenny and Pierce's ghost appearing in front of us identifying Samantha as Vicki, their murderer in disguise. It took me over a year to help solve this murder." After pausing, he said, "I want to thank my friend Alan who made this party." The guests applauded and then Sebastian said, "I want to introduce all of you to Katherine who is the love of my life." The guests applauded again and Alan thanked all his guests for coming.

Sebastian then told Alan that Katherine needs to sit down for awhile because of her pregnancy and he could join them if he wanted. Alan told him he's going to walk around and talk with people. While Sebastian and Katherine were sitting at a table, he kind of smiled as he asked her, "Did you like the way I introduced you this last time?" She said, "Yes I did and keep it that way." He asked her if he could get her something to eat at the buffet and she told him to pick out some food that she likes so he left her for a few minutes. Before long, Sebastian was back with Lobster Newberg on pastry shells, rolls, and salads for both of them. She said, "I'm starving and I'm sure it's because I'm eating for two." He kissed her cheek and then told her he'll introduce her to a Hollywood biography writer after they eat. She said, "Oh, I'm looking forward to that. Hollywood fascinates me."

After Katherine and Sebastian finished eating, he then introduced her to Nina who looks elegant tonight as usual. Katherine liked meeting her and Nina was happy to meet her. She told her Sebastian is a good man and Katherine didn't comment. After talking awhile, they left.

Sebastian and Katherine sat down by themselves to talk for awhile and then they went and found Alan and told him they were leaving because Katherine was tired. He understood that so he and Sebastian hugged goodbye. He then shook hands with Katherine and said, "I'm looking forward to seeing you again." She said, "It was such a pleasure meeting you, Alan, and I'm sure we'll see each other again." Katherine and Sebastian left Alan's beautiful mansion and all of the wonderful guests they mingled with.

It didn't take Sebastian long to get back to his own mansion because Alan didn't live very far from him. He soon parked in his driveway and then he and Katherine entered the mansion and were happy to be back so she could rest. She first stood in front of him and reminded him they're no longer engaged. He believes her now and asked, "Why, Katherine?" She yelled, "Because you told Jenny you may not move!"

Katherine and Sebastian then went and sat on chairs and stared at each other. He apologized for telling Jenny he may not move, and, it was because he was confused about Jenny's baby. Katherine didn't respond, so he said, "I'm sorry. Can you ever forgive me? I got lost in Jenny's world but that has ended. I'm moving on." Katherine said, "I forgive you but right now the engagement is still off." She was tired and wanted to go to bed so she was on her way upstairs to sleep and he told her he'd join her shortly. She yelled, "Not in my bed!" She also wants to go home early tomorrow.

Sebastian and Katherine were soon both in bed in separate bedrooms on the second floor trying to sleep. She didn't want to kiss good night so they just said good night.

Within the next few weeks, surprise! Katherine and Sebastian got back together and are now smiling coming out of a church in Marblehead as the bells chimed! She looked stunning in a silk shantung bridal gown, which concealed some of her almost six month pregnancy, and a veil that trailed nine feet. He looked handsome wearing a single breasted black tuxedo with a champagne colored silk vest.

As Katherine and Sebastian happily walked towards the white limousine, they waived to a crowd of people who cheered them on and kept throwing confetti at them. Some of the guests were: Alan, Nina, Brad, Max, Jonathan, Dr. Louis, Charlie, Phoebe, Veronica, Danny, Saul, Mrs. North, Mr. and Mrs. Marlow, Ultimate Inn's Inspector Bradford, Manager Gerard, Chef André, Bruce, the waiter, Jacque, the waiter, Chief Brooks, Lieutenant Darwin and Officer Martin.

There were many sightseers there who enjoyed seeing Sebastian, the renowned murder mystery writer, criminal psychologist, psychic medium and clairvoyant from New York, tie the knot with Katherine, the beautiful real estate agent from Marblehead. Their wedding along with Sebastian helping to solve the Marblehead Neck 2006 triple homicide was all big news! Therefore, photographers were snapping pictures to sell to newspapers, magazines and talk shows.

While Sebastian and Katherine went to the limousine, people continued to throw confetti. As the limousine started to drive away to Marblehead Neck for their reception, Sebastian and Katherine could be seen kissing in the back window and then smiling while waving to the crowd of people who were watching them.

A large sign was held up: "CONGRATULATIONS KATHERINE AND SEBASTIAN!"

ACKNOWLEDGEMENTS

To my daughter Karen Adreani,

My special thanks to you again, Karen, for your technical support which I couldn't have done without you. I also thank you for always inspiring me with my singing, painting and publishing novels.

You've been exceptionally good to your mother and I'm lucky to have you. You're still that gentle and soft spoken and caring person you've always been to me and everyone. You're as good as they come. To me, you are a perfect daughter and I will always love you.

Your Mom

To my son Keith Walters,

My thanks to you, Keith, for being a great source of inspiration to me in the arts. You have motivated me with my singing and painting more than anyone and you also inspired me to get my first manuscript published. You are a naturally kind-hearted person.

You self-published an art book because you have wonderful artistic and literary skills. You also won First Prize from the Chamber of Commerce in a flag poster contest when you were eight years old; nine thousand children participated in it. You did well in the Navy. For all the above reasons, I'm lucky to have you for my son and I will always love you.

Your Mom

ABOUT THE AUTHOR

BERNICE CARSTENS

BIOGRAPHY OF ACCOMPLISHMENTS

As a painter:
Studied at **Fitchburg Art Museum, Fitchburg, MA,** three years, two as a teenager, one as an adult. Chosen for 3 shows. First Prize Awards in two Major Shows.

Member of **Copley Society of Art, Boston, MA** for 18 years (1990-2008). Participated in eight shows. Five paintings "chosen" for Major Shows. Award-Winner in one Major show. Three paintings in Co/So Small Works Shows. In 2006, she received "COPLEY ARTIST" Status (certificate of advancement) having five paintings chosen for Major Shows. COMMISSIONED FOR 17 PAINTINGS (1961-1986).

As a Singer and Guitarist:
Held her own weekly radio show for one year from age 15 to 16 at Radio Station WFGM in Fitchburg, MA. Sang and accompanied herself with a guitar. She then went on giving numerous stage performances as a pop song stylist. A taped live performance, at age 30 in 1964, resulted in a CD that was mastered by Waltz Audio Mastering in the year of 2009. ELECTRIFYING SONGS OF THE 1960's.

As a Fitness Enthusiast - age 50 & 58:
Featured in Muscle & Fitness and in Natural Physique.

As an Author - by age 68:
   Wrote four screenplays and one novel, all registered.

At age 76:
   Published her first novel, Copyright © 2011:
   "Larry And Nadine In Vegas"

At age 79:
   Published her second novel, Copyright © 2014:
   "The Ghost And Sebastian"
   Proposal for a near future solo art show to sell approximately 38 of her oil paintings.

CPSIA information can be obtained at www.ICGtesting.com
Printed in the USA
LVOW11s1410260315

432146LV00001B/35/P